In a Land of Thieves,
He Was the Grandest of Them All

"Are you going to wear this same dress all the rest of your life?"

She laughed. "I'll change later."

"Change now." He secured her, imprisoned against him, with his hand at the small of her back. She could not even fight free. She tried, still attempting to smile. He loosened the small black velvet tie, unbuttoned the collar of her shirt.

Lily caught her breath. "Why, Ward. What're you doing?"

"I'll show you. I'd rather show you than tell you." Deftly, his fingers pulled downward, loosening the button of her blouse.

Stiffening, Lily tried again to writhe free. He held her effortlessly, slipped her blouse away from her shoulders, down over her arms . . . She fought him now, silently, but fiercely.

"What are you going to do?"

A Saga of
Tropical Passion and Promise

BLAINE STEVENS

THE OUTLANDERS

A JOVE BOOK

First Jove edition published December 1979

10   9   8   7   6   5   4   3   2   1

Printed in the United States of America

Jove books are published by Jove Publications, Inc., 200 Madison
Avenue, New York, NY 10016

To Kathryn

20. And Benaiah the son of Jehoiada, the son
of a valiant man, of Kabzeel, who had done many acts,
he slew two lionlike men of Moab: he went down
also and slew a lion in the midst of a pit in a time of snow.

21. And he slew an Egyptian, a goodly man:
and the Egyptian had a spear in his hand; but he went
down to him with a staff and plucked the spear out of
the Egyptian's hand, and slew him with his own spear.

22. These things did Benaiah, the son of
Jehoiada, and had the name among three mighty men.

23. He was more honorable than the thirty, but
he attained not to the first three. . . .

II Samuel, 23.

THE OUTLANDERS

BOOK ONE:

LILY, 1876

Chapter One

HE STOPPED WALKING suddenly atop a lonely knoll. Stunned, he stood sweating in the sulphurous blast of a Florida sun that galled and seared the raw, red earth. His heart hammered. He quivered in every muscle of his body and felt as if the blood boiled and exploded in his temples; as though he held a desirable and submissive woman in his arms; as if overwhelmed with white-hot passion that would never ebb or release him in this life. This was his first glimpse of this strangely green and lush subtropic veldt, the like of which he had never seen before. It lay before him, a steaming wilderness, a sultry flowering, elemental, intoxicating, languorous, and untouched.

"The village. Not far from here, Masta Hamilton."

Hamilton jerked his head around as if rudely awakened. He stared at the mustee Indian-black. For a heart-stopping instant, he'd forgotten his derbied, gaudy-jacketed guide on that mule. The *os rouge* rode the ridge-backed animal without a saddle, with only a worn and smelly blanket between his buttocks and that knuckled spine. The half-breed was tall, thin, and large-boned. His high cheekbones and hawk nose suggested his Creek ancestry, but those broad nostrils and heavy lips recalled ancient lands and tribes east of Senegal. His tawny body glistened with sweat, but he seemed cool in his black cotton pants and brightly printed jacket. His derby hat sat straight on his black, crisp-haired head. He was probably twenty, though it was as difficult to judge his age as to fathom his thoughts from the sullen mask of his face.

Hamilton hesitated. It was cool under the umbrella of the sweet bay; a soft breeze caressed him lazily and soothed the sweat from his skin. He breathed deeply, dreading to leave. Palms, pines, cabbage palmettoes, and scrub oaks, trellised with velvety green scuppernong vines, stretched as far as he could see. His mind cleared this land and tamed it and owned it. His iridescent vision peopled and planted and paved it, and linked it with iron rails as random and prodigal as those thick vines. His excitement rose and, for this moment, thrust his ugly mission deep into the far recesses of his brain.

"All right, Uzziah. Let's go." Hamilton nodded and swung back up onto the seat of his flatbed wagon. In the bed of the vehicle he'd stacked croker sacks of staples— bacon, flour, corn, and coffee—two guns, a couple of steel shackles, and some chains. He hoped he wouldn't have to use them, but— He shrugged.

The Indian preceded him down the undefined trail. Hamilton slapped the reins, sweat sprayed from the rumps of the sodden dray horses, and they plodded forward between the boles of ancient water oaks.

Hamilton squinted through the shimmering heat. Shielding his eyes with his hand, he gazed across waist-high grass and palmetto, looking for signs of habitation. There was none. Immediately ahead, he heard the unmistakable *whirr* of a rattlesnake, but the guide ignored the sound and Hamilton tried to. One thing he'd never grow accustomed to—those damned rattlesnakes. And crossing a river this morning, he'd watched a fourteen-foot alligator slither off a fallen tree trunk into black water. The sight had sickened him, raising his hackles and moiling his belly. He hated those damned slimy serpents, but even at nineteen, he had learned one truth: there was no paradise on this earth without its own evil.

"Hear folks. Up ahead," Uzziah said over his shoulder.

Hamilton listened, but heard nothing except the irritating hum of deerflies, the singing of mosquitoes, the raging of bluejays disturbed in their rookeries. A six-foot panther

14

slunk across a clearing ahead of them, but Uzziah ignored the animal as he had the snake, and Hamilton shook his head, grinned, and wiped sweat from his eyes.

Holding the reins slack, he let the animals plod forward at their own gait. They trailed slowly in the wake of the half-caste on his mule.

Hamilton slapped the stinging horseflies from about his shoulders, aware of a recurring coolness under every canopy of spreading oaks, the dazzling dapple of sunlight and shadow, the blinding, fiery orange glare of the sun in open places. He let his mind savor the anticipation and challeng this fragrant province stirred and inflamed in his imagination. Dreams raged to match the restless vitality that drove him by day and by sleepless night, the need to achieve, to accomplish, to be first among men, to walk among the powerful and to command them. He shivered under the influence of fantasies that must have spurred DeSoto: the glories to be won, the wealth and power that the future could provide and nourish on this rich frontier. God knew there wasn't another plot of real estate on earth comparable to this fabulous, barbaric territory. This undefiled domain looked like heaven to him and, as a heaven, he would sell it to other Yankees, now freezing their winter asses off up north, never suspecting the existence of such a fertile paradise of eternal sunshine, gentle rain, rich earth, a breeze waiting under every shade tree. Cities would mushroom, cities that would be constructed of lumber and bricks and steel, cities that had to be linked by rails. His rails. His cities. Xanadu. The seven golden cities of Coronado. The Fountain of Youth. He saw all this on the vivid magic-lantern screen of his mind. Nobody could stop him. Nothing could cheat him of this opportunity.

Despite his daydreams, he shivered with an abrupt and irrational chill. He thought of his brother up ahead of him somewhere, and of what he had to do. He hated admitting it, even to himself, but the prospect of the impending pain burned his eyes with tears he refused to shed or even acknowledge. That there would be pain, he admitted. That scars would sear inside him that nobody would ever be permitted to see or suspect and that he would never escape, he was well aware. And still he said to hell with it, and still he pushed it from his conscious mind, and still he plodded forward in the pitiless heat.

He pushed his planter's hat back on his head and mopped at his perspiring forehead. His skin was burnished like old copper, his hands were toughened, his arms thinned down to corded sinew and tendon. His long legs were marble-hard with sculpted muscles; his waist and hips were trim and flat; his shoulders were wide and his chest deep. Southern suns had bleached his tan-colored hair and faded the gray of his eyes. Somewhere in his ancestry lurked the violent Scot and black-mooded Celt. His nose was well-carved, his chin strongly cleft, his forehead classic. His sweaty clothing was cheap, his boots old and worn, but he carried himself erect, with an arrogance that bought him hatred on sight in many quarters. He walked with a swagger and, even slouched on this hard wagon seat as royalty must have slumped on some tired throne, he exuded the aura of authority, the bearing of nobility, the strength of self-confidence, and had not a single gold dollar in his pockets.

He rode into a clearing where stood a rural village. The sun westered, flinging jagged shadows across the dirt road that ran between the scattering of clapboard shacks. Every hut was built with at least a two-foot airspace between the flooring and the damp ground: a precaution against mildew. The settlement smelled like an open outhouse, and his nostrils quivered, offended. He entered the first crosshatching of shadows, aware of people crouched in shade, sprawled on slanting stoops, or standing, unmoving, against dry-rotting walls.

People unlike any he had ever seen before stared at him from hooded eyes, a polyglot of poverty, an immixture of races. The whites—poverty-ridden, dull-eyed, watchful—were suspicious of every stranger. The blacks were troubled because of his skin color and because they didn't know him or his intent. The few Indians he saw were the worst of all: weak with hookworm, malarial, half-starved, without the energy to sustain fear. No one spoke to Hamilton, and he returned their greeting in kind, meeting their sullen gazes, watching them shiver under the lash of his glance and look away, submissive and disturbed.

Farther down the bare road, he saw Uzziah halt the mule before a rude country store where two old men were locked in combat over a checkerboard. Hamilton slowed the horses and sat in the sun, waiting. He sensed instinctively that his long search was almost over.

Uzziah questioned the natives for a few moments, then turned slightly on his mule and motioned toward a hut down the path. Hamilton nodded and urged the horses forward. The creaking of wheels, metal, and wood, were loud in the intense stillness.

Uzziah dismounted from the mule as Hamilton drove the wagon into the meager shade before the shack. Four people lounged on the stoop and peered at him from expressionless, coffee-brown faces. An aging man—he may have been no more than forty, but there was almost Biblical ripeness in the sunken blue eyes, the unkempt gray hair, and the scraggly beard—sat unmoving in a rocking chair. A slat-thin, leathery, middle-aged woman, chewing snuff, her lips and chin stained with it, sat beside him on a cane-bottomed kitchen stool. A young man, lean and vague-eyed in overalls without a shirt, sagged against the wall, his legs spread wide. A teenaged girl, soiled, her tattered cotton dress much-washed and outgrown, leaned against an upright, her briar-scratched legs dangling over the side of the scoured stoop. Hamilton drew a deep breath. If Robert were here, he'd have laid odds there would be a young girl nearby.

Hamilton swung down from the wagon and approached the steps. The people on the stoop made no move to stop him, nor did they welcome him in any way. They merely watched him dully. He hesitated for a long moment, but when none of them spoke, he moved tentatively up the wide pine-plank steps. They did not ask him in or attempt to deter him. He walked to the closed door, still waiting for some response from the squatters. They merely continued to watch him in silence. He heard a sound of movement within the shack. He jerked his head, silently ordering Uzziah to guard the rear doorway. Uzziah nodded, ground-tied the mule, and walked around the corner of the shack in the blistering sun.

Hamilton said, "You in there, Thetis?"

"Yes, Masta, we here." The Negro's voice sounded muffled.

Hamilton glanced toward the owners of this house, but when they remained unmoving, he opened the door and stepped inside. The room was poorly lit, even in the bright

17

afternoon. Clothing hung from pegs sunk into exposed wall studs; an iron woodstove, a bare pine table, a few chairs, a homemade pinewood dresser, one bed, and two cots comprised the hovel's only furniture. Robert lay on one of the cots. The Negro, Thetis, knelt beside the cot, his head bowed as if in prayer. He leaped back guiltily when the door opened. Thetis was about seventeen years old, his hair a tight, kinky cap of curls, his forehead slanted, his brows ridged, his nostrils wide and flat, his mouth full-lipped and wide. He was a well-built youth who moved with effeminate affectedness. His appearance was marred by the loss of three fingers on his right hand. Only the thumb and little finger remained; his fingers had been chopped off by a deeply religious and devout slaveowner who had caught the boy masturbating.

The room was permeated with a sweet-sour odor that was nauseating. At first, Hamilton was unable to understand how his brother could remain in a crib that stank so offensively. Then he saw one of Robert's legs uncovered on the couch, gashed with a bullet wound and discolored with gangrene almost to the knee.

Hamilton shuddered involuntarily and stepped close to the cot. All the symptoms of moist gangrene were immediately evident. He'd seen gangrenous wounds often among soldiers of the army of occupation in Georgia. Both arterial and venous circulation had been disrupted by the lesion, and putrefaction had set in. The flesh of the open sore festered, liver-colored and infected. Robert's whole body was marked with changes flaring upward from the afflicted area: sickening odor, purpling of the toes, foot, calf, and ankle. Robert writhed in agony on the cot, almost deranged by pain, and when Hamilton touched his brother's forehead, he found him flushed and dry with raging fever.

Hamilton peered down at Robert in the hazy half-light. Though they were brothers, with less than twenty months between them, and superficially similar in appearance, here any likeness abruptly ceased. Inwardly they were totally unlike. Even in this filthy sty, fevered and suffering a putrefying injury, Robert's was the effete look of the foppish gentleman of fashion. His hands were pale and soft—as he was soft inside, damn him! Though they were of equal height, alike in their fair coloring, the sun had bronzed Ward to the dark shade of a Caribbean pirate, while Robert looked pallid, helpless, lying in the shadow of death.

When Ward touched his brother's forehead, Robert opened his fevered blue eyes and stared disbelievingly. His mouth quivered. His voice quavered with a strange timbre, a hopeless weakness. "Thank God, Ward. Thank God you've come."

"Yes, I'm here."

"Ward's come to help us, Thetis." Robert's voice broke, tears choking it.

"Don't count on that, Robert," Ward said.

Robert's mouth trembled. "I knew you would come, Ward. I'll tell you why. Because I prayed you'd come. Thetis and I. We ran as far as we could. Then my leg acted up. We had to stop. Every night. All day long, I prayed you'd come and find us."

"Yes. I found you."

The odor of gangrene was stifling. The room was hot and close, with the stink of hopelessness and death coiling in the shadows. Tears welled in Robert's eyes and spilled along his taut cheeks. "Please help me, Ward. Help us. I'm begging you."

"Well, don't. I don't like to see you beg any more than I like to see you cry. You're sick; I understand that. You need a medical doctor and a hospital, fast. I'll see that you get them."

"Why? Why do you want to keep me alive if you're taking me back?"

"I don't know. But let's get this straight, Robert. Taking you back is the biggest favor I can do you. God help you, I'm sorry for you—for the mess you've gotten yourself into—but what in hell good does that do you?"

"I'm innocent."

"Now's not the time, Robert. If you could have proved you were innocent, you wouldn't be here. You had everything, everybody on your side, but you ran like a jackal."

"Oh God. Help me."

"Nobody can help you."

Robert's head rolled back and forth. Tears welled in his eyes and ran down his cheeks. "Please. I'm not asking for me. It's Lily. She does need me, Ward. Without me, she has nobody. She loves me. She believes in me."

19

"She'll get along. Women always have, always will."

"I'm innocent, Ward. I swear it."

Hamilton shrugged. "All right."

"So help me God, that's why I started praying for you to help us. I got to thinking about you, and I started praying. I know this sounds crazy and like I'm sick in the head, but I kept praying to God for you to help me. I prayed all the time. I knew you were smart and I'm not. You figured things all the way, and I never did. I knew nobody but you could help me get away. I knew you'd come. It got clearer and stronger as I prayed, like it was an answer. Oh God, I know how sick this sounds."

"I'm taking you back, Robert."

Robert rolled his face away and flung his arm across his eyes as if shielding himself from brutal blows about the head. He burst into anguished sobbing. He tried to stop crying and couldn't, and he crouched, drawing in upon himself, as if he were being beaten and couldn't take it anymore. Sobs wracked him. Thetis remained on his knees, his dark face wet with tears.

Ward stared down at his brother. Was this the same man who, in ruffled shirts and elegant fashions of the haute bourgeoisie, charmed and delighted the Southern gentry, to whom manners and wit were stock in trade and any Yankee a two-pronged demon? Robert drank their gin and bourbon and relayed federal decisions with such empathy and concern that the overthrown aristocracy accepted those decrees without malice—toward Robert at least—though he may well have handed them a final, crippling blow behind his warm smile. Robert's greatest investment in the defeated Confederacy lay in the triviality of wasted afternoons on plantation verandas.

Ward remained standing, cold. He counted the hairs on the back of his hand, waiting for Robert to stop crying. He could smell the death in this room. The hell of it was, so could Robert. At last Robert stopped weeping and got himself under control. Now that he'd stopped crying, there was nothing in his eyes anymore; they bulged as empty as fish's eyes after a day in the sun. His sunken cheeks twitched as he abandoned all hope. "I'm sorry I cried like that."

Ward shrugged. "God knows you're sick. I can see that."

20

Robert shook his head. "No. That's not why I cried. I need help; I am innocent."

Ward shook his head. "Jesus, you stink."

"It's my leg."

"I know it's your leg. It's gangrenous."

"No. No. I don't think so."

"You don't *want* to think so. Even with your leg stinking with putrefaction, you still hate facing the truth."

"I am facing the truth. Now I know why you're here." Robert shuddered. "You've come to take me back to Atlanta."

"No."

Robert's eyes widened, and his pallid, stricken face lightened faintly. He hoped, without daring to hope. "You have come to help me after all?"

"No. But I can't take you back up to Atlanta, that's all. Not with that leg putrefying. It's too far. You'd never live to make the trip. I'll try to get you to the provost marshal in Jacksonville."

"And turn me in for the reward."

Ward shrugged. "The government offered the reward. They say you stole a hundred thousand in gold."

"You know I didn't."

"They think you did."

"You know I didn't. You know *why* I didn't."

Ward shrugged again. He blew sweat from his eyes. "You'll get a trial. I'm sorry. I am taking you back. There is a twenty thousand-dollar reward for you."

"You bastard—"

Ward's grin mocked him. "Your own brother?"

"You ruthless son of a bitch." Robert's head rolled on the filthy pillow, but he was too outraged to cry now. "You'd send me to prison and let me go into that hell, for money—"

"What else? Every man's got his price, Robert. They met mine." He lifted his shoulders, let them sag. His face twisted sourly as he surveyed the dark shack. "You'll be better off in the federal pen at Atlanta than rotting with gangrene among these crackers."

Robert struggled on the cot. "God damn you, I'll kill you."

"Sure you will." Ward's voice taunted him lightly, then

21

hardened. "We're wasting time. Look on the bright side, Robert—"

"What bright side? When my own brother—"

"A few years in prison, most of it in the hospital. You may lose that leg. When you're out, I'll have a place for you in my organization."

"What organization, you lying bastard?"

"Railroads, Robert. South across this territory, deeper into these tropics." He grinned, paraphrasing Scripture. "In my organization there will be many mansions . . . if it were not so, I would tell you—"

"You sacreligious son of a bitch. I'll tell you this: when I am out, I'll find you. And I'll kill you."

"Meanwhile, let's get on the road. It's a long way to Jacksonville and I'm in a hurry."

"To see me in prison? Tell me, Ward. God damn you, tell me—what the hell is it you want? What do you really want?"

"I want to be richer than God."

Robert's mouth twisted; his agonized eyes glittered. "Is that all?"

"No. I want power, the kind of power I've seen men use casually. Power and money. You can't have one without the other. If you've got enough money, you can buy power. When you get enough power, you can really begin to amass all the money there is. That's what I want."

Robert continued to stare at him, his face rigid. "Is that all?"

"That's all."

"And you have no feeling for me? None for the disgrace on our family?"

"About as much as you had when you stole that army payroll." Ward smiled. "Where'd you hide that money, Robert?"

"I don't have any money."

"Don't lie, brother. You wouldn't have run—a bullet wound in your leg, your reputation destroyed, your engagement smashed, our name disgraced. You wouldn't lie here stinking like this unless you had hope of getting to use that money."

"There is no money, so you can get to hell out of here."

"There's still twenty-thousand waiting for me at Jack-

22

sonville, and a chance to save your feckless hide—if we make it in time."

"So I can rot in prison?"

"As I say, when you get out, you can come work for me. I'll make you rich." Ward glanced about the dank hovel. "If you'll turn your loot over to me, I'll multiply it tenfold—while I pay you ten percent interest."

Robert stared up at him. "If there were money I'd stolen, you'd never get your paws on it. If I did have such money, I'd share its whereabouts only with someone who loved me enough to keep my secret safe to death. So, even if there were money, you could just forget it, brother."

"Robert. For hell's sake, just this once, face reality. You're on your way to prison. You may not even live to get there. If I don't take you in, somebody else will. Since the reward will be paid for you dead or alive, you've got a better chance with me. You've fouled our name until there is nothing left for either of us in ordinary commerce. We either go outside the law, or rise above it. I can use that money you stole, and warrant you a tenfold return you'll never get with it planted somewhere in the ground."

"Go to hell." Robert turned his face away.

Ward's mouth pulled down. "Jesus. I don't mind your being weak and soft. I don't even mind your being criminal. But I hate and despise stupidity, and goddamn it, you're stupid."

"Maybe. But you're the one scrounging for money."

Ward exhaled heavily. He knelt and took his brother up in his arms. Fever made Robert's body fiery to the touch. Robert struggled, cursing and crying aloud in protest, but Ward carried him gently, as if he were a disgruntled child. Ward jerked his head and Thetis took up Robert's gun and rucksack and followed him from the hut.

Ward walked across the shadowed stoop and down the plank steps. When he reached the wagon, he tossed Robert into its bed as casually as if his brother were no more than a sack of grain. Robert gasped, the breath knocked out of him, pain fulgurating through his body, exploding in his skull. Ward didn't glance toward him. "Comfortable, old son?"

"You bastard."

Ward grinned. He took the gun from Thetis and motioned the freedman into the wagon beside Robert. The four people watched silently from the shadowed porch. The slender young girl swung her leg and chewed a stem of grass. Uzziah came around the house and vaulted lightly to the back of the mule. Ward swung up into the wagon seat, turned the vehicle north, and slapped the reins across the glistening rumps of the perspiring horses.

Chapter Two

WARD WALKED OUT of the Dixie Hotel, going downtown on crowded Peachtree Street. He winced, assaulted by sounds, smells, and sights in the raucous, steamy morning. Pressed against a wall, he waited while bareback riders herded cattle through the busy thoroughfare. He held his breath when gaunt-faced drovers harried fat hogs along the rutted roadway. One farmer, armed with a hand-whittled staff, trotted beside the porkers to prevent thieves from stealing strays in broad daylight. Mixtures of odors doused him: burning rubbish, boiling tar, wet feathers, new lumber, new concrete, new money, old corruptions. . . .

He glanced about in the confusion and prettified misery. Atlanta still wore her scars raw, red, open and ulcerated ten years after her pillage and rape by Union troops. Though often—and erroneously—considered the heart and hub of the antebellum South, the town had been a mere fourteen years old when the Civil War began. Its corporate entity dawned only when a tycoon named Thomson chose it as terminus for his midland system, the Western & Atlantic Railroad. Growth was rapid between 1846, when Mr. Thomson brought in his first rail lines, and 1864, when Mr. Sherman casually gutted the place in pyromanic

25

passing to the sea. In 1868, when the twenty-one-year-old town became the state capital, construction and growth quickened, erupting upward from shell craters and debris. More and more trains rolled in daily, disgorging adventurers, refugees, carpetbaggers, scalawags, speculators, and even an occasional honest businessman.

He threaded his way carefully along the red clay streets, which were gouged deeply by steel-rimmed wheels of heavy wagons. Water stagnated in those potholes after heavy rains. Sleet misted, adding to the general mood of misery and discomfort. Blue federal uniforms dominated every street. The oppressive presence of the Third District Army of Occupation increased the burden but, despite all this, the village boomed into a city, buildings mushrooming along encroaching streets, flushing and spewing uncontrolled and haphazardly outward from the railhead.

He paused outside a newly constructed, two-story red brick building that was already pocked and decaying. He climbed narrow stairs to a long corridor of closed doors lettered carelessly by the occupants: doctors, lawyers, realtors, human rights enforcers. The third door on the right bore a small printed card pinned to its facing with two bright thumbtacks: *Phillips Clark, Attorney-at-Law.* Scrawled beneath the name was: *Please Knock Before Entering.*

Ward knocked, then entered a small crib partitioned from the larger space. He knocked on the inner door. A man's voice called, "Who is it?"

"Ward Hamilton."

A pause, then, "What do you want?"

Ward shook his head in mild exasperation. "I want to talk to you." He tried the knob. The door was locked.

"Be with you in a moment," the voice said.

Ward waited a long, silent ten minutes in the cell-like reception area. Minutes ticked away. He tried to be patient, but he was not by nature passive. He knocked again on the locked inner door. Finally, Phillips Clark unbolted and opened the door and stared at him, frowning.

"Is this the way you welcome all prospective clients?" Ward asked.

"I keep my door bolted and locked because it's dangerous not to, in these times. Blacks have determined that freedom means freedom to steal, assault, enter."

26

"Maybe they're just imitating the Army of Occupation."

"Whatever, it's dangerous to walk the streets. Dangerous to leave a door unlocked, a henhouse unguarded."

"Maybe they're hungry."

"There's plenty of work in Atlanta, if they want to work. Maybe they're still too ignorant to handle freedom, too violent in demonstrating their new equality. Someone said, 'For every right, an obligation.' But they forgot to convey that message to the new freedmen. Or maybe there's no way to make them comprehend yet. Anyway, I'm busy."

"Too busy to talk to me?"

"I've nothing to say to you."

"I've plenty to say to you."

"What in hell do you want of me, Hamilton? Selling out your own brother. Jesus. What can I say to you? What can you want of me?"

"I need a lawyer."

"Why? What have you done now?"

"A *good* lawyer."

"What in hell have you done?"

"I haven't done anything yet. It's what I want to do. I can't complete any transaction without a lawyer backing every move."

"My God."

"What's the matter with you?"

"Me? Nothing. I'm just a nice Jewish boy with a gentile-sounding name and a law degree, working hard, trying to exist in Atlanta. Reconstruction, redneck Atlanta, where even local-born Jews are foreigners, aliens. I don't have trouble enough; I have to be haunted by the Hamilton brothers."

"It is because of Robert—because of the way you defended him—that I'm here."

Phillips Clark stared up at him, his thick black eyebrow tilted. Clark was a heavy-shouldered, round-hipped, fat-jowled young man who looked younger than his thirty years, despite a prominent belly accented with a gold watch chain across his checkered vest. His dark, tightly curled hair receded from his high, bulging forehead and turned up over his stiff detachable collar. His aquiline nose jutted between heavy eyebrows and a full mustache, ragged over his dark-lipped mouth. His blue eyes glittered in the musty office light. "The way I defended Robert? My God, man, he's sentenced to ten years in the federal penitentiary."

Ward shrugged. "He's better off there."

Phillips Clark winced. "He told me how he hated you. He appeared to have every cause. According to him, even the payroll robbery germinated in your fertile brain."

"I may have mentioned how it could be done. I never had any idea he'd try it alone and bungle it. He was a damn fool."

"I had no idea you hated him as cordially as he hates you."

"I don't hate him at all. He's my brother. I've always admired him for what he could do. But with his leg amputated and all, his reputation ruined, he has no chance of employment." He shrugged. "They'll take care of him in prison."

Phillips Clark whistled between his bulbous lips, riffling ragged strands of his soup-strainer mustache. He went around his desk, sat down, and pretended to scribble on a pad of newsprint before him.

It grew quiet in the small, overcrowded office. A fly buzzed around an inkwell. Ward said, "You handled yourself well. You were good in that courtroom. I watched you. I decided that if I ever needed a good lawyer, I'd hire you."

"Next to money, nothing warms the cockles of my heart more than flattery. But I am honest, even with myself. I'm afraid I didn't earn such extravagant praise in defense of your brother—pleasurable as it sounds."

"You're hard on yourself because you lost the case—"

"Winning. That's everything, Hamilton. Everything."

"You don't have to tell me that. And I knew you felt that way. That's why I came to you; I've always felt that way—"

"But I lost your brother's case—"

"No. You won a moral victory. You had the best lawyers the U.S. Department of Justice and War Department could send in here to oppose you. You stood against them. You were better than they were. If you're as honest with yourself as you claim to be, you'd admit that."

Phillips Clark almost smiled. "I had them sweating."

"Them? Hell you had *me* sweating. You kept that stupid old judge awake. He was afraid to take a nap for fear he'd miss something. You brought up a point that almost finished them off: circumstantial evidence. And only circumstantial evidence existed against my brother. Where was the money the government charged him with stealing? Where was the proof beyond the shadow of a doubt? He'd had the opportunity, but he'd had that every month for the past year. His record as civilian paymaster was flawless, impeccable, unquestioned. But because he was frightened and in panic when soldiers tried to arrest him, and resisted arrest and fled, the U.S. Government, in its wisdom and impersonal heartlessness, nominated him as the culprit, pursued, indicted, and tried him—on circumstantial evidence. He was the paymaster. He had access to the money. The money was gone. He grew frightened and fled. Therefore he was guilty."

Phillips Clark shrugged. "He *was* guilty."

"I know that, but the jury didn't. Oh, that was beautiful! That's why you were scaring hell out of those government lawyers. A shadow of doubt. If there was a shadow of doubt, that jury had to release him, let him go free, in the name of justice. I thought you had won it." Ward laughed and shook his head. "That judge had to undo all your work, or you would have won it. He bore down on the government's side. He must have said 'a preponderance of evidence' twenty times in his instructions to the jury."

Now Phillips Clark actually smiled. Smiling, he looked younger than ever. "You really did appreciate every nuance, didn't you?"

"I thought you had him free. I'd have gambled on it. The only reason the jury found Robert guilty was that they were afraid not to. The federal government brought him to trial in a federal court in occupied territory. It was a matter of being guilty until proven innocent—as it is every time the government brings a case to court."

Clark watched him. "So you want to hire me? What have *you* done?"

"I told you. I haven't done anything."

"Then take my advice. Your brother lies almost helpless in a prison hospital, bitter, an amputee, about to be fitted for a wooden leg. Whatever you plan to do, think twice about it."

"Whatever I do, it won't be stealing peanuts."

Phillips Clark laughed. "A hundred thousand in government gold is hardly peanuts in a disembowled economy where a rich man touches maybe two or three hundred dollars in a year."

"I admit it's relatively a lot of money. But what good is it to Robert? As you say, he'll hobble on one leg for the rest of his life. That gold won't buy back his leg, or his genteel fiancee, or his place in society. He didn't tell you where he hid that money, did he?"

Phillips Clark stared at Ward coldly, then laughed incredulously. "You get more interesting by the minute, Hamilton. Is that why you came here? You think your brother confided in me?"

Ward shrugged. "I could use that money. Now. He can't."

"Well, Robert didn't tell me where that money is hidden. I wouldn't have let him tell me even if he'd wanted to. I had burden enough trying to defend him without sharing his guilty knowledge. I told him that as long as there *is* no money, he is imprisoned—if not falsely—at least only on circumstantial evidence and not without hope of appeal. Even if appeal fails, in three or four years he'll be eligible for parole. They can never try him on this matter again. When he gets out of prison, he can buy diamond-inlaid wooden legs if he wants to."

Ward laughed. "You're my kind of man, Clark."

Clark winced broadly. "God. I wish you hadn't said that. You and your brother are a one-family crime wave."

"Why do you say that?" Ward waited, but when Clark only laughed, he said, "We're just a couple of country boys from the Midwest. One of us is in trouble—"

"And the other one is grabbing for the brass ring. You want to hire me in advance. Most people hire lawyers only in the extremity of need."

"Well that's where you're wrong about me. I haven't committed any crime. I'm not about to, unless I have to."

"And you want me retained and ready, just in case?"

"Yes. And I'm not asking you to do anything crooked."

"Oh, I have no objection to illegality or immorality—as long as the price is right. Do you mind saying what you have in mind?"

"Only that it's nothing stupid, like stealing an army

payroll and running. I can't believe my own brother could be that damned stupid. No, what I'm after is *real* money, real power, the kind that lifts you above the law. No, Mr. Clark, I'm not like my brother at all. I look at things and I see them as they are. As they *really* are, not as the blind idealist sees them, not as the establishment wants me to."

"For example?"

"For example. When Robert and I grew up in Ohio, the war was going on. I was five or six when it started. It was a long way from Ohio, a farm in Ohio, way down here. This was like another planet to a kid as young as I was. But as the war dragged on and I got older, I saw people choke up when the flag went by. They would yell and wave and cry when young men enlisted and went off to fight. That's when I first realized Robert and I were different. He couldn't wait to get old enough to enlist. He stood like a tin soldier, saluting when the flag went by. But I saw past the parades, even then. I saw the wounded shipped home. Coming home without the bands and the parades. All these cheering, flag-waving patriots didn't really see the maimed and ruined. They didn't want to see them. The war was a glorious fight against a godless enemy, and that's all they saw. You know what I saw?"

"Nothing patriotic and exalting, I'm sure."

"I saw the men who got rich off the war, and off those battered and destroyed men who marched off to fight. By the time I was in my early teens, I knew who those men were. They were the elite of this country—the bastards who ran things for their own profit. And *they* were *my* heroes. There's a man named John D. Rockefeller. He was written up in the Sunday features in those days as a great patriot. He was young enough to fight, but he didn't fight. He was a grain commission merchant in Cleveland. He never enlisted. Probably paid some damn fool to go off and fight in his place, while he stayed home and made millions routing government grain bought from his clients through his warehouses to be sent to the federal troops under fire. That started me thinking and looking around. *Nobody* with any real influence and wealth actually *fought* in the war. They got rich off it. There John D. was, every Sunday in the Baptist Church, leading the prayers, while he gouged the government six days a week. Since then he's gotten richer, more powerful. He wasn't my only hero.

31

Philip Armour and John Wanamaker were too busy profiteering to get mixed up in those glorious hostilities. A fellow named Flagler was in grain routing too, and salt and whiskey speculation. None of them followed the flag into battle; they profited from it. I made up my mind that I was going to be one of them. And I will. Hell, I'm as smart as they are. I just need a chance. And that's why I'm willing to pay you twenty-five dollars a week as a retainer. All I ask is that you be ready to work for me—twenty-four hours a day."

Phillips Clark rocked a moment in his swivel chair. The dry springs squealed like a scalded cat. Finally he smiled and nodded, then rubbed his hands together. "I never met anybody just like you, Hamilton. I won't say I like you. As a matter of fact, I get tears in my eyes when a flag goes by. But I will say this: for twenty-five dollars a week, I'll be ready any time. You own a small but vital part of my soul from the moment you make your down payment."

Chapter Three

THERE WAS LITTLE that was spectacular about the Hotel General Douglas Clayton, which had recently been built on Spring Street, except its newness. Even the paint on the gilt letters that proclaimed its distinguished name to unimpressed Atlantans smelled new. Beds, mattresses, furnishings, and cheap prints of Confederate heroes, locked in futile but noble combat, all glittered with the gloss of novelty. The room was not large, but utilitarian and adequate for the four-poster double bed of air-seasoned, kiln-dried oak and high-gloss golden finish. All the furnishings matched it: the dresser with its cast brass handles and French bevel plate mirror, and the washstand. Such a set must have cost at least thirty dollars wholesale, in quantity lots. Ward acknowledged that the place was commercial, less than swank, but it was not a place he was ashamed to take a woman, even a fashionable and genteel lady like Dolly Marsh.

He supported himself on his arm, looking down at her. She slept on her back, nude, an arm flung over her tousled blonde head, her full lips parted, her body vulnerable. Her vulnerability, if not her fading beauty, stirred something deep in his loins and he felt himself go empty-bellied with the savage thrust of need. She slept so soundly, in such exhaustion, that he did not want to wake her yet. It had been a long night; he had used her body excessively. Faint discolorations showed in her pale cheeks, around her mouth, on her delicate chin, along her fragile arms. God knew he hadn't wanted to hurt her—the precise opposite, in fact—but she had roused him to sweet violence, even if she was probably close to forty, though she confessed only to being twenty-eight. It had been one hell of a party. Empty bourbon bottles lay discarded on a straight chair beside the bed. He hadn't drunk much, watching her swig it down. He was young, but for at least three years he'd been living by his wits, and he'd learned better than to dull his mind with alcohol. Enough brew to kindle a glow, enough to burn out those Ohio farm boy inhibitions, that was all. He didn't need liquor for stimulation. There was excitement enough in just staying alive. Neither could he drown his woes in whiskey; he found no answers at all in the bottom of a bottle. But at the bottom of a woman now, even an older woman, pliable and anxious to please—a woman like Dolly—that was something else. . . .

He folded back the sheet and glanced down at himself, proud of his physical endowments. "Hey, you look great," he told his tumescent erection. "A wonder they don't stand in line for you."

He grinned in satisfaction. He was conscious that he had all the attributes to help him achieve the success he wanted, accomplish all his impossible goals. He had a good mind, sharp wits, an almost photographic memory, and he learned from his mistakes. The mirrors that were women's eyes told him he was good-looking, ruggedly healthy, well-built, and brimming with vitality and zest for life. His excellent body delighted women. He was capable of controlling himself so he could satisfy his partners. He'd studied every woman he met and stored away her reactions. Few men gave a damn about a woman's satisfaction. He was proud of himself, his mind, his body, his physical endowments. He had learned how to use women to help him achieve what he wanted, how to make them want to help him. Yes, he had everything he needed to get ahead, except money, except that one irrecoverable opportunity that would set him on his way. . . .

He had also learned one sad fact of life. He didn't belong among capitalists, and he was excluded from the moneyed circles, the councils of the affluent, and the compounds of the powerful. He had neither family background, rich relatives, nor the patronage of authority, influence, or prestige. He was an outsider.

God knew they'd taught him that in three years. Despite his tender years, he'd already made many stabs at advancement, grabbing at every opportunity, only to be knocked flat by remote, casual, and unmindful men who did belong in the world of money and power. He never escaped the fearful sense of his vulnerability; he was naked and defenseless against them, doing battle with the dubious assets of poverty and youth. The hell with them. He wasn't afraid of anything in this world except failure.

Yawning and pushing his hair back from his face, he sat up and rested his weight against the pillow and headboard. The bare breasts of the sleeping woman tempted him. He wanted to reach out and fondle them, but he delayed, aching pleasantly, watching her.

He grinned coldly. She had been in his plans even before he met her, or knew she existed as an individual. A woman like her would open doors for him that were locked against him now. He'd gone uninvited to the ballroom at the Atlantan Hotel last night, mingling with the guests—the railroad men and their ladies.

Among the women had been the quiet, faintly regal woman who drank too much and danced too infrequently. He saw her toes bouncing with the music at the hem of her rich, watered-silk gown. The neckline was cut extremely low, daring even for the latest fashions, squared across her cleavage and trimmed with a full ruche of tulle that formed the sleeves. The skirt was unadorned and appeared to be somehow wound downward about her hips, thighs, and legs from her narrow waist to pleated hemline. Elegant. Everything about her pronounced her that. The choker at her slender throat reflected the winking gaslights every time she moved her head. Her gaze found Ward early and returned to him often, at first in boredom, then in interest, and finally, in such open invitation that he approached her almost warily.

They danced and drank together. She drank and he watched her in some fascination. She left him once, and he saw her across the crowded room in heated dialogue with a man with muttonchop whiskers who looked to be in his fifties, gray, distinguished, wearing tailored evening clothes. The man held his top hat in his hand and his alpaca topcoat across his arm. He was not trying to get her to leave with him. The opposite was true; obviously, he wished to depart the premises immediately, urgently, and without her.

When she returned to him, Ward waited for her to mention the small, tense episode. She did not. She had another drink, and they danced again. Alone with her on a small terrace overlooking the slumbering city, he could not resist sliding his hand beneath her arm and covering her small, high-standing breast with his palm. "Please don't do that," she said. He apologized, grinning and admitting it was what he'd wanted to do since the first moment he'd met her. She sagged against the balustrade and gazed indolently across the dark night for a long minute. Finally she said, "Are you staying here at this hotel?" He told her he was sorry he was not, but she merely shrugged, and when he left the party, she went with him.

She seemed without obligations to anyone. He wondered if she were an outsider like him, looking, as he was, for contacts with wealth and prestige. It was a hell of a joke on both of them if she were.

When he registered at the General Douglas Clayton Hotel, she said, "We'll need something to drink." He dispatched a bellhop for her favorite bourbon. Inside the room, she slipped the tulle ruche straps down over her arms, baring her breasts. "Do you think them beautiful?" she asked, as if something vital depended upon his answer. He replied truthfully, but in a voice growing taut with fiercely aroused passions. He not only had never met, nor fantasized, a woman like her before, he'd had no idea such liberated females existed in the same world with him. Her breasts *were* lovely, firm and round and taut, unsagging, the nipples rigid and freshly pink.

In bed, she lay in that vulnerable way, her clouded eyes watching him with gentleness and yet such passionate appetite that he was aroused in ways he'd never imagined. She lay back and opened her legs for him, but as he settled between her knees, pulsing and throbbing and breathless with craving, she stopped him. "What's your name, boy?" she said.

36

He stared at her, wild-eyed. She continued to gaze at him as at a stranger, and she waited, naked, open, her splayed hand against his navel. "Ward," he gasped at last. He laughed helplessly. "What a hell of a time to ask a question like that."

"Don't laugh at me," she said. "I think it's important to know. What if there's a fire?"

When he looked at her again, she spoke without opening her eyes. "Are you awake, Ward?"

"I hardly slept," he said. "I've never met anyone like you."

"I know." Still without opening her eyes, she dropped her fiery-hot, slender-fingered hand onto his thigh. "What time is it?"

"God knows. Daylight."

She sighed. "I really should go. If I'm not in my hotel room when Baxter wakes up, he'll go into one of his jealous snits. He's such a fool."

"Who is Baxter?"

"Baxter Marsh. Yale. Wall Street. Railroads. He built the rail lines from Jacksonville to Lake City. That's in Florida."

"He's your husband?"

"In name, dear boy. In name only. It's been ten years since he's had an erection. Five years since he's wanted one."

He laughed. She opened her eyes slowly, wincing against the sharp shafts of light. "What's the matter?" she said. "Don't you believe me?"

"I believe you. I just never heard a woman talk like this before."

"You're young, dear. God, you're young. Beautiful. And it was lovely last night. All of it."

"Was it?"

"Yes. I hope you don't expect to get paid."

"What?" He sat forward, staring down at her.

She shrugged those lovely bare shoulders and her breasts jiggled entrancingly. "After all, it does happen. I *am* a few years older than you are. Some young men, when they're built like Greek gods—as you are—do want money for their favors."

He tried to pass it off lightly, as if the whole idea were

37

not new and unheard of in his life, and somewhat shocking. "I'll have to remember that—if I'm ever with an older woman." He forced himself to laugh and caressed her breast lightly but with urgency. "Maybe next time."

"With me? There won't be a next time for us, sweetheart. After I get out of your bed this morning, I'm out of your life."

"Is that the way you want it?"

"Whether it is or not, it's the way it will have to be. I am an older married woman with all the problems I need for one lifetime. I can't take on a teenaged boy to raise."

"I'm almost twenty."

She laughed, delighted with him, a gentle sound. "Even so. And I wasn't denigrating your manhood, darling. Nineteen or twenty, you *are* a man."

She turned on the bed and reached for him, sending blood throbbing into his temples, making his hands tremble with nervous excitement. "Take it easy, sweetheart," she whispered. "Take it easy." She closed her eyes and clung to him, reaching for something intangible, something he could neither see nor understand. She cried out, chewing at her full lips, thrusting herself upward to him violently.

They lay sprawled, lightly touching, in exhaustion. Pulses throbbed in Ward's temples. His eyes felt as if the pressure behind them would eject them from their sockets. His legs felt weak and clabbery. "I'll order some coffee," he said at last, staring at the ceiling, too tired to turn his head.

"That's sweet."

He managed to thrust himself to his feet. The floor felt strange and chilly against his soles, as if even the extremities of his nerve ends had been stretched taut and tender. He pressed a button on the wall beside the door and, when a bellboy arrived, he ordered breakfast, then toppled almost helpless into a club chair, the fabric rough on his bare flesh.

Dolly had returned from the bathroom, almost fully dressed. "Thank God for the opera cloak," she said. "A hellish hour to appear in a decolleté party gown."

"I wish I thought I'd see you again."

"Well you musn't—or even think about it."

"Where will you go?"

"Home. Baxter and I came just for the conference. He's interested only in business. That's all he's got left at his age. He walked out on me last night for a late-hour meeting."

"Was that Baxter?"

"Yes. He's fifty-eight. A real prig. He's trying to retire. Trying to pull in his horns, he says, dispose of holdings. That's why he's here. Trying to sell off his Florida rail holdings."

Ward felt his heart constrict. He forgot to be tired. He forgot what had happened in that rumpled bed between him and Dolly. "Could I meet him?"

She stopped in the middle of arranging the bodice of her gown. She looked up and stared at him, her eyebrow tilted. "Why would you want to do that?"

"Maybe I could bid—for his railroad holdings in Florida."

She shrugged. "Maybe you could." She patted at her dress. "I had no idea you were that old or that affluent."

"How old and affluent would I have to be?"

She moved those alabaster shoulders again, in a careless shrug. "I have no idea, darling, and absolutely no interest. Still, under the circumstances, you can't expect me to introduce you to him. It makes the whole thing even more commercial than my paying you for it."

His face flushed. If she had thought him ardent and violent in that bed, she could have no inkling of how he felt at this moment. He barely heard what she said. He forced himself to sit quietly. He had from Dolly Marsh all the information he would get. Her husband owned rail lines, obviously in northern Florida, since that was the only part of the state developed to any extent. He was trying to sell off those lines. This was far more knowledge than he'd possessed yesterday. It was the kind of information he spent his life looking for. He felt a rush of tenderness toward her. "Do you want me to find a carriage for you?"

She smiled and formed a kiss. "You're a dear child. Since you can afford it, I'd appreciate a carriage. It's not far to the Atlantan, but it is public, every step of the way."

He lunged up from the chair, kissed her, and dressed hurriedly, forgetting he was tired, forgetting he had ever been tired.

* * *

"How in hell do you *buy* a railroad?" Phillips Clark said. He stared at Ward, thick black brows tilted.

"You bid for it. Along with other bidders."

"You have to deposit at least ten percent of the bid." Clark shook his head and grinned sourly. "Oh, that's right. You've got twenty-thousand burning a hole in your conscience, haven't you? Your thirty pieces of Judas money for betraying your brother. So you make your bid. Suppose you're high bidder. Then what?"

"You either make the highest bid, or the most attractive bid. And that's what I'm going to do. One or the other."

"I *know* the procedure. And I'll lead you by the hand step by step. But I ask you again. How do you pay for it? How do you finance it? How do you keep it running long enough to get any returns? You've got to have money to run a railroad. A hell of a lot of money."

Ward grinned coldly. "I can cross only one bridge at a time."

Clark met his gaze. "You'd better start looking ahead in your pipe dreams. Your contempt for your brother is based, I understand, on his being constitutionally unable to see or plan ahead."

Ward shrugged. "I plan ahead. As far as I have to. But I don't think that's what you're talking about. You're talking about worrying over some future problems. And that I won't do."

Clark gazed at his client, awed in spite of himself. "Hell," he said. "I wouldn't have missed this for anything. To you, operating capital for a company is a future problem you can't concern yourself with now."

"That's right. I don't own the company. Why in hell should I worry about how I'll keep it operating? I'll face that when—and if—I get that far. Right now I've only one problem: getting all the information on the company and making a bid for it."

"With total assets of twenty-thousand dollars." Clark whistled through his mustache.

"If you want out, just say so."

"Oh no. You couldn't get me out with a crowbar. I'm in. You'll just have to forgive my fretting over such mundane matters as capital credits."

"Hell. Go ahead and worry. Just don't bring up such

40

matters as my financial condition or where I'm going to get the money while I'm conferring with these people."

"You don't have to tell me how to do my job, either."

"Just so we understand each other."

"I think we're beginning to."

Ward saw at once that he'd made the ideal choice in hiring Phillips Clark as his legal representative. Clark jotted down the few facts Ward had on Baxter Marsh's rail company and began an instant investigation, survey, and analysis of the firm, especially its line between Jacksonville and Lake City.

Ward and Clark examined the meager interstate records held by the Army of Occupation. Clark contacted Governor Marcellus L. Stearns at Tallahassee, asking about a state railroad commission. He learned that there was no such organization in Florida. There was a Governor's Board on Transportation, but most viable contact between the state government and the rail companies came through something called the Internal Improvement Fund. Clark received brochures, prospecti and statements of assets from the Marsh home office in Jacksonville. Still less than satisfied, Clark interviewed all the railroad officials still in Atlanta for the conference.

Ward was sprawled in exhausted sleep, face down on his rooming house bed, when Clark's fists, pounding on his locked door, woke him.

Ward sat up groggily. He lit a lamp on the bedside table and checked his watch. He stood in his underwear, staring at the rotund young attorney and the sheaves of papers he carried. "You know what time it is?"

"A little after one," Clark said. "You hired me on a twenty-four-hour basis, and that's what you're getting."

Ward was waking slightly, the excitement mounting in his belly. He tried to smile. "Hell, I thought I was driven."

"You aren't even Jewish," Clark told him. "Now sit down and try to listen. I've got a lot of news, and most of it is bad. To me it is totally discouraging, but by now I'm convinced you'll find a golden lining somewhere in these dark clouds. I believe I have all the facts on the East Florida & Gulf Central Railroad. Baxter Marsh is a devious son of a bitch, and maybe I've just seen the tip of the iceberg. But it's enough. It should discourage you."

41

"Is that what you set out to do? Is that why you came running here at this hour."

"Just listen. Since the late, lamented War Between the States was fought to secure Southern commerce for Wall Street, innumerable small lines from Virginia south have fallen into bankruptcy, or have hung on by their teeth in hopes that somebody with cash will buy them out. Now, East Florida and Gulf is not quite in that condition. But it's not much better off, either. There are seventy-two miles of track, switches, and sidings between the railhead in Jacksonville and the terminal in Lake City. There is a railyard at Lake City, owned by the state of Florida and leased to the several linking lines that converge there. Some are just short logging lines, tracks running out to groves, farms, sawmills, or turpentine stills. Others, like EF&GC are a little more respectable. There is a line running from Lake City to Apalachicola, and one to Tallahassee. The biggest line in and out of there is the Lake City, Pensacola, and Mobile line. East Florida isn't the biggest frog in that pond, but it's not the smallest by a hell of a lot. It may well be the shakiest. I got a list of rolling stock, employees, materials, and equipment. I also learned from a guy named Ralph Bracussi, who is the head accountant at Jacksonville for Baxter Marsh, that all prospective bidders are invited there to inspect the physical assets of the company. I elicited no such invitation to inspect company financial records."

"We'll do it."

"My advice is to forget it. you're not dealing with an ordinary rail company. Baxter Marsh is a financier and promoter first of all. Hell, he's in everything: banks, gambling, hotels, a stock brokerage firm on Wall Street— Cushing, Byers, & Marsh—steamship lines, lumber, cattle, oil. You name it."

Ward whistled, wide awake now.

"Yes sir, Baxter Marsh is one of your hero types. He's amassed so much money that he's been absorbing losses on EF&GC for some years now without even breathing hard. But I can assure you he has Bracussi's bookkeepers on triple-entry accounting. You could dig for two years and find nothing he doesn't want you to find."

"Why is he getting out?"

"Because he's smart, a hell of a lot smarter than you

42

are. Obviously he's given up on Florida as a developing area, and he wants out. The only good angle is that I think he's willing to take a bath to get out. That ought to tell you something." Clark grinned at him coldly. "If a man as rich as Midas can't make it down in that wild country, what do you want with it?"

"I've got to start somewhere."

"Why not one of these bankrupt Georgia lines? You could probably buy a seventy-mile line for promissory notes, scrip, and your twenty thousand. You could use any capital credit you could scrape up to make the line productive."

"I want something with bankable assets."

"The liabilities outweigh assets at EF&GC ten to one. You're not talking about a company with cash flow, ongoing income, adequate receivables. You're talking about bidding on, and trying to pay off, a line with a lot of costly-to-maintain assets and staggering operating losses."

"Yes. But you just said it. Marsh is a financial—uh—"

"Manipulator?"

"And not a railroader. He was trying to get something out of East Florida besides income. Hell, nobody knows how much income he might have diverted from that company."

Clark smiled and nodded. "Touché."

"What's with 'touché'?"

"That's French for 'Goddamn, you may be right.'"

They talked until daybreak. There was much to discuss. For every negative Clark presented, Ward provided a positive, or at least a hopeful alternative. He would not be discouraged. "Jesus," Clark said at last, "You'll make a believer out of me yet. A Ward Hamilton follower. I don't believe you can make me like you, but I am a disciple, and that scares hell out of me. I hope it's just because I want to see you get your face smashed in, but I'm damned if I'm even sure about that anymore."

Ward seemed not even to hear him. "I want a line with bankable assets. That's what I've got to have."

"Borrow on the assets even before you own them." Clark shook his head, disturbed.

"If I can. I'm not going to cheat anybody. This I know: EF&GC *has* to hold current working transportation con-

43

tracts. Nothing else makes sense. I don't care how badly the company is being managed. The freight traffic is there. Lumber, fruit, vegetables, naval stores—God knows what all—come from the center of the state into the port and railhead at Jacksonville. Building materials and machinery, fabrics and equipment come in from the North—some of it consigned to central and west Florida. The rails and sidings are blocked up down in Jacksonville every day of the year. Incoming loaded cars are held up by empty cars on every switch and siding, waiting to be loaded. EF&GC *must* get some of this pie now—and I can get more. And EF&GC must have gotten in on the land grants."

"Oh, they did. Land bonuses to rail builders and promoters, along with guarantees for rail and canal bonds, have just about bankrupted the state, according to Governor Stearn's people. Along with thievery, bribery, malfeasance in office, and general corruption and the threat of bankruptcy, that state has problems. And if you think they won't affect the running of a rail company, you're more innocent even than you look."

"What about the land bonuses?"

"I didn't get a chance to tell you. Marsh's company was awarded grants and bonuses for building that line between Jacksonville and Lake City. Those handouts amounted to four million acres of land at ten cents an acre. When this deal was made, the market price on that land was a dollar and a quarter an acre."

Ward stared at Clark. He got up and paced the room, unable to sit still. *Please, God,* he begged, *don't let them take this one away from me. Help me, God.* He managed to keep his voice level. "Is the land included in the bid?"

"Nobody discussed the land. I found it listed among assets. I investigated and found out where it came from. This was the biggest shock I got, and already I'm becoming immune to shock. The land bonuses and sweetheart deals awarded to EF&GC, along with the franchise, could be worth millions. As far as I can learn, Marsh considers the land worthless. I don't know this, but he may never even have seen it, or wanted to. He planned to develop it, but when the boom he expected didn't materialize, he said to hell with it all. That's where it stands now. But even at twenty cents an acre, you might pay off your bid—if you found buyers for that land."

"Whether anybody discussed the land, be damned sure it's spelled out and included in our bid, every acre and every section and every grain."

"I've told you, don't try to tell me how to run my shop."

"All right." Ward wiped his damp face and body with a wrinkled shirt. He tossed the shirt on the floor and walked to the window, trying to suck in a breath of cool, fresh air. "What's our next move?"

"We see Baxter Marsh. We get the proper papers and make our bid, if you intend to try it, and I can see you do. Then you can pray a lot."

Ward remained motionless. "I'll be too busy to pray."

"So. I'll pray for both of us."

Ward stood immobile at the window, with his back to Phillips Clark. He felt alone, completely isolated and removed from those nearest him, as he often had. He stared toward the sky, already lightening with the first hint of dawn. He gazed toward the distant stars. His star, winking brilliantly in infinity. His star. He didn't even know its name. He could have checked volumes on astronomy and learned its name, but he didn't want to know. For him, that star had its own reason, purpose, and destiny, and its fate was wrapped tightly with his. It was his star. The brilliant, gemlike clarity, the way it sailed suspended, alone and sharply illumined in the constellation, one of a million stars, and yet set apart, alone. His star. Fred. He called it Fred. Fred was good enough. It was his star.

Chapter Four

TWO DAYS LATER, Ward and Phillips Clark were in Jacksonville, arriving by stagecoach over Kings Road. Clark advised reasonably priced rooms—a dollar a night for two in a double bed—at one of the upstairs hotels on Bay Street. This would place them near the railroad terminals, warehouses, and piers. Business offices of increasing numbers of railway companies were down there, convenient to their modest lodging.

Ward walked with his lawyer, each carrying his own suitcase and sweating under the weight, along Bay Street. Ward gazed in amazement at the wharves, warehouses, and mazes of rail lines where hundreds of black men toiled, shirtless and glistening in the sun. The rail terminus at Atlanta was huge and bustling, but nothing like this place, because this was not only a railhead, but a seaport. Incredible piles of long-leaf yellow pine logs reared like massive, formless structures waiting to be loaded on oceangoing steamers bound for Europe. Bales of cotton rose like feudal walls as far as the eye could see. Naval stores sweltered and stunk in the unyielding heat, as did the cattle and hog pens and the vegetable ramps.

His pulse quickened. Instinct assured him this *was* the place where he'd get his chance, the goal toward which he'd been running every day of his life. He'd make it here. *Please, God!*

He found no lodgings to suit him on Bay Street. There were plenty of those upstairs hotels, their signs hanging out over the twisting, sandy roadway, still lined and scarred with old and deteriorating pine shacks. There was plenty of action and noise, with Phillips Clark turning to stare over his shoulder at a fistfight, a knifing, or a strange being from some other existence. Piano music blared from barrooms, gambling places, dancehalls, and the whorehouses where the ladies sagged in open windows, their ratty peignoirs revealing powdered breasts. Sailors staggered drunkenly along the walks or vomited into the gutters. Garish women—brown Latins escaping from the Ybor cigar factories at Key West, slattern blacks, and frowsy whites—brushed against them, or sucked their middle fingers suggestively in passing.

"Hell, how would it look if we stayed down here?" Ward said.

"Like we were conserving your money." Clark mopped at his forehead and grinned sheepishly. "Like we're going to live it up down here where nobody knows us on the Barbary Coast of the East."

Ward swung his arm, signaling a passing black man driving an open carriage, pulled by a spavined gelding wearing a derby. The hack pulled into the boardwalk and the driver bent down from his high seat. "Where-at you wish to be taken to, young mastas?"

"The best hotel in town," Ward told him.

The black man's wide smile bared glittering white teeth with large gaps in front. "That would be the St. James, young masta. Yassuh. The St. James Hotel. Finest hotel you find south of Fifth Avenue up in New York City. Yassuh, we foolishly proud of our St. James."

Ward nodded. He tossed his bag into the carriage and swung into it, followed, with some reluctance, by Clark. "Take us to the St. James," Ward said.

He watched the busy town glide past the carriage. The few nondescript frame residences they passed were built close to the street and hedged with red-blossoming oleander, wisteria, trumpet vine, or purple bougainvillea, wilting under evergreen oaks, camphor trees, or native palms. Main Street was a twisting pioneer thoroughfare on the

47

eastern boundary of the business area. Ramshackle buildings of faded brick and clapboard strung out from the wharves and warehouses at the river. Another loud street, boisterous and crowded, its walks were thronged with Spaniards, blacks, seamen, farmers, trappers, soldiers, businessmen, fugitives, and thugs. The town was old, but it had suffered a harried, sometimes tragic history since the north bank of a village called Cowford was incorporated in 1822. It had been named for General Andrew Jackson, the territorial governor whose troops had almost decimated the Indians and their fugitive slave allies, and who had never come nearer the town at the mouth of the St. Johns than the distant Suwannee. This ford where cattle were swum across the river had first been called Wacca Pilatka, an Indian name meaning "cows crossing over." The town had prospered, faltered, failed, and, during the occupation by federal troops during the Civil War, fallen to a population of less than a dozen. The village had to be rebuilt after the withdrawal of Northern troops in 1863. On returning, refugees found their homes burned, trenches instead of streets, outlying farms devastated, and all ferry and dock facilities destroyed. Now the burgeoning metropolis, almost fifty percent black, boasted a population of about 7,500. Restoration was a painful process, but it was being accomplished. The St. James Hotel opened its opulent doors in 1869.

The driver set Ward and Clark down at the canopied entrance of the splendid hostelry. "Ain't been nothin' better'n the St. James built in the last seven year," the old black man said. He grinned. "Ain't likely nothin' finer ever will be built, this side of the Jordan."

"This is more like it," Ward told Clark. "They'll know we're somebody."

"Hell, I don't care. As long as you're paying for it."

They entered the cool, ornate foyer. Ward said, "If any rail people are here to bid on EF&GC, they'll likely stay here at the St. James. If we meet them, maybe we can get a line on Baxter Marsh."

They needed a line on Baxter Marsh. Pausing only long enough for both of them to shave and Ward to dress, after a night of discussing the assets and liabilities of Baxter Marsh's rail line, they'd walked downtown from Ward's rooming house to the Atlantan Hotel. Ward had managed to curb his impatience. They'd had an enforcedly leisurely breakfast of wood-smoked ham, scrambled eggs, grits, and coffee. By nine A.M., Clark agreed that it was not too early to inquire at the desk for Baxter Marsh.

Ward walked across the foyer, followed by the young lawyer. Ward felt empty-bellied despite the heavy breakfast, the four cups of black coffee, the buttermilk biscuits. Inside his mind he kept repeating, *Please, God. Please, God.* But in his loins and at his nerve centers he was conscious of the fact that when they met Baxter Marsh, Dolly would be with him. Even with this urgent business spurring him, he wanted to see her again. *One more night, God. One more time.*

But his hopes of meeting Baxter Marsh in Atlanta were quickly dashed. The Atlantan Hotel desk clerk—slender, fair-haired, and more than faintly effeminate—didn't even have to check the files. Baxter Marsh was so distinguished and outstanding a personality that the clerk recalled him instantly. He was different from ordinary people, richer, more arrogant, more compelling. One noticed him instantly and didn't forget him easily. The clerk shook his head, smiling down his drooping nose. "No, I'm sorry, gentlemen. Mr. Marsh and his party have checked out."

Ward stood for a moment immobile, as if he'd walked into an unexpected wall. Then he drew a deep breath, exhaled it, and swung around, striding across the quiet lobby toward the street exit.

"Ward," Clark said.

Ward paused, glancing over his shoulder. "Yes?"

"What now?"

"We'll find Marsh in Jacksonville. What else?"

Phillips Clark hesitated a beat, then spread his hands in a gesture of surrender and followed at his heels. "A Ward Hamilton follower, for God's sake," he said aloud.

The Southern regional offices of Baxter Marsh, Inc. were within sight and smell of the loading wharves, but their decor was like a world removed. The entire interior had been newly and glossily renovated, sound- and heatproofed. Ceiling fans, their large blades battery-powered, swept in lazy circles in every suite. The office furnishings gleamed with polish and whispered of affluence. The Persian carpeting was ankle-deep in Near East texture, pattern, and

49

design. Ward was unable to overcome a sense of being an interloper, an outsider in a masquerade, a crass country bumpkin confronting third-generation prestige and respectability. Bookkeepers, statisticians, routing people, dispatchers, and controllers worked in silence in a hive of flat-topped desks. The whirr of ceiling fans was the loudest and most intrusive sound.

They were ushered into the private cubicle of accountant Ralph Bracussi. This mid-level executive appeared to be an ethnic mongrel of a man, swarthy-skinned, his thick black hair long and carefully brushed to his collar. His bushy brows flared like a protective cover for dark eyes somehow too busy to be impaled or delayed for longer than a second or two at a time. He laughed easily and smiled often. He provided Phillips Clark with all papers pertaining to the bidding, and Clark carefully eased them into his briefcase.

Baxter Marsh remained an elusive quarry. Ward and Clark were assured by Bracussi that Marsh was in Florida, but not in Jacksonville. Bracussi shook his head, smiling. Marsh had come· into the EF&GC office, read his mail, conferred with his top-level executives, and departed.

"Where can we find him?" Ward said.

Bracussi shrugged and laughed. Baxter Marsh was never that easy to contact. His efficient male secretaries and executive assistants screened out all but the most important visitors. Still, Bracussi agreed with a smile, meeting men who expected to bid for the railway corporation was urgent. "If that's not important, what is, eh?"

Bracussi provided them with additional literature, identification materials, and railway tickets. "All interested parties are expected as guests ón an inspection tour of the EF&GC line. You'll undoubtedly get the opportunity of an audience with Mr. Marsh himself before that junket ends."

They had to be satisfied with this.

The train gathered speed, leaving the newly constructed Union Depot at Jacksonville. It raced out of the dusty, poverty-stricken environs of the town into the north Florida pinelands.

Ward sat in the elegantly appointed chair car and gazed out the open window at these thickly timbered regions where lumbering, naval stores, and new orange groves were the priority industries and the businesses most dependent upon rail service, and potentially the most profitable for the carriers. They raced past cotton and tobacco farms, speeding, whistles screaming, through sleepy plantation towns dating back to antebellum days and sunk in the morass of an unprecedented depression.

"Hell of a lot of landfill through these swamps," Clark observed. From the inner chair, he gazed over Ward's shoulder to the farm and forest land. "Maintenance through here must be ruinous."

"If you're dealing with those turpentine stills, lumber mills, and logging camps, it's worth maintaining and the hell with the cost," Ward said, without turning from the steamy countryside. Pines, finger-thin, tall and straight, topped with tufts of green needles like cheap parasols, denied shade. Spreading water oaks and ancient live oaks gave way to hammocks of scrubby jackoaks, an occasional squatter's shack, the occupants running out into sunstruck bare yards to watch the train race past on soot-streaked windstreams.

Marsh's private train scarcely slowed for crossings or settlements along its path. All rail traffic had been relegated to the sidings. This junket had the right-of-way, and the train's whistle screamed like trumpets heralding its passage. Logging trains—flatcars loaded crosswise with five-foot lengths of sawn logs, securely braced with heavy iron bars and channel-iron chains to prevent logs from shifting in transit—idled patiently on switches or sidings as the polished special hurtled through, as did the daily passenger and mail service, freight carriers, and track-working crews. Inside, company employees became proxy hosts, stewards, and bartenders, conscientiously and continuously soliciting the comfort of Marsh's guests.

The towns looked deadly quiet, poverty-stricken, untouched by any influences of the embryonic tourism industry. This section of the state profited from tourists only in their casual passing. The settlements sprawled like clapboard patches along the serpentine right-of-way. Beer halls and saloons, small, soot-pocked depots, a general store, a church or two—all segregated by skin color—flared for an instant into view and then were jerked away on the winds of passage.

Dull-eyed Negroes and thin, ill-clad whites fished in the

51

creeks, ditches, and cypress swamps along the tracks. Huge alligators sunned on wet logs; deer, wild turkey, panthers, and black bears took mindless flight at the clatter of wheels on railings or the capricious whistle blaring from the engine.

The names of the communities snagged at Ward's attention for a brief flash in time: Whitehouse, Baldwin, MacClenny, Glen St. Mary, Eddy. On the south rim of the dank Okefenokee Swamp perched Sanderson and Olustee. Huge turpentine stills with galvanized tin roofs, smoke, black and pungent, belching from tall metal stacks, nestled in thoughtless clusterings of the surrounding clapboard cabins of Negro workers. As the train raced past each settlement, everything for that moment stopped. It would be generations before the passing of a train through the piny backwoods ceased to provide a momentous occasion, a suggestion of a world outside, a hint of unknown places never seen, of strangers from a different existence, thundering past on their way somewhere.

Ward's gaze sought to drink in every sight along these tracks—the towns, the flat pine woods, the swamps. It could all be his some day. It had to be. It would be. His eyes burned from soot and heat and windburn and something unspoken and unspeakable inside him. His heart clattered in rhythm with the racketing of steel rims against rail joints. It was, to him, the loveliest sound in God's world, the click and hammer of wheels on rails, and it had been since the first time he rode a train in the Ohio backcountry of his boyhood—soothing, stimulating, promising. . . .

Chapter Five

THE TRAIN WHISTLED for a lonely pig-track crossing in the flat pinewood wilderness. The crossing was an unimproved clay road just wide enough for a single wagon. If carriages met, one was forced to pull off to the side and sit tilted precariously over the watery ditches while the other passed. A small beagle, its tail tucked protectively between its legs, stood bowlegged in the middle of the roadway. The little animal's expression was so forlorn and morose that Ward felt instantly that the dog was lost or abandoned. A sharp sense of shared panic and dismay flared through him. He stared back until the crossing and the unmoving stray vanished.

Company employees swayed along the aisles bearing heaped trays of condiments, spices, triangular sandwiches—turkey, ham, lettuce and tomato—mixed drinks, ice in bowls, coffee or tea. They proffered the hors d'oeuvres, persistent, unflappable, and unyielding hosts.

In knots, groups, and loosely formed circles around the chairs where Ward and Phillips Clark sat, people laughed and talked. They all seemed acquainted, casually at least. Ward sighed. Perhaps the rail industry was like the law or medical professions or any specialized business community—a village of common interest where everyone knew everybody else; or at least, where one stayed aware of laughed, visited, helped in time of crisis—and kept one's guard up. You had to know your friends, and you had to be equally as conscious of who your enemies were; they sometimes wore the same smiling face.

He gazed about the superbly appointed chair car, feeling more closely allied with the abandoned beagle on that crossing than with his smartly attired fellow travelers. Marsh had spared no expense in making his guests as comfortable and relaxed as possible. They hadn't even reached Lake City, and already one middle-aged man was sprawled snoring on the floor with his head in some young girl's lap. The girl chatted as if the man didn't exist. In the next car, a string band, with a black man at an upright piano, played requested songs and segued into fast rinkytink numbers between requests. The laughter, excitement, pleasant camaraderie, and shouted insults that were warmer than endearments, swirled around Ward and added to his sense of being excluded, an outsider looking in. This was the company of people to which he wanted to belong. So far, he and Phillips Clark remained a small, isolated island across an impossible, invisible bay from the haven of communal revelers. He took a bourbon highball from a proffered tray, turned it up, and found a middle-aged man standing in the aisle beside their chairs, braced against the yaw and pitch of the speeding train, smiling down at them so warmly and without reserve that Ward almost felt it was a case of mistaken identity.

"Hell of a fun junket, huh?" the man said. He had been drinking, but was not drunk. He looked like a man too entirely in command of himself to drink to excess. Though perspiring, he looked distinguished. He was the sort of man who'd look elegant somehow in any situation. He held a half-empty glass of bourbon-on-ice negligently, but without losing a drop to the sway of the car.

He bent at the waist over their chairs, smiling. A man in his forties, he wore an air of affluence like an expensively tailored suit. It set well on him. He had an attitude of arrogantly accepted wealth that Ward recognized; he'd seen it often; he'd begun to look for it as a distinguishing mark among prominent rail, business, and professional figures. This man exuded self-possession and fiscal security,

54

though its gloss may have been marred slightly by a faint disenchantment of his eyes, a wariness, a mussed, dry disarray of his silvering hair. His wasn't smooth elegance; he had his problems, no matter his financial rating.

He raked his glance across Ward, discarded him as too young and beardless to be worthy of attention, and gave Phillips Clark a tentative grin. "Are you on Baxter's little trek for business or pleasure, sir?"

"We're on business," Clark said.

"Are you? Plan to bid on EF&GC, do you?"

Clark didn't answer his smile; he felt no obligation to reply. Ward said, "Yes. We intend to."

The man tilted a brow in Ward's direction, but continued to address Clark: "Are you bidding on your own? Or do you represent some of the Northern boys? More and more of them are coming down here. Some of them are like vultures picking up the pieces after wartime, reconstruction, and depression-caused bankruptcies. Do you mind saying whom you represent?"

Clark jerked his head toward Ward. "Him."

The man enjoyed this hugely. "Won't say, eh? Or not permitted to divulge that information. Is that it?"

Clark merely shrugged.

The man sank into the chair across the aisle. Holding his drink out from him like a weapon, he leaned toward them, supporting himself on his elbow. "I'm Dayton Fredrick. You may have heard of me?"

Clark shrugged again, but Ward nodded. "You own a narrow-gauge line south from Lake City to Port St. Joe on the Gulf."

Now Dayton Fredrick condescended to consider Ward directly for the first time as a human being worthy of his notice. Not even the mightiest are inured against flattery. He even smiled. His smiling rendered him handsome, if tired, somewhat drawn and tense about the mouth, and too thin. "Very good, youngster. You know railroads, don't you? You have to, to know about a little feeder line like mine." He laughed. "My line has proven to be an anachronism. One of my mistakes. Not my first. Probably not my last. When I got involved in development down in the Port St. Joe area, I believed all feeder lines in Florida—hell, in the South for that matter—would be narrow-gauge. Sort of like tributaries off the main stream of

55

the big cross-state and interstate lines, eh? I was convinced of the feasibility and reasonableness of such planning. I was so convinced of it that I laid narrow-gauge against the advice of my own people. It seemed the economical thing to do. In a lot of ways, it still does. Less costly to install, to maintain, to equip. You can see that, eh? Well, it was all I could see. But I overlooked the fact that it meant changing trains at every main line junction, because the big system cars can't move on my narrow tracks and my stock can't roll on the wide-gauge rails. Well, some of us live and learn. Others of us just live, eh?"

"There are dozens of other narrow-gauge lines in Florida," Ward said.

"And all dying on the vine." Dayton Fredrick laughed ruefully. "Oh, I don't suggest I'm the only damn fool. Short logging lines, short excursion runs, milk line connectors, farm and grove feeders. But nothing that asks winter tourists to detrain and wait uncounted hours in a backwater settlement like Lake City while they connect with narrow-gauge feeders. I'm learning that people simply will not do it—not more than once. And as financially distressing as this fact is, I can't blame them. Schedules are totally erratic on any Florida lines. No competition, so hell, there's no *reason* to run on schedule. People from New England, the middle Atlantic states, and New York City—places where they set their clocks by trains—are not about to tolerate the inconvenience of mosquitoes, no facilities, no decent restaurants or hotels, just to come down and winter at Port St. Joe."

"You own that huge new gambling and resort spa?" Ward asked, awed.

Dayton Fredrick eyed him with increased interest and grudging respect. "I do. My hotel and racetrack and gambling facilities are the finest south of Saratoga. As a matter of fact, I tried to duplicate Saratoga down here in the sun, sand, and bright waters. Sounds reasonable, eh? A place for the moneyed crowd to congregate from January to April. And I managed a respectable kind of hybrid replica of Saratoga. If you gentlemen are interested, I'd like for you join these other folks as my guests at Port St. Joe. Matter of fact, this entire excursion is scheduled to wind up down there—guests of Baxter Marsh. He's opened and

56

staffed my hotel for his caravan—no mean feat, this far out of season."

"Will Baxter Marsh be down there?" Ward asked.

"He's already down there," Dayton Fredrick said. "He, his wife, my daughter, and a few relatives and friends, getting a head start on us."

The luxurious excursion train continued to roll west through pine and wire-grass country. Fredrick told Ward and Clark that before the state financed a plank toll road between Jacksonville and Lake City—called Alligator, after the Seminole leader, until the start of the Civil War—the seventy-two-mile trip had required four days over nigh-impassable and ill-defined trails.

The train, despite the fact the passenger cars were of the latest design, rattled and shuddered at times on the roadbed.

"Poor maintenance," Fredrick said, speaking loudly to make himself heard. "I think Baxter gave up on this line at least two years ago, and he's allowed the roadbed and ties to go to hell. Like I say, no competition. You ride the train or you go by toll road. If you ride EF&GC, you don't expect a smooth ride. That's another factor that's hurt my business down at St. Joe. Getting there is a real battle. If it weren't for the steamboats from Mobile, New Orleans, and around the Florida straits, I'd have gone under last winter. Rail service is atrocious—and that's on good days. I don't know what I'll have to pay Marsh for this line, but whatever it is over ten dollars, it'll be excessive."

Ward glanced around at the other people in the cars, laughing and ignoring the shaky condition of rails and ties, the flat, hot country outside, the soot and inconveniences. There were incredible amounts of wealth represented here, people who never bothered with how or why their investments functioned. He said, "You sound convinced you'll bid EF&GC in."

Fredrick nodded and smiled. "Oh, I am convinced. With me, it's not a game. It's a matter of survival."

"There may be other compelling reasons for buying a line like this," Ward suggested.

Fredrick laughed. "Name one. No, these are experienced railroad people, all right. Most of them. Some are Wall Street. Finance. Steamship lines. Most of them are

57

along for the ride. It's another party—or a wake, with dancing on the corpse. Look out there—" he swung his arm to indicate the swampy, sun-prostrated countryside fleeing past on soot and wind. "This country looks godforsaken. Baxter Marsh is smart, and he's given up on it. Try to imagine how desolate it must look to people who've lived in Manhattan, Boston, Philadelphia, or Baltimore all their lives. It's the hole beyond hell to them, I can tell you. That's the way they see these pinewoods. That's all they can see. Can you blame them? It takes an optimistic land developer to see possibilities in that raw wilderness." A young woman came swaggering along the aisle. She dropped into Dayton Fredrick's lap and stroked his throat, face, and tousled hair. He grinned, levered her to her feet, slapped her smartly across her shapely bottom, and continued without hesitation, "Me, I don't care about this country. I want this line to connect me with Northern cities. If I'm to attract Yankee tourism and money down here, I've got to run comfortable trains on good tracks, on schedule and with as few changes of trains as possible. I'm the only one who gives a damn, the only one whose goddamned existence depends on owning excellent accommodations between the North and my spa on the Gulf Coast. I've got everything they could want, if I can just get them down there, but that gets harder every winter." He laughed self-deprecatingly. "I had one great year—the winter I opened the hotel. Hoopla. You'd have thought I was P. T. Barnum himself. Champagne fountains. Press junket. We entertained European royalty that winter. We got the Saratoga crowds, the wealthiest tourists, the high-roller gamblers, the horse breeders. We had three months—the entire season—ninety-percent occupancy." He exhaled heavily and shook his head. "The past two seasons have been less spectacular. I figure one more losing year and, even though I'm offering those people a sun-bathed paradise with gambling, drinking, horse-racing, bathing, swimming, swanky surroundings, and discreet prostitutes, I can go under." He laughed, an empty sound. 'Hell, I *will* go under."

"But you don't agree with Baxter Marsh that Florida's going back to the Seminoles, alligators, rattlesnakes, and mosquitoes?" Ward said.

Fredrick laughed. "My boy, I don't agree with Baxter
58

Marsh about anything on God's green earth—well, maybe with his taste in wine and women."

The train slowed, pulling into Lake City. Dayton Fredrick shook hands cordially with both Ward and Clark, repeating his hope to meet them on his narrow-gauge line for the run south to Port St. Joe. Then he disappeared, with two laughing young women in tow. Most of the older men were circumspect—at least overtly—in their conduct toward the attractive young females, but no one criticized Dayton Fredrick. In many ways, he appeared as young as Ward Hamilton, as young as the girls enclosed in his embrace. He was a man Ward could admire, even while he feared him.

Ralph Bracussi hesitated beside Ward and Clark, watching the tycoon stride through the train with his women in tow. "Dayton's one hell of a guy," Bracussi said. "He must owe—conservatively—twenty million at least. . . ."

Ward left the train in a blaze of sunlight. Lake City lay somnolent in the heat. It had been established on a site near an Indian settlement ruled by Chief Halpatter Tustenugee, called Alligator. At first the whites named their village in honor of the incredibly brave and formidable foe of the invading United States forces. Eventually, worn down and ill, Alligator had been employed by the U.S. military authorities to persuade his tribesmen to capitulate to army terms for removal west to the Oklahoma territory.

Bracussi gathered the inspection party and led them toward the sidings. Most of the group glanced casually toward the polished and gleaming rolling stock displayed in the yards, and then unceremoniously repaired to the nearest hotel dining room where they could find ice for their drinks. When Bracussi called one of the new passenger locomotives, built by Baldwin of Philadelphia, "a great innovation," one of the older men laughed. "Son, there ain't been but one real important invention in the State of Florida. That was when ol' Doctor Gorie got his ice machine working in 1845." The other guests laughed appreciatively, and the tour rapidly deteriorated.

Ward was left finally in the yards with only Phillips

Clark lounging patiently in a patch of shade, awaiting him.

Ward moved along the tracks, noting the age, size, and condition of the EF&GC rolling stock. The others had repaired to the coolness of bourbon over Dr. Gorie's ice, but he could not. He envied those happy souls who accepted life as it appeared on the surface, who never dug beneath outward appearances for the truth, and never wanted to. God, how he envied them.

He was not like them. He doubted that he would ever be, even if he somehow struck it rich and joined their exclusive coterie. He had told Clark he was driven, and it was true. And at this moment, he stood on the threshold of the paradise he'd sought all his life.

He stood alone, his heart thudding, in the cab of a silent Baldwin locomotive. His gaze moved over the valves, the steam gauge with its steam-operated illumining lamp, the automatic lubricator for oiling the main valves, the fire box levers, the brake handles, and the motion gears.

He placed his hand on the brass facings almost reverentially; this was as close as he'd come in a lifelong romance. He felt—besides excitement—awe, as he might facing a perfect twenty-foot Bengal tiger, a mastodon, a sacred elephant of some other culture. In this finely crafted monster reposed incredible power and great beauty. One looked at these iron-and-steel giants and wondered how they could be improved, even knowing that at this moment, on some distant design board, this venerated monster was already obsolete. He felt dread and admiration for these great, pulsing, breathing, fire-eating marvels. He would change nothing, except to refine and improve. Yet they were constantly changing, already as different from the DeWitt Clinton steam engine of 1831 as if it were entirely unrelated, and it was this change that he respected as much as anything else. This was his religion, this great god he could touch and feel and believe; its rugged presence left no room for doubt.

Somehow he'd known from early boyhood why he loved the railroads as he'd never love another human being— family, woman, or saint. The railroads were free and independent; they could not be hemmed in or mastered, any more than he could. Growing older, he learned that these roads were granted powers greater even than the states themselves. Rail lines crossed state boundaries at will, thrust over the public domain, through huge cities, small towns, and hamlets, going everywhere, belonging everywhere, but under no narrow jurisdiction or niggling authority.

And he saw that the railroaders were a free and rugged breed, as he had to be free, as he would prove his ruggedness. They moved unfettered and uncontrolled like the privateers, pirates, and freebooters of another age; they roamed the hills and valleys, the plains and mountains and deserts, instead of open seas.

From their inception, the huge train companies had controlled the controlling forces of government. The earliest grants were franchises, anxiously and freely bestowed, with liberal provisions piled on open charters. Many of the transportation laws—from the first—weren't even subject to governmental interference, alteration, or repeal, without prior consent of the railroad corporators themselves. These railway men were awarded grants that limited or even excluded competition. Monopolies could only expand; they could hardly be restricted or curbed once created. The right to incestuous multiplication of rail lines came with the territory. A man had to fight his way into that close-gathered community of corporators, but once in, the ranks closed against outsiders, enemies, competitors, antagonists, or even against legislators on the highest levels.

American railroad locomotives had evolved far beyond anything in Europe because America's working engineers had nothing but contempt for the so-called authorities on the subject of what a locomotive could do and could be asked to do.

In his small Ohio town, people ran out to watch the trains enter and depart. The arrival of the Limited became a high point of the day—for young Ward more than all the others. All the romance of living roared past with the fast trains. The old excitement of heading west—in Conestoga wagons, of fighting battles and opening territories, was now involved in this restless new high-speed industry. The highest ambition of any of the other Lumberwood, Ohio boys was perhaps to be an engineer, a firemen, a flagman, blowing the whistle on those great engines to let folks know they were coming. By the time Ward was sixteen, finishing his last year in the school at Lumberwood, his desires were crystallized in his mind: those trains carried you to wonderful places, but the most wonderful place of all must be in those boardrooms where the engines and dining cars and sleepers and day coaches were owned and managed and bought and sold. This was where he wanted to go.

Robert was twenty months older than Ward and already a teller in Lumberwood's only bank when Ward got out of school. Ward was restless. He had grown up with the Horatio Alger "dream of success"; a boy had pluck and luck and daring and virtue and he saved some tycoon's daughter from runaway horses, thugs, or broken ice, and the tycoon started the boy on the way to success. The amazing irony was that such things did happen in that new industrialized society. A man had only to be on the lookout for the chance to strike it big.

Through his connections at the Lumberwood Bank, Robert tried briefly to get Ward jobs in the town. He soon gave up, afraid Ward would fail and blacken the Hamilton name, even at the bank. His father wanted Ward to manage the farm. Ward listened impatiently, if at all. He and Robert were so unlike that they could scarcely communicate without yelling and coming to blows. Robert was dependable, careful, industrious. He never took chances. His greatest excitement was in singing with the local barbershop quartet before church, social, fraternal or business luncheon groups. He had a lovely, lyric tenor voice.

Young Lumberwood women and their mothers rated Robert and Ward Hamilton as extraordinarily handsome, good catches, men with potential as well as good looks. The Hamiltons became locally renowned for having two poster-type men in one family.

Ward disappointed the town females and his family, and disgusted Robert, by accepting work as a traveling drummer. Traveling salesmen were regarded as rootless gypsies, going where the stagecoaches went, or the trains, living in hotels, doing God only knew what. Ward sank one rung lower in their estimation. He sold whiskey to taverns, inns, and restaurants around the state. The whiskey was all of the same quality, same proof, from the same run, shipped in the same barrels, but it was sold for as many different prices, under as many different brand names and labels as Ward and his distillery-owner employer could discover ethnic tastes.

Robert found this fraudulent, dishonest, and little better than thuggery. "You're robbing unsuspecting people. Don't you feel even a twist of conscience?"

"I'm giving them what they want. Germans don't want a French whiskey, anymore than the Poles or the Italians do. They want their own kind of liquor, at the prices they're accustomed to paying."

Ward became first proficient and then expert in poker. He was seldom in Lumberwood more often than once a month, and then only for a night or two, during which time he slept around the clock and ate ravenously at his mother's table. She found him thin, hollow-cheeked, and, she suspected, godless. Robert found him hard-eyed and tough-talking. "What are you trying to do to yourself?" he demanded.

"Get rich," Ward told him, if he bothered to answer at all.

He enjoyed the nights in hotel rooms, back rooms of small-town barber shops, or in Masonic lodges. He had friends and poker-playing cronies all across the state. He met people, sounded them out, discovered what craft or trade they followed and what was its potential. He was always willing to gamble on some commodity—grain, corn, wheat, or lumber. Sometimes he made a few dollars, which he sent home to Robert to deposit in his account.

When he'd saved a few hundred dollars, he bought land that looked promising for one reason or another. Most of it he was able to sell at a small profit, but he was almost eighteen and he certainly wasn't getting rich. When his employer expanded the distillery, Ward drove out into the farmlands, and bought up grain. But his employer was smarter than he was, and let him hold the grain until it was ready to spoil and too costly to store. He bought it all at bargain rates.

Robert raged, pacing up and down, "Doesn't that show you what a thug and criminal you work for?"

Ward didn't see it that way. "He outsmarted me, that's all. I hold no grudge. My turn will come."

He learned accidentally from an Internal Revenue representative visiting the distillery that there would soon be levied by Congress the first new tax hike on whiskey since the Comprehensive Internal Revenue Act of July 1, 1862 had placed a tax on malted and distilled liquors—and incidentally enriched many distillers and liquor speculators, among them a man named Flagler and another named John D. Rockefeller.

Ward raced home to Lumberwood, horse galloping, slavering, the runabout buggy rattling and dancing on the roadway. He arrived after midnight and woke Robert. "How much money in my account?"

"You're plucked, chicken," Robert told him with some self-righteous satisfaction. "That crook you work for cleaned you out."

"How much have you got?"

Robert stared at him, incredulous, wide-eyed, sleep forgotten. "Me? For you? For another one of your hare-brained schemes? Not a dime, Mr. Hooligan."

"Will you help me borrow a few thousand from Mr. Melton at your bank?"

Robert went pale. He looked as if he might vomit. He staggered back and sank into a chair, his nightgown tight about his bare legs. "I won't even mention your name to Mr. Melton. Not even in his presence. I'm ashamed enough to have you in the family. A whiskey drummer, a gambler, a card-playing, harlot-chasing traveling salesman, for God's sake. Now you want me to help you defraud the bank where I work. Well, I won't do it." His laugh was cold, rasping with contempt. "If you want money from my bank, I advise you get a gun and a mask. They're too intelligent down there to give it to you any other way."

Robert began shaking his head from side to side, stunned, when Ward walked into the Lumberwood Bank at ten o'clock the next morning. Robert's cheeks went pallid. He stared in horror at his brother. Ward looked rested, freshly showered and shaved, decked out in a derby hat, a three-button, single-breasted, sack-cut suit of woven brown worsted. His brown shoes gleamed with polish. His wing collar was high on his neck, fresh and spotless; his tie was of striped brown silk. People turned to gawk at him, to admire him, or to stare at such midweek finery where most men wore open collars, suspenders, and work pants. Robert admitted that Ward attracted attention, but the sight of him made Robert ill. He got even sicker as Ward was ushered into the railed-off area where Harmon Melton sat at his big rolltop desk.

Robert looked ready to cry when Mr. Melton crossed the lobby with Ward at his side twenty minutes later. "I want you to credit your brother's account with five thousand dollars, which comprises our loan to him, Robert." The bank president cleared his throat. "And another five that I want to invest with him—on my own." Melton cleared his throat again.

Robert managed to nod his head, but his eyes brimmed with tears and he chewed anguishedly at the inside of his mouth. Mr. Melton was saying, "A superb investment opportunity is the way I see it. As for Ward's loan, you know I'm insistent on collateral, Robert."

"Yes, sir, I know."

"But Ward's a hometown boy. And he does seem to have an ironclad proposition lined up. We don't want to stand in the way of a local boy's bettering his position, eh? Do we? And a main consideration, Robert. He is your brother. I don't see how we can go wrong trusting him one thousand percent, eh?"

Ward didn't see Robert again for almost a year. For some reason, understood only in the bureaucratic labyrinths of Washington, D.C., Congress did not hike the tax on domestic distilled liquor. Perhaps it was because Ulysses Simpson Grant had been elected President in 1869, and five years later, Congress was still timid about angering the general and his lobbyists and supporters. Anyhow, Ward was left holding ten thousand dollars worth of whiskey for which he was paying storage and for which there was no inflated price, no quick return.

Robert resigned from the bank in Lumberwood. When Ward went home infrequently, his mother stared at him in silent accusation and reproof. Robert had departed the town rather than face disgrace generated by his brother's fraudulent deception of the bank and its president.

Ward tried to tell his mother he was repaying the bank in installments at three-percent interest, but she didn't understand dealings in finance; she knew only that he had robbed Robert of his splendid opportunity for advancement at the Lumberwood Bank. For this she could not forgive him. She was sorry, but she would never forgive him for hurting Robert like that.

Ward stopped going home more than once every three months to see how his parents fared, and then he was quickly in and quickly out. He went home for all holidays. His mother smiled when she saw him, but it was a smile tinged with sadness. Robert never returned to Lumberwood.

Ward's stomach was becoming inured to hotel and restaurant food. He didn't gain any weight, he was leaner than a winter coyote, but he no longer suffered gastritis, indigestion, flatulence, or stomach cramps.

Then, suddenly, Congress passed a Distilled Liquor Tax hike, amending the Internal Revenue Act of 1862. Overnight, Ward almost doubled his investment. He drove home to Lumberwood, with the U.S. banknotes in a wooden box nailed under the seat of his buggy. A light snow fell, but he was not even chilly. The town had never looked more beautiful. He repaid Harmon Melton in full. Melton clapped his arms about Ward, maudlin. The way to Melton's heart was through his pocketbook.

Ward drove out to the farm. He tried to explain to his mother that he had repaid Robert's bank in full. There was no scandal, no disgrace. Robert could come home to Lumberwood if he wanted to. But his mother didn't understand. He couldn't wait to get out of town. . . .

Robert stared up at him from his civilian paymaster's desk at army headquarters in Atlanta. A dozen emotions flared in Robert's eyes—pain, rage, disbelief, shock—everything except pleasure. He glanced around as if ashamed to be seen talking to Ward. "What are you doing here?" he whispered tautly. "What have you done now? What are you running away from this time?"

Ward grinned. "Relax. I only came to see if you were all right. Mom worries. And I came to tell you you can go back to Lumberwood if you want to."

Robert's eyes were icy. "I don't want to." He set his shoulders stiffly. "I couldn't ever go back there. And I'll never forgive you for what you've done to me. I've made a new life, do you understand? I want you to stay away from me. I don't know you. I don't want to know you. You ruined my life once; you won't do it again."

Ward grinned. "I'm sorry for anything I've done to you. I never meant to harm you—"

"You never gave a damn."

Ward glanced about the bustling army of occupation headquarters. "Looks like you've landed on your feet."

"Whether I did or not has nothing to do with you. You stay away from me."

For two days, Ward wandered around reconstruction Atlanta, looking for an opportunity. The carpetbaggers had arrived ahead of him and, along with the military, had bled the region white. Fortunes were being amassed at the expense of these defeated people, but all the best veins were already being mined.

Railroading fascinated him. The rail center drew him back again and again. The train yards expanded daily. Freight, materials, cotton, and lumber equipment were stacked everywhere. Army cars, grain and gun carriers, and army freight haulers crowded every siding.

He never meant to stay in Atlanta, but his poker playing brought him into contact with Simon Shaffer, who dealt with the federal army as supplier. Shaffer learned, from bribing junior officers, supply sergeants, and poker-playing cronies among majors and generals, what the Army of Occupation wanted to buy, and then he tried to supply it first, in greatest quantity, and at highest prices.

"The military wastes," Shaffer told Ward. "The whole War Department is like a monstrous garbage dump. Material is dumped in and never seen again. If the quartermaster needs one freight car, they never look on the sidings, they order a gross. If somebody needs a horse, they requisition a herd and all the grain and equipment and supplies to support them. But that's not even the real waste. The real waste is not even knowing—or caring— what they've got. It's just too big; they can't keep up with it, so they don't try. It's cheaper not to, and nobody cares anyway. It's not only money, it's government money, and comes from a bottomless reservoir. Once they've used something—equipment or whatever—out it goes, to rust or melt or disappear. Hell, I could sell their own materiel back to them, but I don't have to. No matter what I pay, I've got an automatic seventy-five-percent markup and nobody even questions it. If anybody questions anything too much, he gets transferred—sometimes out West, where being in the army can be downright dangerous. I tell you, old son, a man can get rich down here, helping reconstruct the South."

Rich was what Ward wanted to be. He learned that Shaffer had become so wealthy—having arrived in Atlanta in 1865 with a carpetbag and ten dollars—as military supplier, grain router, distributor, and procurer, that he had bought the railroad that connected Atlanta with Richmond, Virginia, and, through that shattered city, the industrial North. He'd gotten sick of paying high freight rates to thieves.

Ward went to work for Shaffer. He learned that military personnel at army headquarters were easy to deal with; he didn't even bother with the kickback. Shaffer handled all that through regular channels where he was welcomed warmly.

He learned that supply sergeants ran the army. They bought what they wanted to buy; they ignored the highest-level requests unless there was some rebate in the deal for them. Master sergeants and duty sergeants simply filled out requisition sheets of their own among the hundreds completed officially each morning. These requisitions were placed in piles on the administration officer's desk for his signature. This harried or preoccupied officer seldom read the papers he signed. If he were a conscientious officer, or new in the Third Division, the sergeant simply left blank spaces in the requisitions to be filled in after they were signed.

Ward was stunned at the profligate wastage of the military in this storm center of misery, poverty, and literal starvation. The army thrashed about in the morass of destitution like a bloated blue ogre chewing up and spitting out, gorging and discarding. He was soon as cynical in his approach to army supply as was his employer. He stopped questioning the officers and noncoms as to their needs; he began, as Shaffer directed, to sell them the materials, surplus, and discards Shaffer had on hand or had carted in from bankruptcy and distress sales and other army bases, which closed down and sold off supplies at ten cents on the dollar.

Learning where he could get a million tons of grain, Ward tried to sell it to General Maitland O. White to be used as food for the destitute people of Georgia. He failed. White yelled at him. The army had no money to waste like that. The army was no philanthropic organization. Finally he sold the grain in smaller lots, as fodder for army horses.

"Now you're learning," Shaffer told him through a cloud of cigar smoke. "Never go against the establishment. Always go with it."

Ward's discontent mounted because, while Shaffer was getting richer, he was not. He remained on salary and an infrequent, grudging bonus. Investing all the money he'd made from his whiskey-tax bonanza, he went into army supply for himself.

He quickly found himself in over his head. He knew how to deal with army personnel as well as Shaffer. He got along with brass and noncoms even better than the abrasive Shaffer, because he made friends quickly and was amenable to almost any rebate deal. He liked people and they responded to him. But Shaffer had formidable connections in the Third Division. Shaffer was an affable, if tight-fisted, friend; he was an implacable foe. Ward would have thought there was gravy enough for everybody in army supply, but obviously Shaffer did not share these sentiments. His contacts and material sources quickly dried up and he found himself broke again.

He did not see Robert except infrequently. He heard through the grapevine that Robert was engaged to a girl who belonged to a respected plantation family out beyond Decatur. Ward didn't envy him. It was a hell of a long trip out to the Lawrenceville Road just to visit some girl. He heard *about* Robert, if not *from* him. Robert was doing well, was highly regarded in the federal military, and yet was accepted by the local gentry as few Yankees were. In Atlanta, the lowest forms of human life were the niggers, the Jews, and the Yankees, in that order. Robert had somehow surmounted all obstacles among the defeated people of Georgia; he had even been named liaison between the army and the community. Robert was gaining in stature, both with the military and the faltering Confederate establishment, even though he was not getting rich. One thing the military did not waste: payroll money for its enlisted personnel or civilian employees.

Ward visited Robert's home only once. He sought him out one night to let him know their father had died. He found Robert living in a two-bedroom, Georgia brick cottage near Fort McPherson. The house was sparsely furnished, but immaculately kept by a live-in male servant, houseboy, and cook, a freedman named Thetis. Robert didn't explain to Thetis that Ward was his brother; he didn't even want his servant to know. "Thought you might want to go home to Pa's funeral," Ward said. "I thought we might travel together."

This idea appalled Robert and he shook his head. "I won't ever go back to Lumberwood. I can't face the disgrace."

"What disgrace?"

"I'm not going back. Mother will understand. I could never face those people again."

"Jesus." Ward stared at his brother. "You don't ever forgive, do you? You really know how to bear a grudge."

"Now you know. Just stay away from me. I've met and been accepted by good people down here. Good, churchgoing, Christian people of excellent families. Genteel, quality people, socially prominent—real Southern aristocracy. They wouldn't interest you, however. They are poor, in money and worldly things. I want you to stay away from me. I won't have you spoiling my life among these people of breeding and culture.'"

"God forbid."

"Make your jokes. But make them out of my sight."

Chapter Six

THE TREK SOUTH renewed two hours later. Ward and Phillips Clark boarded the narrow-guage passenger car and gaped incredulously. It was like entering a small-scale world after Marsh's latest-model luxury chair lounges. The fragile, gondola-like cars rested on thoroughbraces and had narrow windows without screens or glass panes, seats cane-bottomed and cane-backed, hard and rigid and straight. Canvas curtains on rollers were the single protection offered against sun, soot, rain, heat, or cold. "Fredrick's got guts at least," Ward said, "inviting these people to ride on this contraption—even as guests."

Though the standard-gauge lines continued west from Lake City to Pensacola, through the state capital at Tallahassee, passing stations within forty miles north of Port St. Joe, Fredrick's line wound south and west through swamp, wilderness, and, in places, almost impenetrable subtropical forest, 180 miles to the Gulf Coast town. None of his guests knew Florida geography, so none were prepared for the incredible voyage ahead of them at forty-miles an hour top speed across godforsaken backcountry. It promised to be the longest seven hours in their existence. If Fredrick had planned this leg of the excursion as a joke, it would have made more sense than as an extension of Marsh's lighthearted junket.

The departing train whistled—a petulant, petty sound like a small lapdog's yapping. Passengers and onlookers along the rails laughed derisively.

Soon after the narrow-gauge departed the station at Lake City, rattling and bumping along the close-set tracks, laughter died among the travelers; the drunk sobered; the sober devoutly wished they were drunk; the incredulous believed they were being duped as part of a practical joke. But they did not laugh. It was suddenly not funny at all.

Only Dayton Fredrick remained unruffled, laughing, joking, and expansive. He walked along the aisles of the swaying coaches, reassuring his guests that after a brief few hours of discomfort, they would live like Near East potentates at his spa at Port St. Joe. Few of them believed him anymore. By the time the train had traversed the first sixty-odd miles to Perry, most were ready to mutiny. Many would have abandoned the junket at this point, but they dreaded a return trip, and Fredrick constantly assured them that the ordeal would soon be over. "A little physical discomfort to whet your appetites for paradise," he told them.

Fredrick paused beside the seat Ward shared with Phillips Clark. The tycoon smilingly but peremptorily jerked his head toward a vacant chair across the aisle, and the attorney moved into it. Clark listened to Ward and Fredrick for a few moments, then tilted his derby forward over his eyes and tried to sleep.

Fredrick toppled into the seat beside Ward. He said, "Well, what do you think?"

"About this train? If you're serious about transporting these people a hundred and eighty miles on this deathtrap, I don't know what to think."

Fredrick exhaled, looking around. "It seems fine to me. Only a few hours. And yet you're right. It has driven off more potential hotel guests at St. Joe than mosquitoes. I'm getting too old for this modern generation, I guess. It happens to all of us, in every business. Fashions demand change. And I guess while us older fellows get more and more set in our ways, younger people want more and better, and get softer, demanding more luxuries. When I grew up, if you wanted to go any distance more than ten miles, why, you rode stagecoaches. There's no more torturous way on earth to travel. To me, after those coaches, these smart little narrow-gauge cars seemed like a step into paradise. I thought everybody else would think so too."

"You can't be that old," Ward said.

Fredrick laughed. "But it's true. One generation's discomfort is another's luxury. The broadsword, the rapier, the crossbow, gun powder. Progress. But that's not what I meant. What do you think of Marsh's rolling stock? You inspected every vehicle, eh?"

"Yes. I think it could be a good line. I think it could be made to pay."

"Any ideas how you'd do it?"

Ward smiled inwardly. Fredrick took him seriously now, for some reason. A couple of hours had made a lot of difference in the tycoon's attitude toward him. Fredrick no longer thought him naive or ill-informed. He said, "I'd grab all the freight-hauling contracts I could, and I'd repair the roadbeds."

"That would take a lot of money. Latest figures show that the cost of railroad construction this year, per mile, is over fifty-seven thousand dollars! It costs more than fifteen hundred dollars to repair one mile of track. It all adds up to a cost of about thirteen cents a mile run by engine. A corporation has to have heavy capital support to do anything in railroading these days."

"I wouldn't do it all tomorrow. I'd let the line finance itself, maintenance, repairs, replacement, as much as possible."

"That's always a lot easier said than done, if I may coin a cliché, son. Even the biggest corporations have to scrounge for credit sometime. An independent in this cutthroat market today has two chances—slim and none."

"I'd expect to have to borrow."

"Borrowing can be difficult. Borrowing will take you to Wall Street. And then they've got you by the tail. I know. Hell, Whitney Cushing and Burden Byers are both in this party. They're Wall Street; ask them. As long as you're strong, as long as you control the game, as long as you hold the dice, you've got a chance. But the minute you let the money boys take the play away from you, you're dead. I know that too." He stared for a moment at the backs of his hands on the bar of the seat ahead. "You get one

73

chance, one throw of the dice. It's for everything. There's no second roll for anybody."

"You don't sound real optimistic."

"I sound pessimistic because I'm telling you the truth." He breathed in deeply and exhaled. "There are no rules set in this game yet, except the rules made by the man with the whip—the money and the power. This railroading is all new. There are no textbooks for any of us. We learn about railroading by building railroads, by running them, by being wrong part of the time, but, with luck, right most of the time. By changing. But by changing in time." For another long beat, Fredrick was silent, his thoughts turned inward, sour-tasting. "We use everything we learn, and we don't make the same mistake twice and survive. Different mistakes once, one to a customer, but never the same error twice, or we're out. Like I say, no rules exist, except the rules we make—as we need them—to pull our own tails out of the fire. And we bend and change the rules; as fast as we make them, we need to alter them. That's just the way it is."

Ward smiled tautly but good-naturedly. "If I didn't know better, I'd say you were trying to discourage me."

Fredrick laughed with him. "Hell no, boy. I'm offering you a job. I'd like you to work for me when I take over Baxter's line. I'd give you a free hand."

Ward stared at him. "What brought this on?"

"During the break at Lake City, I found out what I could about you. You're the only unknown element in this game. I liked what I learned, and I'm an instinct man. My instincts tell me to go with you. I've given it a lot of thought since we left Marsh's train at Lake City. I need somebody to build that line, make this one work."

Ward shook his head. "There's no way to do that. This line is doomed, you must know that."

Fredrick nodded. "I smile a lot to hide the crying. I do know it's doomed. That's why I've got to have Marsh's line from Lake City. I'd try to buy the Mobile people out, but they're too strong, too well-fixed. It's got to be Baxter's company. Then I'll cross over the standard-gauge through Tallahassee, beyond Chattahoochee to the Appalachicola River, then lay a narrow-guage spur of forty or fifty miles—"

"Narrow-gauge? Again? You just won't ever learn, will you?"

Fredrick spread his hands. "All right. Standard track."

"What would you do with this line?"

Fredrick winced. "Abandon it, it looks like. Either I take bankruptcy and abandon it and all its liabilities, or I lose it to creditors. The money boys like Cushing and Byers or the Seligmans will take the whole play away from me. Losing this and all I've sunk into it will cripple me, but it might be the best thing in the long run. You are right, you know. I've got to change, to think as modern as my daughter does. In this business, we don't stand still. You know why? Because we can't stand still and exist. We've come a long way in fifty years of railroading. Of course, the war gave transport a hell of an impetus. Even so, we've moved from the old rocket-type locomotive that weighed six thousand tons and drew—on level grades—up to forty tons. Our very first improvements brought huge engines weighing twenty-five tons and drawing, on level grades, sixty loaded freight cars at a total of twelve hundred tons. This looked great. But already, consolidation locomotives weigh fifty thousand tons and can pull more than twenty-four hundred tons on level stretches. Heavier and more powerful engines are being designed that will test the limits of present-day tracks. Nothing can stop us because nothing is as beautiful as a full train racing along an open track."

"If you feel that way, how'd you ever get in narrow-gauge?"

"I told you, I guessed wrong. I was up to here in debt for the Biltmore down at St. Joe. I was hanging by my fingernails, and I meant to hang on no matter what Wall Street did to me."

"You don't think much of Wall Street."

"I honestly don't know what my opinion of Wall Street is. I probably distrust the whole idea, even when I personally like men like Whit Cushing. Mostly it's because I'm an independent and had to struggle to reach the place where I didn't need them before they'd even deal me in."

"I guess that's true when you deal with a banker or any other loanshark."

"My capital needs soon went beyond the most liberal of

bankers. I had to deal on Wall Street whether mutual mistrust and hatred was real or imagined."

"That didn't matter."

"No. Not as long as I got my bonds floated, my money to operate. But let's get back to what we were talking about. If you don't want to come to work for me yet, I'm still going to try to sell you on the idea. I just thought it would be good to have a place to start, an understanding of what we both are up against! I know now what you want; I know what I wanted when I was your age. I'd just like to help you see things as they really are, and not as you wish they might be."

"It's no good, as much as I appreciate your offer and your confidence, in spite of my lack of experience."

"Hell, nobody's got that much experience. You work on guts and gall. The toughest survive. I think you might be tough. And you'll get tougher as you have to."

"Thanks. But you know what my trouble is, if you know anything about me. I've tried to work for other men. In every case, we got along great personally. But I wanted more than I could get, and that let me out. No matter what else, this would be my toy. Mine. And I believe I can make it work."

"Don't count on that. It'll take a long time to get any money boys behind you. Ask Whit Cushing, he'll tell you. You can start with me. The sky is the limit to where you can go, in time. Right now, low pay, but—"

"I've got expensive tastes, Mr. Fredrick. And running my own line—that's where the money is. I know other men have made it starting out with damned little more than I have."

"Damn few."

"That's what I mean, though; it has been done. And I'm as good as any who ever made it. Better."

"Maybe you are. But the odds are greater. I wish to God somebody had offered me what I'm offering you when I was your age, and I had self-confidence that would make you look like a shy violet. Nowadays, it seems young fellows want it all. They don't want to sweat it out, serve their time. They make a choice and grab at it. The fact is, boys nowadays seem to get exposed to more pomp and pageantry than when I was that age. We believed we had to work for what we got, with our hands and our backs, as well as our wits. Now youngsters are told it's out there waiting, go out and grab right at the top." He shook his head. "I guess it doesn't do too much harm, as long as they don't kid themselves."

"Maybe I am kidding myself, Mr. Fredrick, but it's a chance I've got to take."

Fredrick offered Ward a cigar, and lit one himself. He grinned through a wreath of blue smoke. "I get the gut feeling you wouldn't come to work for me, even if you believed I'd bid in EF&GC. Do you mind saying why?"

Ward laughed. "You're probably a hell of a poker player."

"I'd rate you pretty fair, too."

"Maybe we can get up a friendly game sometime."

Fredrick smiled. "Why not when we get down to the Biltmore? The game rooms are open. We'll ask Whit Cushing, Byers, and a couple of others who believe, as I do, in old-fashioned, straight five-card stud, nothing fancy and nothing wild."

"Sounds interesting. Expensive but interesting."

"Maybe we can teach you one of the most valuable lessons of your life. Maybe you'll come to work for me, after all."

Ward grinned but remained silent, watching the unhappy people squirming, trying hopelessly to find a comfortable position on the unyielding chairs.

Fredrick said, "I read you as a gut-instinct man, too. And you've voted me out. That's fair enough. But do you mind saying why?"

"I like you. If I could work for anybody, I could probably work for you. But I wouldn't do it."

"What you're not saying is that you've also heard about me, about my debts."

Ward shrugged.

Fredrick laughed. "I can tell you, son, it's all relative. I feel a hell of a lot less concerned about fifteen million in debts than I did when I owed some grocer ten bucks for food."

"I admire you. I really do. What makes you hang on?"

Fredrick laughed. "That's easy; my daughter. My daughter's lovely. And she's all I've got. She thinks I'm the number-one greatest male in the world. I can't let her down, now can I?"

It was after ten at night when the train pulled into the station at Port St. Joe.

The irreconcilably angered, physically distressed, and mentally agitated travelers debarked in cold silence or rasping sarcasm. Horsedrawn carriages, brightly bedecked with gas lamps, flower streamers of hibiscus, roses, and gardenias on ropes of fern, awaited them, manned by formally attired black coachmen in top hats. The guests remained unmoved. It required more than ostentation to revive these pilgrims. They climbed, protesting and fault-finding, into the carriages, loudly expressing concern for their luggage.

The carriages bore them, like tumbrels carting doomed aristocracy to some somber guillotine, through the sleep-stunned streets of the fishing village on the shores of St. Joseph's Bay. Beyond that silent inlet, a reef stood as a guardian against the Gulf. The main street was paved with red bricks, leading to the gates of the Port St. Joe-Biltmore Hotel complex. The clatter of horses' hoofs and the grating of metal wheel rims on sand-covered bricks were the loudest sounds as the sad little parade passed make-shift houses, small stores, and docks where fishing boats idled at anchor.

Even in the darkness, the freshly scrubbed façade of the rambling frame hotel loomed like some magnificent chateau of a gentler age. Built on rolling dunes, among ancient water oaks, palms, pines, sweet bays, and magnolias, the Biltmore promised unaccustomed luxury and escape.

None of Baxter Marsh's guests was impressed by the opulence at that moment. An orchestra played muted love songs in a salon off the elegantly appointed main lobby, but few of the arriving guests even glanced in that direction. The mosaic dance floor gleamed, empty and waiting. Equally, the guests pointedly ignored the late-night repast of roast turkey and chicken breast, melons, cantaloupes, avocados, pears, bowls of iced mixed fruit, pickles, tomatoes, hearts of lettuce, celery and carrot stalks, along with heaps of sliced rye, pumpernickel, Greek, Italian, and Cuban white breads. Most demanded their room keys and departed via grilled elevator, or stalked, stiff-backed, up wide, winding staircases to their suites. They exacted a bitter, self-satisfying vengeance upon Dayton Fredrick by despising and denigrating every touch of elegance he put on display for them.

Swearing that his back was irreparably damaged, Phillips Clark stumbled off to his suite, cursing under his breath and leaning against the pure Italian marble stairway railings for support.

Ward was as impressed as Dayton Fredrick had wanted all of Baxter Marsh's retinue to be. He had heard fantastic stories about this beautiful hotel, racetrack, and gambling casino overlooking St. Joseph's bay, but nothing had prepared him for his first view of its splendid and breathtaking richness: tall windows set deep in thick walls; high, vaulted ceilings; Persian carpeting; handwoven draperies; gilt-framed paintings. The architecture was clean and simple in line, substance, and purpose, yet so plush and dashing that it always verged on the brink of vulgarity. But there wasn't anything cheap or vulgar about it; it exuded a quality of having been crafted in love and devotion and pleasure. This momument to sybaritic tastes revealed more about the real, hidden Dayton Fredrick than all his financial statements, resumes or biographies could ever expose. He'd admired Fredrick before, but he respected him warmly now, his awe mixed with understanding and real affection. Dayton Fredrick was one hell of a man.

Ward was too restless to sleep. Carrying three-decker sandwiches, he wandered through the gambling casino, walked down to the ill-lit and abandoned paddocks and guests' riding stables, empty and eerily silent so far out of season. He stood for a long time beside the sixty-foot indoor swimming pool, hearing in his mind the laughter of pampered guests long departed. He surveyed the dark tennis courts: open, paved places, characterless and voiceless without their nets and competitors. The eighteen-hole golf course wound darkly through walls of bay trees, wisteria, oleander hedges, and sand traps.

Like fluffy woolen carpeting, a long, white stretch of pumped-in beach sand lay ghostly gray between the hotel and the bay. He walked down to the edge of the water, small waves lapping almost to his feet. He could sense the triumph and exultation, the sheer pleasure Dayton Fredrick had realized in making his dream come true out here. He had made a dream come true. That's all this really amounted to, a dream that was so real inside him, he had to build it for the world to see and marvel at. Dayton Fredrick had made his dream a reality, as Ward would make his own dream come true.

He gazed westward, across the sibilant bay and the humpbacked shadows of the reef that was like a feudal and fatally flawed wall against the savage assault of the Gulf. He tilted his head and searched the sky for his star, but the heavens were occluded, black with boiling thunderheads. He couldn't see his star, but he felt good about it, because he knew it was there. He was more certain of it in that moment when he couldn't find it than he had ever been in all his life before.

Chapter Seven

By DAY, the Biltmore was even more extravagantly elegant than by lamplight. Baxter Marsh's requisitions had staffed the luxury inn impressively, six months out of season. Bellboys, clerks, maids, polite and efficient waiters—bowing and better-trained than the senior class at West Point—cooks, bakers, and gardeners, operated the place with oiled precision. Except for the blaze of summer sun, one might have believed this to be the height of the winter season. And all for a single party. God, what swank.

Ward lay luxuriating on the firm yet pampering mattress. He'd slept until 10 A.M. after lying restlessly on the seductively comfortable double bed for a long time last night, unable to sleep. The orchestra in the hotel salon had played for dancing, if not for dancers, until one, precisely as ordered, love songs haunting and somehow faintly melancholy in the lonely dark. For a long time, he'd felt as if he were still being shaken, blended, and mixed well aboard Dayton Fredrick's narrow-gauge nightmare. Gradually, in the languorous silence, he had fallen asleep, lulled by the whisper of the waves upon the shore, and he slept dreamlessly. He woke once, at four-thirty, troubled by those thorny, brambled agonies that bristle with fearful substance and urgency most relentlessly in the dark hours before dawn.

He thought about Dayton Fredrick, admiring, wary, uncomfortable, sweaty, and irresolute, all at the same time. He admired the way Dayton Fredrick fought for existence. Hanging on. Owing, Bracussi had said, at least twenty million dollars, needing that Jacksonville-Lake City line desperately to keep it all glued together, prepared to do anything to get it. Totally amoral. He was awed by Fredrick, even when he knew him to be conscienceless and driven. He even felt a *rapprochement* he'd never felt toward any other man—a sense of knowing that Fredrick was his kind of privateer. He liked him and all the time knew him to be a clever, cunning, resourceful, and remorseless enemy. Probably one of the most dangerous places to stand on this earth was between the grinning, easygoing Dayton Fredrick and what he wanted. And Ward knew this was where he stood. He rolled his head on his pillow. The whisper of the gentle waves was no longer restful, but taunting and irritating and distressing.

He showered, shaved, and dressed casually. This suite was so far superior to any accommodations he'd known in the past, that there was no basis for comparison. It had a fifteen-foot ceiling, with cupids carved across the dome of the room as in some Sistine Chapel consecrated to pagan eroticisms. A ceiling-high mirror doubled the depth of the room and destroyed any frame of reference by which to judge scale. French windows opened on a courtesy balcony overlooking the sun-drenched bay, the green reef, and the milk-blue Gulf beyond it. Jesus, luxury was enchanting. It could be habit-forming. Imagine, some people lived like this all the time!

He encountered other guests on the wide stairs and in the lobby. Most had slept fully and rebounded from their ordeal aboard the narrow-gauge train, even if they remained unforgiving. They spoke to him, if not warmly, at least politely. He was not one of them, but they almost recognized him, almost recalled him from yesterday's agonized cavalcade, almost admitted his existence in their world, even if only on the vaguest periphery.

He entered the dining room, where swift, ubiquitous servants kept a buffet lunch set up, including a pick-me-up bar. The black waiters were fun to watch, moving fluidly, unerringly, performing, like mind-readers, little niceties before they were asked, the dark faces smiling, remote, alert.

Whitney Cushing touched Ward briefly on the shoulder at the long, linen-draped serving table. A slender, blond, faintly aloof man, he smiled. "Hear you fancy yourself a stud poker expert?"

Ward grinned. "I play, but I'm just a country boy."

"You make the prospect sound irresistible. Dayton proposes a joust this afternoon. I look forward to opposing you."

"Might be too rich for my blood."

"Hardly. We set table stakes by common assent. The size of the pot is not significant. Winning is." Cushing smiled palely, his faded eyes crinkling. "All any of us want to do is *win*. We couldn't care less how much or how little. To win; that's all that matters."

"That's all," Ward agreed.

He sat alone, attended by a smiling, precognitive waiter, at a small table beside an open window overlooking a green shard of the golf course, a sprig of white beach, a rectangle of empty bay and cloudless sky. The waiter held his chair for him, shook out the large linen napkin, placed it across his lap, and poured coffee before Ward could ask.

Ward smiled. "As expert as you are, you must amass a fortune in tips during the season."

The grinning waiter glanced around conspiratorially and shook his head. "Pardon me, Cap'n, but rich people are the stingiest tippers in this world."

"You figure I'll come through pretty good."

"Yessuh. Figure you ain't that rich yet."

Ward glanced around. He would have been happy to have joined any of the tables. Here were people with so much wealth they didn't even realize that a few dollars in gratuities meant anything to lesser beings. They were enjoying themselves, and everyone was in better humor this morning, but their remote courtesy effectively excluded him. Some of the women eyed him with covert interest, but it was a tentative, frangible curiosity.

Laughter rose and washed around him. The urgent topic, at every table and among them all, was vengeance.

"Vengeance to fit Dayton's crime," a woman said. "I'll get revenge on him if it's my last act."

"I'm referring the whole matter to my attorneys," a man said, laughing.

"Legal redress?" Burden Byers shook his head negatively. "Entirely too humane, too soft. Even if the trials dragged on for years, Fredrick wouldn't really suffer the way I want to see him writhe."

"Besides, he's always being sued by somebody, every day."

"He'd hardly notice another lawsuit, civil or criminal."

"I was thinking more of drawing and quartering."

"Or maybe the rack."

"No good. After his trains, he'd sleep like a baby, stretched on a rack."

"Castration might work."

"At his age? Darling, you'd be doing him a favor. It would be a conversation piece for him."

"Most of his pieces are conversation pieces nowadays."

"What is scourging? I'm always hearing about people being scourged."

"Where?"

"In the Bible."

"When have you ever read the Bible?"

"In a hotel room once."

"Didn't he show up?"

"Yes."

They laughed their way through the leisurely brunch. Their methods of wreaking vengeance on Dayton Fredrick became more and more creative, cruel, and unusual.

"May I join you?"

Ward looked up. Ralph Bracussi stood beside the table in dark suit, tie, celluloid collar, vest, as excluded as Ward from this laughing company. When Ward nodded, Bracussi told the waiter to set out his food.

Ward said, "I haven't seen Baxter Marsh this morning."

"You probably won't." Bracussi left the thought dangling. Ward recalled that Fredrick had called this excursion a wake—"dancing on the corpse." This was Marsh's corporation being liquidated. Perhaps, in a way, it was a wake, with Marsh respectfully out of sight. The rail tycoon had marched into Florida, meaning to conquer and develop and exploit it. He was retreating, his tail between his legs. Bracussi spoke, his mouth crammed with a doughnut consumed in one bite, "He'll be talking to prospective bidders sometime today. You'll probably be notified."

"How many serious bidders are there?" Ward asked.

Bracussi shrugged. "One."

"Dayton Fredrick?"

"I couldn't say that."

"But you wouldn't deny it?"

Bracussi gulped his poached eggs as if this were an ordinary hash-house breakfast. He chewed with his mouth open, seeping at the corners. "I will say this much. Mr. Marsh has set a floor for the bids. That's why I say there's only one serious bidder."

"Could you say what that floor might be?"

"You know better."

"But Fredrick will be safely above that floor?"

"He wants that rail line."

Ward felt himself sweating uncomfortably. "Would a hundred thousand dollars be a safe estimate?"

Bracussi met his harried gaze. "I can only say Mr. Fredrick will be above that."

"Above that, eh?"

"Yes. Oh.yes. Well above that."

They sat for some moments in silence. Bracussi ate hurriedly, without any genuine appreciation for the excellence of the meal, chewing loudly, gulping his coffee black, sucking air through his teeth. He was quickly finished from old habit, eating as if he had to run this morning, as he did every morning, to answer the tyranny of a time-clock.

Ward managed to keep his voice at the level of polite disinterest. "Do you plan to stay on with Marsh or go with the railroad, after the sale?"

Bracussi sucked his teeth. "Those are the options I'm considering. I've been an accountant with EF&GC for over ten years. I'll be worth plenty to whoever does bid it in."

"I'd say invaluable."

"Still, Mr. Marsh pays well. He's generous with his employees. He's not tightfisted; you've got to say that."

"Any employer could afford to be generous—to a man with your qualifications."

Bracussi met his gaze levelly, somehow having suddenly taken control of the situation. He was being bribed, but he

85

was too intelligent even to permit the knowledge to show in his eyes. "Yeah. Like I say, I've got my options."

Ward sighed heavily. "If only I weren't so damned new at this. I hate to underbid."

Bracussi wiped his mouth and tossed the linen napkin on his plate. He said, "Wish I could help you. You know my hands are tied."

"Maybe you can. Would a one-five bid top Fredricks?"

"I couldn't say anything like that."

"One-ten?"

Bracussi shrugged. "A bid like that—one-ten—would have to be gilt-edged. Mr. Marsh would want proof that the transfer could be executed."

Ward sagged in silence against the upholstered back of the heavy chair. Bracussi got up, smiled, and hurried from the room. Still sweaty, empty-bellied, and yet somehow afraid that if he ate another morsel of this excellent food, he'd vomit, Ward sat unmoving.

He felt an odd prickling at the nape of his neck, unexplained, unreasonable.

He turned, glanced across the dining room toward the lobby entrance, hesitated, then looked again, staring at Dolly Marsh.

She stood alone, beautiful, her slender body as shapely as any of the women fifteen years her junior. Her blouse was open at the throat, her skirt lightweight spun cotton. She looked desirable, especially desirable because he had been in bed with her.

She had been staring intently at the back of his head. He had, through some extrasensory perception known only to lovers, idiots, and mind-readers, sensed her presence. Now she looked through him, beyond him, remote as any stranger, unaware, uninterested.

He sighed heavily, unable to look away from her, aware of others calling to her, waving, speaking her name. Her smile glittered in the golden morning.

She turned, slightly smiling, when someone spoke her name behind her. Ward gaped, expecting to see Baxter Marsh. But it was not her husband she awaited. Dayton Fredrick joined her. Fredrick slipped his arm about her slender waist, overtly possessive. Chiding laughter peppered them like bright confetti lovingly thrown.

Dayton and Dolly moved down the carpeted steps into

the dining room. A half-dozen attendants leaped to attention.

Watching them, Ward felt emptier and younger and more alone and forlorn than ever. Dayton Fredrick made him feel like an awkward and callow boy, fresh off the farm. Fredrick was everything he was not, everything he aspired to be: urbane, sophisticated, debonair, self-confident.

Ward sat, feeling helpless against impossible odds. Dayton had casually appropriated the woman he wanted. How could he hope to oppose Fredrick in the financial world where Fredrick was knowledgeable, expert, and he the green outsider? Why didn't he get up and walk out of here and keep walking? Was Fredrick laughing at him? If he gave him a thought, he probably laughed.

Ward stared at his hands. He wanted to laugh at himself. He was more than a little desolated, but he could have been stabbed, wounded with jealousy. God knew, he had looked forward to seeing Dolly Marsh again. But he was not jealous. Discouraged, but not jealous. If Dolly Marsh had to choose anyone but himself, he was glad it was Dayton Fredrick. At least he understood her.

When he walked out into the lobby from the dining room, the desk clerk whispered his name. The man was at the register forty feet away. Ward heard him clearly. Astonished at the acoustics of this chapel-like rotunda, he crossed the deep carpeting. "Message for you, Mr. Hamilton."

Ward's heart lurched. Was Baxter Marsh inviting him up already? Where was Phillips Clark? Where were those bidding forms? What in hell would he say to the man?

The clerk removed a small, perfume-scented envelope from the mail rack and handed it across the dully polished desk. Ward carried the letter gingerly out to the veranda. He didn't know Dolly well enough to recognize her cologne. He was not well-heeled enough to attract any of the other women, and Dolly was the only one he wanted to hear from. He felt let down, and yet a sense of relief, that his confrontation with Baxter Marsh had been postponed.

He found a fan-backed wicker chair and sat down, the breeze from the bay fresh-scented and cool across his fevered face. He ripped open the envelope, read the hastily scrawled message, then reread it. The note was brief, bright in tone, and final:

If you wish to do business with my husband, you will stay away from me. He truly is insanely jealous. Many impotent men are. He has industrial and personal spies everywhere. You don't know me, and I certainly don't know you, darling. This note was left at the desk by a dear and devotedly loyal friend who traveled down here yesterday on the train with you and thinks you're cute. I think you're a tiger. But this is not my lifetime for ambitious young tigers. So beware! Isn't intrigue fun? If you're really smart, you'll chew this note up and swallow it. Conspiratorially and affectionately, D.

His heart thudding against his ribcage, Ward folded the note and placed it in his pocket. He went on sitting there, trying to look casual. He was twisted like barbed wire inside, staring warily about the shadowed veranda. The wide, brightly tiled porch was columned, with low balustrades against thick pepper bushes, hibiscus, and gardenias. Italian pines grew at every columned break in the hedge. Everything was neatly manicured and verdantly green.

He found himself watching people's faces almost suspiciously. Near him, people laughed and chatted, as untroubled and carefree as immense financial security and social status could render them. A young man in a white shirt, white duck slacks, and white slippers gently batted tennis balls to a young woman in a white ankle-length skirt and matching shirt with sailor's collar, down on the courts. A foursome had already staked out an area and set up bridge tables. Couples sipped liquors from tall, frosted glasses; pleasant fragments of disjointed conversations drifted by him.

He saw Dolly often that morning. It proved hard to get her out of his mind and just when he did, she suddenly reappeared, arrestingly tall and regal and unapproachable. Usually she was with Dayton Fredrick, invariably laughing up at him, intensely involved, her eyes nursing him publicly.

He studied every person moving in and out of the perimeter of his vision. He laid his head back, but remained taut and troubled. He admitted he was no judge of human quality or social status, as that waiter had been at breakfast All these people appeared relaxed, contentedly wealthy, at ease, untroubled. Yet among them slunk Baxter Marsh's paid spies. Who? Which one?

He admitted he was in a rarified world entirely alien to him, but he felt like Alice, fallen in a rabbit hole where everything was wonderful, but strange.

A buzz of excitement spun up and down the length of the tiled veranda. Suddenly guests discarded lovers, books, cards, and whiskey, and lined the brink of shade along the veranda balustrade like a Greek chorus, some even venturing unawares into the blaze of sun, shading their eyes with their arms.

Something of terrible import was happening on the beach, and even the worldliest, the most blasé, stood gaping like rubes at a carnival. Ward felt a little reassured. No matter how rich, they were just ordinary people after all, *ordinary*. Curiosity was a great homogenizer.

Ward got up and joined the people lined along the sunlit terrace.

He squinted against the blast of sunlight reflected off the basin of the bay. In the distance he saw a girl on a horse. At first there seemed nothing very unusual about her. Then he saw that she wore a black bathing dress, her fair hair dank and wild in the wind. Whoever, whatever she was, she had grabbed and riveted these people's attention and, for some reason, did not release it, though she appeared wholly unaware of the sensation she created. The guests stood staring at her, as if in thrall.

The full-bodiced, high-collared bathing waist hung open, the entire bathing suit mutilated, skirt ripped away, pantaloons chopped off raggedly, high above her suntanned knees. "Undressed like that in public," a woman whispered. "That would be entirely unseemly in a child under ten."

But the rent and abbreviated bathing costume was the least disruptive and shocking aspect. The girl rode an incredibly beautiful white stallion, running it, fetlock-deep, along the shoreline. But even her racing the animal in the dangerous, potholed shallows was not as disturbing to her audience as the *way* the girl rode. She sprawled, legs

89

apart, on a Western saddle, riding like a man, rather than posting decorously sidesaddle.

From this distance, Ward could not guess her age, but he was provided a clue that she must have been in her teens, for more than one of the women pronounced her "That brat—that incorrigible brat."

The girl had tied a forty-foot lariat to her saddle horn. At the end of it she was pulling three scantily clad black children, all under ten, on a planed watersled.

The children on the sled were just far enough offshore to ride the gently breaking waves on the bouyant board. Their yells, urging the rider "faster, faster, faster," rode in across the veranda on the wind.

"Somebody ought to go down there and forcibly remove her," a man said.

"Not even sidesaddle," a woman said, horrified.

"She cut off the skirt to her swimming outfit—"

"Disgraceful. Revealing her body like that—"

"She's chopped it off halfway up her thighs."

"And playing, big as you please, with niggers."

"What the hell? The pickininnies are having fun. Listen to them laugh."

"It's entirely unseemly, a girl her age. There's no excuse for such behavior."

The cresting waves lifted the board precariously and hurtled it toward the shore. It skidded as lightly as a snipe across the shallows. The joyous laughter of the children carried like music, although it was unwelcome and discordant to the people along the veranda. The chortling cries only aggravated the situation as far as the onlookers were concerned, though they were vocal in declaring their interest only in "what's best for that girl."

"It's not her fault. Not really. It's Dayton's fault—"

"Dayton lets her run wild—"

"He's let her go like a gypsy since she was five—"

"She'd behave if Corrinne were alive—"

"I doubt if even Corrinne Fredrick could do anything with that brat."

"She can do no wrong in her doting father's eyes—"

"Riding straddled across that saddle. Looks like even Dayton wouldn't want her to do *that*—"

"Half dressed—"

"Half naked."

90

"Somebody ought to paddle that young lady's behind before it's too late."

"I can't believe—as lax as he is—that Dayton knows about this."

"Not even he could countenance such unseemly behavior."

"Where is Dayton?"

This caused them to glance at each other knowingly, but to deny aloud any knowledge. "Who knows where Dayton is?"

"Cherchez la femme," somebody said.

Mordant laughter slashed its way along the file of the righteous.

"If Dayton won't look after her, he should hire governesses—"

"My God, he has. By the gross—"

"They learn from *her*—"

"And run shrieking for shelter."

"I'm afraid nothing less than a female prison guard could control her now."

"Dayton's going to regret this. To the day he dies, he'll regret letting that child grow up wild, headstrong, spoiled rotten, undisciplined and unprincipled—"

"Sounds like she takes after her father."

"The fruit don't fall far from the tree."

"She adores him. She'd be just like him if she could be."

"She's made a valiant start."

"Dayton just doesn't know. He doesn't know half the time what she's doing—"

"Or, if he knows, he doesn't care—"

"And if he cared, she'd laugh at him, and he'd laugh with her."

Some instinct warned Ward that something was going wrong down there on the sunstruck beach. Dayton's daughter prodded her heels harder into the stallion's flanks and the beautiful horse responded, and it seemed they sailed, fluid on the wind, without touching the ground.

"Damn," somebody said. "If that horse steps in a hole, he'll break a leg and kill her."

That feeling of impending danger clutched Ward deep in his belly. He leaped over the veranda balustrade and ran down the grassy slope toward the beach. The board suddenly lunged upward crazily, out of control. It bal-

91

anced for a long heartbeat, like an awkward albatross catching an air current. Then it tipped, dipped, and bounded along on its edge in the shallow water. The children laughed louder, terror and delight in equal mixture.

One of the children was hurled outward. His small arms flailed, his chocolate body tensed, his skinny legs battered at the insubstantial air. He struck the water, face down, screaming and kicking.

The board righted itself, but the terrified wails of the children struck at the girl on the horse. Jerking her head around, she pulled up so fiercely on the reins that the stallion reared, its tender mouth agonized. The horse squealed and lurched, its front hooves pawing mindlessly. The girl clutched leather and hung on, coolly talking to the horse until she got it quieted and under control.

Ward ran across the beach and into the water, fully dressed. The child lay struggling weakly, face down, strangled and half drowned from trying to wail out its terror underwater.

He took the child up in his arms, turning him first upside down to drain the water from his lungs, throat, eyes, nose and sinus cavities, then holding him close and well out of the water to reassure him. The boy, not more than five, eyes round and brown as buttons, shuddered, whimpered, and pressed close in Ward's arms, sniffling raggedly, his terror subsiding.

Most of the people from the veranda had moved, entranced and silent, to the white brink of the beach. The girl walked the white stallion back to where the other two children still perched on the polished board.

Gazing up at her beseechingly, they chanted, "Sled some more, Julia, sled some more."

Laughing, ignoring the thick miasma of disapproval emanating from the crowd across the narrow, sugar-white sand, Julia agreed. Then her gaze touched tentatively at Ward's, fell away contritely, leaped back. She slid lithely from the saddle, watching him intently.

Looking at her, Ward felt a tremor of shock and surprise. Was this child the center of that tempest on the veranda? She *was* a child, and, despite the fullness of her high-standing young breasts, she was no more than thirteen years old. She wasn't, at first glance, even pretty, with lank hair plastered down the side of her incomplete child's face. Her odd-colored eyes were hard and defiant until she realized he was not going to accuse or upbraid her.

"Thanks," was all she said. The rage and defiance clouding her strange off-hazel eyes receded, replaced by something else, something new and totally alien inside her. Her face flushed pinkly, blood-bright even under the deep suntan, and her lips parted. For a long moment in the blazing sun, she didn't move, but stared up at him unabashed, unblinking.

Chapter Eight

WARD WALKED THROUGH the hotel and went up to his room. He removed his sodden, sandy clothing, and sent his shoes out to be dried and polished. Awaiting his summons into Baxter Marsh's august presence, he sat bare-chested and barefooted, wearing white duck slacks, in a club chair pulled to one of the open windows. Seagulls raced the wind. Pelicans lumbered along the shoreline, fishing. The bay-and-pine-scented breeze was cool and tranquilizing, soft and pleasant against his bare skin.

He stared down at the narrow, royal white carpeting of beach and smiled, thinking about the furor the Fredrick child had created. He tried to relax; this place was consecrated to relaxation. It was pleasant and restful to be sprawled there, and yet he couldn't rest. He wondered where Phillips Clark was with those EF&GC bids. When would Marsh call him? Would the old boy call him at all? Or had he checked his credit rating and found him unworthy of consideration? Twenty thousand dollars in an Atlanta bank would be laughable to a man like Marsh.

Ward felt his face burn. What no credit rating could show was that one hundred thousand in gold that Robert had stashed away. He had recognized, all along, in Phillips Clark's undeceived eyes, that the lawyer understood what he called Ward's "unrealistic dependence on Robert's stolen money." In many ways, Clark was right. If the army recovered the money, Robert was uselessly in jail. And Robert would never willingly lend him that money, even if he could return it tenfold. He didn't know where that money was hidden, or how to find it, and yet he went on depending on it, because he was driven by his dreams and he had to. He had nothing else. Once he got his hands on that railroad property, he could wheel and deal and make it pay. He vowed he'd find that money and, in the meantime, he'd keep driving forward, as if it were already banked and waiting. He swore to himself that when the moment arrived when producing that cash was crucial, he would get it. He had to believe in that; there was nothing else to believe in. The money existed; it was hidden somewhere. If anyone could find it, he could, and knowing it was there made it possible to take daring chances—like bidding for Baxter Marsh's railroad.

The gentle breeze, fragrant and soothing, lulled him into a half-sleep. He laid his head back and watched the sun lash thin silver chains across the dark face of the bay. Behind his eyes, he saw Julia clearly. He had no idea why he would think about her now. She had seemed totally unexceptional at first, and yet he had not been able to get her out of his mind. She spun and pirouetted there like a laughing imp, an irritant, an unwelcome and unlikely aphrodisiac, taunting, provocative, promising, her naked girl-woman eyes gaping at him, vulnerable and unreservedly open to him, even at thirteen. What the hell, he had to put her out of his thoughts. Yet it might be fun—if dangerous—to be around her when that willful child grew up, which could happen in a week or two! She had, the longer he observed her on that beach, grown quite extraordinary before his eyes. She was more than just a pugnosed kid. She had begun to exude a gamin appeal he'd never encountered before. She'd begun to look—hell, the only word was "adorable," a word he'd never speak aloud in masculine company, in that mutilated bathing costume, too old for her years, too knowledgeable, too direct and artless, her odd green eyes defiant and her breasts bouncing, too full and unfettered under that proper fabric. Hell, her breasts were fuller, shapelier, more disturbing already than—than even Dolly Marsh's.

Smiling, he reminded himself that child-molesting was antisocial, a criminal offense, perverted and sick. Yet he grinned and sighed. He'd never felt healthier, more robust, more in tune with God's universe, than at this moment. Maybe his pulse was pounding a little fast; perhaps his blood pressure was up slightly. Hell, he knew how young she was. He wouldn't touch her, but he sensed that of all the important, worldly, and fashionable people he had met at Port St. Joe, it was Julia Fredrick's strange, upsetting, pixy image he would carry in his mind away from this place.

A knock on the corridor door brought him from his reverie to his feet and across the room. It occurred to him that this might be his summons to Baxter Marsh, or at least it might be Phillips Clark, turning up with the bid forms.

He opened the door and caught his breath, staring at Julia Fredrick. Her gaze touched his face and loitered across it. She smiled tentatively.

"My daddy said I could come and thank you."

"For what?"

"For saving little Ethy's life—"

"Ethy?"

"Ethyopia. The little boy who fell off the watersled. That's his name. He's named for a country somewhere. His sister is Gaza and his brother is Revelation Two. May I come in?"

"I'm not dressed."

"Good lord, I don't care."

"Maybe I do. Maybe your father would. Or his friends."

"Those sticks, those absolute sticks! I'm coming in. I don't intend to stand out here in the hall." She walked past him and thrust the door closed. She turned and grinned at him wickedly, staring at his hairy chest. "Don't put a shirt on," she said. "It does something really weird to me to see you like that. Makes me feel all bubbly inside, like hot champagne."

"Those feelings can get you in trouble."

"Don't lecture me; I'm really very selective. I see men without their shirts on all the time, working down in the kitchen or on the railroad, and out in the paddocks. I can tell you it doesn't affect me in the least. It never has." She swung her arm toward him as if to indicate an unknown vista. "But you affect me."

He laughed. "Are you trying to seduce me?"

"Seduce? What does that mean? Would I like you to kiss me?" She considered this and nodded. "I'd like that."

"Come back when you know how to kiss."

"Maybe when I know how, I won't come back."

"I'll have to take that chance."

"Is it that I don't appeal to you?"

"My God. Appeal? You're a child."

"You're not exactly a doddering old gobbler yourself. What are you? Seventeen? Eighteen?"

"I'm almost twenty. Twenty means I'm grown and thirteen means you're still a little girl. There's a hell of a lot of difference between thirteen and twenty. Maybe when you're twenty, seven years won't mean that much. But it does now."

"No. You're just right for me. Thirteen-year-old boys bore me to tears. They're such pills, such droops. Playing tag, grabbing hair ribbons, for God's sake. Really now, can you imagine ever being that young and stupid?" She nodded seriously, watching him without blinking those strange eyes. "You think you're too old for me now. But when I'm nineteen, a nineteen-year-old boy will still be too young for me—and you'll still be just right."

He laughed at her. "You've got it all figured out."

She nodded, wandering about the room, gazing at herself critically in the mirror. "I'm really quite pretty naked," she said. "Really. Everybody says so."

"Everybody?"

She laughed over her shoulder. "You know what I mean."

He said nothing. Unwillingly moved, he watched her feast on herself in that vast reflective glass. She wore a pale pastel lavender shirtwaist and skirt, ankle-length, with no more than one petticoat under it, if any. Her blouse gaped open three buttons—the way Dolly Marsh wore her crisp shirtwaists—revealing the shadowed gap of nascent cleavage. Her only ornaments were a small diamond ring and a bracelet of woven gold design. Her sun-damaged, dark golden hair gleamed, scrubbed dry and painstakingly brushed two hundred strokes, parted precisely but spilling casually about her square-jawed face. It was her pixy face that grabbed at him and twisted him inside, even when this made no sense at all. He smiled, meeting her unde-ceived green eyes in that mirror. She was thirteen all right, going on twenty-eight. She met his gaze artlessly, smiling oddly, her lips parted. Those almond-shaped eyes admired him, large in her little girl's face and accented by straight, winglike brows.

"You are beautiful. Even with your clothes on," he said to her reflection. "It's all true, kid, just the way you see it." He grinned, retreating. "But for both our sakes, give yourself time, little girl."

She stared at him in the mirror. "I haven't been a little girl since my mother died. She left my father with no-body—oh, those stupid women who chase after him, but they don't mean anything and they don't really care about him, as I do. You're the first person except Daddy I ever have cared about." She laughed without mirth. "The mo-ment I saw you down on that beach, I just melted, just plain melted. How long do you expect me to wait for you?"

He laughed. "Until you're ripe, at least. Or legal. Whichever comes first."

She turned. "You would like to make love to me."

"No. No, I wouldn't."

"You are afraid of me, aren't you?"

"God, yes. You're a penitentiary pullet. I don't need you—or anybody—bad enough to go to jail for it. That's an automatic life sentence."

She preened, standing on her toes. "I might be worth it. I'd certainly try to be."

"Not to me. I've got other things to do."

"Nobody else would ever know."

"They might. There's such a thing as statutory rape. That means it's rape even if you're willing. You might talk in your sleep." He winked at her, forcing himself to keep it all in perspective. Despite her tone, she was just a young girl, an ordinary little rich girl one might see a dozen times over in some polite finishing school for fashionable young ladies. Her uptilted nose underscored and left no doubt about how young she was. Despite all the taboos against it, he was certain she wore lip rouge. A brat. A spoiled brat, playing at being grown up.

She walked over and sat on the bed, her bared ankles dangling over the side.

He returned to his chair at the window and sat down, the languid breeze chilling the sweat on his flesh. "Are you playing a game? Are you trying to find out how much willpower I've got? I can tell you, damned little. You've thanked me now. Why don't you run and play?"

She seemed not to hear him. "You're really pretty."

"Don't be ridiculous. Men aren't pretty."

"Of course they are. Some of them. They're just too cold-fish to admit it. Now, you—you're too thin, but your shoulders are great, and I love those muscles in your chest. You're built like a god. You're the prettiest man I ever saw, except my daddy."

He grinned. Dayton Fredrick again. And once more he ran second. He was relieved they were back on a safer plateau.

When he turned, she was wriggling on the bed, watching him, lips parted, green eyes hooded. He felt a sharp constriction deep in his loins. He said, "Your dad's going to worry."

"About me? Don't be a stick." She nodded, satisfied about something. She was thinking that he was handsomer than all the male models in the magazines and catalogues, or even the knights of her fantasies. Whatever man she dreamed about from this moment on would always have his face. Finding Ward Hamilton was for Julia an encountering of an image unexpected, unsuspected, and unknown, until she had looked up and seen him on that sun-braised beach. He became the standard, in that brief instant, against which all young males were measured—and found wanting—her fantasies. This thirteen-year-old found his self-mocking smile and ease of manner irresistible. In her romantic dreams, she'd promised herself what her lover, when he appeared, would be. But now she amended all her old dreams. Even if, by some terrible prank of fate, she never saw him again, she would never forget him.

She drew a deep breath and smiled palely. "I'm glad you're coming to work for my father."

"Did he tell you that?" He reacted, wincing. The prospect sounded unpleasant even when she said it in anticipation. *Maybe he'll work for me*, he said deep in his mind, where she couldn't detect it. "I think you've got a crush on me," he said, making another effort to laugh her out of this dangerous mood. Despite everything he could do, it was closing in on both of them. Not this, he told himself savagely. You've done enough unforgivable things. Not this, especially not with a young girl playing games. "A crush," he repeated firmly.

"Haven't I, though?"

"More grist for your father's friends' gossip mills," he warned. "Do you know how much they disapprove of you already?"

"Of course I do. The prudes. They all scream about such stupid things. Good manners, good conduct, social form. Good lord! They get ill when I straddle a horse. Ugly, vulgar, unladylike, disgraceful. They're convinced it's too—stimulating. It might feel good." She lay back across the comforter, laughing. "It does, you know."

The knock on the door came, a welcome sound of release for Ward. No matter how valiantly he tried, things were getting out of hand between them. This child meant to gratify her desires, even if she was too young to know what she wanted.

He strode across the room, as if fleeing from purgatory. She went on lying indolently across his bed, watching him with sleepy-eyed approval.

Ralph Bracussi pushed past Ward, speaking as he entered the room. When his gaze struck Julia Fredrick lying across the bed, Bracussi grinned knowingly.

Ward winced. Thank God the bed was made, unmussed. If this gossip got spread around, it could be trouble.

"Well," Bracussi said. "Sorry I bolted in like this. Didn't know your tastes ran to young girls."

"Jesus, Bracussi."

Bracussi shrugged, still grinning, finding pleasure in this situation. He had little faith that Hamilton would buy control of EF&GC, but stranger things had happened in this business, and it was always good to cover all bases. "I should have known you had company."

"Oh?" The word was cold.

"Yes. The way your face was all flushed and the way your eyes bugged out. And those veins in your neck." He laughed in good-natured mockery. "Yes, it was obvious you had company."

Ward's voice crackled, humorless, steel-hard, "What do you want, Bracussi?"

"Me? Nothing. Just delivering a message from God. That's what we in the Jacksonville office call Baxter Marsh—when he's in New York. He wants to see you. Suite 314, at your convenience—which means ten minutes ago."

"For God's sake." Ward searched around frantically, found a fresh shirt, pushed his feet into shoes, knelt and laced and tied them. His hands shook. He stood up, shoving his shirttails into his trousers. "Tell him I'll be there as soon as I find Phillips Clark."

Bracussi shrugged and grinned. "Tell him yourself. I'll just stay around and entertain the chicken. I like to pluck 'em young, too."

Julia slid off the bed, her murrey mouth twisted sourly. She idled past Bracussi on her way to the door. "Bull," was all she said.

Within ten minutes, Ward had located Clark, glanced through the bid sheets, and walked with him up the stairway to Baxter Marsh's suite.

Ward fully comprehended for the first time the true connotation of the word *dread*. He understood what emotions assaulted the minds, bodies and kidneys of the doomed, unfortunates bound for beheadings, the gallows, or boardrooms.

"Have you got everything?" he asked Phillips Clark for the twelfth time on the stairs.

"Everything except the money."

"Very funny."

"As I understand it, you're required to deposit ten percent of your bid. You assume operating control of the company in twenty days and final transfer—with payment in full—in ninety days."

"That gives us ninety days."

"That's not reassuring as hell to me."

"Did you cover everything?"

"I've told you a dozen times. I put in every clause, subclause, and addendum, every 'whereas,' every loophole known to man."

"Good."

"Then why do you look like you're about to throw up?"

101

"I'm fine, I'm fine. Leave me alone, Phil."

"Sure, you're fine. Setting out without a dollar in your pocket to buy a railroad. Well, I left open only the bottom line. I've a weak stomach. Whatever you bid is up to you; I'd rather not know."

"You're helpful as hell."

Baxter Marsh sat alone in the Louis XIV suite, which was obviously designed and appointed for royalty. A massive painting—*The Pursuit*, by the master of the French rococo period, Fragonard—highlighted in massive, handcarved framing of rosewood, dominated the south wall. Beneath the painting, almost as formidable as the room itself, Baxter Marsh sat in a high-backed French baroque chair, carved in rare decorative satinwood. Before him, a polished, hand-crafted Louis XIV table served him as desk and buffer zone between himself and his antagonists.

It was as foes that he received Ward and Clark, staring stonily at them, without speaking. He seemed younger and a hell of a lot more redoubtable than when Ward had first glimpsed him briefly, formally attired, in the ballroom of the Atlantan Hotel. He wore a starched white shirt with attached collar open at the throat, revealing his gray chest hairs. His muttonchop whiskers were grayer than Ward recalled, and elegantly barbered. His face was graying with age, going white about the eyes and gaunt in the cheeks, but his eyes remained strong, probing, unwavering.

Phillips Clark followed Ward across the room. They waited for Marsh to stand and shake hands. He did not move from his chair, but simply sat, regarding them with an attitude almost of aloof contempt.

A well-stocked bar, holding a wide selection of liquors and wines, glasses in many shapes, and a bowl of melting ice had been set up near the opened windows. Marsh did not invite them to have a drink. Ward exhaled between his teeth, feeling as if he'd been holding his breath for ten minutes. Too bad Marsh didn't offer them drinks. Ward could have used a whiskey, straight, on ice.

The silence remained brittle. Marsh made no effort to put them at ease. Ward felt the nerves tightening in his gut, thinking that anyone who suggested that men of great power, men who controlled one's destiny even tangentially, didn't inspire apprehension, wet armpits, and dry mouths,

102

simply hadn't encountered such a personage under adverse circumstances. Ward said, "Mr. Marsh, this is my attorney, Phillips Clark."

Marsh barely nodded toward Clark. He didn't take his gaze from Ward's face. The beginnings of panic fluttered deep in Ward's belly, butterflies taking wing. "Is that so? And who are you?"

Ward's anger flared. He abruptly felt more at ease. If Marsh was going to be a son of a bitch, he could match him in spades. "I'm sorry, sir. You had an appointment with me. I assumed you knew my name. I'm Ward Hamilton."

"I know your name. And your attorney. I must congratulate you on your defense of Mr. Hamilton's brother recently in federal court."

Clark smiled. "I got the shit kicked out of me, sir."

"No. My report has it that you did admirably against those government lawyers. Well. This is all preliminary inquiry, Mr. Hamilton. We won't need your attorney present." He almost smiled, those anguished eyes lightening faintly. "I have no lawyer present. You wouldn't want to take unfair advantage of me, would you?"

Clark handed Ward the folder of papers, elevated both of his brows, pushed his tongue in his cheek, and withdrew. The older man waited until the door had closed behind the lawyer. "You've seen my rail line, my base in Jacksonville. You've inspected my rolling stock quite minutely, I understand. You wish to submit bids for my company. Is that why you're here?"

Ward frowned. "What else?"

Marsh leaned forward across the cluttered table. "I know who you are, Hamilton. All about you. I know you bedded my wife in Atlanta. And now you hope to screw me, is that the idea?"

Ward staggered. He didn't waver physically, but mentally he toppled, stunned with shock, and sank to his knees, helpless. He stared at Marsh across that paper-littered table. It looked to him as though whatever he did, no matter how pleasant it seemed at the moment, he hurt somebody unforgivably. They never forgot, never forgave. This hard-eyed man looked as if he'd never forgotten or forgiven a trespass against him since kindergarten. He had piled them up and stored them behind those wounded eyes.

Ward's stomach churned, his legs went weak, his mind whirled in confusion. He remembered thinking, with such high hopes, when Dolly Marsh had told him her husband was divesting himself of a rail company, that knowing Dolly might smooth the way toward the purchase, at least. It was ironic as hell. If he had not spent the night with Dolly, he wouldn't be here now, clutching bids in his clammy fists. Yet going to bed with Dolly had abrogated any chance he might ever have had of acquiring this property.

Obviously, Marsh hadn't sent for him to discuss the bidding. Marsh was taut and icy with rage, but controlled, as half a century in industry boardrooms had taught him to be.

Ward tried to regroup his thoughts. It was almost impossible for him to think clearly in the face of Marsh's charges. His mind raced, flitting, jumping, as if short-circuiting. It was never like this in Horatio Alger. When the poor but honest boy, with daring and pluck, finally met the aging tycoon, everybody lived happily ever after. Jesus, such fairy tales. Ward managed to keep his voice level. "I didn't know her as your wife, sir."

Marsh's pained eyes glittered. "No, you didn't. I have to give you that, don't I? You didn't know. The refuge of every knave. Well, I give you that. But do respect my intelligence enough not to ask me to believe it would have mattered a damn to you if you had known."

"I can't honestly say, sir. Maybe if I'd known you—as a person. Liked you, respected you."

"Or feared me."

"I'm not afraid of you, sir. I'm sorry. I regret what happened in Atlanta, if it causes you anguish. I never wanted to do that."

"No. You just wanted a piece of tail, didn't you?"

When Ward didn't reply, Marsh's voice lightened slightly, but only by a decibel. "Maybe that's the reason I hate you so deeply. Because you're so goddamn young. Something I can't ever recover. Youth. The hot, mindless excitement, the overwhelming needs."

"I've said I'm sorry."

Marsh tilted a thick, graying brow and gazed at him

from those fishbelly-white-rimmed eyes. "Did you believe, when you walked in here, that I didn't know?"

Ward shrugged.

Marsh's quiet voice lashed out across the table. "Of course I knew. I know what I have to know. I know you not only took her from our hotel, I know which hotel you took her to, and which room." He shuddered slightly. "I know you kept her all night long . . . all night. I hate you deep in my guts for that also. The voracious appetites of youth—those are denied me, too."

Ward wondered if Marsh hated him more for what he had done with Marsh's wife, or for the fact that age had destroyed him, leaving him prey to young bucks like Ward Hamilton. It was a hell of a thought. For the first time he felt a stricture of regret, a sense of compassion and pity for the older man. "I don't know what you want me to say, sir."

"You don't have to say anything. I don't care to listen to you any more than to look at you. I just want you to know. I read my wife's charming and utterly deceitful little note left for you at the hotel registry desk this morning; I suppose you chewed it up and swallowed it, as directed?"

Ward flinched. Well, so much for Dolly's dear and devotedly loyal friend. You couldn't trust anybody anymore.

The large, high-domed room grew silent. From the beach rose wan sounds of distant laughter, the muted scream of gulls, the remote lapping of waves on the shore, intensifying the taut silence inside Marsh's suite.

"There is this," Marsh observed almost as an afterthought. "I won't pretend you're the only man who's bedded my wife. But you are the one, among them all, whom I resent and refuse to tolerate. I have but one weapon against a man as young and virile and conscienceless as you—violence. I am not a violent man, Mr. Hamilton, but I assure you of this in all sincerity: if you ever touch my wife again, I'll kill you."

Ward remained standing there because he didn't know what else to do. He supposed he could turn and walk out, but no matter with how much dignity he accomplished his retreat, it was going to look as if he were running with his tail between his legs. Damned if he would do that. Sorry, Marsh, my own brother doesn't forgive me, either. He

105

wants to kill me too, and he has priority. You'll have to take a number. Get in line.

He stiffened, waiting. Marsh watched him. "You've a certain arrogance, haven't you?" When Ward said nothing, Marsh continued in that flat, unemotional tone. "I hope you understand that I'm quite serious. I've lived a long and fouled-up existence—a life that no longer holds very much for me. I'd just as soon end it in a melodramatic, asinine act of revenge. If I killed you, I'd die satisfied. Do you understand that?"

Ward continued to stand unmoving. Now that the initial shock had worn off, anguish welled up in him. He was going to lose whatever opportunity he'd had here. Maybe he couldn't have pulled it off, but now he would never know. It had all crashed down around him before it had ever really started. He was thankful it had been great in bed with Dolly Marsh. God knew there had one hell of a price tag attached. He felt empty and desolated, even when he admitted not a gram of contrition or regret for having cuckolded this baronial bastard.

"Is it clear to you?" Marsh said again.

"I heard your threat, if that's what you mean."

"All right. We can discuss the bidding now if you wish."

Marsh nodded toward a chair, but Ward remained standing. They faced each other, adversaries in an arena where Marsh was a seasoned gladiator. Ward held a single advantage: as long as he stood there across that table, Marsh had to look up at him. How the old hellion must hate that!

"I can tell you this, Hamilton, as I've told each prospective bidder: I've set a floor. If none of the bids exceeds that base amount, the sale is simply nullified."

"All right."

"I've told none of the others; it was not expected or necessary. But I tell you so you won't waste my time. The bidding floor is one hundred thousand dollars."

Ward didn't flinch.

"So far, there have been eight bids submitted. I personally know each of the bidders or the corporations they represent. I'm confident of their fiscal competency. I have no such knowledge of you. I know you only through my wife. I don't know that I'd accept a bid of over one hundred thousand dollars from you."

106

"If you're going to get revenge, do it with a gun."

"Don't be so hotheaded. Why should we accept a winning bid from you, only to have you default? I'm personally convinced that is what you'd have to do—unless there is more stable support behind you than my operatives have been able to uncover. You have an Atlanta bank account of slightly under twenty-five thousand dollars."

Ward did not waver. He nodded. "All right, so that's all you know about me. If I'm to be allowed to bid, I must also provide you assurance—"

"Gilt-edged warranty—"

"That I would not default."

"All bids are accompanied by draft deposits amounting to ten percent of the total bid. That will not be acceptable in your case."

"I understand that."

"Even to accept your bid, I'd require a great deal more from you than that."

"All right." Ward withdrew a draft drawn against his account in the Atlanta Commercial Bank. "Either I'm an adventurer without credit, or I have financial support. You know I have twenty-five thousand on deposit in this bank. I say it's there simply to cover the deposit with my bid."

"You're such an arrogant young bastard. Maybe I ought to sell you that rail line. That would be my truest revenge, in the long run." He accepted the draft note. He studied it, his brow tilting. "You've made it out for twenty thousand—almost your total account."

"That's right. You demand a guarantee. There it is—twenty thousand, nonrecoverable deposit. If I default anywhere along the line, you have it all. My gift. Cash it now, today. It's yours. It's my warranty that I'll pay off the total amount of the bid the day it's due."

Marsh almost smiled. His gaze raked over Ward, something new, less violent, and less hostile in his eyes. "I think you're bluffing."

"Sure you do." Ward took up a pen and wrote "$110,-000" on the bottom line of the bidding form. He shoved the papers across the table and straightened. "Maybe I am," he said. "But there's just one way for you to find out; call me."

Chapter Nine

HE SAW HER first as a flash of color sparkling in patches of sunlight on the distant shadowed veranda. Then she darted, a bright wraith in a summery dress, into the yard and down the long driveway toward him, convoyed by small black children and half a dozen yapping and yowling dogs.

Ward pulled up on the reins and halted the buggy just inside the stone gates. He sat frowning, watching the girl run in the crosshatching of shadows beneath the aged live oaks lining the narrow clay driveway.

He urged the horse ahead, slowly. He pushed his planter's hat back on his head and stared, awed at the fading magnificence of this estate. Count on Robert's selectivity. He would choose only the superlative among the remnants of the old elite. It was odd to find a splendid old chateau standing intact, since Atlanta and the village of Decatur had been in the path of Sherman's fiery march to the sea eleven years ago. As a matter of fact, Ward had glimpsed fragmented remains of several gutted and abandoned homes on the road out of town. A few miles away, the nearest neighboring plantation house was recalled by only a blackened and crumbling chimney, that persisting symbol of total defeat.

He'd hesitated outside the natural fieldstone gate where the small cypress sign named this estate: *Errigal—Where Peace Lives.*

There was only a hint of the elegance this estate had possessed in antebellum years, like the melancholy memory of the enchantment of yesterday's aristocracy. Tall and protective oaks shadowed and softened the ravages of time, hiding from passersby the peeling paint, the weed-scabbed lawn, the anemic luster of gardenias, roses, portulaca, bells of Ireland, and climbing morning glories. A somber silence pervaded the place, a stillness not disrupted by the joyous barking of dogs and cries of children. The serenity and dignity was really all that remained intact. Errigal was a survivor.

The girl hitched up her long skirts about her calves as she ran. Even in the distance, he could read the delight illumining her face. Beyond her on the misty veranda, a man and three women had stood up from their chairs and now stood on the rim of sunlight, watching expectantly.

She was near enough now so that he could see she was young—somewhere in her late teens—slender, fragile, dark-haired. Excitement glowed in her heart-shaped face, and died there, lingeringly.

She hesitated, slowed, let her skirts fall about her shoe tops. Then she stopped, gesturing sharply toward the children to silence them. They paused beside her, puzzled, watching her. The dogs milled about, tails whipping frantically.

She lifted her arm, shadowing her eyes, staring at him. For no logical reason, the forlorn sight of her, disappointed like that, clutched at him and stirred him deeply whenever he thought of her as long as he lived. His first vivid image of her was always this brief vignette.

He pulled the single-seated runabout buggy close, seeing her expression alter from expectancy to disheartened loss to confusion. Keeping her arm lifted to shade her eyes, she smiled timidly, self-consciously. "I don't know whatever in this world you'll think of me," she said.

"You must be Miss Lily."

"Running out here like this, like I've got no more manners in this world than a billy goat. Whatever will you think?"

He swung down from the carriage and removed his hat.

109

Smiling, he bowed. She *was* beautiful, fragile, with a sweet and innocent purity, her eyes direct, artless, incapable of any but that petty dissimulation all Southern females practice, even in their cradles. Her dark hair grew richly about her face, highlighted with faint red tint. Soft tendrils, silky, baby-textured, curled across her small, straight forehead. Her eyebrows were natural, dark, unplucked, above ash-blue eyes and thick, upcurled lashes. Though her complexion was Dresden china—suffused with blood under its delicate surface when she laughed or flirted or ran—there was no hint of a freckle or blemish. Her nose was slight, cast in perfect proportion with all her dainty features. Her smile charmed, eager, ardent, lively, unsophisticated, and interested, reaching out to everyone she met.

"You are Miss Lily?" he said.

She gestured vaguely, still uncomfortable. "Well, there's just no question about who you are, is there? You *have* to be Robert's brother." She waved her arm toward the manor house. "From way up there, from up on the terrace, we thought it was Robert. I declare, we all did."

Ward smiled. "Robert admitted he had a brother?"

She let him take her fingers now in his hand. Her eyes touched at his, then fell away. "Of course he did. What a perfectly terrible thing to say, Mr. Hamilton. He told us all about you."

"Did he really talk about me?"

She laughed. "Well, not very much. But you do look the spitting image of him."

"Oh, I'm much prettier," he said with a wry smile, remembering what Julia had told him.

"Pretty? Goodness. Men aren't pretty, Mr. Hamilton."

"I always say that."

"Men are handsome. You and Robert truly are handsome. But as to which is handsomer—well, I'm sure plenty of girls think you are." She laughed. "But I must be loyal to Robert. We're all foolishly fond of your brother here at Errigal, Mr. Hamilton."

"You haven't seen him since—"

"He was—imprisoned?" She winced. Even saying the word seemed to hurt her. "No." Her pale, aster-colored eyes clouded. She'd wanted to see Robert; she'd been desolated with loneliness without him. She wanted to visit him at the federal penitentiary in Atlanta, but this whole notion was unseemly and impossible. Ladies didn't enter pestholes like that in her world, where genteel womenfolk never even ventured into the business district. To go, even escorted, to a prison? To visit Robert now was impossible, no matter how devoutly she wished it. Prison conditions were too crude, too ugly, too brutal. She had to cling to memories of him. She wanted to be near him, and without him, she lived in an empty void. She drew a deep, ragged breath. "Have you seen Robert?" she said. "How is he? Tell me. How is he?"

He nodded. Yes, he'd seen him recently. He shivered, remembering.

Robert had received him in almost violent reluctance, forced to because he could not escape his prison hospital cot on the stub of one leg.

Robert glared up at Ward, his desperate eyes brimming with tears of hatred. "What do you want here, you son of a bitch?" Men in other cots turned, watching. Robert continued to stare into Ward's face. "You want to see what you've done to me? You want to gloat? You want to see the stump of my leg? Is that what you want?"

Robert yanked the covers away, exposing the slowly healing surgery, raw with sutures, flesh bunched like a bloody bouquet, the leg ending just above the knee. "How do you like it, brother? How does it look? Are you proud of yourself?"

Ward stood unmoving. "I'd hoped we could talk Robert."

"About what? Money? Is that what you want to talk about?"

"Phillips Clark is my lawyer now, Robert. He—"

"I know. I heard. He's a son of a bitch too."

"Why? He did everything for you he could."

"He's still a son of a bitch. He has to be a son of a bitch. He associates with you."

Ward tried to smile. "I have to pay him to do that, Robert."

Robert's head rolled on the pillow. "In time you won't even be able to pay people to come near you. You're a leper, Ward. I've lain here and figured it out. You've got leprosy of the soul."

111

"I'd hoped you'd forgiven me a little. I know now that you haven't."

"Forgiven you? You're goddamn right. I'll never forgive you. Not as long as I've got this bloody stump to remind me. And I'll hound you, you smiling bastard, as long as I've got one leg to hop on."

"Meanwhile, Robert, I can make you truly rich. Financially secure. Both of us."

Suddenly Robert threw his head back, growling out his rage. "The money. That's why you came. You didn't give a goddamn about my leg, did you? Go to hell, you bastard. I've told you, there is no money."

Guards and orderlies came running. They stood near the foot of the bed, watching warily.

"Get him out of here," Robert said.

"Your fiancee, Robert—"

"What about her?" Robert came up on his elbows, his face pallid. "You stay away from her."

"Doesn't she worry about you? Doesn't she want to know about you?"

"There's nothing you could tell her."

"Don't you want me to see her?"

"No. I saw her the night I—ran. She's all right. She understands everything between us. You stay away from her, you filth. Stay away."

"Does she know you've lost your leg?"

Robert stared at him, his eyes bleak and wild. "Does she have to know that too? You sadistic son of a bitch. Does she have to know that, too?"

He tried to tell Robert he'd been awarded the option to buy the East Florida & Gulf Central Railroad. He believed—perhaps for no better reason than that he wanted to believe—that his getting this opportunity could mean a great deal to both of them, might make some difference, cause a lessening of the hatred Robert felt toward him. Robert refused to listen, so he was unable to impart that bit of news.

In the two weeks since he'd left Port St. Joe, Ward's world had been capsized, catapulting him into a strange new existence. Always before, he'd desired opportunities. Now he had one in his fist, his one chance at the brass ring.

Phillips Clark had stared at him, still incredulous, holding the sheaf of papers and legal documents forwarded from Jacksonville.

Clark read aloud, his voice oddly empty, "This is to advise you—" He broke off suddenly. "I don't believe it, Ward. They've granted you the option to buy EF&G—lock, stock, and barrel, on the basis of your bid." He reread the body of the letter silently, shaking his head disbelievingly. "On terms mutually agreed upon. A bid of one hundred and ten thousand dollars, for Christ's sake, with a twenty thousand-dollar nonrecoverable deposit. You don't need a lawyer. Shit, you need a keeper."

Ward stared at the lawyer, unable to speak, his eyes brimming with tears. His heart felt constricted in his chest, as if it were malfunctioning, compressed in a space too small to contain it.

Clark stared back at him. "What are you going to do now?"

Ward shook his head, laughing and crying at once. "I don't know. Hell, I don't know, Mr. Vice President and General Counsel of the New East Florida & Gulf Central Railroad. How about celebrating, for a start? How about getting drunk?"

Clark laughed exultantly with him, nodding. "How about getting laid? I've been drunk plenty. I never have got enough poontang."

The railroad became Ward's obsessive passion from that moment. He worked with single-minded purpose to make it successful and profitable. The very first day, he called on his old boss, Simon Shaffer. "I need freight business in north central Florida," he told Simon. "What do you buy from Florida?"

"Hell, anything the army needs, or anything I can convince the brass it needs."

"Naval stores? Lumber? Vegetables? Cotton? Fruit? Anything from central Florida. If you get it shipped on my line, I'll give you a ten-percent kickback."

"Fifteen and you've got a deal."

"Fifteen, if it's worth it. I can pick up crappy jobs for nothing."

"Hell, I'm talking big." He gestured broadly as if exaggerating the size of some monstrous fish. "General Mait-

113

land White himself told me the army is building a base at Jacksonville, on the site of some old fort down there."

Ward managed to remain cool. He laughed, remembering old shady deals with Shaffer over whiskey and branch water. They joked together for thirty minutes during which no further business was discussed. "Always liked you, Ward," Shaffer said in sodden sentimentality. "Ought to come back with me. Don't try to be too big for your britches." Twenty minutes after he left Shaffer, Ward was in Phillips Clark's office.

"The army will need millions of feet of lumber, naval stores, God knows what, from north central Florida," Ward told Clark.

"Where'd you hear that?"

"Hell, it's as sure as if it came from the Secretary of War himself. More definite. I got it from Simon Shaffer. The army can't shit that he doesn't know about it."

"The army of occupation is to be pulled out of the South next year."

"Jesus, don't waste time arguing, Phil. You know what it really means when the army pulls out of any occupied territory. They march out with flags waving and bands and big machinery. But quietly, they leave policing troops on hand—in case of disorders. The War Department never willingly yielded an inch in its existence. Hell, who cares *why* they are building? They are building a base. Shaffer thinks they'll be buying through him."

Clark grinned tautly. "But you don't think so."

"I know goddamn well they won't. Why should they pay a middleman when we can transport for them?"

"Why indeed?"

"I want you to bid on all freight hauling. Everything. From the heaviest lumber to a bale of cotton. Now, I've worked with Shaffer long enough to know how to bid and how to win that bid with the army."

"Shaffer's got friends in high places."

"Yeah, but Shaffer's a greedy, carpetbagging hog. He'll bid his usual eighty-percent markup. But we're pure at heart. I want you to bid on everything. Figure each cost and add ten percent to every transported item. Figure the total and add another ten percent."

"Is the army going to accept a bid like that?"

"The army, when it gets a bid that's not inflated from

114

forty to a hundred and twenty percent, is going to believe they've found a sucker. They won't even believe we're for real. But we'll show 'em."

"Jesus." Clark stared at him. "I think you will."

"I know I will. We're going to get rich, Phil. But not in one day, like Shaffer and the other carpetbaggers. We're going to milk the War Department. They wouldn't deal with us unless we did. But compared to what's been happening to them, we'll look downright honest."

Clark nodded. "I'll buy the deal. But one thing doesn't change. You've got one hundred and ten thousand dollars to produce in a couple of months, or they're going to take your toys away from you."

Ward nodded. He strode about the office as if it were a cage ten times too small for him. The walls pressed in upon him. Sometimes it was hard to get a full breath. What was it Dayton Fredrick had said? "As long as you hold the dice, you've got a chance. But the minute you let the money boys take the play away from you, you're dead." Ward spoke savagely across his shoulder. "I told you I'd get that money."

Clark spread his hands. "Jesus, you're still trying to come up with that money your brother stole."

"Wouldn't you?"

"If you got it, the federal government would take it away from you."

"I've planned ahead better than that. I'll fence the gold when I find it. There are plenty of places."

"Yeah. All you've got to do is find it."

"He hid it somewhere. Hell, he's not that much smarter than I am."

"Maybe he's a hell of a lot dumber. Maybe what he's done with that loot is so stupid you'll never figure it out. Time's running out on you. You ought to know your own brother, how his mind works."

"I don't. He's like a stranger I grew up in the same house with."

Clark flopped in his chair behind his desk. "I shouldn't even discuss this illicit money with you; after all, I'm your attorney. But for God's sake, since we've got a puzzle here and I'm fascinated, can't you think as Robert might?"

"God knows how Robert thinks. I always liked girls. He loved to sing tenor in barbershop quartets where a bunch

115

of guys stand with their arms around each other. Hell, I don't know."

"What sort of plans for disposing of that loot would your brother make?"

"Stupid ones."

"All right. Think stupid. Because unless you meet that payoff deadline, you're out twenty thousand and out on your tail, and I have to go back to honest law practice. Either come up with Robert's swag, or give up on it. You can't give up on it, so how does Robert's mind work?"

Ward stared at him, his eyes bleak. "What color is shit before the air hits it?"

"Jesus Christ. Who knows?"

"That's what I mean. Who knows?"

The days hurtled past like a locomotive out of control on a downgrade. Phillips Clark assumed responsibility for bidding in freight contracts with General Maitland O. White's office.

Clark came back from White's offices with the bad news. "White says Baxter Marsh refused to bid to haul freight for the army project in Jacksonville."

"Why, for God's sake?"

"Marsh said he lacked flatcars to haul lumber. It would take a corporation with the money of Cornelius Vanderbilt, or the Morgans, or the U.S. Government, to supply enough flatcars for that job. And Marsh was right. One-use basis. It's just not practical."

Ward pased. "We sure as hell can't back out now. These contracts will put us in business. Here's what I want you to do, another little trick I learned from old Simon Shaffer. Put a clause in each bid, somewhere about page fifteen. Buried. Not too near the end, and nowhere near the front. Don't try to hide it, but we don't have to flaunt it. We don't have to explain it unless somebody asks specifically. What we want is a simple line I've seen in a hundred contracts Simon Shaffer gets passed by army brass. It'll read: 'The U.S. army agrees it will lend every assistance where feasible to expedite and insure delivery of all army-requisitioned materials.' "

Clark stared at him in disbelief. "You are a son of a bitch."

"I worked for carpetbaggers. I learned well. The federal

116

government is gouging the shit out of these crackers. Rubbing their faces in it. And the carpetbaggers are getting bloated fat off the federal government contracts. There's room for us at that trough, old son."

"Hold it. I knew it sounded too good. Shaffer could get away with a clause like that. But General White *knows* EF&GC is short of flatcars. He'll snort blue smoke when he sees that innocent little clause."

"He's a busy man. Rushed, harried, egotistical. God was built in *his* image. Who knows if White will ever *see* those contracts? Unless somebody brings them to his attention, they're just another bunch of bids. Are you going to point them out to him?"

Clark grinned guilelessly and spread his hands. But he put into words a fact both of them knew to be irrefutable. Those lucrative government contracts wouldn't pay off in time to save him. No amount of hauling would return profits in six figures in the time left to them.

The swiftly approaching date of transfer of EF&GC was like something that hung over the edge of a precipice and defied gravity—for a time—grinding at first with terrible slowness over a yawning abyss, then suddenly plummeting earthward, as one had known all along it must.

This brought them back to Robert's money.

Ward lay sleepless at night, seeking answers, but there was only one answer. Like a squirrel on a treadmill, he kept coming back to Robert's stolen gold. There was no sense—and no humanity—in tormenting Robert further by visiting him at the prison hospital.

Too restless to sleep, he dressed and stalked the downtown streets. The house where Robert had lived offered no clue. It had been searched inch by inch by army intelligence.

Ward kept telling himself the answer was there in front of him, if he could find it. He blanked out the sounds of the street, the shouts of soldiers, the laughter of women, the braying of animals, the crack of gunbutt on concrete.

He walked blindly in the darkness. People spoke to him or bumped him. He was unaware of them. What had Robert said about that money? He'd said he hadn't stolen it. This was a lie. It was there, all right. That day he'd found Robert and Thetis in the squatter's shack in the

Florida wilderness, what was it Robert had said: "If there were any money I'd stolen, you'd never get your paws on it. If I did have any such money, I'd share its whereabouts only with one who loved me enough to keep my secret until death . . . so, even if there were money, you can just forget it, brother."

One who loved Robert enough to keep his secret safe until death. Melodramatic as hell. But then, Robert was melodramatic. Still, if there were truth in what Robert had said so feverishly on that cot, the answer had to be where Ward had believed it would be all along, with Robert's beloved fiancee, Miss Lily Harkness.

Chapter Ten

THEY WELCOMED HIM warmly at Errigal because he was Robert's brother. This warm acceptance shocked him for several reasons: primarily because, so it seemed to him, if they loved Robert as they protested, they would hate him. Either they didn't know that he had trailed Robert and brought him back to trial and ultimately to prison, or they found extenuating circumstances Robert certainly didn't discern. More likely, they didn't know the truth yet, and this was discomfiting. It might be worse to be accepted first and then banished. Whatever happened, he had a reason for being here, and, though he hadn't Robert's charm, he would do the best he could to ingratiate himself as long as possible. Further, he didn't see how it could be easy for them to tolerate him, a Yankee with his Midwest accent constantly to remind them. These people had suffered degradation at the hands of the invading army; they still suffered. And yet they returned his smile when he had even feared they might reject him because their affection for Robert may well have soured—Robert had turned criminal; they had received him in their home, their family. His crime could well have brought disgrace on them among their friends, they had taken a Yankee to their bosom, and he had proved to be only another demon. With the grinding poverty they endured, intolerable taxes, confiscated lands and money, and anguished memories, they didn't need to be humiliated by an outsider, one of their own mortal enemies whom they'd befriended. Yet they did everything they could to put him at ease.

Lily's mother, Miz Marcy, spoke kindly of Robert: "Everybody out this way loved him. He was so gentlemanly. Friendly, yet reserved, shy, and lovable. He sang so beautifully. We miss that, his sweet and gentle voice. He was so respectful toward me, our girls, all our friends. Not at all our idea of a—" she stopped, her wan face flushing.

"A Yankee?" Ward laughed. "Some Yankees don't have horns."

"You must overlook our chill toward people from the North. We're intelligent enough to know they must be just like we are—really. I don't think people are that different, no matter where they live," Miz Marcy said. "Still, our memories are—evil memories. I'm sorry."

"My brother was killed at a place called the Wilderness," Lily said. Her pale violet eyes filled with tears. The others nodded silently. She tried to reconcile her brother's death in some alien place. A place called the Wilderness. Some faraway landmark with no reality for her except heartbreak.

"You've been gracious toward Robert, and now to me," Ward said. "And forgiving—to accept either one of us."

Marcy Harkness's head tilted. Her smile was rueful and self-accusatory. "Don't give us too much credit, Mr. Hamilton. Forgiveness may not be all that unselfish with us now. It's all we have left anymore."

They sat on the shaded veranda. A silent black woman called Aunt Molly served lemonade. Miz Marcy Harkness explained that several black families lived in the old slave cabins as sharecroppers. Some of them were slaves at Errigal before Lincoln's proclamation; they had wandered away, but now returned home.

"They're almost as well off as we are these days," Miz Marcy said.

"Poor devils." Charles Henry Harkness laughed without mirth. He was in his early fifties, rail-thin. His hair was already cottony white and his sun-bleached blue eyes were permanently haggard and he got around poorly, limping slightly. But he held himself erect, and Ward learned that many of Harkness's neighbors still called him "Major." But he didn't like this and discouraged it brusquely. The war, whatever it had done to him, and obviously it was considerable, was behind him. "Even with sharecroppers, we don't sell much any more. Don't grow much. Now— eleven years after the war—we should have found our directions. But we don't seem to have. We flounder. We knew *one* way of life. I suppose we're a dying breed because we don't adapt well."

"We certainly try," Miz Marcy said, touching his arm.

"Yes." He nodded, his smile gentle. "Yes. We all try. All the families, the darkies, and our girls—" His faded eyes touched lovingly at Lily and her two sisters. "All the families have kitchen gardens, a few animals, chickens, cows for fresh milk. We do eat; all of us at Errigal." A faint pride toughened the fiber of his voice. "Black and white. All of us."

"Many people don't," one of the sisters, Beatrice, said. The two older girls were not as pretty as Lily, but they seemed resigned to it. Beatrice's hair was a mousy brown, her features drawn in a narrow face. Lavinia's hair was a faded red, and her skin was freckled, despite all she could do. But they laughed, teasing Lily about the way she wrapped her hands and wore scarves like masks, and old straw hats pulled down to her eyes when gardening, to protect her skin from the sun. "Even on the hottest days," Beatrice laughed, "Lily is out there wrapped up like an Eskimo."

Ward glanced at Lily. She always looked fresh, as if she'd just loitered her way across dew-drenched pine hammocks. But now he saw that her fingernails were broken and stained. Lord, how she must hate that!

He listened to the loving, teasing talk as it volleyed back and forth. Lily didn't care how she looked weeding in the garden patch; she refused to ruin her complexion. Her sisters used every remedy known to mail-order cosmeticians to restore their skins, particularly one cerate—which, their father quietly reminded them, was only some unctuous preparation, essentially an oil base and wax, using resin or spermaceti mixed with lard. They didn't care. Lily told, laughing, how both Lavinia and Beatrice plastered themselves with the odd-smelling concoction every night. "A

121

wonder the cats don't lick your faces in your sleep," she teased. They also rubbed raw cucumbers on their necks, shoulders, and wrists. In season, they even crushed strawberries and generously laved the potion over their faces. They all laughed and admitted there was just no hope for the backs of their hands. "Not as long as Daddy acts like we're boys when there's work to do," Lavinia said.

"The Lord never saw fit to bless me with boys," Charles Henry Harkness said, his smile loving. "Only nagging females and shiftless darkies." He spread his hands. "Though, helpless as I am, I don't know what I'd do without them."

"I wouldn't care so much," Beatrice said. "If it just didn't *destroy* my skin."

"When everything else fails," Lily teased, "Bea and Lavinia bathe in buttermilk. Yes, they do." The girls blushed and laughed self-consciously. "One thing we have no lack of—buttermilk. I declare, sometimes I think our cows give *sour* milk."

"Maybe it's the way you milk them," Bea said. "You hate it. You probably hurt them."

"Well, Miss Priss, at least I don't try to sleep in masks of cornmeal paste like you and La."

"Lily is blessed. She never needs those remedies," Mrs. Harkness said.

"She never exposes her skin to the sun," Lavinia said. "Bea and I both hate her." She laughed. "As much as we envy her."

"No," Beatrice said. "As much as I envy Lily, I think I hate her more."

The unhurried, loving banter livened the afternoon on the tiled terrace. They idled because, as Harkness had said, they'd found no direction, no purpose in their lives; they didn't know what to do. Their way of living had been brought to an abrupt end when the war drove down into Georgia. Errigal survived, but without its slaves, its hundreds of plowed acres, without purpose. The Harkness family lived in enforced otiosity, Charles Harkness said, because they had not yet managed to find a way to pick up and repair the broken pieces of their existence.

Ward detected no rancor, probably because all dialogues carefully skirted rancorous issues—the onerous taxes, property confiscation, the aftermath of war, Reconstruction, the blacks wandering lost across the face of the South, huddling in cities, waiting to be fed and told what to do—all aspects of life as it truly existed off this lovely, quiet, distressed farm.

Ward heard words unknown to him in their chatter. "The safe," where the girls were constantly dispatching the servants, proved to be a pantry cooler. The girls reminisced about a vacation they'd managed last summer "on the salts." This meant they'd been to the seashore near Savannah. They talked of their sewing circles and rose gardens and church clubs at Decatur. They'd gone to a ball recently, carrying their "dance slippers" in homemade but quite elegantly trimmed "slipper bags." Lily admitted they made their own clothes nowadays. They all thought it hilarious that the one slowest to learn to be a seamstress was their mother! She'd been taught fine hand stitching. Nothing else was considered ladylike in her girlhood in quite a different world.

"Anytime we can get a bolt of shirting now," Lily said, "We all blossom out in fresh new dresses. I can tell you, making our own dresses is *very* ladylike."

"Preferable to appearing in public in sackcloth," Bea said.

"What's sackcloth?" Lavinia asked.

"Who knows?" Lily shrugged. "You wear it with ashes."

The talk drifted to the high cost of trading in the village. Calves' liver, ten cents a pound! "Can you imagine ten cents a *pound* for calves liver?" Marcy Harkness said. "I can tell you, we used to *give* it away. Gladly."

"I still would," Lily said.

"That's why I love you best, Lily," her father teased, reassuring his other daughters with a quick touch and brief smile intended only for *her*. "You eat like a bird. You're the only one of us I can afford to feed."

"And we had oysters packed in ice from Savannah recently," Mrs. Harkness said. "At fifty cents a quart."

"Well, at least, Mrs. Harkness, they were opened for you on delivery," her husband said, addressing her formally as he always did in public.

"Well, I should certainly hope so! Fifty cents a quart for oysters. They multiply by the millions. Can you imagine, Mr. Hamilton? How will we ever go on living in these terrible times, what with these prices and all?"

Ward tried seriously and insistently to refuse their invitation to dinner. But they persisted. "Cook's already prepared for company," Lily said. "She'll just have to throw it out. Nothing keeps in this heat."

"We have nothing elaborate—far from it—but you are welcome," Charles Harkness said.

"And we're having other guests for dinner," Beatrice said. "We do every night. It's a custom around here. It'll be fun. You'll see."

"We haven't even shown you around the farm," Lavinia said. "Every guest gets a conducted tour on his first visit, whether he wants it or not."

"And we haven't talked about Robert." Lily's pale face was bleak, her smile wan, but pleading. "I do want you to tell me about him. All about him."

"The poor boy," Mrs. Harkness said. "I know he made a mistake. I suppose he must pay. But when one steals from thieves, one can't feel much repentance in one's heart, can one?"

The three sisters conducted Ward on a tour of the interior of the old manor house. Despite the desperate lack of money and the resulting lessening of maintenance, the plantation home was imposing, a striking reminder of what it must once have been.

Obviously, much of the furniture—the best pieces that would bring the highest prices when sold to Yankee buyers for shipping North—had been sold to meet taxes, upkeep, daily expenses. Once, to maintain this mansion would have cost in a day more than Harkness was able to spend on it in a year. He would gladly have made repairs himself, but he was helpless with carpentry tools in his hands—far more helpless than the girls. When he was a boy, he hadn't been taught to do anything. He'd been taught rather to do nothing, and do it with flair.

Ward stared, awed at the somber beauty—the memory of elegance—in the quiet old chateau. A Chickering piano was stacked with sheet music; its keys were open, its bench out as an invitation, and it was often used. It could build a mood, or sometimes it could rescue one from a mood. Near the old piano was a violin in its case, a flute tossed atop the stacks of songs. The Harkness girls and their guests provided their own entertainment.

With pride, the girls displayed satin glass antiques, overlay glass colors, Battiglia carvings, small objects of alabaster—all slated eventually for the pawn shop, the auctioneer's table, or some rich Yankee's distant home.

Ward discovered, in the fifteen-foot ceilings, the thick, pegged oak floors, the inset windows, the kind of quiet, tasteful beauty he wanted in a home. Errigal Plantation was no longer a showplace. It was more a musty old barn of an ill-furnished house, lost out of time, too expensive to maintain, too lovely to condemn, but retaining a dignity nothing except fire could erase.

Ward found himself drawn to Charles Henry Harkness as he had not even been attracted to his own father. A troubled, self-deprecating man, Harkness was so warm and outgoing that he was like a friendly St. Bernard. He was, however, so exaggeratedly polite—an ingrained flaw pounded into him from the cradle—that he never entered a door, lit a pipe, sat at a table, or sought the least comfort, until his guests had preceded him. This was irritating until one realized it was a learned part of him, as characteristic as his limp, as his easy smiling. He was concerned for the comfort of others; this was his training. In many ways, despite four years in college and the Grand Tour that always followed graduation, it was his *only* training. "It was pounded into me. Others come first. No matter who they are. This way you demonstrate your own value. A stupid idea being rapidly unlearned in this generation, but I can't go against my training. Not at my age."

Harkness laughed and said he'd tried to farm but learned too late that he'd even planted the potato settings with their eyes down. He could milk "a cow in fresh that day," and she abruptly went dry. If he painted a room, a dozen people with mops scoured it to remove his excesses and mistakes. "I even tried to distil my own cane whiskey, but I burned the syrup. Until you've tasted scorched liquor, you haven't really suffered."

He walked with Ward about the yard, the barns, the gardens, the inadequate fields of tobacco that was their only money crop. Somehow the talk turned to the old custom, of which Ward had heard even in the North, of supplying black bed wenches for overnight guests. Harkness shook his head. "It never happened in my father's house or the house of any of my friends. I know. I've heard the rumors. And perhaps among redneck farmers, half-literate

125

or illiterate, no matter how wealthy—it may have happened among them. I don't know. I just know I never saw it. None of my friends ever did. Not that some of them didn't chase down pliable black wenches in the throes of passion, but most of us were too afraid. No, it didn't happen. I don't believe it happened—not among my people."

They sat together on ancient, cane-bottomed kitchen chairs in the shade of the barn. "I think old Sherman had heard of that custom, whether it existed or not. He didn't ask for a wench, but he suggested he wouldn't kick a dark-skinned beauty out of bed. I told him, 'General, I'm sorry, but your president has freed all my black wenches.' He looked sour. 'My God,' he said, 'didn't you keep a couple around for pets?' I think old Sherman liked me. I hated his guts so badly I could have killed him, but I was unarmed and on crutches at the time, and at his mercy in this very house. He had that very day ordered the Curtis placed burned to the ground. Nothing left but a chimney. I expected to be burned to a cinder. I remember I had some melodramatic notion of staying inside the burning house. I could not stand to think of life, for me or my girls, after it was gone. But I laughed at his jokes. Trained to charm. A man of leisure, manners, and courtesy. Sherman must have responded. Otherwise, I don't know why we were spared."

Harkness sat sucking at his pipestem in silence. Agonized, even in retrospect, he recalled the incredible arrival of the bloated blue troops on their scourging passage to the sea. Despite his hatred, he saw that Sherman, like the generals of the Confederacy, was simply the latest version of the military mentality: the supreme commander who saw other men only as pawns, servants, or hostiles to be eradicated. Human life and human property were no more than factors on a gameboard.

Harkness had known the Yankee forces were descending upon Errigal, destroying, burning, pillaging. The girls were children then. He would have fled—the roads were clogged with refugees fleeing from fire into nowhere—but his life and fortune and three generations of his family were entangled inside the boundaries of Errigal. It would never be the same again, but he could not let go. "A dying breed. I could not adapt, not even to hell."

And where would he go? His healthy dray animals had

126

long since been commandeered by the retreating Southern army. He'd stood in a kind of catatonic trance and watched the refugees, afoot, homeless, dispossessed, mindless with fear, adrift in sweat and hunger and misery and terror. He could not subject his gentle lady and three small children to this debasement.

He had stood there, God knew how long, on his crutches, rooted, chilled, and helpless as the first blue wave engulfed Errigal, followed by the main forces and finally by the commanders. Sherman appropriated the big house for temporary headquarters. All remaining fowl, animals, and plant stock were consumed or ordered destroyed by the troops.

Sherman himself was calm, domineering, aloof, unapproachable, coldly courteous, and wary. Perhaps the wariness at the highest echelon had, in the end, kept Errigal from being put to the torch.

The federals were ready to march by dawn. Sherman and his officers walked out to the veranda and stood there in the blue morning mists. Harkness could not say why, but he was convinced that one of Sherman's executive officers had passed down the order to burn the mansion, stables, and barns.

Before that decree could be sent down the chain of command to a rank low enough in the pecking order to carry it out, a young line officer ran across the yard. He was harried, his eyes as bleak as those of ancient messengers of ill tidings who know they'll be beheaded for delivering unpalatable intelligence to superiors. The line officer almost lost his life because garrison guards leaped to attention, ready to annihilate their own rather than allow a junior line officer inside the command area. But the lieutenant's urgency prevailed over all military protocol and he was permitted to deliver his message to a captain temporarily out of favor. As soon as the message was relayed up the chain of command, the top officers moved out swiftly. Sherman and his senior advisers were carefully horsed, surrounded by phalanxes of cavalry, infantry, and militia. They departed unceremoniously, almost at a full gallop.

The entire army followed at double-time. By the time the first prongs of the Confederate forces arrived, there was not even the dust of the federal troops visible in the still morning. There proved to be less than two hundred Confederates, hungry, hollow-eyed, and stinking of dysentery.

Errigal had been unable even to feed them because what the federal troops had not consumed, they had confiscated or destroyed. Gaunt, sleepless, crawling with lice, the bedraggled rebel forces stumbled across the fields, planning to intercept the massive blue juggernaut somewhere ahead and extract every possible ounce of blood by hitting and running, barefoot and empty-bellied, as they had done every mile of their trek south.

Perhaps, Harkness mused, Sherman had not ordered Errigal burned. Or perhaps, after having put the torch to old houses all day, he had hesitated because he was, for that moment, sickened on his own gorge, a glutton sated by gluttony, overwhelmed by the immensity of his own evil. Not even the least sensitive civilian did not know the Confederacy was humbled, crippled, permanently destroyed. God knew, the military must have possessed that total knowledge, must have known that this final retribution, this scorched-earth retaliation, was no more than a mindless scarification of the corpse.

But he admitted he was attributing motivations and reactions to a man he did not know. Perhaps Sherman felt nothing but a sense of duty; he had been assigned a campaign task and he was executing it. For whatever reason, the invaders had denuded the fields, the garden, the livestock pens, but had spared the manor house, leaving behind many of the less conspicuous valuables.

Ward wondered why Harkness delayed talking of a subject that was painful to Harkness and alien to Ward. But about five, he learned the answer. Two neighbors arrived, riding in across the fields on horseback. Extravagantly polite, Harkness introduced them to Ward. Just as extravagantly, they greeted and welcomed him. His acceptance by Harkness was his passport in this region. He could not carry a better reference. They were all so polite, their voices so mushy and drawling, their smiles so broad, that Ward missed their names entirely.

Names didn't matter. They'd come for an afternoon nip of moonshine, which Harkness provided from a jug stashed in a haystack. They drank thirstily and smacked their lips. They talked of poor crops, persistent heat, up-

128

pity niggers refusing to work and begging, stealing, or assaulting for food and money.

"God knows where it'll end," they said, shaking their heads. "God knows."

But none of this was important. They had come for another reason. On a discarded kitchen table, Harkness set up whiskey and a deck of cards. In moments, their jackets off, they were involved in stud poker, with matchsticks for chips. No money changed hands. There was no money. But the competition was fierce, the male ego demanding to be supreme among its peers, even in a game where winning was the only reward, the only justification, the only goal. Winning was all that mattered here, as in Port St. Joe at the Biltmore, where the pots had built up to five hundred dollars on the turn of a card.

Ward was glad there were no financial stakes. These fellows loved poker, but he could have bankrupted them all, taken land, home, and shirts from them. It was a simple world out here, totally unlike the brutal, savage conflict over those upholstered gaming tables with Whitney Cushing, Burden Byers, and Dayton Fredrick. That had been poker at its most dangerous, silent, taut, deadly. . . .

The Harkness girls had not exaggerated about company for dinner. When Ward and Charles Henry came into the manor house at seven, there were four guests for dinner. They seemed to have materialized from the woodwork.

The only guest who impressed or interested Ward in the least was a young Georgian named Hobart Bayard.

"Hobart is a banker, a most promising banker," Lily said with pride, holding Hobart's stout arm. "Really. A vice-president. The Atlanta Stockmen's and Farmers' Bank. A vice-president. And so young! We're all just so proud of Hobart."

Hobart tried to stifle and conceal his swollen pride long enough to demonstrate a seemly humility. "Reckon I am a mite young to have so much responsibility. But I reckon it's really because there's just a shortage of qualified men. The bank lost most of its personnel during the war. They take what they can get these days. Even me."

Hobart's voice was as runny as watery grits. Like Harkness, he was extraordinarily refined, pretentiously retiring, and self-effacingly, almost arrogantly humble, osten-

129

tatiously courteous and respectful and attentive toward all womankind. He was eternally leaping up to hold a chair, open a door, fetch a drink, remove a glass, fluff a pillow, or redirect a draft. There was one aspect of his inner feelings he was unable to conceal or disguise: he hopelessly, passionately idolized Lily Harkness.

Hobart was over six feet tall, heavy in torso and hips, slump-shouldered and potbellied from too much starch and too little exercise. He parted his dark hair low on one side and brushed straight across his crown, a lank shock spilling over his bulbous forehead. His eyes bulged; his nose was round, his lips giving him the look of a pouter pigeon. He spoke often of how he'd been reared by two old maid aunts after his parents became war casualties when he was only eight years old. He demonstrated precisely the results of this upbringing. He was fussy, patient, and unable to express rage.

Lily was obviously flattered by Hobart's unyielding devotion, but she was also indifferent, unmoved, bored. This very remoteness was precisely the response Hobart saw as proper because it placed her just beyond his fingertips, unsullied, on a pedestal where every genteel Southern lady deserved to perch.

After dinner—sugar-cured ham, sweet potatoes, lima beans, a cabbage slaw of sugar and vinegar, and angel food cake—Hobart played the piano, heavily, rough on the retard pedal. He sang, an aggressive Baptist-choir baritone, the lyrics almost totally unintelligible in that strained-grits accent. Once Ward's gaze touched Lily's and she smiled and almost winked. He smiled back, entranced by the candlelight that accented the tender texture of her face. Jesus, Robert's taste was impeccable, the poor bastard.

Then, with Hobart smiling and nodding encouragement and approval, Lily played the piano—gently, lightly—Beatrice, the violin, and Lavinia, the flute. They played lilting or melancholy love songs, extravagantly applauded.

Lily suggested a walk in the garden before the evening ended. Hobart Bayard sprang to his feet, smiling, and caught at her elbow—gently, shyly, frantically.

But Lily lightly twisted free. "I'm going to let you walk with my sisters tonight, Hobart. I know I've just been too selfish with you lately. And I do want news of poor

Robert. Mr. Hamilton has promised to tell me all about him."

The garden concealed its damaged and run-down condition in darkness. Gardenias and sweet bay perfumed the languorous breeze. The moon, a ragged sliver, tipped the waxen leaves of overhanging magnolias, glittering like tiny, winking candles. The aged paths, worn and bordered by verbena, lantana, and hedge roses, had been laid out before Charles Henry Harkness had been born. The faint moonlight concealed all signs of decay. In the softening darkness, one almost forgot the cancerous desolation visited on Georgia in the name of retributive justice.

Lily's fingers touched his arm lightly. Hobart walked ahead of them between Beatrice and Lavinia, heavy-handedly gallant, laughing, anguished.

Hobart and the sisters turned on a winding path between rows of boxwood. Lily tightened her fingers on Ward's arm and indicated a bench of Georgia marble set along the lane.

They sat together for long moments, silently. It was as if Robert were there between them.

Ward exhaled. He recognized in Lily Harkness the Southern belle he'd heard so much about in drama and sentimental fiction, and had so infrequently encountered in the flesh. Here she was, all surface beauty and sweetness and gentility proportioned breathtakingly over what he would bet was a core of steel. He was convinced she knew what she wanted, knew all the stratagems invented by femininity to achieve it. Her ash-blue eyes danced, catching pinwheels of fragmented starlight in the darkness. Those eyes flirted without even meaning to; they never for a second dropped their watchful guard. Her lips looked soft and full, inviting, tilting in an unfaltering smile. She exuded charm not so much practiced as absorbed over generations of genteel society, capped by heroic coolness in the fiery struggle against barbarity, but which put evil aside and recalled only the languor of twilit terraces.

She *was* lovely. Her body was fragile and slender, her rich, dark hair framing her pale and delicate face as the night frames a star. No wonder Hobart Bayard drove out here, evening after evening, all the way from downtown

131

Atlanta over execrable roadways. No wonder Robert had robbed the payroll of the army of occupation.

"Robert says he came out here to see you, the night he ran away."

Lily nodded, her face bleak in the wan moonlight. "Yes. It was the last time I saw him."

"I suppose he had—secrets for you?" He watched her face. He wasn't dumb enough to expect an answer, but the question was blunt and direct enough. If she knew about the money, she knew what he was talking about.

She shook her head, staring at the backs of her hands. "No. Only that he loved me. That he would always love me. He wanted me to promise to—wait for him."

"And nothing else? Did he tell you why he was running away?"

"No. We—my family—learned that later, from the Atlanta papers. Just as we learned from the newspapers that my poor love has been sentenced to ten years in prison." She cried suddenly, like a little girl.

He put his arm about her, pulling her head against his shoulder. "Please don't cry."

"I can't help crying. I'll always cry. I did love him—I *do* love him so."

He exhaled heavily. She was too upset to talk anymore. He could not persist. Coquette she might be, but her grief was honest. It got inside him and hurt him, as she hurt.

Her forehead was still pressed against his shoulder. He felt her quiver and gasp for breath in the throes of the lost and lonely agony that shattered her. He tightened his hand on her shoulder, trying to make her aware of his nearness, his understanding.

Agony and self-hatred welled up in him, without, however, regret or any sense that he should have acted differently. "Please don't cry."

He gave her his handkerchief. She took it, sniffling, and blew her nose loudly. "Oh, I'm so sorry," she whispered. "To go to pieces like this."

"It's all right."

"I hold it all inside as long as I can. Then, suddenly, I can't anymore. I can't stand to talk about him, and I can't stand not to. I can't stand thinking about him—in that terrible place. But he's in my thoughts all the time."

Her voice trailed off. Ward felt empty-bellied, insufficient. Either Robert had not told her where he'd hidden that money or she truly loved Robert enough to keep his secret to death. But he had no instinct that she was hiding anything. Her heart was broken. She had no room in her thoughts for anything else.

His mind raced, retracking, leaping forward, digging, searching—and coming up defeated and frustrated. Maybe Robert had not told Lily where he'd hidden that money; the knowledge would be far too dangerous for her to hold. Army intelligence knew Robert had been engaged to marry Lily; they would have no scruples about arresting, interrogating, harassing, or terrorizing her. Even Robert would have been too smart to expose her to such a threat of mental and physical torture.

But Jesus, what had happened? Perhaps, on that last night, he'd given her a gift—some simple-appearing object with a key inside. Melodramatic as hell. But then, he reminded himself once more, Robert was melodramatic as hell. Still, he couldn't badger this heartbroken girl by requesting an inventory of Robert's gifts to her. He could do nothing. He could frighten her away by pressuring her, drive her deeper into melancholy, or he could be patient, cautious, and observant—and wait. There was only one thing wrong with waiting: time was running out for him, racing mindlessly.

They sat, his arm about her, not speaking, watching faint and distant stars flickering like small candles about to die out.

Chapter Eleven

HOBART BAYARD LOOKED UP, alarmed, when Ward walked into his railed-off area at the Atlanta Stockmen's and Farmers' Bank, two days later. Though the bank was less than twenty years old, it possessed the austere atmosphere of an established institution. The furnishings were massive, polished; the wickets were of heavy wrought iron, the people behind them serious and sedate.

Bayard stood up, looming tall and round-shouldered behind his desk. His first words were about Lily. "Miss Lily—she's all right, isn't she?"

Ward grinned. "She's fine. She's well, probably all bundled up, working in the garden."

Bayard's heavy-jowled face relaxed. He smiled, musing over the sweet mental picture evoked by the idea of lovely Miss Lily, with outsized straw hat pulled down to her eyes, working in the kitchen garden at Errigal. He apologized, shaking his round head, his lank hair bobbling over his bulbous forehead, his full lips pouting into a smile. "I just get afraid something will happen to her."

Ward shook his head, gently taunting the young banker. "She can't marry my brother. He's in prison."

Bayard was caught off-guard. He laughed unaffectedly

in amused relief. In that second, with his guard down, he was almost honest in revealing his emotions.

He spread his sausagelike fingers. "I shouldn't say such things, or even think such things," he said, flushing. "I do have the deepest compassion for your brother in his distress."

"But you hope he stays to hell in jail."

Hobart retreated behind the simpering smile. "I could wish no one such torment, sir. No one. It's just that I do devotedly love Miss Lily. And I have done for many years."

Ward nodded in sympathy, grinning. "And you thought you had a chance—until Robert came along."

Hobart stopped smiling and bent forward confidentially, his eyes clouded. "Is it true—has he lost a leg?"

"Yes, it's true. He was shot. Gangrene set in."

"Poor devil."

"But Lily shouldn't waste her life waiting for a man with a prison record, only one leg, and ten years to serve."

"Oh, I'd never say such things to her, sir. Not even in her presence."

"It's all right. You should. It's the God's truth. Somebody ought to tell her, make her see she's wasting her life for nothing."

Hobart sweated, licking at his pouting lips and shaking his head. "Oh well. No. I never could. The very thought of hurting her like that—why, the very idea terrorizes me."

Ward shrugged and stood waiting, rolls of paper in his hands, until Bayard cleared his mind of agonizing over Miss Lily, the cruelty of fate, and the pain of this life. Hobart slowly became aware of him as a possible client.

He gestured meaninglessly, swinging a stout arm, indicating a mottled, hand-carved chair, deeply upholstered. "Oh, I am sorry, sir. My apologies. My good lord! How crude of me. Please sit down, please do. I see it is business—" he laughed self-effacingly—"and not Miss Lily that brought you here."

"Yes. When I met you at Errigal Plantation the other night, I was impressed by you. It seemed to me that you and I had a great deal in common, Hobart. I mean, besides our mutual concern for Miss Lily's beauty and well-being."

Hobart flushed, flinched, and then realized he was being

gently teased. "Oh. You're joking, of course. What *do* we have in common, Mr. Hamilton?"

"Our ages. You're twenty-one and an executive in this bank. That's unusual. It's a big responsibility. You can be modest, but you weren't promoted into such a position of trust for any reason except capability." He swung his arm, indicating the plush surroundings. "Not in a place like this."

"I like to think that's true, sir."

"I'm sure it is true, or I wouldn't be here. And I'm twenty. And I've recently been awarded the option to buy the East Florida & Gulf Central railroad line."

Hobart reacted, eyes widening at this news. He pressed his stubby fingers together, making a tent. He nodded, smiling, concealing his incredulity. "My heartiest congratulations, sir."

Ward nodded, brushing that thought aside. "We're both doing well. Some would say *extremely* well—for our ages. We've got that in common. And we're both ambitious, Bayard, driven. Both of us. Unfortunately, that's as obvious in you as it is in me. We have that in common. We both deal *first* in money; we've got *that* in common."

"Just how you do mean, sir?"

Ward's grin disarmed him. "You've got money. And I need it."

Caught off-guard, Hobart smiled, then laughed. They both laughed. Hobart put his head back, laughing. He also recovered first. "What do you have in mind?"

"We represent a lot of talent, resources, intelligence. What I'm suggesting is almost a merger, a pooling of talents, a consolidation. A partnership, you might say. Oh, I don't mean that literally—"

"I *am* totally loyal and dedicated to my career here in the bank—"

"And this is where I want you to stay; I wouldn't have it any other way. Stockmen's is a solid institution with excellent capitalization. Secure, for a Georgia bank in these times. No, you couldn't do better than devote your career to this bank."

"That's the way I see it."

"Under ordinary conditions, you should earn reasonable returns. But both you and this bank could be bigger, stronger, fiscally healthier. It could grow—"

"We expect to." Hobart nodded his head vigorously, his bulbous lips bouncing in his enthusiasm. "Right along with Atlanta. Yes, sir, as Georgia grows—"

"How about as Florida grows?"

Hobart withdrew slightly, cautious. "I don't know that we're prepared for interstate banking."

"But you could be. Now we've talked about you—who you are, what your potential is, as things are right now. How about talking about me for a few minutes?"

"I'd be most pleased and gratified, sir. You'll find me an interested and attentive listener." Hobart sank back in his high-backed, upholstered judge's chair. He smiled, nodding, encouraging.

"I expect my rail line to grow. It has to grow or fail. That's where I am right now. Either I grow in such fantastic giant steps, in extravagant ways we'd both find so incredible and hard to swallow that it would sound more like a braggart's dreams than possible goals, or I fail completely. I make it as big as I suggest I will, or I fail totally and lose the line. I mean, there's no halfway. It's one or the other; midas or misery, feast or famine. But I won't lie to you, or minimize the risks, the obstacles, the odds against me. Those odds are fantastic. Right now they might look insurmountable.

"But for the sake of argument, let's say I meet the mortgage deadline and assume full control of EF&GC. In the meantime, I've bid for contracts with the Third Division army headquarters as carrier for lumber, naval stores, supplies, materials, and equipment—any supplies to be delivered into Jacksonville from north central Florida sawmills, turpentine plants, logging outfits, and cotton gins. Now, this should secure my basic operations, because it's a huge government contract." He smiled, watching Hobart's incredulous, fascinated face. "And there are two reasons why I'm going to be awarded that contract—"

"You do sound confident."

"I *am* confident. Reason number one why I'll win that contract: my bid is going to be forty percent below the next bidder—"

"How can you hope to earn even a slight profit?"

"I'll make out like a bandit, Hobart, if you'll excuse the expression in this place."

Hobart smiled, but was shaking his head. "If such a low

137

bid can be profitable, why is it so far below your competition?"

Ward straightened. "For one reason. Because every one of those other bids is coming from carpetbaggers."

He couldn't have done better if he had waved the Confederate flag, hummed a bar of Dixie, or crooned about the old folks at home. Hobart almost stood up and saluted. He began to nod his head vigorously, his face pallid and set.

"You need say no more, sir. I understand." Hobart found no irony in the fact that Ward Hamilton was an outsider from Ohio. Ward was accepted in the Harkness home; his poor brother had been engaged to marry a Harkness daughter; that brother was incarcerated in a federal prison for a crime against the federal army of occupation. Ward was bidding against Yankee carpetbaggers, submitting a relatively honest bid, almost worthy of a Georgian-born. Hobart Bayard felt his throat constrict; he was totally enlisted in Ward's support.

Ward held up his hand, a finger extended. "That's *one* reason I'll win the contract. It's pretty solid, you'll admit?"

Hobard nodded. "If there's one honest man in the Third District Army of Occupation, you *will* have that contract."

Ward smiled. "There's an even more compelling reason why I'll have it."

"Sir?"

"EF&G is the *only* rail line between Jacksonville and Lake City. It's either use my line, or mule-haul over toll roads."

Hobart Bayard laughed with him, as if Ward's triumph were his victory as well.

Ward spread out the rolled survey sheets. Hobart anchored them with books, inkwells, ornaments, holders, vases. "These are surveyor's maps. They don't show a lot to an uneducated eye like mine, but each one of these four pages represents a million acres of Florida land registered in the name of East Florida & Gulf Central. Some may be swamp, some may be overflow land; I don't know yet. I haven't inspected it, but you can bet I will. As owner of EF&GC, I also own that land. Four million acres of Florida land."

"Good lord."

"It's land granted by the state of Florida to EF&GC for

building the railway system between Jacksonville and Lake City. The state made those land grants in order to encourage companies to come in and build railroads. At first, the land granted was part of the right-of-way. This got sticky because, naturally, a rail line runs through every promising town and hamlet. So they started packaging land from different regions of the state and making grants of that. That's what this land is. It is in several packages which your bank's real estate appraisers can decipher in ten minutes. They'll know where this land is. I know this much: it was deeded to EF&GC at ten cents an acre when the going market price, at that time, was a dollar and twenty-five cents per acre."

"Good lord."

"So I've come to you with viable assets. How much that land is worth today, I don't know. I want *your* real estate appraisers to determine that to *their* satisfaction, to the satisfaction of this bank. I've come to you because I met you at Harkness's home. That's a hell of a reference."

"As it is for you, sir."

"We're both young. We can work together for a long time. We've both got a future. The limits of that future are determined only by the limits we *ourselves* put on it. Do you believe that?"

"My head's reeling, if that's what you mean."

"I can come to your bank, or I'll go to another one. I'll find one that will want my deal. And let me make this clear; I don't want a one-time loan, no matter how big your people offer to make it. I want *loans,* overlapping, concurrent—"

"A line of credit."

"That's right. I'll never ask to borrow one dollar that isn't secured by two—never. But I want to be able to get what I need, when I need it. At that moment."

"I understand that."

"I mean, if your bank decides to lend me money on this land as security, Stockmen's becomes my bank—EF&GC's bank. Deposits, checking, security, everything. As EF&GC grows—and I swear to you it will—so this bank will profit.

"I don't know what personal goals you've set for yourself, Hobart. I don't know what your expectations or hopes are, how high you want to go in this bank. But if this loan is approved, and if I repay it satisfactorily, if

139

Stockmen's then agrees to provide me a line of credit, the kind of capital support I need, that can't help but reinforce your position in this bank."

"That's true."

"It's got to be a feather in your cap. It's got to make your bargaining position strong. It's got to make you a person to be considered. Isn't that true?"

"It would solidify my position immensely, if all went well."

"Look at it clearly. Make up your mind now. I can't get into this, need backing, and find it's not there. If I fail, it all fails, it all goes sour. You look bad here in the bank. It'll be your rotten tomato then. I want you to see that, too."

"I appreciate your consideration and concern, Ward. I really do."

"I want you to see what I want, what I must have. I want you to see what it might do to improve your position, but how it might backfire as well."

Hobart nodded, a faint dew of sweat across his upper lip. "I see it all, Ward. I do. I get your picture, I appreciate your warning. Give me a little time; we'll get back to you as soon as possible."

"Take your time." Ward grinned. "Three hours will be fine."

Hobart laughed and extended a hand as soft and damp as thickened grits. "A few days will be more like it, Ward. I've got to sell the board of directors as you've sold me." He laughed again, almost chortling. "But I think we can do business."

In slightly more than a week, the president of the Atlanta Stockmen's & Farmers' Bank notified Phillips Clark that the bank directors had approved a line of credit for the New East Florida & Gulf Central Railroad. The bank, as directed, had established, on a first level, an amount of credit amounting to one hundred thousand dollars on deposit in Atlanta, secured by EF&GC Florida land holdings as certified by the Florida secretary of state.

Phillips Clark stalked around his office, stiff-legged, head back, thrusting his fist high in the ancient gladiators' signal of victory. "You did it! I bow to you. I admit myself unworthy, a man of little faith. You did it! You smooth-talking, conscienceless son of a bitch, you did it! A hundred thousand. On deposit. My God. My God. My God. You can pay off Marsh. That screwing rail line is *yours*."

"Yeah."

Phillips continued to prowl. "I want a raise in pay."

"You've got it."

"In company stock."

Ward didn't answer. Phillips hesitated and turned, puzzled. "Hell, I'm full of piss and vinegar—and you look like you've lost your last friend."

"I'm just thinking ahead." Ward stood at the window, staring down at the busy Main Street. "Get us tickets on the first train to Jacksonville."

"What for?"

"Why do you care what for? We'll be making a lot of runs to Jacksonville."

"We don't take over there for ten days."

"I want tickets now."

"Wait a minute, Ward. Something's wrong. I'm against it."

"But it's what we're going to do."

"Still, you hired me to counsel you. My guts tell me this is all wrong. Do you mind saying why we're going to Jacksonville?"

Ward grinned coldly. "We're going to do some shopping."

As Ward spoke, Clark began to shake his head, his eyes going bleak. "No, Ward, no. Spend that hundred thousand for *anything* except to satisfy Baxter Marsh's note? No." His voice rattled against the walls. "I won't let you. I've followed you this far, and you've been lucky. I've listened to you, I've connived with you, but I'm damned if I'll let you throw away the chance to secure the rights to this rail line. It means too much to you. Hell, it's even come to mean too much to me. You've got to listen to somebody else now."

"Why?"

"You can't throw away the single opportunity you'll have to walk in there and take possession of that property. Damn it, that land you've hocked isn't even *yours* unless you finish paying off that note to Marsh."

"We've got almost a month and a half. We can't let that

money sit there—not even in certificates at two-percent interest. We've got to get it out where it'll help us, where we'll get real return. I don't have to remind you, we've got to repay the bank as well as Marsh now."

"That's why I'm trying to talk some sense into you. Don't screw around and lose the rail line. Even if you lost that land—"

"Are you stupid? I'd rather lose my eyes, my arms, my skin, even you, kid. That land proves Baxter Marsh is a blind, pigheaded, unimaginative old bastard. That *land* is my whole base, not the goddamn seventy-two miles of railroad. That railroad can fall apart, locomotives run off rails or collide head-on, and I've got troubles. But that land—" he kissed his fingers— "that land, old son, just lies there, growing more valuable every damn day. Did you notice that the bank didn't even *offer* to suggest a total market price for that four million acres? But they *know*. There's nothing more conservative than a bank. They know to their own satisfaction. I knew that if they went for it, we were on our way. They're *glad* to secure a paltry hundred thousand dollars with that land. And I'm happy if they are. No, kid, we've got to protect that land like we protect our balls."

The most astonishing and gratifying difference in Jacksonville, for Ward, was the change in the atmosphere at EF&GC toward him and his attorney. Where they'd been shunted around on their first visit, and he had been ignored as a beardless kid unworthy of corporate attention, and any substantive answers had always been directed to Phillips Clark, now, magically, everybody on the staff knew them, and they all knew *him*. They knew which was Mr. Hamilton, and which the attorney.

They were practically bowed into the EF&GC office complex overlooking the rail terminals. Everyone smiled, spoke to Ward by name, and offered to be of service.

Ward's first order as head of New East Florida & Gulf Central Railroads was to change the name on the doors, letterheads, bills of lading, reports, and invoices. This order was implemented immediately, the doors repainted, relettered, and smelling of fresh paint before noon of the first day.

"Now I know how God felt," Ward told Ralph

142

Bracussi, who trailed in his wake all day until he was finally able to be alone in an office with him. Ward grinned, enjoying his exultance, the newness of his triumph, the sense of gratification and anticipation. "Let there be light, and there was light. Let the name be *New* EF&GC." He laughed, then glanced around, frowning. "Where's Phil Clark?"

Bracussi grinned unctuously. "He dropped down to Bay Street. Says he hasn't been bedded down in two nights. His satyriasis is killing him."

Bracussi sank, completely at ease, into an upholstered, black leather-covered conference chair. He had shown Ward into the private suite Baxter Marsh had occupied in the Jacksonville headquarters, and which Marsh had vacated, down to the last scrap of paper, rubber band, inkwell, and paper clip.

Ward sat down on the deeply comfortable, maroon leather high-backed chair behind the large, polished, completely nude desk. Behind him, windows opened on a smoke-darkened rail terminal, jagged buildings, and a glimpse of the wide St. Johns River in the distance.

"We'll have office supplies and materials in here this afternoon," Bracussi assured him, hooking his leg over the arm of the chair. "We want you to be comfortable. We just didn't know you were coming in so soon. Though, of course, there's no reason why you shouldn't."

For some moments they sat in silence. Ward watched the auditor without speaking, letting the tension boil. Bracussi somehow felt in control of this situation. Because he was fifteen or twenty years older? Because he was an old hand at railroads and Ward a youthful novice? Because his experience would put him in the catbird seat? Did he really believe Ward couldn't get along without him? Or was it because he'd walked in on him and Julie in that St. Joe hotel? Did he really think this provided him leverage? Or was it that Bracussi believed, with all the smart railroad money, that Ward Hamilton's tenure in these rarified surroundings would be brief?

Finally Ward said, "I see you've decided to stay on with us?"

Bracussi moved his shoulders negligently. "That's up to you."

"Oh?"

143

"Yes. Mr. Marsh did ask me to stay with him. I promised I would give him an answer right away. His offer was—substantial. But I might be persuaded to stay on with you here at EF&GC—even if you can't yet meet his salary offer. This is the work I know."

"This company is now NEF&GC. And you might be happier with Marsh."

Bracussi blanched. He swung his leg down from the chair arm, taut, wary. "I know railroads. I know this railroad. I can be of invaluable assistance to you. Even Mr. Marsh said that."

"Unfortunately, Mr. Marsh doesn't do my hiring, does he? I have to weigh several things I know about you that maybe Marsh never took the time to learn."

Bracussi's taut face flushed. "My books are ready to be audited—twenty-four hours a day."

"I hope so. That would certainly be a plus for you. On the other hand, you're not as loyal as hell. Not to Marsh—"

Bracussi stiffened. "I was trying to do you a favor."

"At your boss's expense."

"Well, I didn't see it that way. He wanted to peddle the railroad. I made it possible for you to bid down this company."

"That's just it. You expect me to hire you because you think I'm indebted to you."

"I did help you place the right bid; you can't overlook that."

"I'm not overlooking it. It's the blackest mark against you. I never hire people I'm indebted to. I hire people I can trust."

Bracussi was silent for a long beat. "I can keep my mouth shut, Mr. Hamilton; I think I proved that at Port St. Joe. I happened into your room on a very delicate situation. I never breathed a word of it. I never will."

"Unless you think it'll profit you. Well, if you do work for me, Ralph, you'll happen in on a lot of delicate situations. The first one you try to collect on, you're going to find yourself out on your ass, with your nose bleeding."

Ralph Bracussi nodded. Ward relaxed. At least the son of a bitch didn't sit with his leg slung over the arm of the chair, and he called him Mr. Hamilton. "You're a devious bastard, Bracussi. You're always looking for the jugular."

Bracussi shook his head, looking gray, trying to smile reassuringly. "You keep me on, Mr. Hamilton. It's a job I like, a job I know. My home is here. And we understand each other."

Ward nodded. "I think we do. I don't mind hiring bastards. But I've got to hire only bastards I can trust."

Phillips Clark returned from his assault on Bay Street about dusk. He looked gray, haggard, but happy as a briar-eating mule. He smiled tiredly at Ward. "I love this town. I've decided I'm moving here from Atlanta, permanently."

"You keep fooling around down on Bay Street, you'll move here permanently, all right. With a tombstone to prove it. You're going to get killed fooling around down there."

"Oh, don't be provincial. That's excitement. Whatever you want, there's a woman—or women—on Bay Street to provide it. That's why they call it the Barbary Coast of the East."

Ward exhaled, watching him. "That's one of the reasons."

Ward's male secretary—Clifford Stone, a holdover from Marsh's regime—knocked on the door and announced a visitor.

Ward got up and came around the desk, admitting a rising excitement, an empty sense of expectancy that didn't make sense, a quickened pulse. He put out his hands. "Julia! What are you doing here?"

"Daddy and I are passing through Jacksonville. He's got to find some new interim financing for the Biltmore."

He looked over the top of her gleamingly brushed, severely parted hair. "Is he with you?"

"He's at the St. James. He was slightly disturbed that you are staying at the same hotel with us." She stood and stared up at him artlessly, with longing in her eyes. She may have been too young to understand fully what was happening inside her body but, at the same time, she was too fiery with natural desires to misunderstand what she wanted. Her whole body was a heated mass of exposed nerve ends. She had looked forward breathlessly, ever since the Biltmore, to the moment when she would see him again. She'd asked her father to come with her, and had been happy and breathless with anticipation when he refused. She trembled with a need to touch and to be touched—whether she fully understood it or not. The very thought of his hands on her—even accidentally brushing her shoulder blade—set her to trembling, sent molten juices flooding downward in her, increasing her ache, her need.

She was still young enough that if he touched her hand—as he touched it now—spoke her name, or touched her hair, it would be enough for this moment—it would release and relieve the sweet agony roiling deep inside her.

She burned, she shivered with chill, her hands felt awkward and weak. She knew that anyone, even the stupidest yokel with one good eye, could see she could not take her eyes from his face. She could exist only in the immediate orbit of his presence. She wanted him to talk to her, as long as she could keep him, look at her, smile at her, hold her hands.

She laughed emptily. "Daddy says he isn't ready to see you yet. He hasn't forgiven you yet for topping his bid."

"And you?"

Her face colored faintly, reminding him, along with that pug nose, how young she was. "Oh, I admit I hated you at first. I'll always hate anyone who hurts Daddy. But he thinks you're just a temporary setback. He doesn't think you'll last. Neither does Baxter."

"And you?"

Her face color deepened. "I hope you won't last. I have to be honest, I hate to see you hurt. Truly. But Daddy does need this line, and you *could* work for him. He thinks you will, eventually. And so does Baxter."

"Nobody has a very high regard for me."

"That's not true. But you are *very* young for such—responsibilities."

"I've got to start somewhere." He drew her after him to a comfortable conference chair, aware that she was still holding his hands and that her icy fingers trembled slightly. "I was hoping you'd be in my corner."

She sat on the arm of the chair. "I'm afraid that can't ever be. Not as long as you and Daddy are—competitors. Oh, if you'd just come and work for him, as you should."

He sat behind his desk, watching her. Before him lay re-

146

ports on sawmills, lumbering, logging, and naval stores operations located in Lake City, some with executive or administrative offices in Jacksonville. Clark had gathered the material and it was imperative that he study it before he confronted any of the owners of these industries. But he was not in a hurry to have her leave; it was pleasant being idolized, even if it was a dead-end street. She was still a very young girl, even in a fashionable, wasp-waisted street dress of pastel green cloth. Her skirt was ankle-length—her sole concession to her extreme youth; ladies wore their dresses over their shoes that year. Still, that designer model made her look at least three years older than her actual age. He forced himself to tease her, to tease himself for even thinking about her as anything but a child. "Sure. Come work for Daddy. Wait for you to grow up and then we'd get married and live happily ever after."

"That's not the worst thing that could happen."

"Thanks for the compliment. Tell me, have you met any boys your own age you find attractive?"

"No. And I'm not constipated, and I'm doing everything I can for my face pimples. Stop being condescending."

"I'm not. I'm interested. In you."

"God. I wish you were."

He shook his head. "Will you stop that? I don't know if you mean this, or if you're playing a game, or if you're truly willing to face a fate worse than death just to insure your father's railroad."

"I mean it. I don't need to get you in trouble—if you're going to start that statutory rape talk again—to help my father. I think he'll get this railroad; it's just an inconvenient delay for him. But anything between you and me is just that—between you and me."

"There's nothing between us. There can't be."

"Bull. Don't sound so frantic. I couldn't think about you so constantly, and you be totally unaware of me."

He spread his hands. "I'm not unaware of you. But isn't that enough for you?"

"No."

He laughed and Julia said, "You like to believe it's just a crush, don't you, what I feel for you? Well, it's not. I come from a long line of one-man women. Do you know that my mother never even walked out with another man except my father?"

147

"Things were different, there were fewer chances for a girl to get around, when they were young."

"Yes. But it would have been the same for Corrinne. I know. The Fredricks are fierce in their emotions—love or hate—and single-minded in their devotions. You can trace them back to 1066, when they came over to England with William, and they're all the same. Violent, steadfast, loving, jealous, demanding. They love one person for life, and only one. It's nothing I want. It's just the way I am—my bloodline."

He laughed. "You scare me. Don't tell me you don't expect even to *date* anyone but me."

"I'll probably date hundreds while I give you time to come to your senses. But it doesn't matter. That's just what they'll be—blank faces. Hundreds of blank faces."

"How many times have you been desperately in love like this?"

"Once. Now." She got up, came around the desk, and leaned against it beside his chair. Her eyes burned into his. "You may as well stop talking down to me. I told you, I've gone everywhere my father's gone, ever since my mother died. I'm no little girl; I never have been. I've kissed other boys. Grown men. You'd be surprised how many grown men like to kiss young girls when they get them alone and think nobody will know. A forty-year-old man wanted to give me an engagement ring. I took it. But then he wanted to ask Daddy to let me marry him. I talked him out of it."

"I hope so."

"One of us had to be sensible."

He grinned up at her. "That's the way it is here, with us."

"And you think you're being the sensible one?"

"I'm trying."

Her eyes glazed oddly. "You could just let me—sit across your lap. Just hold me."

"My God." His neck grew hot and he flushed.

She continued to stare at him. "How many girls have you kissed?"

"Hundreds."

"How many have you loved?"

"Loved?"

148

"You know what I mean."

"No, I don't."

"The hell you don't. And stop laughing at me."

He sighed. "Would you rather see a grown man cry? I guess the only way to figure you out is to understand that you've always gotten everything you wanted."

"If I wanted it bad enough." She nodded. "In that I'm like Daddy."

"You've always been rich, haven't you?"

"We've never been rich. Not *money* rich, like the Cushings or the Vanderbilts. But we've lived rich."

"It's the same thing."

"How do you know?"

He shrugged. "It seems the same."

She shook her head, wise far beyond her years. "The cost is higher."

"I don't see how it could be."

"That's because you've never really looked into Daddy's eyes, or seen him when he's dead tired and scared. That's because in many ways you're younger than I am. It's because you don't know anything about it. Wait until *you* owe twenty million dollars."

In the next few weeks, Ward was seldom in one place for more than a few hours. When he was in Atlanta, he found Hobart Bayard watching him, troubled but admiring. Hobart had cast the die; he was with him all the way. Ward felt real affection for the fat young banker; there's nothing like money to weld a friendship, especially when that money promises a profit.

He was welcomed warmly at Errigal. He found few moments to be alone with Lily. He could not hound her with questions, and she proffered nothing helpful about Robert's hidden money. She appeared to have forgotten all about it. He wished he could, but with the weeks racing past, this was impossible.

Lily and her family did look forward to his visits. Yet he didn't know if it was for himself or some news he might bring about Robert. They were good and kindly people at Errigal. They never forgot Robert; like all Southerners who abolish woes by refusing to think about them, they never discussed *where* Robert was, or why. Their memories were warm, and spun around the good times they'd had when he had come almost every afternoon, as Hobart Bayard now did.

Ward was there only infrequently, for a few quick hours, and he always left feeling frustrated, insufficient, unsettled.

There were always some young men hanging around Errigal that summer. A young Yankee officer, more tolerated than accepted, painfully in love with Lily, was begging her to return with him to his home in East Aurora, New York. Lily only laughed. it sounded like the name of some place without reality, a cold city on the dark side of the moon. There was a Southern boy of a once prominent family. He was now reduced to the status of common laborer; like the master of Errigal, his training had prepared him for no practical commerce. There was always some man or other, in the company of more exciting guests, and, in between and eternally present, there was Hobart Bayard.

The quick, unrewarding runs to Atlanta and Errigal were sandwiched between inspection trips out of Jacksonville aboard his own rail line. He inspected logging operations, a naval stores plant, a saw mill, and a wholesale lumber distribution company in the bustling Lake City vicinity. He wrote four breathtaking drafts—they took away Phillips Clark's breath and all his sense of security—on his line of credit in the Stockmen's and Farmer's Bank. He came away from Lake City the outright owner of a sawmill-lumber yard and a logging operation, and having made a substantial investment toward full ownership of a naval stores production and shipping plant.

The owner of this naval stores company had his headquarters in downtown Jacksonville. He and his attorneys met with Ward, Phillips Clark, Ralph Bracussi, and the railroad lawyers in the conference room adjoining Ward's private office.

Selden Stokes, the naval stores company owner, was a self-made man. He'd seen the need for turpentine, resin, and other stores, and had set out to supply that need. Forty, portly, his hair parted in the middle and brushed down on either side of his head, he was frankly astonished when he met Ward for the first time. He could not credit that a man as young as Ward Hamilton could direct a concern like NEF&GC, to say nothing of branching out so rapidly and so radically.

"I see nothing radically diversified about these companies," Ward told him. "They all depend on shipping to reach a market. And the rail company depends on their freight for a profit, or even to stay alive. I can certainly offer myself better carrier rates than I could an outsider. My lawyers wouldn't let me charge you the low freight fares I'm going to charge my own company."

Selden Stokes agreed. "Will you plan to run our naval stores company?"

"No, sir, I plan on your running it," Ward told him. "You have the know-how, you built it. I hope you'll go on running it as you do now."

Stokes nodded, smiling. "Sounds like a good working arrangement, Mr. Hamilton."

"Just call me Ward, sir," Ward said with a wicked, quick glance toward Bracussi, a look lost on all present except the auditor. Ward was still Mr. Hamilton to Ralph Bracussi.

"Right, Ward. And we'll do our best to go on showing a profit."

"Oh, we're going to show a profit," Ward said. "We'll be sure of that. As I said, you'll run things just as always. One little change, Selden. I'll send my own auditors in each month."

Stokes laughed. "Sounds practical. And wise, Ward. I think we'll work well together."

When all the guests were finally gone, Ward sagged in his big chair behind his now cluttered and high-stacked desk. Across it, Phillips Clark slumped deep in a conference chair, exhausted.

Ward sensed a recurring moment of panic. He had not really been free of panic, of the faint fluttering of moths in the deep closets of his belly. There were more moments of panic than those free of concern. There were two things he said to himself: *Please, God;* and, *What did you have before you got into this?* Still, common sense told him he was getting deeper into debt, not really finding a solution to the most pressing problem of all: the approaching due date on the Baxter Marsh note for the remainder of one hundred and ten thousand dollars. That morning—bright or cold—he had to come up with ninety thousand. At this moment it might as well be Dayton Fredrick's twenty-million-dollar liability. What had Julia Fredrick said to him in this office about the price of living as if you were rich? "Wait until you owe twenty million." He tried to consider that astronomical sum, but they were numbers without meaning. The vision of that sophisticated yet little-girl face kept flaring disruptively behind his eyes. He pressed his fingers hard against his forehead, massaging, trying to erase that image, and failing. He couldn't be in love with her; even the thought was untenable. Yet nobody has ever proved that a love had to be expedient or reasonable to be real. He realized that Phillips Clark had been talking to him for some moments. He winced and apologized. "What, Phil?"

"I said, what now? You own down payments and investments in half of north central Florida, none of which can be either liquidated or mortgaged for enough to satisfy Baxter Marsh."

"Still, when we bid to deliver the Third Division's naval stores, lumber, and materials, they'll be our stores, our lumber, our profit."

"Sure. Except for one thing. You don't pay Baxter Marsh, and you'll be making deliveries piggyback."

"If I do, Phil, I swear I won't ask you to help me. A drink of water now and then, that's all."

"Jackasses bray loud, too."

"I told you, kid, I'll pay Baxter Marsh. With minutes to spare."

Clark swore. "That's what I was trying to find out. That's the real truth, isn't it? You're still deceiving yourself that you can find Robert's cache of stolen Yankee money. And in time, for Christ's sake."

Ward shrugged. "I don't know. But I have made one decision I believe you'll find interesting. I'm going to marry Lily Harkness."

"Robert's fiancee? A girl whom you've told me yourself appears to love only Robert? I don't buy that one. Why would you do a thing like that, to her and to Robert? Oh God, Ward, just when I'm about to like you."

"I don't give a damn whether you like me or not."

Clark's eyes filled with tears. "When did you decide to do this heinous thing?"

Ward drew a deep breath, exhaled it. He shook his head as if bemused. "I don't know, I really don't. Maybe the first time I saw her."

Chapter Twelve

HE HAD NOT dared believe the Harkness family would so readily and amenably accept the idea of his marriage to Lily. They lived in rigid conformance with the strictest mores. What people thought of them and of their conduct was their first consideration. Yet they must have enraged and infuriated social arbiters when they accepted Robert as a potential son-in-law. Still, Robert had ingratiated himself with most of the local tribes; only the most obdurate resisted his charm. It was different when they had received Ward. They welcomed him at first for one reason only: he was Robert's brother. And even his and Robert's consanguinity seemed to Ward—who cared not a damn for what people thought—not much of a mending strap to secure such widely unlike cultures as rural Ohio and plantation Georgia, especially in a time when bloody fratricide still writhed in aching hearts and stormed in unforgiving minds.

He got a reason for this affront to convention from Marcy Harkness in the days before the wedding. "Lily has been heartbroken, too withdrawn, too wrapped up in her grief," Miz Marcy said. "Your brother was the first man Lily ever truly loved. Before, they'd all been merely passing acquaintances, flirtations, casual friendships. But her devotion to Robert was different. We all knew this from the first. This was the compelling reason everyone in the family immediately put aside all prejudice or hostility and accepted him as warmly as we could, even though his background was—well, alien to ours. We soon learned a very valuable lesson. No Georgia-born boy could have been sweeter, kinder, more intelligent, lovable, and sensitive than Robert. I think his presence did more than any other one thing to make us see the terrible hatreds dividing North from South as lies disseminated by people who—for reasons of profit or warfare—had to foment and enflame deep hatreds in order to achieve their goals. Looking at dearest Robert, we could see that all you young men, like our own sons, were good at heart, decent, home-loving boys from families as heartbroken and heartsick as ours."

"We're taught to hate you just as fiercely—Negro-beating, drunken, godless, thieving, wanton." He laughed.

Miz Marcy sighed. "I suppose ordinary people must be incited and manipulated like this, or there could be no wars. But I was talking about Lily. Though she's made every effort to hide her true emotions from our guests, she has been terribly depressed and melancholy. Some days, she'll sit alone in her room, not speaking, simply staring along that road out there. Both Mr. Harkness and I believed if we could just afford to get her away—perhaps on the salts—for a little while— But of course, we couldn't afford it. And it wouldn't be fair to send her at the expense of the other two girls."

"I am sorry," Ward said, "for the grief my brother has caused your family."

"Oh no. You mustn't say that. We've forgiven Robert. We are even, though we never speak of it, fearful that Robert may have stolen that money to make life better and more bearable for us. Northern oppression and confiscation became an obsession with him, a personal burden, a guilt he carried inside himself. He felt sick over what his people were doing to us. Every time the unbearable taxes were raised—to pay for the army of occupation, or to support the misguided, homeless blacks who had been promised paradise and now wander hungry and confused and lost—he was angered, tormented with guilt. He never for a moment condoned slavery, but mistreatment of human beings, he said, is not a matter of skin color. To lie to

155

blacks about what instant freedom would mean to them, to enslave a whole region, to bleed it, to scourge and devastate it in the name of retribution or reparation for wrongs as old as mankind, was its own brand of cruel and inhuman enslavement. Poor Robert."

"Yes. Poor Robert. But Lily must not go on waiting, grieving over something that can't be changed, throwing her life away. Ten years, unless Robert is paroled. And that's unlikely unless he produces that money he stole."

"Yes. We do want Lily to start to live again. Perhaps you can help her find the way."

Another night, but the same Georgia marble bench on the same secluded and winding pathway in the Harkness garden. Lights from the parlor splayed saffron across the dark lawn and the flower beds, touching the boles of ancient oaks.

Ward sat with Lily, aware as ever that Robert was like a tangible form between them. He had the certain sense that Lily preferred him to the other men who haunted Errigal's summer evenings, even the ever-present Hobart Bayard. Perhaps it was only because he was Robert's brother. He *looked* like Robert. In a way he talked like Robert, reminded her of Robert. This was why she suffered him at all. She was far too imperceptive to see all the differences between him and Robert. Perhaps she didn't want to see them; perhaps she even minimized them. And perhaps she did not even give him that much of her attention. He was Robert's brother; this was enough for her.

"I've missed you, Lily," he said.

"What? Oh, I'm sorry . . . why, I've missed you, too. We all have."

He laughed. "Yes. But I haven't missed the others at all. I haven't given them a thought. All my thoughts have been for you."

"How gallant." She touched his arm lightly, flirting from ingrained habit. "I know you've been so busy with your railroads and all that you haven't given me a thought, stuck away here on a farm. Still it is gallant—and sweet of you. But you mustn't. Why, you'll turn a poor girl's head."

156

He caught her arms, frustrated. "Listen to me, Lily. Really listen, will you? I said I *missed* you—"

"Why, I heard you. I'm sure you're just being kind and darling. You just feel sorry for me—"

"Stop it. Stop flirting. I don't want you to flirt with me, Lily. I'm serious. I'm trying to make you see me. Not Robert, me."

"I am sorry. I never meant to hurt your feelings."

He pulled her nearer. She was so slender, reedlike, fragile. He almost felt she might break like fine China in his hands. Her face was drawn up close under his. Something flared for a moment in her eyes, then she sagged, waiting, almost resigned. He wondered what doltish attack the young Yankee officer had committed upon her in a desperate, frustrated effort to reach her, to make her aware of him and his anguished longing before he retired in defeat to East Aurora, the dark side of the moon?

Ward held her rigid so that she was forced to meet his gaze, her eyes mirroring the faint moonlight. From the house, Hobart's aggressive baritone, delivering a Foster melody, was like the anguished baying of some bereft stag calling in the night. Ward forced himself to proceed cautiously. He had to be careful; casual flirtations were no new experience for Lily, but honest emotion, honestly expressed, might well be. "I'm not talking about empty feelings, surface feelings. I'm talking about deep inside—"

"I do know. It's the way I've felt about Robert."

"It's the way you must not feel about Robert."

Her delicate body shivered. "Why don't you ask me not to breathe, Mr. Hamilton?"

"Because I'm asking you to live. To throw out memories and regrets and useless wishful thinking about Robert. I'm sure you did love him. I'm sure he loved you. But he is not worthy of you."

"Please don't—"

"He sits in a prison, for a stupid crime he committed. A criminal, imprisoned for ten years. He betrayed you when he stole that money. Whether he meant to or not, he betrayed your name, your trust in him, your love, his right to love you. Maybe he's not truly bad, but only a fool. The end's the same."

"Even if you're right, I can't just stop loving him."

"You can't throw your life away waiting for him, either."

"If I thought he wanted me, I'd wait forever."

"Would you?" His voice hardened. "Is that easier than facing the truth?"

"The truth, Mr. Hamilton?"

"The truth. Robert has lost a leg."

She shuddered, her body stiffening, her face twisting as if she looked unwillingly upon some repellant disfigurement in a sideshow.

His voice attacked her, unyielding. "Are you going to spend your life in seclusion, feeding on a hopeless sorrow?"

"Please don't . . . I know I can't . . . you don't have to . . . please don't."

"I'm only trying to make you see, Lily. You mustn't waste your life."

"I know you mean to be kind. I know you want to help me." She burst into sudden, helpless tears. "It's just that I can't be helped . . . I just feel all dead inside. How can I care about anything, when I'm empty?"

He drew her against him, more gently, protectively, yet firmly within his arms. Her small, high-standing breasts crushed against the corded muscles of his chest. He put his arm about her and placed her head against his throat. She clung to him, crying. One of his hands, supporting her beneath her upper arm, covered her breast, but she seemed unaware of his touch. It was as if he lacked reality to her, like something lost in her memory.

"I love you," he whispered.

"Please don't."

"It's true. I want to make up to you the hurt Robert has caused you. I want to help you forget. I want to help you start living again."

She sniffled, breathing raggedly, and her weeping subsided. Holding her close, her small, shapely breast still cupped in his hand, her body pressed on his, Ward vowed that he would take care of Lily. He would give her good for all he took. He wasn't sure what love was, but if he had any inkling, he did not love Lily in that unbending, world-shattering way. Perhaps he never could love like that. Maybe he was too deeply committed to his own crusade, his own Holy Grail—money and power and affluence—luring him like some unquenchable beacon. Maybe he had no time for love, only for that maddening sexual need that overwhelmed him sometimes. But whatever he did have inside, he vowed he would give to Lily. He would care for her. He would make her believe he loved her as poets described love. He would be attentive, loving, gentle. In silence, holding her, he made a bargain with her and with the gods, almost as he had with Baxter Marsh—a nonrecoverable deposit: he would give her everything he could. If he did not love her passionately, she would never guess it from anything he did or failed to do.

"I want you to marry me," he said. He laid out in his mind all the material things she might desire, and said, "I'll give you everything you want. I'll be loving, Lily. I'll try to be a good husband in every way I can. If you don't love me yet, I'll teach you to love me. I'll teach you to love."

She did not speak or move. He turned her face up and kissed her, at first gently, under the tolerant eye of the moon. The music from the parlor seemed distant, removed. A rising breeze stirred, whispering in the oak trees. She remained silent, submissive, fully aware of him now, of his hands caressing her body, touching her, yet leaving her untouched.

Her mind spun, half in confusion, half in terror. She tried to think what she had to give a virile, demanding man like Ward. In his arms she found the differences between Ward and Robert intensified, magnified, terrifying. Robert was gentle, even withdrawn. Ward was aggressive, powerful, even when he spoke of giving. Was there anything she could bring to Ward except despair, hammered out in her grief like coins? She knew only what her answer would be, what it had to be, and yet she could only reach backward, emptily, to the dust of another summer.

She lay her head back on Ward's shoulder. The things she should have said to him she could never say. Her eyes brimmed with tears, but she did not cry again. She let him kiss her, but his kisses did not arouse her. There was nothing in his rough, heated kisses to remind her of Robert's gentle mouth. If only he did recall Robert! But he did not. She longed for Robert, but he was lost to her. She longed to run away and hide until Robert came back to her. And she could not do that, either. She could only go on living, whether she wanted to or not.

She felt his hand slip inside the bodice of her dress and close on her bare breast. She shivered and bit her lip, recoiling, dismayed, and even a little disgusted at his animalism. She hid her distaste, letting him caress and fondle her rounded breasts and pink-tipped nipples, knowing, her eyes burning with unshed tears, that he was trying to make her come alive. She tried to respond and she could not. His mouth over hers was fiery hot, suffocating, his lips parted, his tongue probing at her teeth in a way she despised, forcing her own mouth open. His tongue drove deeply into her mouth. She lunged back, trembling, afraid she was going to vomit. "Oh, don't," she whispered. "Please don't."

He smiled in the gray concealment of the night, convinced that her protest was as formalized and meaningless as all the other poses she struck in her role as the ultimate reigning Southern belle. Every Southern gentlewoman must pretend, at least, to be unapproachable, inaccessible, unmoved by sexual advances, virtuous and chaste. Well, let her play her games.

The second greatest surprise came with the alacrity with which the Harkness family consented to an early wedding. By this time, Ward knew well the rules of conduct in the Confederacy: an engagement could be a matter of months, and a wedding date within a year was somehow obscene.

Ward pleaded the press of business. He was rushed, under pressure; his and Lily's honeymoon—from necessity—would have to be combined with work. He promised her an extended honeymoon later, when his business affairs were in order.

He suggested a wedding date a month ahead. This would coincide, within a week or two, with the due date of the Baxter Marsh mortgage. He did not mention this. To his surprise, the family, although reluctantly, agreed.

They said they could not be unaware of his harried rushing in and out of Atlanta, his hasty visits to Errigal, his preoccupation, over these past weeks. He was so thin they were worried about his health. He assured them he had never felt better! And Charles Henry told him that

160

Hobart Bayard had explained in great detail the nature and potential of his business, his urgent need to batten down all loose hatches, the pressures under which he worked in competition with conscienceless and predatory Yankee carpetbaggers. They understood. "We want to do nothing which might burden or inconvenience you, my boy," Harkness assured him.

The next weeks at Errigal were hectic. There had always been three or four "extras" for dinner or overnight, or half a dozen guests for the weekend, at the plantation. Suddenly these numbers of friendly invaders were multiplied. On those infrequent occasions when Ward was able to be there, able to snatch a few moments from his work to try to convince Lily that what she felt for him *could* turn into love and desire, he found the house crowded and bustling with strangers—smiling, soft-accented people congratulating him. Relatives arrived from every cranny of the old South. Almost-forgotten friends appeared from the past, to linger for the duration.

The only acquaintance Ward did not see at Errigal in those weeks was Hobart Bayard.

Ward gazed at these people, milling about the foyer, on the stairwell, in the sunroom, rocking and laughing on the veranda, singing at the piano in the parlor, dancing, crowded around the formal dining table, or staking claim to one more guest room. Not one of these thoughtful, charming people ever paused to consider what all this must be costing Charles Henry Harkness. Ward couldn't see how Harkness could afford even to feed so many mouths. A meal at Errigal might last over two hours, with laughter, talking, reminiscing, third helpings, and smiling requests for "just one more slice of that delicious pecan pie, Aunt Molly. I am just foolishly partial to your pecan pie."

Ward watched in disbelief. At his home farm in Ohio, they had done reasonably well financially, though neither he nor Robert could endure the backbreaking labor and had escaped as soon as possible. But they'd entertained maybe a dozen guests over a year. Each was a burden—in extra work, food and expense. He didn't see how Harkness, already strapped by a big family, increasing numbers of black sharecroppers' families, each of whom had to be

161

staked for the first year or two, and an incredible parade of visitors, could manage. One afternoon, alone with Charles Henry at the barn over a jug of bourbon, he broached the subject of helping with the expenses, though he was afraid he would insult the older man. There were so damned many unreasonable rules of conduct in this society. "Oh, I couldn't let you do that, my boy." Harkness sloshed him another drink. "But I do appreciate the offer and your concern. It's the spirit, the goodness of your heart that touches me."

Finally, Harkness did accept five hundred. This too became a little secret custom at Errigal. Ward always managed to leave five hundred with Charles Henry when they drank together out behind the barn, with Charles Henry protesting. Protesting.

Ward mentioned to Phillips Clark that Hobart Bayard no longer appeared at Errigal under any circumstances.

Phillips stared across his desk at Ward. "Have you seen him at the bank?"

"Yes. I make a point of going in to see him at Stockmen's, whether I have business there or not. He's always very cordial."

Clark shrugged his heavy, round shoulders. "I've never seen a Georgia cracker who wasn't cordial, even if he hated your guts. *Especially* if he hated your guts. As I've believed all along, this marriage to Lily Harkness can ruin you with Hobart Bayard and his bank. As a practicing satyr who knows the indispensable value of female flesh to a healthy male, I can tell you in all sincerity, I think you need Hobart Bayard and his bank a hell of a lot more than you need Miss Lily Harkness."

"My marriage shouldn't have anything to do with the bank."

"It shouldn't, but it will. Even bankers are human. Especially hurt bankers."

"I'm betting you're wrong. Hobart is hurt, I know that. But he's no damn fool. He's smart enough to know love's fun but business is money."

"Well, we can pray you're right."

For Lily, their engagement period was a time of agonizing characterized by long hours of melancholy sleeplessness.

Alone in her bed, she returned Ward's ring a thousand times and kissed him goodbye, sadly but finally. Thinking ahead to her marriage, she felt her heart thundering crazily, all out of rhythm in her chest. She felt as if she were suffocating. She had to bite her lips to keep from crying out. Thinking back to Robert, she lay numb, too filled with hurt and despair even to cry.

She tried to blot out her fears, to overcome her sense of dread. Ward was a good man, and everybody said he would be fantastically wealthy some day. She had never seen a man as ambitious and dedicated. She supposed many Northern-born boys were driven as Ward was, but the young men she knew had been trained to hide their raw emotions, even in business. In a way, Ward's single-minded concern with industry might prove to be a blessing. Being fair to Ward, she felt terribly inferior, unable to please a man with his rugged sexual appetites and enthusiasm for life. Her face burned. She had never known a man like Ward, and, deep in her mind, she admitted she was afraid of him.

She had grown up, warm and protected, sheltered in the bosom of an insulated world at Errigal. She had been loved and petted and spoiled, even in the terrible war years she was too young to remember. No matter how evil times were, her parents provided food from somewhere, and surrounded her with love and comfort. She grew up expecting rarefied male devotion, a male respect which proscribed the physical and accented the spiritual in every relationship. Her love with Robert had been ideal. He demanded nothing; he was far more gentle even than the Southern boys she'd grown up with. He understood her fears and her needs exactly. It was as if she had been reared for that day when she met Robert. She had flirted, flitting forward and retreating like a butterfly, and, like a butterfly, she was so fragile a touch would destroy her. She reached out for love on her terms and found it waiting, soft and yielding, fragrant as jasmine and unrelated to harsh reality. Love was another of the games at which she had always played, until Robert came along.

But like everything else in her life, Robert had failed her at the last. He lay on a hospital prison cot—she could not endure to imagine how he must look with one leg amputated. She'd seen amputees struggling back home some-

163

where from that glorious struggle, but they had been remote, awkward strangers, quickly gone. Her own father's slight limp was sad, but somehow romantic.

She got out of her bed and stood at her window in the blue-misted, pervasively fragrant night. A whippoorwill added its own melancholy song, and a mockingbird mimicked all the calls it had stored up during the day. She stared across the darkness toward the unseen, unseeable, unknown and unknowable penitentiary at Atlanta. Robert was there. He was lost to her, and pragmatism told her she had to forget him. She did not see how she could live without him, yet she did have to go on among the living. She had a hundred reasons for marrying Ward, none for refusing him. She belonged in the remnant of that lost, sad world where a gentle and well-bred girl could never do anything really wrong or ugly. But this privilege carried obligations too. She could not knowingly hurt others; she must first hurt herself. There were all the practical considerations. Ward had money, a brilliant future. He would try to be good to her. In return, she must blot Robert out of her mind, even if she never got him out of her heart. She would be practical and wise and pragmatic. Life was not what she wanted it to be, or what she had dreamed it would be. She felt she was doomed to look through all the empty rooms of her life for someone who should be there, and never was.

Black, stout Aunt Molly waddled into the parlor on pink-soled, sandaled, and flat-arched feet. She cleared her throat self-effacingly. "They somebody to see you, Masta Ward, suh. He at the kitchen door."

Ward followed the heavy-hipped woman to the rear of the house. Aunt Molly opened the kitchen door and said, "You can come in now, boy."

Ward stared. "Thetis."

Robert's manservant burst into tears. He stumbled forward, dusty, thin, shaken. He had lived in terror since Robert had been imprisoned. He had not dared to cry, alone and friendless. Now he'd found someone onto whom he could shift his intolerable burden. He fell to his knees in front of Ward, sobbing. He scrubbed at his dark face with the two-fingered stub of his right hand.

"Thetis. What is it? What's the matter?"

"I hongry, Masta Ward."

"Well, don't cry. Get up. Aunt Molly will fix you a good meal."

Thetis stayed where he was, shaking his head. "I scairt, too, Masta Ward. I powerful scairt."

Aunt Molly and the three black girls helping her in the kitchen watched Thetis in silent contempt, but he did not care. He had been in hell. He was totally unaware of them.

"You've no reason to be scared here, Thetis," Ward said.

"No, suh. Not here. But I scared. All the time. Ever since they put Masta Robert in that big jail. I go there and tried to see him. Every day. I went every day. But they just turn me away. Then one day they let me seen Masta Robert—for just a few minutes. Pore Masta Robert. That pore boy."

"Why are you afraid, Thetis?"

Thetis stared up, his tear-brimmed eyes wide with fear. "I got nowhere to go, Masta Ward, nowhere. After they close Masta Robert's house where we lived, I got no place to stay. They hundreds of colored boys like me. Nowhere to stay. They steal to eat, to stay alive. I cain't do that, Masta Ward. I scairt."

"Well, it's all right now."

"Yassuh, that's what Masta Robert say. Masta Robert, he say if'n I find you, it be all right."

"Did he?"

"He say to ax you to take me in. To work for you. He say to tell you I a good worker. I work hard. I do anything you want, Masta. Anything."

Thetis caught Ward's arm with his mutilated hand, trembling. Looking down at the boy, Ward wondered savagely why Robert hadn't come himself? He might as well, sending Thetis constantly to be in front of him. Well, he couldn't refuse to help the poor devil, but he was damned if he could endure having him underfoot all the time. He'd have to find something for him—somewhere out of sight.

"Thetis! Oh, Thetis! It's you!"

Lily came running across the kitchen. She caught Thetis's head against her thighs, holding him, rocking him. "Oh, my poor Thetis. What's the matter? What have they done to you?"

"Thetis wants me to hire him," Ward said.

Lily swung her head around, her smile bright and anxious. She nodded, laughing. "Of course you will, Ward. Oh, of course you will."

"Yes. But . . . I don't know exactly what to do with him. I don't—need him with me."

"He was Robert's manservant."

"I know he was. I don't need a manservant."

"Oh, Ward, I do! Truly I do. Thetis can work for me. Please. I need him. I truly do."

Ward nodded. Somehow, Banquo's ghost had achieved substantiality—a doleful black face, an effeminate manner, a constant reminder of Robert for Lily. Which, of course, was exactly what she wanted.

Lily threw up the morning of the wedding.

She dressed early, before seven, in a simple cotton morning frock, flowered and full in the skirt, the dress she would wear into the First Baptist parsonage on Church Street in Decatur. There, arrangements had been made for her to be dressed by mothers, sisters, relatives and close-friend volunteers, in her grandmother's wedding dress. Handmade of silk and lace, feathery, light, faintly yellowing, it was the gown Miss Marcy had worn when she married Charles Henry Harkness.

Lily entered the hectic dining room, crowded with overnight guests at the morning meal. Some of the dozen diners—Ward not among them, of course—laughed and teased her about a bride's wedding-morning jitters.

She tried to smile at them, aware of the bland smell of scrambled eggs, the oily fragrance of smoke-cured ham, the heat and mist of grits, the pungency of black coffee. Suddenly she cried out, "Oh, Mamma!"

She clamped her hand over her mouth and ran toward the kitchen. She made it only as far as the corridor. She toppled against the wall, gasped and heaved, and vomited helplessly.

She sagged to her knees and slumped there, head down, her clothing wet and sour.

In the dining room the guests sat back, alarmed. Some even stopped eating for that first unsettling moment. Miz Marcy raised her hand calmly and smiled. She reassured them. "It's all right. Please don't be upset. Aunt Molly and

166

I will handle it. It isn't important. My poor baby . . . she's been—indisposed like this before lately. Nerves, it's just her nerves."

Aunt Molly was not so certain it was a simple case of nerves. She saw uglier portents. She shoved the quavering Thetis aside, and gathered Lily up in her arms as easily as she had when Lily had been a little girl. Aunt Molly ordered Thetis to "clean up that mess, boy. Scrub it up good." Followed by Miz Marcy and Beatrice, Aunt Molly carried Lily up the wide staircase and along the cavernous upper hallway to her bedroom.

She laid Lily down on her bed, washed her face, and brought her a glass of water and a basin so Lily could rinse out her mouth.

Lily lay as if lifeless—pale, melancholy, staring at the ceiling. Beatrice found a fresh dress and Miz Marcy gathered up clean underclothing. But for a long time, Lily refused to help them undress or dress her. She remained unmoving.

Aunt Molly shook her head in its faded bandanna. "I knowed something fearful was going to happen. I knowed. Purely could have told you. I heard that ol' stopped gran'father's clock of Master Charley's strike—yes I did. I purely heard it strike—once—loud and clear—last night."

Bea laughed. "Oh, Aunt Molly, you dreamed it."

"None of the rest of us heard it," Miz Marcy said. "Someone else would have heard it. You must have dreamed it."

"No, ma'm. I swear, 'fore Gawd Hisself. I heard it. Ain't no sign worse for a weddin' than a stopped clock what strikes in the night."

"Oh, Aunt Molly, what a terrible thing to say," Bea told her.

"Well, look at her. Look at my pore, pale-cheeked chile. Ashy as death. I did hear that ol' clock. Struck jus' one time, but hit put the fear of Gawd in me. I laid, chilled and scared to move. I waited, but hit didn't strike no more. Jus' that one dreadful time. I laid, wakeful and listenin' and prayin' it would strike again. And then—and then I heard a cow moo. Then I *was* too scared and upset to sleep anymore all the rest of the night. No wonder my pore Missy ain't slept none. No cow *ever* moo after mid-

167

night—but when one do, no way but hits a shore omen and sign of death in the family."

Lily spoke softly, awed. "Robert isn't dead, Aunt Molly."

"He worse than dead, Missy. He locked up like he dead, while he still livin' and alive and lively."

Lily burst into helpless tears, rolling her head back and forth on her pillow, her fist pressed fiercely against her lips.

"Now look what you've done with your superstition, Aunt Molly." Miz Marcy shook her head impatiently. "You've got poor Miss Lily all upset with your old wives' tales."

"Just tellin' you what I heard. Just tellin' you what I know."

Miz Marcy gestured sharply downward. "Well, it isn't true. Please, Lily, you must put Robert out of your mind. We all deeply regret the terrible thing that has happened to him. We all loved him as you do. But it can't spoil this lovely day for you. This should be a happy day, darling, the happiest day of your life."

Ward was dressing in his room at the Decatur Inn, with Thetis and Hobart Bayard to assist him. This was Ward's first dress suit. He had never even seen a tuxedo until he left Lumberwood. He admitted as much to Bayard, who had reluctantly agreed to serve as his best man. Bayard had thought at first Ward was joking about the tux. Bayard's maiden aunts had bought him his first dress suit to wear to a cotillion when he was in his early teens. "There aren't a lot of chances to wear a dress suit on an Ohio farm," Ward said.

Thetis answered the knock on the corridor door. Ward turned from admiring his reflection in the mirror. He stared at Julia Fredrick standing just inside the doorway. She merely smiled, a gray and forced warmth. She did not speak. An air of tension swirled through the room. Hobart mumbled something about checking with the minister. Thetis too withdrew, closing the door.

Ward smiled. "Hello, Julia. You look very grown up."

"Don't condescend."

"My God, I'm not. I'm glad, but surprised to see you. What are you doing here?"

Her voice sounded odd, as empty-timbred as if she had a cold, but calm, controlled. "We came to your wedding, Daddy and I. We wouldn't have missed it." She laughed, a mirthless sound. "Well, Daddy would have missed it. But I wouldn't let him. An old friend and all."

"That's very thoughtful of you."

"Yes, it is. Daddy's in our room down the hall. He says to tell you he's got a headache or something."

"I understand." He watched her. Her white shirtwaist was pleated and caught with a tiny bow tie at the base of her slender throat. There was a brief, taut silence.

"Ethy sends his best wishes too."

"Good. How is he?"

"He's fine. They all are. Gaza and Revelation Two. Gaza thought you were going to marry me."

He tried to smile. "I guess we all did."

"No. I told her it wasn't true. I admitted I lied."

"It would have been a long wait."

She shrugged. "That would have been up to you." She looked him over critically. "You look pretty. Real pretty."

"First fish-and-soup I ever had on."

"It becomes you, it really does." She sighed. "The only thing is, you look a little nervous. Daddy says you've got to remember to keep a go-to-hell look on your face when you wear one of those tuxedoes."

"I'll try to remember."

The silence settled brittlely between them again. Julia looked as if she wanted to leave, but didn't know the appropriate word for goodbye. "Guess Daddy will be worrying about me."

"Oh? Has he started worrying about you now?"

"I'm growing up."

"Yes. You look—great."

"No. You needn't lie. I'm right in the middle of the awkward age."

"Not you."

She winced slightly, forced another smile. "I can't wait to see—the bride. She must be lovely."

"Yes."

"Have you known her a long time?"

"She was engaged to marry my brother."

"It figures." She retreated to the door. "Remember, keep that go-to-hell look on your face."

169

"I'll remember, Julia."

"So will I," she said. "So will I."

Julia sat with her father at the wedding of Ward Hamilton and Lily Harkness. It was a quiet and somehow faintly sad wedding—an odd marriage really, a belle, loved and admired, and a boy from the enemy North. Perhaps to some onlookers the union was unforgivable, symbolic of the already deteriorating quality of life among respectable people who were able to forget horror and evil in a little more than a decade, an era blackened with oppression and injustice, tinted with the fading blood of brothers and fathers. To Julia, the ceremony was unspeakable too, but for far different reasons. She didn't give a damn about the war or the mores of a bunch of mindless sticks living in the past.

She stood close beside her father, feeling the security of his solid presence, as the bride came down the aisle toward the altar where the groom and minister waited. Julia felt her heart constrict. God, she was lovely. As fragile as an Easter lily. You couldn't hate her. The bride raised her veil, her face gravely sweet and lovely. All brides are beautiful, Julia told herself emptily, but she could forgive this one because she looked so sad and forlorn. She watched the dainty bride cry openly, tears streaking down her wan, alabaster cheeks. There were few dry eyes in the crowded, flower-banked church.

Julia saw the two sisters of the bride break down sobbing. The bride's mother dabbed at her eyes and tilted her head higher, refusing to cry. Even the best man was frankly weeping, from a heart that was a haunted vault.

Julia watched the crying, her own face chilled, her mouth set, her hazel eyes bleak with contempt. It was like a wake. It was nothing like the joyous wedding she would have. And she went on staring until the bride turned up her face for her new husband's kiss.

Julia sagged against her father. She pressed her face to his shoulder and sobbed helplessly, if as silently as she could. It didn't matter; no one noticed her, not even her father, except to pat her shoulder awkwardly. After all, everybody cried at weddings.

Chapter Thirteen

THE HAMILTON WEDDING PARTY advanced, laughing, across the crowded Atlanta railroad station. Train depots were becoming the small cores of the universe, each tiny cosmos teeming with its own passionate brief existence, without past or future. People paused, hesitated, then stared, watching the happy procession, fascinated by their laughter, the spicy admixture of tears and mild ribaldry, the comparative elegance of dress. Such bittersweet hilarity, such carefree and infectious laughter, shouted advice, and unrestrained bussing and hugging was new again in this sad place, somehow renewed, like something lost out of time.

They were late driving through the bad roads and heavy army and construction traffic between Decatur village and Atlanta. The Jacksonville train was made up, engines watered and idle, steam escaping from pressure valves, conductor and porters standing beside the awkwardly high steps to assist passengers to a small portable stool, and then up the metal stairs.

Seeing the train breathing visibly, its engineer slouched in his window, passengers hurrying along the platform, the tearful partings, the open crying, the faces framed in day coach windows, Lily slowed involuntarily.

Walking close beside her, his arm about her tiny waist, the fox-fur collar of her dove-colored traveling suit ticklish and fragrant against his face, Ward tightened his embrace and laughed, whispering in her ear, "It's all right, darling. This is the easy part."

Lily seemed not to hear him. She gazed about, abstracted, almost frantic. She found her mother and sisters, and reached out forlornly. Miz Marcy caught Lily's fragile hand and squeezed it reassuringly.

"Which is your car, Lily?" someone called. "You're not in the day coach, are you, Ward?"

Everybody laughed. Ward spoke over his shoulder, taunting, "Is there a day coach?"

The laughter fluted again in the noisy station. He felt Lily go tense at his side. She dug her fingernails into the back of his hand to demonstrate her displeasure with his vulgarity. She tried to keep her voice light. "I prefer to sit up."

"Of course you do," someone called in derision, and everybody laughed again.

Lily's face flared a fiery red. She pressed her head hard against the sleeve of Ward's heavy topcoat.

The laughing knot of well-wishers paused at the entrance of the Pullman car. This coach was fatter, broader, quieter than the others, like some grand dame, not as garishly lit with gas lamps, not as frantic with people's hurrying, stowing luggage on overhead racks, and calling farewells through open windows.

"It was a lovely wedding, Miss Lily." Hobart Bayard bent slightly over Lily's hand. "I only hope your life is nearly as beautiful as you were today."

"You were such a lovely bride," a girl said.

"You didn't look real—"

"Like an artist's ideal—"

"I never saw anyone look happier—"

"Did you notice? Even the minister seemed to sense how extraordinary and beautiful this ceremony had to be. He didn't just rush through to tie a knot. He lingered over each sentence, as if he knew it had to last forever."

"It will." Ward nodded, smiling. "I've set my mind to that."

"Set your heart," someone said.

Ward laughed. "That too."

Miz Marcy caught Ward's hand in both of hers. She smiled up at him through her tears. "You will be good to her? I know you will. And—be patient with my little girl. We have spoiled her. She's still our little girl. You must be patient."

Ward kissed the backs of his mother-in-law's hands. "I promise."

The conductor called, "All aboard!"

They all crowded around, kissing Lily goodbye, clasping Ward's hand tightly for a moment. The women all kissed Ward lightly, quickly, embarrassedly, but ardently. "Take care . . . take care . . . take care of her. . . ."

Thetis went aboard first, carrying Lily's bags and hat-boxes. Lily clung to her parents, sobbing openly. When the porter touched her elbow, wishing to assist her aboard, Lily cried out and her knees gave way. She would have fallen, but Ward caught her, supporting her against him. He half-carried her aboard the train.

Twice, the pullman porter suggested Lily might wish to retire to the ladies' lounge to "get comfortable" while he made up their berths. But Lily shook her head, gray about the lips, rigid in her refusal. "Please, Ward. I want to sit up a while longer. I do."

Ward shrugged and spread his hands. He tipped the porter five dollars. The black man smiled again, touched at his orange-crowned cap, and made up the rest of the berths, swinging them out on their hinges, making the beds quickly and expertly, then closing them in with thick green draperies, each closure darkening the coach a little more. Ward's and Lily's chairs faced each other, a vaguely lit island in the darkened car.

"A man named George Pullman invented train cars that could be converted from day to night coaches. They could have been called Smith Cars or Jones Cars or Rasmussen cars—"

"You don't have to entertain me or be nice to me, Ward."

"I'm not being kind, or entertaining. One way to make you sleepy is to bore you stiff." He smiled and held her hand in his. "Old George Pullman rode on a new, so-called 'sleeping car' back in the 1850s, but these things were so uncomfortable he couldn't sleep. So he copied the idea of comfortable berths from steamboat sleeping accommodations. Even Abraham Lincoln slept in one of his upper berths."

"Thetis," she said. "Is Thetis all right?"

"Thetis is fine. Tell me, Lily. What did Robert actually say to you—about the robbery?"

She stared into his face for a minute, then glanced about, as frantic as a trapped rabbit. Why was he questioning her about his brother? She believed in terror that he was reading her thoughts, trying to trap her. "Robert? Why nothing. I told you. Nothing."

"Or about the money?"

"I told you, no. Oh, Ward, what is it? Why do you question me like this?"

"You didn't want to talk about George Pullman or Abraham Lincoln. You're not easy to talk to."

"I'm nervous."

"I know you are. But I don't know why."

She bit her lower lip, and exhaled heavily. "And you don't make it any easier, nagging me about—about Robert."

"I wasn't asking about Robert. I was asking about the money."

"Money?"

"There is money, Lily. A fortune. Money I could use right now."

She shook her head. "Robert's money."

He drew a deep breath. "I could make Robert ten times richer if I had that money right now." He leaned forward, looking into her troubled eyes. "Did he leave something in your care that last night he saw you, Lily? A letter? A key?"

She writhed in her seat, looking about wildly. "Please." Her voice quavered with tension. "Please, stop badgering me about Robert. I don't know—about that money. I know nothing about it, nothing. Robert left me nothing. He didn't mention the money. He left me nothing." She broke into tears, covering her face with her hands.

The Pullman car was quiet, darkened now, with only the wan yellow island where Lily sat, rigid and unyielding. The porter bent over her, smiling but insistent. "Hit gittin' mighty late, Missy. I sho' like to make up yo' bed. Got to

174

git mah sleep twixt here and Jacksonville, even if you ain't sleepy. I has to git my bones up at five o'clock in the mornin'."

Abjectly, Lily gazed at Ward, her eyes brimming with tears. "Please," she whispered. "I—can't—go to bed—with you—on this train. All these people." She caught back a sob. "It's so . . . public. What will people think?"

Ward stared at her. "They might think we're married. We could pin the license on our drapes—"

"Don't you make a joke—"

"You can't fool people, Lily; they know you're married. There's still rice in your hair."

She shook her head, exhausted, her nerves raw and her eyes wild. "I—can't."

Ward gazed at her for a long moment. He spoke in a cold, flat tone. "Make up the berths, porter." He bowed toward Lily. "I'll sit up. In the day coach."

When Ward returned to the Pullman car a little after eight the next morning, the berths and bedding had been stowed away and fastened. For Ward, to whom the staccato rhythm of the wheels on the rails and railjoints was an aphrodisiac, Lily's almost morbid hatred of the "palace" car was puzzling. He was irritated and more than a little provoked by the sight of her rumpled traveling suit, which she had not removed, and by her wan, sleepless face and haggard blue eyes. Obviously, she had slept no more during the interminable night than he had. Quick exasperation flared up in him.

He sat down beside her, forcing himself to smile, to ask how she felt this morning, though he was damned if he wanted to hear. But if this was a battle in which patience was weaponry, he was well-armed. He had vowed to himself to wait, to be patient. He took her icy hand in his. "Let's go into the dining car and have breakfast."

"I'm not hungry."

"You'll feel better after you've eaten. Everything looks better on a full stomach, as the fat lady said to her lover."

"Don't talk like that, Ward."

He laughed. "Come on, let's go eat."

She shook her head. "You go ahead. I look too rumpled, too messy. I couldn't face people."

"People. People couldn't care less, Lily."

175

"Ward, *I* care."

"You'd care a hell of a lot less after a cup of hot coffee and maybe some pancakes and an egg."

"I couldn't eat anything. I'd be sick. Please, go without me. I don't mind."

He flung himself into the upholstered chair across from her. "To hell with it. I'm not hungry, either. We'll be in Jacksonville soon. We'll have breakfast at the hotel."

She pressed her sodden handkerchief against her lips. "You must hate me. I don't want you to hate me, Ward."

"I don't hate you, Lily; you're far too pretty. I never hate pretty girls."

She sniffled and laid her head back against the seat rest. She stared upward, without blinking, the swaying and vibration of the car moving her head from side to side. Her perky little feathered traveling hat bobbled. Tears filled her ash-blue eyes, squeezed from the corners, and rolled forlornly along her cheeks.

"Don't cry," he said. "Please don't cry. I will make you happy, Lily. I swear I will."

"It isn't you. That's not why I'm crying. You've been sweet. More than good. I miss—my folks. I'm sorry. I've never been away before, not knowing when I'll get back, w-when I'll see them again. I miss them, that's all. I'll be all right." She gulped suddenly and sagged forward, a dejected, fragile little figure in her fox-fur-collared traveling suit, tiny princess Eugenie hat, soot-stained gloves. She cried helplessly, trying vainly to get herself under control.

He swung across to the chair beside her. He drew her gently to him. She pressed her face to his chest, her nails digging into him. She cried quietly but brokenly for a long time. He went on holding her tenderly, whispering to her. The heated warmth and cologne-tinted aroma of her body, her fragile, helpless loveliness, assaulted his senses. He felt himself grow empty with desire. His hand moved under her bicep and closed over her small, resilient, upcurved breast.

Lily lunged away from him, her face gray and taut as papyrus. She looked about wildly at the other people in the car, sick with embarrassment. "Don't," she whispered. "Don't. What will people think of us?"

"God knows," he said. "God knows." He told himself it

176

would be better when they got to their suite at the hotel, but he was no longer certain that this was true.

The St. James Hotel bellhop unlocked the door to their suite and pushed it open, smiling. Ward jerked his head, motioning the porter and Thetis ahead of them with their luggage. Before Lily could protest, Ward swung her up in his arms and carried her across the threshold. He stood holding her for a moment while the bellhop applauded and Thetis grinned, his dark face wreathed in smiles.

Ward set her on her feet. He tried to send Thetis off to his room in the servants' quarters of the hotel, but Lily insisted that before she could spare him, she needed the boy to help her unpack her bags and hang up her dresses.

Ward ordered brunch sent up. When Lily came out into the parlor, she'd removed the small hat and the fur-trimmed traveling jacket. Her pleated shirtwaist, buttoned at the base of her throat, looked wrinkled and stained with perspiration. She gazed about the suite, smiling. "Oh, Ward," she said, "everything is so lovely. It's all so lovely. A suite like this—it must be awfully expensive."

He smiled, setting down his cup of black coffee on the serving table. "I used to stay in a boardinghouse for two months for what this suite costs per day," he said proudly. "I want to give you the world, Lily, if you'll let me." He touched her arm and led her to the small table, set with china and sterling silver service and centered with a single rosebud in a spun-glass vase.

She shook her head. "I couldn't eat."

"Couldn't you try? You can't go on forever—"

"You go ahead. Eat, Ward. I'll just get my things straightened. Some of my dresses need ironing—"

"We'll have a hotel maid do them, Lily."

"Oh no." She looked about helplessly. "What will I do with myself?"

He went to her, put his hand against the small of her back, and drew her against him. "Relax, for a start."

"Why, whatever do you mean? Why, I am relaxed."

"Are you going to wear this same dress all the rest of your life?"

She laughed. "I'll change later."

"Change now." He secured her, imprisoned against him, with his hand at the small of her back. She could not even

177

fight free. She tried, still attempting to smile. He loosened the small black velvet tie and unbuttoned the collar of her shirt.

Lily caught her breath. "Why, Ward, what're you doing?"

"I'll show you. I'd rather show you than tell you." Deftly, his fingers pulled downward, loosening the buttons of her blouse.

Stiffening, Lily tried again to writhe free. He held her effortlessly, and slipped her blouse away from her shoulders and down over her arms. Pulling the garment free from the waistband of her skirt, he tossed it behind him. "What *are* you doing?"

He unbuttoned the waistband of her shoe-length skirt. The material fell about her feet. She held her breath, trying to cover her voluminous petticoats and lacy undergarments with her bared arms and splayed fingers. "In broad daylight?" she cried out.

"The better to see you, my dear." He rolled the shoulder straps down her arms, forcing the fabric over her hips. She fought him now, silently but fiercely. "What are you going to do?" she demanded, breathing frantically. "Rape me?"

"Not if you relax and enjoy it."

"Ward, please! You can't undress me like this—in broad daylight. Why, not even my own mother has ever seen me—naked like this."

"She doesn't know what she's missed." Still pinning her hips against his, he bent down and took the rose-pink nipple of her breast in his mouth. He felt her whole body tremble.

He straightened, staring at her. Naked, she was lovely. Her cuplike breasts, standing taut, nipples rigid, her waist and hips slightly fuller than he'd imagined them, but the dainty triangle at her thighs delicately dark, shapely, her sculptured legs and trim ankles—she was lovely. God, she was fragilely beautiful. He lifted her in her stocking feet from the bundle of her clothing about her calves, and carried her into their bedroom.

The bed was littered and strewn with her dresses, hats, and underthings. He caught the counterpane and threw everything on the floor over the foot of the bed. He laid her down across the gleaming white sheets and lay down beside her. "Lie still," he said. "I'll take off your stockings. You look like a whore with your stockings on."

She gasped, raging. "What a vile, insulting thing to say to me."

Ward laughed. "If you don't know yet the difference between loving you and insulting you, Lily, you soon will."

"You can't talk to me in such a vile way."

"When I'm excited, Lily, I may say anything. You'll get used to it. You might even get to like it."

She tried to struggle free. "No. I never will. I am a lady, and you'll treat me like a lady—"

"Damn it, Lily, I'm trying to. Lie still."

Breathing heavily, but without a trace of shared passion, Lily sagged into the mattress and lay motionless. For a long time, Ward kissed her mouth, her eyes and cheeks, her earlobes, the base of her throat, the warm cleavage of her breasts. As he nursed at her nipples, he moved his hand across the slight rise at her navel into the warm wetness at her triangle. She pressed her legs tightly together, then suddenly relaxed. He moved his fingers on her in a gentle, yet swift and circular motion. "Oh God," she whispered. "What *are* you doing?"

"I'm trying to love you, Lily, to show you I love you—"

"Don't. Please don't. I hate it. It makes me feel—dirty."

"Jesus, I'm trying to *love* you, that's all. There's nothing dirty about loving you. I'm trying to make you want to be loved, as I want to love you. God, Lily, I'm only trying to—excite you, as I am excited."

She rolled her head back and forth on the mattress, her lips pale and taut across her teeth. "Well, it doesn't excite me. I don't like it. Do it. Do whatever you must do, whatever you want. Do it. You will anyway. Get it over, Ward, please."

He stared down at her, a tightness gripping his chest. He studied her face, taut, gray, set, resigned, waiting. Waiting for something she hated to be over and done with. Rage and hatred welled up in him. He felt deceived, tricked, outraged. If she hated the thought of his touching her so terribly, why had she married him? If she'd known she could never want him, why had she agreed to marry him at all? Frustrated, defeated, rejected, he felt the bristling rigidity that had throbbed, driving him, subside. He remained tumescent if not rock-hard, because he was fool enough still to want her lovely body, bared to him, because she lay naked, her form incredibly lovely and alluring, scented, heated. He was torn inside, hating her, wanting to get up from this bed and stalk out of here. Maybe he could salvage a little pride, enough so he wouldn't be haunted by this stunning rejection every time he came near another woman. But even ill inside, he didn't want to leave her. If he left her now, he lost her forever. She had no right to reject him like this. Not now, for God's sake, of all times.

Empty-bellied, confused, he moved his hands woodenly on her, not knowing how to arouse her, afraid to give up for fear he would never come back to her. God knew, she was a young girl—inexperienced, protected, sheltered, and frightened. She came to him with only whatever misinformation she'd gathered in a repressive society, dominated by a straitlaced Baptist Church and an overly fastidious mother. Maybe it was up to him to free her, to help her, to enflame her, to make her want to love, to share loving, to be loved. Maybe she could be aroused, despite her narrow and restrictive background. Their whole future might depend on how well and passionately he performed, how much he pleased her.

He pushed her legs as far apart as she would permit without growing rigid and withdrawn. She lay stiffly, her eyes closed, as he came down upon her. She winced when he thrust himself into her, and lay chewing distractedly on her lip until he had battered at her unprevailingly and poured himself into her in halfhearted ejaculation. When she remained unmoved, unmoving, he fell away and lay silently beside her.

She stayed where she was upon her back, her limbs spread across the rumpled sheet, and then she turned on her side, away from him. She drew up her knees, lying curled, drawn up in a knot. He thought she might be crying silently. When he lifted himself on his elbow and looked down at her profile, laced with strands of her dark hair, she was not crying. She had escaped him for the moment. She was asleep, breathing deeply and raggedly.

Ward returned from the NEF&GC offices at seven that night. He found Lily wan but smiling, determinedly lighthearted. Thetis had put away her clothing. She'd or-

180

dered their meal sent up at noon. Everybody had been so nice, sweet, and thoughtful all day. She'd eaten her lunch on the small balcony overlooking the busy downtown. She had found the river in the distance.

She wore a freshly pressed summer dress with pelerine wrap and half-sleeves of lace with ribbon loops. Her skirt was sprigged muslin, plainly draped, slightly gored, hemmed, and gathered. She looked lovely, heartbreakingly lovely. He had tried all day to thrust her rejection from his mind, but he could not. He found the thought of her repudiation of his manhood driving him, forcing him to attempt to prove himself in every transaction all day.

Lily was in a warm, sprightly mood. The ugly scene this morning in their bed seemed forgotten. She accompanied him, with excitement lending color to her cheeks, to the hotel dining room. She was not unaware of the favorable attention they attracted in this elegant atmosphere. They were an attractive couple; people smiled on them, or whispered, nodding pleasantly in their direction.

Lily agreed to white wine with her dinner. She tried to keep conversation bouncing between them; she was animated and lively. He could hardly share her mood. His failure with her this morning had hurt him savagely, struck him where he was most vulnerable—in his pride—and, though he tried, he could not forget that easily.

After dinner, they sat over iced drinks and watched beautifully dressed couples dance to the muted music of a small ensemble. When they danced together, it was as if a space, especially illumined, widened around them, and they were the center of attention and approval.

At eleven, they returned to their suite. They found their bed freshly remade, her gown and his pajamas laid out across it. "I told you how wonderful and helpful Thetis would be," Lily said.

He nodded and took his pajamas, robe, and slippers, and retired to the bathroom. When he came out, Lily went into the dressing room and closed the door. He heard the lock click shut, and winced.

He walked out on the small balcony. They were on the top floor of the old hotel. The view was matchless in the murky night. The yellow ribbons of aged streets wound from the vaguely lighted expanse of the river, a few lights winked in unknown windows, and gray banks of clouds

181

piled beyond the black horizon. He located his star in the western sky, but drew little pleasure from finding it. "Please, God," he whispered once, but didn't know why he begged or what he asked for. For the first time in his life he felt lost, unsure of himself, capable of being stopped, defeated.

Lily was in their bed when he came in from the balcony. She had trimmed the wick of the bedside lamp so its light glowed softly across her. He stood for a moment, looking down at her. Her eyes were closed, her lips parted. His eyes burned. She looked as perfect as some matchless jewel against the white pillow.

He blew out the lamp, removed his robe, and tossed it behind him. The suite settled into dark silence. It was as if Lily lay holding her breath, as if the old hotel itself waited, as if the world held its breath as she did.

He turned back the covers and got into bed beside her. He wanted to reach out and touch her. She would submit, he knew this in advance. But he didn't want her submission. What would happen when he touched her was that she would quiver, withdrawing inwardly, and it was this rejection he couldn't take just now.

Sweat broke out across his forehead. He felt himself growing rigid, his body betraying him. Unmoving, he stared at the ceiling in silence. Not even the most raucous night sounds from the streets reached up here. There was only the waiting stillness.

Beside him, Lily did not move. He winced. It was as if she were afraid any slight movement might be misinterpreted as invitation. He did not know how long it was, but at last he heard her deep, regular breathing and knew she was finally asleep.

He pressed his arm across his eyes, forcing them closed. He lay unmoving for what seemed interminable hours, begging for sleep.

Sometime during the night, he fell asleep and dreamed. In his dream, Lily was screaming, wailing in terror and agony, reaching out for him, and he could not get to her. His legs were rubbery, stretching, refusing to move in the insubstantial muck that stalled him. He tried to call out and could not. He felt as if he were choking. He came awake suddenly, sweating and shaken.

182

Lily sobbed uncontrollably. Coming to full awareness, he lunged forward, stunned.

Lily's cries were almost the ululations of an animal gone mindless in agony. She sobbed hysterically, crying out, moaning, sobbing brokenly.

"Lily. For God's sake, Lily, what's the matter?"

He sat up, drugged with sleep, sick with her weeping. Frightened and helpless in the face of her sobbing, he stared at her.

Lily crouched on the side of the bed. Her feet were supported on the slat board, her shoulders slumped round, her head sunk low between her shoulders, her dark hair spilling forward into her lap. Her whole body shook with her sobs.

For some moments he stared at the slight, heartbroken figure huddled on the side of that bed. He had never felt such compassion and pity for anyone. He had never been so helpless to console her. "Please, Lily. For God's sake, tell me, What's the matter?"

Lily only shook her head, without raising it. Sobs wracked her. He touched her shoulder gently, trying to comfort her, but she writhed free of his hand, crying out.

"My God, Lily. People will think I'm beating you."

"What do you care?" Sobs shook her. "You don't care what people think."

"I care about *you*, Lily. Please, Lily, don't wail like that; they'll break down the door. They'll throw us out of here." He tried to laugh. "They'll probably arrest me. You won't even have to swear out charges."

She went on weeping loudly, inconsolably, in the late night stillness. Even when he forced her to lie down inside his arm, her head on his shoulder, she cried. At least this muffled her sobs. Jesus. What *would* people think? He wondered if they'd ever let the Hamiltons back in this hotel. He whispered, "Tell me, Lily. What is it? What have I done? What do you want? Tell me. Whatever it is, I'll do it for you."

"I want to go home."

He felt as if she'd hit him. He held her for a long time, then nodded. "Will you not come back to me, Lily?"

"I don't know. I don't want to leave you, but I want to go home . . . I want to go home . . ."

"All right, Lily. It's all right. I promise you. Today. This

183

morning. Daylight. As soon as we can get a train, I'll take you home."

She sobbed raggedly for some moments. She pressed her face against his throat, muffling her waning sobs. She pressed her body close to his. Her small, pliant breasts, the heated triangular outline of her femininity, the supple lines of her thighs yielded to the corded musculature of his body. He felt himself respond to her moist, warmth, but he reined his emotions coldly, in a way he hadn't even believed he could. She didn't want *him;* she wanted only the comfort of his physical nearness.

At seven the next morning, breakfast was served in the parlor of their suite. Lily sat across the small table from Ward. She ate ravenously. There were no outward signs of her agonized sobbing a few hours earlier.

Ward sat slumped in his chair, without appetite. He drank black coffee, hearing Thetis in the bedroom packing Lily's clothing for the return trip home.

"They'll be so surprised to see us," Lily said. "Maybe we won't stay long, Ward. Maybe just a few days."

He shrugged. A knock sounded at the door. "Maybe it's our tickets," he said. He got up and crossed the room.

Phillips Clark entered. He nodded toward Lily, surprised to see her awake at this hour. She invited him to share their breakfast. "There's plenty for an army," she said. "Why, Ward has hardly touched a bite."

"I've already eaten, Miss Lily," Clark said. "I've got some news for Ward that just wouldn't keep." He winked at Ward. "I ran here, all the way from Bay Street. It's that vital."

"All right," Ward said.

Clark peered at Ward, astonished at the complete lack of enthusiasm in his tone. "It is good news. First, the U.S. Army. The Third Division, office of General Maitland O. White, has signed *all* our contracts for freight hauling." Clark could not suppress a triumphant laugh. "Those contracts change everything, Ward. *Everything*. We've got a whole new posture. We're no longer hanging on by our teeth. We can make it. Whatever in hell—pardon me, Miss Lily—you want to accomplish, now we can do it."

"Yes." Ward exhaled heavily. "What else?"

"What else? Is that all the response that news is worth?

You've made it, Ward. You'll make that rinkydink line pay. Good lord, I thought we'd do a short gavotte at least."

"What else?"

Clark stopped smiling. He felt a faint prickling at the nape of his neck. "Baxter Marsh is in Jacksonville. He wants to see you—at your office—at ten this morning. You've still a few days of grace on that note. I don't know what he wants, but the word is it's urgent."

Ward's voice chilled. "He'll have to wait."

"Why? Why get him riled now? We're about to pay him off. We *are* going to pay him off, aren't we? Maybe he'll offer a deal of some kind—an extension, if you want one."

"I don't care what he wants. He'll have to wait. I'm taking Lily to Atlanta this morning."

Phillips Clark started to speak three times. He swallowed his words each time as ill-chosen, inappropriate. His face pulled taut, bleak. He glanced toward Lily but she continued to eat hungrily, giving her food her total attention. Ward's face was a graven, inscrutable mask. Clark shivered slightly, looking at him. "All right, Ward," Clark said at last. "Do you know when you'll be back?"

"Probably on the first return train." There was a rustling of movement, a sharp intake of breath at the breakfast table, but Ward didn't glance that way.

"What will I tell Baxter Marsh?"

"Tell him if he wants to wait, I'll see him when I can. Otherwise, tell him to go to hell."

Chapter Fourteen

THEY RODE THE TRAIN, side by side in silence, north and west through the flat Georgia lowlands. Lily seemed glowing, looking forward to returning to Errigal. Studying her, Ward tried to think how she might have behaved in bed with Robert. "What would Robert have done differently?" he said aloud.

Lily jerked her head around to face him. Her pale blue eyes searched his face. Looking for what, he had no inkling. She said, "What? What about Robert?"

He kept his voice low. "If you'd married Robert, you'd still have had the same problems—in bed, wouldn't you?"

She dug her nails into the back of his hand, checking around guiltily. No one seemed to have overheard his coarse remark. She whispered, "This is a very uncouth subject to discuss in public."

His voice remained pitched low, but it was chilled. "Maybe it is, Lily. But we *are* married. If we have any hope of staying married—"

"Why, of course we do." Her eyes darkened, grave, brimmed with tears. He stared at her, shocked by the unhappiness clouding her face. Why would she want to stay married to him if she despised and dreaded everything marriage truly entailed?

"If we have any such hope, we've got to talk about it, Lily. Openly."

"Oh, Ward. We *can* be happy—without *that*."

"*That* always seemed a big part of marriage to me."

"Well, it shouldn't. It's not to me. People *can* live happily together without the vile and vulgar things—"

"Is that the way you and Robert planned to live?"

She was silent a long beat. She studied her slender fingers, the nap of her jacket fabric, the pine and sawgrass country hurtling past on the wind. At last, she nodded. "Robert was gentle. His gentleness was what I loved about him first. We did talk about marriage—and after. Though not in a public place like this."

"Jesus. And you decided—what?"

She was silent again, the clicking of the rails and wheels loud. "Robert agreed that—sex—was not the most important part of life to him. Robert wanted what I wanted, what I believed you wanted. A good Christian marriage—like my parents'. That ugly, distasteful, animalistic side would only have been a small part of our life together. Something we could share, gently and understandingly, when we wanted to. Oh, we agreed we'd have a sex life, but it would be a sane sex life."

"The two terms are totally contradictory."

"Perhaps to you." Her voice hissed like the steam valves of the engine. "Not for us. We agreed. There would be so many other things—important things—to think about and to share."

Ward stared at her, empty-bellied. The hell of it was that he *could* imagine Lily and Robert having a conversation like that, in all seriousness. He believed her. Robert had loved to be around pretty girls, but he never plotted or connived to get them alone, to take whatever advantage chance offered. He said he respected a woman's virtue. Ward had decided that what Robert really meant was that sex just didn't mean that much to him. In some ways, he envied Robert this passivity. The quiet, the peace, the freedom from turbulent emotions and the agonizing ache of unrelieved needs, the driving needs that would not release you.

He stared at his hands. He did not try to answer Lily. What could he say to her?

* * *

The entire Harkness *menage* spilled out across the shadowed veranda to greet them when they arrived at Errigal in a rented buggy, with Thetis sitting on the trunks in the rear. No one—from Harkness himself to the least grinning kitchen servant—appeared to find it odd that Lily had returned within three days from her honeymoon.

Lily sprang from the carriage lithely and ran to her parents, her arms outstretched. They enveloped her in their arms. Ward tied off the reins and swung down. He jerked his head and Thetis unloaded the bags, carrying them into the mansion. The family was crying and laughing together as if they had not seen Lily in months.

Ward exhaled heavily. He glanced around the yard, the fields, the shacks, the red and scarred land. When he brought his gaze back, his eyes brushed across Lavinia's freckled face and leaped back. Lavinia's eyes were faintly smiling, undeceived, mildly amused. For a brief instant their gazes met. Then Lavinia turned negligently away, and it was as if the incident had never happened, except that it *had* happened, and it troubled him.

"I missed you so," Lily was saying, clinging to her parents. "I was so homesick." She broke down suddenly, sobbing. "Ward was so good to me. He brought me back home. We'll stay a few days, if you'll let us."

"Of course you will," Miz Marcy said.

Ward and Charles Henry Harkness walked across the fields, the dogs flushing small coveys of quail in their path. They strolled slowly through the lane between the sharecroppers' cabins, Harkness speaking to the people on the porches, questioning, listening, nodding, promising. As always, they arrived at the barn with its discarded kitchen chairs, the jug of bourbon, the cracked cups. They drank together, and Harkness smacked his lips. "When a man marries a Southern girl," Harkness said idly to his whiskey cup, "he finds life a little different than he's been led to expect."

"He consumes a lot of bourbon," Ward suggested.

"A lot of bourbon."

"I never meant to frighten her."

"Of course you didn't." Harkness poured more liquor into Ward's cup. "You wanted to love her, to let her know how much you loved her, to prove what a proud lover you could be." Ward winced, his pride still raw. They watched a rooster pursue a fat hen across the shadowed barnyard. Harkness smiled. "You probably had no idea in this world that you were coarse, impure, offensive, crude, and maybe even perverted."

Ward had to smile, despite his savage hurt. "You sound as if you were there."

Harkness didn't look up. His voice sounded vague, reticent, reluctant. "Oh, I *was* there, my boy. Only it was a long time ago, a different place. But in this same world. I doubt that much else was different, except the time and place." He exhaled heavily and shook his head, recalling ruefully an ancient encounter, an old defeat that still rankled, in memory at least. "I was proud of my manhood. Thought anybody ought to be. In no way did I consider it—in its glory—an imperfection."

Ward drank. He tried to laugh, to match Harkness's light, taunting tone. "I truly thought a man and woman married for the socially approved *privileges* of wedded bliss."

Harkness nodded emphatically. "And you were right, my boy. It was only that you confused priorities. The *privileges* of marriage—here in the South, anyway—have little to do with conjugal rights. They have more to do with a well-ordered household, furniture polished and chairs in place, courteous children, obsequious servants, a plethora of relatives at table."

Ward smiled. "I had no idea you were so bitter."

"Bitter? Me? Bitter?" Harkness shook his head and drank deeply. He wiped the back of his mouth with a handkerchief. "Don't misunderstand me, my boy. I am far from bitter. I am *old*. I am resigned. I have been *old* since my wedding night. I went gray in my pubic hair. I learned, that first night, that whatever my expectations, they were—in that place—base, vile, villainous, hateful, and detestable."

"I know the feeling."

"Yes. A man walks dumb into that room, but he learns quickly."

"Maybe it's part of a plan, to teach a man the right, from the first."

"I suppose. Later, I learned that my needs—which had seemed so urgent to me before—were indifferent, petty,

189

unimportant, something shamefully to conceal. I learned to live with that. It made an old man of me. But what the hell, I aged anyway. And I did go willingly to war. I fought furiously, with rages inside me I hadn't suspected. But when I came home, I returned to the same life and I resigned myself to it."

"I never will. I can't. I hate to say this to my wife's father, but I'm driven. I have needs—"

"They'll pass, my boy." Harkness took another drink. "You will resign yourself. You will. After enough rejection, a man comes to accept the imposed way of life. It's easier, far easier, maturely considered."

Ward drew the back of his hand across his sweaty face. He tried to smile with Harkness, but there was no laughter in him, no room for laughter in the bubbling cauldron of hurt and outrage. "What about your body? What about your mind?"

"You make a virtue of rejection. Women are quite placid about it. They will tell you that if they can be healthy and happy without such ugliness, you too can find the elusive bluebird of abstinence."

"What can you do?"

"A lot of Southern men run for political office, even for positions quite beyond their capabilities; they sit often on councils of war—though they're called peace missions, of course. They excel in business. They're away from home a lot."

"My God. You knew all this. Why didn't you tell me?"

Harkness smiled. "Lily is my daughter, my beloved daughter. You appeared quite deeply enamored of her. She has been reared precisely as has every other well-bred young Southern girl. What she believes is universally held as true. Would you have done better down the road?"

"I might have. God knows."

"God knows. But I doubt it, my boy. I couldn't have told you anyway, even had I been disloyal enough to the code of the South to tell you. You wouldn't have believed me. There are lessons in this life one learns and accepts only through discovery."

Ward nodded. "I've learned. Everything you've said is true. But I'm damned if I'll accept it."

Harkness winced, serious, troubled. "Does this mean you're going to divorce Lily?"

"I don't know what it means. It's all too new to me, too agonizing. I *hurt* inside. I try to laugh because I hate to cry. But I hurt. So I don't know what it means. I think it means I won't give up so damned easily. She'll learn to enjoy sex. My God, it *is* enjoyable. It's the greatest single gift God gave human beings. Sharing, belonging, giving. Jesus, it's what makes us better than other animals, and we make something filthy and forbidden out of it. My God, my God. It is not dirty or filthy. The artificial, affected lives of hypocrites who call it base; *they* are evil. I'll teach her to love it—if it kills me."

Harkness smiled crookedly. "I promise you a hero's funeral, my boy, with tears shed—mine. Yes, sir. Headaches have killed more good men in the South than ever died from Yankee bullets."

"I don't have headaches."

"Few *men* do. Headaches—as you'll learn, if you persist in your plan to *re-teach* a Southern female the truth about sex—headaches are a female malady. If a husband doesn't learn his place the first night, headaches will find a place for him. I believe, dear boy, that headaches may have been invented south of the Mason-Dixon line. They can be fatal. If you fight them, they can be lethal."

Ward was aware that his hands were shaking. He took up the jug and poured himself a drink. Harkness leaned back against the rough planking of the barn, sipping his bourbon and smiling oddly. "My God," Ward said. "What are you telling me?"

"I'm telling you what Lily was telling you in Jacksonville that night, what I was told and what all my friends have learned. I'm telling you to build your own life somehow. If you do, you may feel guilty, sordid sometimes, but you *may* cling to your sanity. If you do, and are wise, you'll gain a well-run home and a good wife in every other room in the house but the bedroom. A faultless housekeeper, an impeccable mother, excellent with servants, wonderful with guests and patient with invalids."

"And teaching her daughter *her* way of life."

"It's what she knows. It's what she believes."

"My God. What will I do?"

Harkness laughed and poured each of them another drink. "There you are, my boy, the question that proves

191

you have reached the first plateau—the beginning of wisdom."

"Jesus Christ."

"He's never been much help to me. Even He said, 'Go forth and sin no more.' Sin, for Christ's sake. You'd think He'd have known better, wouldn't you?"

"Jesus." Ward stared at the ground. It wavered before his eyes, spun and wheeled.

Ward found his first answer late that night, after Lily and the girls and the last of the guests had gone upstairs.

"How long can you stay, Ward, dear?" Miz Marcy asked.

"I should leave tonight. I must go in the morning, early. I won't need breakfast."

"Of course you will. Aunt Molly would be hurt if you went away on an empty stomach. Aunt Molly will have everything ready, and I'll have breakfast with you. Why, I look forward to it."

Ward's gaze touched Charles Henry's. Harkness smiled faintly. "Wonderful with guests," he'd said. Southern women were "wonderful with guests." Then Marcy added, as an afterthought, thrown away, what had been on her mind all the time, with steel ribbing reinforcing each gentle word. "You are going to leave poor Lily with us for a brief visit, aren't you?"

"Yes, I guess so. It's what she wants."

"I think it best." Marcy nodded. "The excitement of a hurried wedding, the upheaval in her life and all. And she's never been away from us."

Ward felt a muscle work in his taut jaw, but he said nothing.

"When you do come for her, she'll be so glad to see you," Miz Marcy said, nodding. "Anxious to go with you, I'm sure."

"How long do you think she'll want to stay?" Ward inquired, trying to conceal the cold rage underlining every word.

Miz Marcy glanced at Charles Henry. Unless one knew better, one might have believed decisions at Errigal actually were the sole province of its master. By now, Ward knew differently. Only the unpleasant pronouncements were left for the master. The good lady sat by, gracious and helpless in the face of his decision. "Why don't you leave Lily with us for a while, my boy?" Harkness spoke as though the notion were his own, recently arrived at. "You are so busy, and you are in and out of Atlanta often—sometimes twice a week."

"Yes."

"Very little inconvenience, it seems to me, to drive out to Errigal. Stay as long as you can, each time. Lily will look forward to your visits, regret your departures. Give her time to adjust to a new way of life."

"I see."

"Perhaps when you build your home," Miz Marcy said, smiling. "There are so many nice sites near Errigal. The old Curtis place, which was burned down—our nearest neighbor down the road."

"I'll be based in Jacksonville."

"Oh?" Miz Marcy's back straightened slightly. "I see."

There ensued a brief and brittle silence. Harkness said, "No doubt you'll want to build Lily a beautiful home in Jacksonville?"

"Yes, I'd hoped to."

Harkness nodded enthusiastically. "Then why don't you do that, my boy? Build Lily a home. When you visit Errigal, share your planning with her, let her suggest and plan with you. Then, when she has her own home waiting in Jacksonville, things will be different. You'll see. They'll be different then. I'm sure she'll be anxious then to go with you."

"Oh, anxious," Miss Marcy said. "Oh, I'm sure of it."

Hobart Bayard looked up across his work-piled desk at the Stockmen's and Farmers' Bank when Ward approached.

Hobart stood up, tall, slump-shouldered, fat-bellied, that lock of lank hair bobbling on his bulbous forehead. He shook hands, but did not smile at once. For this, Ward liked Hobart better than he ever had before, admired him as he had not done. "Sit down," Hobart said. "Is Miss Lily all right? I'm surprised to see you back in Atlanta so soon."

"I brought Lily home to Errigal."

"Oh? She's not ill?"

"No. Just visiting her folks." Ward saw in his mind his last glimpse of Lily early this morning. As he'd stepped up into the carriage, she'd run out across the veranda and

193

down the steps toward him. She was crying. For an instant, his heart lurched. She wanted to leave Errigal with him. He swung down to the drive and Lily pressed herself against him, her body slight, fragile, trembling. Did he have to go today? He did. Did he have to leave her? He had to leave. Business. She could come with him if she wanted to. She seemed not even to hear this. Her fingers dug into his arms. When would he be back? As soon as he could. She clung to him. She would miss him, she truly would. She was sorry she was like she was—it wasn't what she wanted. She wanted to be what he wanted her to be. Only she couldn't. She wanted him to know. She *was* sorry. For everything. She had stood there until he was out of sight, her arm raised, waving goodbye in the blue, misty morning. He brushed the thought away. He said, "She got homesick in a hurry. Maybe she didn't like my cooking."

Hobart nodded. He understood Lily. "She's never been away from Errigal without her family."

"No."

"You're very understanding."

"Yes."

Now Hobart did smile. It was friendly, admiring, warm—and genuine.

"I've a little business I hoped we could settle before I go back to Jacksonville." Ward laid the stacks of government freight-carrier contracts on Hobart's desk.

Bayard checked them, smiling, as pleased as if the triumph were his own. Ward sighed. Hobart looked as exultant as Phillips Clark had. He wished to God he could regain some of that old enthusiasm—for anything. But he could not. He felt dead inside.

Hobart excused himself, and returned with a senior vice-president and the bank's executive officer in tow. They congratulated Ward. Ward said, "It'll cost a great deal to meet the terms of these contracts. But at three cents per mile for each ton of freight hauled—" He left the thought hanging over the stack of signed contracts.

"Excellent potential. Excellent," the vice-president agreed, smiling. "Eh, Hobart? Eh? Eh?"

"I'd like to increase my first loan—by another one hundred thousand." Ward's voice was flat and unemotional because he felt dead inside. His future depended on what these men said here in the next few minutes, but he couldn't give a damn. "If you are at all uneasy, I'll go along with whatever interest you'll require on short-term notes."

"My dear boy. My dear boy. I see no problem at all. Hobart will handle the details for you. Won't you, my boy? I can tell you, Mr. Hamilton, we consider you a prime customer at Stockmen's. More than that. We share your pride in your accomplishments. We see your potential. We feel like you're one of our family, eh, Hobart? Eh? Eh?"

Baxter Marsh entered Ward's private office at NEF&GC at ten the next morning. He gave Phillips Clark a quick glance, a diffident nod. The stern, pained endurance in Marsh's whiskered face had subsided. He looked mellow, less tense. He glanced around the spacious room that had once been his. He found few changes yet; the change was in the atmosphere. Things were happening here since he'd relinquished control.

Marsh shook hands with Ward across the desk and sat down in a deep conference chair. He smiled. "I may as well confess right off, Hamilton; you've astonished me. I'm completely overwhelmed by what you've accomplished in these months. I gave you ninety days of control of this line—the period of grace to the day the final payment was due. I can say truthfully, I thought you a young, brash, and cocky adventurer who had a lesson to learn—a lesson that would be learned the hard, expensive way. But I have kept in close contact with this office. You could hardly expect me simply to turn my back, when you owed me more money than you'd ever seen in your life."

Ward smiled coldly. "Is Mr. Bracussi still reporting to you?"

Marsh shrugged. "Let's say Ralph and I keep in touch. After all, if you *had* failed, Ralph would have needed a friend and a job."

Ward scribbled on a pad, waiting.

"Ralph's reports have been glowing. His admiration for you—like mine—has multiplied every day for the past ten weeks. He reports that this last month, for the first time in over three years, East Florida and Gulf has operated in the black. No appreciable net, but no loss, no red ink. I'm stunned, Mr. Hamilton. I am as pleased for you as I can be."

"Thank you."

"Frankly, I never believed a rail line in Florida could be made profitable. Perhaps you will succeed. As of today, there are still less than five hundred total miles of rail line in Florida. Most of these lines go nowhere. Despite a good life for the wealthy farmers, cattlemen, grove owners, and rich tourists, life is not all that elegant or remunerative for the crackers. It's not a rich state."

"It can be."

"Perhaps. I see you believe that. Unfortunately, this wealth won't be realized, not in our time. Florida is still a frontier—a rough frontier. It was a refuge for murderers and scoundrels when it was a territory. In many ways, it still is. And the sons of these murderers and scoundrels are now Florida's first families. No, I'm glad to be out of it. I shall, however, watch you with great interest."

"Why?"

"For many reasons. I'll always have a soft spot—in my head—for my old railway line. I, too, arrived in Florida with my dreams! You are up against formidable obstacles. And now, I believe you have increased those odds by undertaking what may prove to be a ruinous contract to haul freight for the U.S. Army."

"Bracussi is certainly thorough in his reports. And up to the moment."

"I learned of this contract from your attorney."

Ward glanced up. Phillips Clark winced and sank lower in the big overstuffed chair.

Marsh continued, "As you may know, I refused to bid on these contracts."

"Three cents per mile per ton was more than I could resist," Ward said.

"Anyhow, the important thing is that with gilt-edged government contracts, you'll have no problem meeting your obligations to me."

"No."

"Or perhaps you'll find dealing with the army a bigger bite than you can masticate. You've got to produce a hell of a lot more rolling stock than you bought from me. However, you are an astonishing, resourceful young man. I am willing to gamble that you will do it."

196

"I will do it. But what is in it for you?"

Marsh smiled. "You forget, I still hold a note for ninety thousand, plus interest. That's why I came down here. You've put EF&GC on a solid base, in the black, in a matter of weeks. Remarkable. Out of the red for the first time in three years. But we both know the rails, crossties, railbeds, and roadways are in poor condition. They must be repaired to hold up under the kind of traffic they'll carry, hauling for the government. You'll need new rolling stock, equipment, and material. I have two courses: I can demand payment on the due date. If I don't cripple you, at least I can make an almost impossible job tougher. But I've no wish to destroy you, or even to delay or obstruct you. I am a railroad man first. I want to see this line progress; I'd like to see you make it work, despite the facts of life as I know them." He spread his hands and nodded. "And so that's why I'm here. We can extend our note another ninety days, if you like. Remove a lot of pressure."

Ward heard Phillips Clark's exhalation of relief in the silent room.

"It's like handing you working capital," Marsh said.

"And what will you get out of it?"

"Why, ten percent. Pay me ten percent interest now, and I'll carry you another ninety days at the same terms."

Ward sensed Phillips Clark stirring in his chair, trying to attract his attention. He did not glance toward the attorney. He said, "Now, Mr. Marsh, it's my turn to tell you, I'm as astonished as you. After our—little conversation, at Port St. Joe, I never thought I'd find you offering to help. Not even at ten percent interest."

Marsh shrugged. "A man can't let personal jealousy discolor his business acumen. Eh? It takes two to waltz, Mr. Hamilton. I've known that all along. It's just that now I've resigned myself to the truth."

"And ten percent."

Marsh laughed. "Love is a luxury, Mr. Hamilton. But business is business, eh?"

Ward had been scribbling on a sheet of paper. He handed it across the desk. Marsh took the draft drawn against Ward's account in the Stockmen's and Farmers' Bank.

"Payment in full?" Marsh scowled. He sounded almost disappointed.

Ward nodded. He still did not look toward Phillips Clark. To hell with him. To hell with all of them. The New East Florida & Gulf Coast Railroad was his. It was all he had, and, by God, nobody could take it from him. He grinned coldly. He couldn't make a woman love him, but he could own a railroad. What the hell? That took balls. He'd started out owing Marsh ninety thousand, plus interest. Now he owed Stockmen's and Farmers' Bank over two hundred thousand dollars, plus interest. He'd come a long way.

Chapter Fifteen

GENERAL MAITLAND O. WHITE peered across his desk, his face savage, when Ward entered his command office at Third Division headquarters in Atlanta. The general was a hulking man, broad-shouldered, imposing, with an underslung jaw—an impressive figure in a tailored blue uniform, unborn-calf gloves, and gleamingly polished boots. He stood up, scowling, and gripped the riding crop he always carried. "Come in, Hamilton." His voice rang with authority and chilly dislike. "You sure as hell took your time getting here."

"I came as quickly as I could, General." Ward almost matched White's arrogant tone. If the officer wanted a skirmish, he could have it. One thing an unsatisfactory marriage had done for him: it had exposed his nerve ends, raw and edgy. Once, he might have cringed—at least inwardly—under General White's glaring, unblinking gaze, the sarcastic lash of his tongue. But not now. Lily's behavior over the past weeks had so frustrated, outraged, and depressed him that he could not truly react to other outside pressures. He simply could not give a damn.

It was less than strictly true that he had reported directly to Third Division headquarters upon arriving in Atlanta. Though General White's summons was marked 'urgent,' he had spent a day and a half at Errigal. He had gone to the old plantation hopefully, if for no better reason than that hope does spring eternal and that desire often does nurture hope. If we want something badly enough, we convince ourselves, against all evidence, logic, or reason, that we will be granted our wish.

He had missed Lily; he wanted her with him, convinced still that he could teach her to enjoy lovemaking. This very instruction itself would be a delight, for him as well as for Lily. He *would* arouse her, make her respond, make her eager to be held, to be caressed, to be loved and to return love. When she was away, he did not remember her anguish at being touched as he touched her, or her distaste for the words he whispered in his excitement. He remembered instead the fragile beauty, the soft hands, the fragrance of her, the elegant suppleness of her body. He would teach her. She would want him if only he had the chance to prove himself with her.

He worked hard, fourteen and eighteen hours a day, long after Phillips Clark had repaired to the forbidden delights marketed along Bay Street. But Lily was never truly out of his mind. It was easier to convince her of his urgent devotion in his fantasies, and in them, she responded. He missed her.

He was exultant to find her happy to see him when he arrived at Errigal. She ran out to him when he swung down from the carriage and flung herself into his arms. She appeared to have put on weight slightly in the weeks since he'd seen her last, but it seemed undiplomatic to mention this. She looked elegant, radiant, her hair brilliant with life and care, her eyes rested and smiling. She clung to his arms. There was a dance at the home of a circuit judge in Decatur that night, and she insisted that they go; she wanted all Georgia to see Ward, she was so proud of him.

Lily was the loveliest girl at the dance, though it troubled Ward slightly that Lily had now pressed Thetis into service as if the black boy were her maid. Thetis had helped her dress—deftly, certainly, as respectful and blind as blacks were required to be. He had laid out her underthings, helped her arrange her hair, made sure she carried a small lace kerchief. It seemed unwise to question Lily about the propriety of this, so he said nothing. None of

200

the Harkness family found it at all unusual that Thetis served Lily so intimately. She paraded in her underthings before Thetis as though he were not even there. Yet she was reticent and shy before Ward. Still, he tried to accept it gracefully. He wanted a truce with Lily, not further division; he wanted her back. And after all, Thetis had practically dressed and undressed Robert when the boy worked for him. It was hardly the same, yet he felt it impolitic even to mention the arrangement.

Lily clung to his arm in the large, brilliantly illumined parlor at the judge's home. She was sweetly, artlessly possessive and wifely. She danced first with Ward, laughing almost coquettishly up into his face, pleasantly conscious that they were the center of attention. Each man who wanted to dance with Lily asked Ward's permission first. Even when Ward nodded, Lily would press her hand on his arm, as if assuaging any jealousy rising in him, and ask smilingly if he were certain he did not mind. During the interminable evening, a dozen elderly women told Ward repeatedly that he and lovely Lily were "the ideal couple, ideally happy, ideally suited in just every way, ideally handsome together—as if you were born for each other." Ward bowed and thanked each of them, considering it a victory over his baser nature—and the emptiness gnawing inside him—that he didn't laugh in their fat faces.

Alone in the high-ceilinged bedroom at Errigal, now furnished as Lily's and Ward's suite, Lily chattered brightly about the dance, how everyone had complimented her on her handsome husband, her perfect marriage. "Ideal," Ward said in some irony, but she did not hear him and, anyhow, irony was lost on Lily.

She said nothing about returning to Jacksonville with him. She seemed not really to hear him when he spoke of it. The sense of frustration and insufficiency overwhelmed him.

He tried to take her in his arms, gently, almost diffidently, when they were in her huge, high-mattressed old bed, a wooden, handcarved four-poster. But Lily tensed at his touch, pulling away from him. Sickness flooded down through him. "Someone might hear us, darling," she said. "I'd just die of embarrassment. Anyway, honey, I'm just so tired. I must have danced every dance. Oh, Ward, I had such a lovely time. And I do love you so." As she spoke, she extricated herself expertly from his embrace. He did not pursue her. In minutes she was asleep, breathing deeply in pleasant exhaustion. He lay sweating in the darkness, staring upward in self-hatred and rage, no longer believing in anything, sick with rejection, nerves frayed and taut.

Now, in General White's office, he stood braced for any attack. He became aware that they were not alone, though General's White's summons had specifically requested that he appear unaccompanied. Simon Shaffer sat in a comfortable chair a few feet from the general's cluttered desk. Simon met Ward's gaze, grinned coldly, and gave him a cavalier little salute.

"I'll be damned. I will be damned," General White was saying. "I *thought* I remembered you, Hamilton. You're the brassy fellow who came in here with the lamebrain idea of the U.S. Army feeding these bastard Rebs! By God, I might have anticipated something like this."

"What's the problem, General?"

"The problem, Hamilton, is you. You're trying to defraud the U.S. Army, that's the problem, and I'm goddamned if I'm going to let you do it."

"Pretty strong words, General. Especially in the presence of a witness." Ward jerked his head toward Simon Shaffer.

"Hell, those are mild words. Compared to what you're going to hear here today, those are love notes, Hamilton. Fraud is the least of the crimes I'll charge you with. And as to a witness, I'd better tell you, Mr. Shaffer is here because he was astute enough to catch your trickery, and loyal and patriotic enough to bring to my attention the base fraud you are trying to perpetrate against our great country and our magnificent flag."

"Mr. Shaffer, General? What has Mr. Shaffer to do with my contracts with the army?"

"Never mind, young man. I'll do the flaming interrogating. You'll get nowhere with me, questioning Mr. Shaffer's integrity and patriotism."

Simon cleared his throat. "I always liked you, Ward, when you worked for me. But I felt, and I still feel, you're getting a mite too big for your britches. And you are trying to defraud the government and trick my great friend General White. So I did feel duty-bound to point out certain irregularities in the contract you pushed through the general's office." Shaffer nodded emphatically. "After all, I was directly involved. Because of your chicanery, my contracts were rejected."

"We're just about to rectify that little mistake, Mr. Shaffer," General White said, cracking his crop against the desk. "It may be a bit irregular, not going through the War Department in Washington and all, but I'll see that you are awarded these contracts—because of the loyalty of your actions in exposing this young crook."

Ward's voice lashed out. "I've told you once, General, about slandering me. If you have charges against me, you make them. Slander me, and Simon Shaffer will testify against you under oath, whether he wants to or not."

White laughed, his face going red. "Listen to that arrogance, will you? Eh, Mr. Shaffer? Coming in here, high and mighty. No better than his criminal brother who languishes in a federal penitentiary for stealing from the U.S. Army. Likely you'll join your criminal brother in prison."

"Fraud is something you'll have to prove, General. Theft—like my brother's bungled attempt—is stupid. Business practices, even sharp or tough ones, are still only good business. Mr. Shaffer will agree to this."

"Never mind Mr. Shaffer. This matter is between you and me—and the U.S. Army, which I am sworn to uphold and serve and protect with my life," White said. "If I had seen these contracts of yours, they'd never have gone through at all." He flipped open a page and read a marked passage: "Clause 57-A: The U.S. Army agrees it will lend every assistance where feasible to expedite and insure delivery of all army-requisitioned materials. Now, goddamn it, Hamilton, did you honestly expect to get away with raw thievery like that?"

"There you go again, General. Slander. That is a perfectly honest clause which merely considers obstacles which might delay delivery of vital materials, thereby inflating construction costs to the U.S. Army. Delays the army itself might wish to alleviate in its own best interests."

"What you mean is, your monkey railroad doesn't have adequate rolling stock to meet the terms of this contract. You knew that when you submitted it, and you expect the U.S. Army to bail you out."

203

Ward met General White's gaze levelly. "Are you interested in completing construction work in Jacksonville—on time and on budget—or are you interested in proving your own righteousness?"

"You cocky son of a bitch. I *will* see you in jail—"

"If you're interested in saving time and money, you'll be glad to cooperate with NEF&GC, glad to furnish the contractor any assistance—as you always have other contractors in the past."

"What the hell are you talking about?"

"Freight cars and flatcars, General, owned by the army of occupation, uncounted and unaccounted for, rusting on sidings, taking up valuable rail space in every railyard in this state. Cars that haven't been used in three years or more, that's what I'm talking about, General. New East Florida & Gulf Central has cars. We'll make every effort to deliver freight, stores, and lumber on time. But not even Gould's railroad or Vanderbilt's has rolling stock in unlimited numbers. Hell, only you have. You, the U.S. Army. If you want me to write to the senator from Ohio, or to Mark Hanna, about idle rolling stock rusting on sidings, which the army refuses to use on army projects, in an attempt to discriminate—"

"Wait a minute, you young bastard. Hold on to that 'discriminate.' We're making no effort to discriminate against your rail company. You simply cannot fulfill the terms of your contract. That constitutes deliberate fraud, and I want these contracts terminated, returned, voided."

"Well, General, as to whether we can fulfill our contracts, you can't say that in advance. You can think it, but you can't prove it. You'll just have to wait until NEF&GC fails to meet *any* of the terms of our contract with the army before you can nullify or void them. Otherwise, I'll bring charges of discrimination—"

"Damn it, boy. I told you not to use that word. I am merely doing my duty, trying to get honest delivery for my country's money. That's my duty, not discrimination."

"And I say it *is* discrimination. You're willing to accept a bid at least forty percent above ours; that's discrimination of the rankest kind." Ward opened the thick leather case he carried and removed a fat sheaf of yellowing legal-sized documents. Shaffer sat forward on the edge of his chair.

White scowled. "Now what the hell is that stuff?"

Ward did not reply at once. He leafed through the first packet, and found a page with a clause encircled in red ink. He placed it carefully before General White.

The general read the clause, his lips moving, going gray. He reread it. The wording in that clause was precisely that of the contract with NEF&GC.

By this time, Ward had placed a second and third copy of different contracts before him, all precisely worded with the "feasibility" clause.

"You son of a bitch," White whispered. "Where'd you steal these government contracts?"

"They're waste paper, General, thrown out by Simon Shaffer. I worked for Mr. Shaffer. I admired his business acumen, his sharp practices. I kept these contracts which he threw out—as models." He continued to leaf through the stack of papers before him.

"Enough," White raged. "Goddamn it, I get your point." He wheeled around and slashed his riding crop down on his desktop. "Goddamnit, Shaffer, why'd you let me box myself in like this?"

"Only trying to help," Shaffer said, voice weak.

"Goddamn it. You could have brought a stinking Senate inquiry board down on my ass. Discrimination. That son-of-a-bitching Mark Hanna of Ohio thinks anything the thieving railroads do is God's own handiwork. You trying to get me crucified?" He jerked his head back around, facing Ward. "Don't worry, fellow. I'm not through with you, either."

General White pressed a battery-powered button on his desk. A buzz was heard distinctly from the adjoining office. Almost immediately, Major Richard Milner appeared, a gray-faced, ramrod-straight man sporting a small blond mustache. General White's voice shook with suppressed rage. "Milner, do you know this—this man Hamilton?"

"Yes, General, I know Mr. Hamilton."

"I don't know whether you do or not, Milner. He's a devious, unprincipled, civilian scalawag. He's got the idea I should furnish flatcars to supply *my* materials over his railroad to a U.S. Army installation, and pay *his* freight rates, to deliver my material on my rolling stock, to fulfill *his* contracts."

"Furnish them or don't," Ward said. "That's up to you,

General. Major Milner, Mr. Shaffer, you and I know the U.S. Government has hundreds of flatcars sitting idle on Georgia sidings. Whether or not you permit us to use them to transport material you need is your decision. The only important thing is the contract you've signed with me, which states clearly that the U.S. Government obligates itself to 'assist in every way feasible' to deliver necessary equipment and materials."

White gestured cuttingly with the riding crop. "Milner, give this civilian son of a bitch any army flatcars or freight cars he *requires—as* he requires them—from any siding or tracks, or any not presently in use. *As feasible*, Major. And, Milner, get the army lawyers studying this bastard's contracts with us. I want them gone over with magnifying glasses. If he fails to deliver by as much as a dotted i or a crossed t, I want his contracts voided, nullified, rescinded. Don't delay waiting for a clearance from me. Nullify the goddamn things on the spot. Is that clear?"

Ward was still quivering deep inside his belly when he got back to Jacksonville. But by the time he was in his office again, he was able to laugh. He related to Phillips Clark in detail the entire scene in General White's office. "You should have been there. You should have seen his face."

"You've made one hell of an enemy," Clark suggested.

"Hell, he's hated me ever since I advised using surplus army funds to feed the starving crackers."

"He'll really hate you now."

"If you think he hates me now, wait until he finds out the naval stores, lumber, and materials he's contracted to buy in Lake City, to ship to Jacksonville via my railroad, come from my sawmills, my plants, and my companies. That's when watching his face will be fun."

Chapter Sixteen

FOR WARD, it was an event without precedent, his being ushered, without waiting, into the office of the Governor of Florida at Tallahassee. In fact, everything that happened to him each new day—the triumphs, when there were any, and the problems that beset him from every unexpected cranny—were all conditions without prior example. He learned as he stumbled forward. He felt as insulated by his ignorance as he was soothed by his vices in dealing with other men in business competition.

Governor Marcellus L. Stearn's secretary was a thin, pinch-faced Yankee, bent-shouldered and obsequious. "Come in, Mr. Hamilton," he said. "Do come in, sir. The governor's expecting you."

Ward grinned inwardly. The atmosphere around him had altered radically in the past six months. He'd enjoyed few victories, but NEF&GC was operating in the black. His peers regarded him with respect, if no real affection. To the natives he was an outlander; to the money and railroad people he was an upstart. But people listened when he spoke; they jumped to obey him; the doors to the Governor's office were swung wide open for him. . . .

It was almost Christmas, crisply cold in the capital city morning. Ward had planned, until yesterday, to return to

Errigal for the holidays. But something had happened—for the first time in Florida's history—at the state prison, which changed any preconceived plan. He dispatched a telegram to Errigal, stating that he would be delayed, and caught his own train to Lake City. There he transferred to the Tallahassee, Pensacola & Mobile line, finding it no more efficiently operated than his own seventy-two-mile company. He even sat at the window, watching the countryside deepen in color and in vigor as the train climbed, and dreamed of owning this line. What an addition to NEF&GC! All development in the state followed an east-west line across the north. Census figures showed six to eighteen inhabitants per square mile across the north central area, with eighteen to forty-five inhabitants per square mile in a thirty-mile corridor between the Georgia line and the Gulf Coast below Tallahassee. The rest of the state lay undeveloped: frontier, swamp, overflow land, the Everglades, or Indian territory, with less than two inhabitants per square mile. The man or corporation controlling northern Florida railroading held the world in his fist. And God knew, Ward Hamilton wanted no more than this. And no less.

His heart pounded under the influence of that pleasant fantasy. He vowed that once his base was secured in Jacksonville, once the government contracts were fulfilled and paid, and the bank at Atlanta at least partially satisfied, he would make his move west. Business accomplishment was about the only dream left to him, and he sublimated everything else to it.

He spent most of his waking hours planning untried ways to build freight and passenger income, improve service, and expand his holdings. He had no existence away from the office. Even Phillips Clark found release and gratification on Bay Street. Clark regaled him daily with erotic sagas of the girls he met and hired and satisfied, the incredible pleasures available to a man with money down near the wharves, where life was good and uninhibited and basic.

Ward worked tirelessly in his office until midnight. The last train from anywhere would have coughed into the terminal yard and expired before he quit. Then, in the silent darkness, he'd walk to his rooms at the St. James. This hotel and his sumptuous meals in its restaurant were his only luxuries. There was a kind of wry self-torment in residing at the St. James. It kept clear and painfully in his mind his failure with Lily—his failure as a man.

He had seen Lily only a few times in the past six months, and no visit had any sufficiency for him, no remedy, no restorative effect. He had not been to Errigal since Thanksgiving—almost a month. When he left that time, he'd vowed he would never go back there. If Lily wanted him, she could come to him in Jacksonville. Even as he laid down this silent ultimatum, he knew better. She never would come to him. She grew plump and serene at Errigal. In some ways, she seemed hardly the slender, willowy girl he'd married. In other ways, she'd changed not at all.

"Husbands and wives live together, Lily." He tried to keep his voice light, to conceal his anguish and outrage.

"And we shall," she said brightly, touching his lips with the tip of her index finger, a touch as light as a butterfly, and as meaningless. They sat together on the wisteria-shaded veranda in the late afternoon. "Just give me a little time."

"They live together," he persisted in that forced, light tone. "Or there is no marriage."

"Please don't talk like that." Her lips quivered. Lovely lips, carved to be kissed and kissed and kissed. Her pale eyes, tear-brimmed, searched about frantically—for what, he had no idea. "Do you want me to come back to Jacksonville with you now? Do you insist? Is that what you demand of me, Ward? If you do, I'll go. We'll go now."

He felt helpless against her, as always. "Jesus. You make it sound like a jail sentence. I only want to know what *you* want, Lily. What do you want?"

"I want you to love me. As I love you."

"My God. Do you love me?"

She stared at him uncomprehendingly. "Do you doubt me? As wonderful as you've been to me? There's no one else as wonderful as you. No one. Do you think there's anyone else, some other man around here?"

"No. I know better."

"Then how can you doubt me? I'm proud of you, I'm grateful to you, I'm awed by you. I never stop talking about you. Ask anyone."

He put his arm about her shoulder, and drew her to

him. "Loving, to me, Lily, means sharing. Loving *you*, to me, Lily, means holding you in my arms like this. Playing with your tits by the hour—"

"Stop talking like that." Her face bleak, she sat up and moved away from him. "I hate that disgusting poolroom talk. I won't stay out here another minute."

He stood up. "No. You stay here, Lily, where it's cool. I'm going out to the barn for a drink."

"You do spend an awful lot of your time here at the barn, don't you?"

He paused at the wide steps, and glanced over his shoulder at her. "Yes, don't I?"

There was no pleasure, no satisfaction, in these sad skirmishes, in trouncing her straitlaced accusations with some acid retort. This only rendered a bad situation intolerable. Lily did seem happy to have him around—for show-and-tell. She took him visiting proudly—to the Baptist minister and his string-necked, unbending wife, to the nearest large plantation, to the melancholy homes of displaced people who'd been affluent before the war, but who obviously barely subsisted now living on cold pride and dried memories. On these trips, Lily took roast chickens and pumpkin, peach, or sweet potato pies topped with three-inches of golden, toasted meringue. She was a delight to watch as she concealed the obvious charity behind a warm, open smile and the statement that "Aunt Molly made extra, because she knows how you folks just dote on her pecan pies." It worked. These genteel folk, defeated, threadbare, and often gaunt, smiled and received the gifts as a favor to Lily and Aunt Molly.

On all these visits, Lily pridefully placed Ward on display. She talked about his rail lines, how well they were running, his government contracts. "Do you know, on some lines a schedule means nothing? Why, from Savannah to Jacksonville, it's supposed to be sixteen hours. Sometimes it's nearer twenty hours—and you can never plan ahead. On Ward's line, no train is ever more than a few minutes late. Ever." She repeated verbatim items he'd never even supposed she'd heard at the dinner table at Errigal, as if Ward's career were the supreme interest of her existence. She fooled her auditors; hell, she almost fooled Ward. A man could look at her, radiant and enthused, with her lovely, enchanted, unaffected, and guileless smile, and believe she *did* care, truly cared. . . .

However, a man made such an assumption at his own risk. Late at night, on his last day at Errigal, Ward lay beside Lily on her bed, aching and tantalized with desire. Lily slept soundly at his side, the sleep of the angels. He felt himself grow heated, rigid—and agonized.

He turned toward her, the heady, warm fragrance of her hair and body attacking him. His throat aching, his breath harsh, he moved closer. This was ridiculous; it didn't make sense. He behaved furtively, as if she weren't even his wife at all. She *was* his wife. She *belonged* to him. Yet she had placed some invisible barrier between them; she was more like a stranger sharing his bed. No, more than a stranger. He could at least approach a stranger with an honest proposition: "Hello, stranger. I'm suffering. If you feel at all the same way, we can work something out." Lily was no stranger, but they couldn't work anything out.

Hell, he didn't have to be apologetic, stealthy, or prurient about it. And yet he was in agony, feeling all these things. He turned back the heavy covers, revealing her body in its sheer, twisted gown.

Lily whimpered, shivering. He lay gazing at her, entranced. He loosened the small lace bow at the bodice of her gown and opened the garment, exposing her high-standing, supple breasts. Supporting himself on his elbow, he lay for some moments enjoying the visual delight of her alabaster body, illumined in faint moonlight. How could anyone who was so beautifully made refuse to be loved, to love? He lifted her gown upward over her thighs, and placed his hand gently on the dainty dark triangle.

She lunged away from him, crying out, only half awake, but thoroughly antagonized, "Let me alone." She whispered tensely, "If you touch me, I'll scream. I will. I swear I will."

"What's the matter with you?"

"Let me alone. I can't stand for you to touch me like that. Not now. I'm sorry. I can't."

"Lie down," he said. His voice lashed at her in the filmy darkness. "Shut up. Don't scream. You don't have to scream to stop me. Go to sleep." He threw the covers back over her. "Go to hell."

He had not been back to Errigal since.

His unhappiness with Lily clouded everything he did at the railroad offices. He knew he was drawn, his nerves ragged. He needed release, and yet he was afraid to become involved with another woman, even briefly. Lily had erected such a hellish barrier in his mind that he had a terrible fear that he would fail any other woman as well.

"Impotent?" Phillips Clark taunted. "You?" He shook his head, laughing. "Hell, all you need is variety. That's all any man needs."

But Ward resisted his urges, compulsions, and desires. The women who passed him in the lobby of the St. James were the loveliest and smartest south of Charleston. Wealthy tourist females looking for brief and unobligating pleasures, they all looked good, they smelled delicious. He was tempted as the months dragged away, sorely tempted.

"No. All I've got to do is try with some woman—and fail," he told Phillips Clark in his office. He pressed his hands over his face. "It would finish me, I swear it would."

Clark only laughed. "Buy yourself a girl. I know some beauties on Bay Street who can't be over sixteen or seventeen. New, clean, beautiful. If you pay, it won't matter if you please her or not."

Ward absently picked up and unfolded the copy of the morning *Jacksonville Union* that was lying on his desk. "It won't matter to *her*," Ward said, exhaling heavily. "It would destroy me." His harried gaze struck the headlines on the *Union* front page: STATE PRISON INMATES RIOT.

He read aloud. The prisoners, overcrowded, idle, cramped in airless quarters, had gone on a rampage of destruction, fighting and maiming each other as well as the guards, prison officials, and army reinforcements rushed in from Third Division garrisons. At first Clark thought Ward was merely trying to shut him up, but the more Ward read, the more Clark followed the direction of his thoughts.

"It's our answer," Ward said. "We've found the way we can afford to repair the right-of-way between here and Lake City. I'm taking the next train to Tallahassee."

* * *

212

Tallahassee, like ancient Rome, was built on seven hills. The name was an Indian word meaning "old town," and it *was* an old town by now, established in 1824, just south of the ancient Tallahassi Trail and the plains where native tribes had conferred for hundreds of years. The cornerstone for the statehouse was laid and one wing completed in 1826. The town grew around this center of government. The site had been chosen for the state capital because it was two hundred miles east of Pensacola and two hundred miles west of Jacksonville. It was then the center of the populated territory.

Ralph Waldo Emerson had visited the village and found it: ". . . grotesque . . . capital of the territory . . . rapidly settled by public officers, land speculators, and (other) desperadoes. . . ."

Florida's first railroad, the Tallahassee-St. Marks line, was built in 1834 and the area became a cotton shipping center. At the time Ward first arrived in the state capital, the Republicans had been in control of the government for almost twenty years, and nineteen Negroes served in the legislature.

Ward drove from the railway depot to the Capitol Hotel on Adams Street near the capitol building. He sent word to Governor Stearns's office that he would appreciate an audience with him at the governor's earliest convenience. His reply came by the same messenger: His Excellency the governor looked forward to seeing Mr. Hamilton at precisely nine the next morning.

The business section was brightly decorated for the Christmas season. Ward loitered along streets crowded with shoppers, lawmakers, lawbreakers, farmers, speculators, touts, businessmen, and assorted thieves. Glittering tinsel, fake snow, huge packets of red-berried holly, branches of loblolly and long-leaf pine, and clusters of red poinsettias framed toys, wearing apparel, and every kind of gift suggestion.

Ward paused, staring into those windows. He thought about Lily, trying to decide what gifts he should take to Errigal for Lily and her family. He'd have to go to Errigal for the holidays, whether he wanted to or not. And, like the man who keeps hitting himself in the head with a hammer, he missed Lily, longed for her—not as she was, as she had learned to be—but as she could become, as she might learn to be, as he would teach her to be if only she would let him. And he wanted to see her.

On the other hand, as Phillips Clark suggested, why not just find a pliant, rentable young woman and stay home? It would be easier all around.

He walked out of the dining room of the hotel at eight o'clock the next morning on his way to the Capitol Building on South Monroe, between Pensacola and St. Augustine Streets.

Someone spoke his name. There was no real enthusiasm in the call, but it was pleasant and unexpected in a place of strangers. Startled, he paused, looked back, and recognized Dayton Fredrick.

Smiling, Ward extended his hand. He glanced around, and found Julia standing beside her father. She looked old for her years and very elegant in a showy brown sealskin coat. She gazed at Ward, her almond-shaped eyes somehow wounded. She did not smile.

"What are you doing here?" Both Fredrick and Ward asked the question in the same breath.

"I'm hoping to see the governor," Ward said.

Fredrick nodded. "I'm trying to deal with the Internal Improvement Fund people. If you hope to accomplish *anything* in Florida, in land, hotels, or rails, you'll find yourself sooner or later dealing with the IIF—and God help you."

"You're looking lovely, Julia," Ward said. "What's Saint Nick bringing you?"

"Are you trying to annoy me, Mr. Hamilton? If so, you're succeeding beautifully."

Dayton laughed. "Julia no longer loves you blindly, Ward, since you actually assumed control of EF&GC. She—like me—didn't think you'd make it. We could forgive you for trying, or even for failing. I forgive you for succeeding, but your success sits hard with Julia."

Julia had not taken her gaze from Ward's face. "Oh, I still love you," Julia said in a hard, flat tone. "I guess I always will."

"I'm glad."

"I love you, it's only that I hate your guts. Whoever hurts my father has me for an enemy."

"I'm truly sorry, Julia. I never wanted that."

214

"I don't think you give a damn. But you should. I hear your railroad is a success, hauling millions of tons of freight for the U.S. Army." Her oddly green eyes glittered. "I do hear your marriage isn't all that great."

Ward laughed and Dayton smiled, amused and indulgent. Ward said, "I'm still married."

"With your pretty little ol' Southern belle wife living in Atlanta? Do you really call that *married*, Mr. Hamilton?"

"I don't call it anything, Julia, because I don't explain myself to anybody."

She laughed. "I'll bet you can't explain such a modern design for marriage."

"That's enough, Julia." Her father's voice was mildly reproving.

"Of course," Julia said. "I never did get to tell you how much I enjoyed your wedding. Your simpering little Southern belle. She's just real pretty." She drawled the words.

"Thank you."

"I think you deserve each other. I hate you for what you've done to my father, but I am pleased you married Lily. I couldn't imagine a more perfect revenge."

Ward laughed at her. "You ought to be restrained, Miss Fredrick—with ropes. What *will* you be by the time you've grown up?"

"Whatever, it will be no concern of yours, Mr. Hamilton."

"Thank God."

Dayton laughed. "Stop this. You two sound like lovers. Julia, behave. Whatever Mr. Hamilton has done to me, it was impersonal. Business. I hold no grudge."

"Well, I do."

"Then you'll have to be mature enough to conceal it," her father told her, his voice suddenly chilled. He smiled toward Ward again. "Hell hath no fury like a woman scorned. Listen, come to dinner with us tonight, here in the hotel. I hear the Capitol Hotel dining room serves a Kansas City strip steak that melts in your mouth."

"If Julia won't feel compromised, sitting across a table from me," Ward said, teasing her.

"Come with us," she said. "My mind hates you. My heart hates you. But there's more to me than heart and mind, and the rest of me would still go to bed with you, low and unprincipled as you are."

"You'll never forgive me, will you?" Ward said.

"No."

Dayton Fredrick enclosed his daughter in his arm. "You'll have to forgive Julia—or ignore her. Julia's a daughter of her father. We hate well, but we love even more fiercely, eh, Julia?"

"Amen," Julia said.

"Come in. Come in, Mr. Hamilton." Governor Marcellus L. Stearns got up and came around the desk, an ash-gray man, harried by political battles. "I've just heard so much about you, sir—the boy wonder of the railroad world. You're making them sit up and take notice of you; I've looked forward to meeting you. In what way may I serve you, sir?"

"If you like the plan I offer, we may be able to serve each other—and the state."

Stearns smiled, nodding him into a chair. "Anything that will benefit this poor harassed state, Mr. Hamilton, finds in me an avid supporter. Florida has come through eleven years of hell. How much more is ahead of her, I can't say. Anything that might alleviate that agony, in any small way, finds favor with me, at least."

Stearns said, "My party has done much to promote railroads, much to assist the builders over the past eleven years or so, Mr. Hamilton. But my party is facing trouble now, we're between a rock and a hard place. We're where we've got to collect support from our friends."

Stearns was a tired, exhausted, disenchanted politician. He had been a leader of embattled Florida's Reconstruction nightmare. When the state had been put under martial law, arrival of federal troops had prevented the natives from seizing any abandoned Confederate supplies that might have lessened the hardship on them at first. Their lands were confiscated, and though the black freedmen were fed, the ex-rebels were not, and nothing dissuaded the occupation army officials from rounding up any existing cotton stores for personal profit.

Republicans—and Stearns was a party executive—seized control of the legislature and the statehouse as soon as

216

federal martial law was declared. Incumbent officials were arrested and stripped of power, property, and voting rights. Stearns's people convinced the blacks that even one Democratic victory at the polls would immediately reinstate slavery. Republicans were able to control the vote; they registered blacks in three and four counties; where they did lose a close election, their party-appointed judges tossed out election results and declared all Republican candidates elected.

Democrats used terror—fire, whips, guns, knives—to frighten blacks away from the polls. Sumner and Seward, avowed enemies of the former slaveholders, found Floridians "more hostile than they have ever been" and ordered new reprisals.

The Freedmen's Bureau and the Lincoln League were established to promote the interests of blacks. A Freedman's Savings Bank & Trust Company was instituted, with branches at Tallahassee and Jacksonville, but, because of inept and dishonest administration, the Freedman's Bank failed, swallowing up the savings of more than two thousand black depositors. Promised by their Republican Party supporters that "next year" Florida's confiscated lands would be distributed among the freedmen, blacks refused to work, preferring to wait until they were granted property of their own. Conflict between the ignorant, illiterate, and pridefully prejudiced poor whites and the black freedmen kept the state in constant turmoil and seldom free from bloodshed.

Men like Stearns, in an honest attempt to solve a grievous problem, formulated a "Black Code" to protect and at the same time direct and control the illiterate, naive, and gullible blacks. But the code was never enforced.

Ex-Confederates or Florida citizens not proven federal loyalists were prohibited from voting by a Republican-backed "Ironclad Oath" of allegiance which no rebel could take without perjury. Whites were either discouraged from voting, unless they registered Republican, or were disenfranchised.

Stearns grew physically and mentally old in public service, looking, when Ward met him, at least twenty years older than his actual age. He first became governor in 1873 when Ossian Hart died in office. Stearns was elected to the office in 1874, serving as honestly and fairly as pos-

217

sible under existing conditions. He was now realizing that if he lost the next election, he would leave office a comparatively poor man. Many army and state officials were retiring as multimillionaires. There had been a huge cake, and Stearns had helped carve it up. Somehow he had not gotten his share.

There was plenty to age, distract, and disenchant him. Bitterness flared everywhere between carpetbaggers and scalawags—as Southern Republicans or federal sympathizers were called by conservative neighbors—and the defeated natives.

Civil government finally came out of a convention where forty-six Republican delegates were elected, of which eighteen were black and unable to read or write. The rest were carpetbaggers and Southern loyalists.

Republicans under Stearns in the final years of Occupation steadily lost ground, adherents, and voters. Though its top echelon leadership was white, the Republican Party was a black man's party; its existence depended on Negro votes. Negroes crossed county lines to vote repeatedly as directed; the party's strength lay solely in the presence of federal troops. Dishonesty was so rampant in state government that a governor named Reed was brought up for impeachment four times by a legislature dominated and controlled by his own party.

As fewer promises of land and food and instant prosperity were kept, the blacks became restive, aggressive, violent, demanding, and unruly. Many were shot or hung by the very army that only yesterday had vocally supported their goals. Whippings, murders, fires, and intimidation of every kind grew daily more commonplace.

Stearns was physically exhausted and mentally depressed, but he was politically astute. He saw the coming end of Republican rule in Florida when and if President Rutherford Hayes kept his vow to recall the army of occupation from the South early in 1877.

"We're going to need the support of influential men like you, Hamilton," the governor was saying. "Aggressive young men with their roots in the North, who want to build their fortunes here in Florida. I can tell you, things won't be as easy for you railroaders when the Democrats take over again.

218

"We've done everything we could—especially to help you railroad fellows. We Republicans kept the 1855 provision promoting railway construction by exempting railroads from taxes for thirty years. Democratic control would change that, and taxes could swallow you up, I can promise you. They're already talking about a law that says tax exemption applies only to those lines operating under the original 1855 franchises—of which, by now, there are none.

"It's good cracker propaganda. The crackers hate you railroaders because all of you are outlanders; you don't belong here. You're holding huge land grants, sometimes grants for railway extensions that were never completed. Anything that threatens to clip your wings is popular with the cracker vote. They'll tear you down if they can, I promise you that.

"On the other hand, we Republicans have done everything possible to help keep railroads out of the hands of receivers. That makes sense for the state, but it's not popular with the redneck voter. I can tell you, one narrowgauge line from Lake City to Port St. Joe would have gone into receivership without IIF assistance."

Ward recognized Dayton Fredrick's line. Fredrick was in even deeper trouble than he admitted. Loss of even that poor little line might isolate his multimillion-dollar resort, especially if the creditors abandoned the narrow-gauge line, and nothing else made sense. An image of Julia's lovely young face and odd green eyes flashed across his mind, lingering like an afterglow.

"As long as we can," Stearns said, "we're giving land grants to our railroad friends who undertake new territory lines or extensions of older lines. But, under rules being formulated, some lines must be improved or laid down in certain time limits, or the grants are forfeit. Such lines could be reclaimed and auctioned by the state. We're trying to do all we can, but I warn you: time is running out if we don't get a lot of support from people with influence, people like you, who can use pressure to get friends and employees out to vote—and vote right."

"I'm quite willing to support you," Ward said. "But I need help too."

Stearns smiled wryly. "Nothing is ever free, young man. What do you want? And what will it cost me?"

"It won't *cost* you anything. It may save the state hundreds of thousands of dollars. And I know it will buy the kind of support you want from contractors, lumbermen, loggers, and railroaders who would benefit from the plan—anyone who can use convict labor."

Stearns winced and sat back in the chair.

"I know it hasn't been tried enough to be proved," Ward said.

"No. A dangerous thing. Putting those men out working unshackled."

"You can leave those prisoners crowded double-capacity in airless cells, or you can put them out—under guard—and let them work off their hostility. Let them work in the sun ten hours a day. They'll be tired. They won't have energy enough for destructive riots like you had this week."

"What about the guards—where would they come from?" Stearns asked.

"The army can supply guards, the state can supply guards, the employer can supply guards. Whoever does it, it'll be a hell of a lot cheaper than prison uprisings and murders."

"And what do you propose the state will get out of it—monetarily speaking?"

"I'd think the state would be happy to buy safety from prison wreckage and wholesale murder and escape. As for me, I'll be willing to pay the working convict ten cents an hour—a dollar a day—to be placed in his parole fund. Money set aside in his account to help him start out when he's freed from prison."

"I see." The governor still looked less than totally convinced.

Ward said, "And to prove my loyalty and willingness to support you and your administration, I'll pay thirty-five cents per man into the governor's reelection campaign fund."

Stearns swallowed hard and stared out the window. "Is that thirty-five cents *a day* per man?"

"Yes."

Stearns hesitated again. "I hope I didn't hear you right."

Ward's heart sank. Was Stearns going to label his offer bribery and refuse it? Bribery wasn't ever bribery until someone so designated it. It looked like a good deal all around. He could easily afford $1.35 a day for laborers.

He would pay the thirty-five cents into Stearns's campaign fund. What Stearns did with the money was none of Ward's concern. But he saw in that moment that he could lose the project, and no matter what Stearns said against it, it would benefit the prisoners, the prison system, and the state. It could certainly benefit the governor, whether he was reelected or not.

Suddenly Stearns smiled. "I hope I didn't hear you right, Mr. Hamilton," he repeated. "I'd be most disappointed if I did. I do hope I heard you say forty-five cents per man per day."

Ward strode back across the busy street outside the Capitol, exultant. He wanted to yell out his pleasure. He saw his lines repaired, restored, reinforced, lessening any chance of ruinous or costly accidents and derailments. He felt the need to celebrate. He sent off a triumphant telegram to Phillips Clark in Jacksonville, and started walking briskly toward the railway station to buy a ticket on the South Georgia line through Thomasville to Atlanta. But his steps slowed, and he paused, turning back. He was looking forward to dinner tonight with Julia Fredrick and her father. God knew, this made no sense. Despite her surface sophistication and superb development, the child was thirteen years old! But at the moment, *he* made no sense. He was too happy to be totally sane. It would be fun sitting across the table from her, looking at her, listening to her sniping at him, laughing at her. It would be insane, but it would be fun, and he deserved a little pleasure, even if he found it in the company of a penitentiary pullet.

Thinking about Julia, he walked along Adams Street. The moment he entered the Capitol Hotel lobby, he was summoned to the registry desk and handed a telegram, stamped *urgent* in red ink.

He thanked the clerk absently and turned away, opening the yellow envelope. The message was terse: LILY DESPERATELY ILL STOP IN ATLANTA GENERAL HOSPITAL STOP COME AT ONCE STOP C H HARKNESS

Ward wrote out a brief, hasty note of regret, addressed it to Dayton Fredrick, and left it at the Capitol Hotel desk. He was on the first train to Georgia. He sat immobile beside a window, staring unseeingly as the locomotive rumbled through the swamplands. He was troubled by Lily's illness, puzzled and deeply worried, but it was Julia's pixy face and almond-shaped green eyes looking at him from the glass pane beside him as he rode north to Atlanta.

Charles Henry Harkness awaited Ward in the reception room of the Atlanta General Hospital. People walked past them on both sides. Neither man was aware of the movement or the faces around them.

Harkness looked drawn, gray, sleepless, and, somehow, as if he'd slumped inward upon himself. His clothing was rumpled, his tie awry, his gray hair mussed, his mouth pulled down at the corners. His anguished eyes searched Ward's face.

"How is she?" Ward asked. "Can I see her now?"

Harkness winced. "We'd better talk first, my boy." He indicated a small alcove off the larger reception room. Ward was unwilling, but he allowed himself to be convoyed by the slender, limping man into the cubicle where they were alone. The area was furnished with a small, gray, uncomfortable-looking couch, two chairs, and a mismatched table littered with old magazines and newspapers. A large bay window, its drapes drawn back, opened out on the street. Reception room activity was vaguely reflected in the long, dark panes.

"Sit down," Harkness said. "Let's sit down, my boy." But Harkness did not sit down. He and Ward stood facing each other in the dimly lit room. Hospital sounds filtered in around them.

"I should see Lily."

"Yes. Soon."

"How serious is—her illness?"

"It was very serious. Critical. But she appears to be doing better now. The doctors were afraid it would be a breach delivery—"

"Delivery?"

Harkness bit his lip and nodded. "It hasn't been easy. We were afraid we'd lose her—and her baby. Twenty-four hours in labor. . . ."

"Baby? We've been married six months. It must be a miscarriage."

"No."

"Such a premature infant—can it live?"

222

"The doctor says the baby will live, my boy."

"I want to see her."

Harkness shook his head. "You can't see her now. Doctor's orders. I must tell you, my boy—this is not a miscarriage, not a premature fetus. The baby is a full-period—" His voice trailed off.

Ward stared at Lily's father, uncomprehendingly at first. He was numb for a moment, then sickness flushed up through him, as he fully understood. Full-period. Nine months. Longer even than he'd known Lily. He swallowed the bile which gorged up in his throat.

Harkness was unable to meet his gaze. His voice was low, ineffectual. "I'm sorry, my boy, for everything. I am so sorry. I can't tell you how sorry I am."

Ward shook his head. His legs felt weak, his thoughts spun. So much was clear to him that had puzzled and distressed him before. This clarity did not release him, but only added to the confusion and despair roiling inside him. His jaw was tight, his voice barely a hoarse whisper. "When—may I see her?"

"Miz Marcy promised to tell us as soon as it's possible."

Ward nodded. Unalloyed horror oozed through his mind. He walked away from where Harkness stood slump-shouldered. At the window, he stared out into the night street. Labor. Delivery. Full period. He could not see her. It did not matter. He did not want to see her. He didn't want to see anyone. He held down his sickness.

A rustling of petticoats behind him was like a physical threat. He heard Miz Marcy's voice, determinedly cheerful: "It's a little boy, Charles. A fine son, Ward. A beautiful baby, my dear. Lily is—doing quite well."

"I've told him, Mrs. Harkness," Charles Henry said in a low, dead tone.

Ward remained unmoving. He heard Miz Marcy's sharp intake of breath, then the quick rustling of undergarments. She came close to him, standing at his shoulder. She touched his arm, her fingers like steel clamps. In the dark street, horsedrawn carriages moved desultorily.

"You must understand, Ward." Miz Marcy's voice was gentle, with steel in it. "Lily's such a young girl. A child. Inexperienced. Innocent, really—despite everything. You must understand. . . ."

Ward did not move. Miz Marcy's voice trailed off. At

223

last she said, her voice firm and resolute, "Lily is sleeping now. She's had a bad time. Why don't we go to a hotel? We can see her in the morning."

"That will be best. Things will look—better—in the morning," Harkness said.

Ward shook his head. "I'll wait here." His voice was cold, final.

"For what?" Miz Marcy's tone hardened slightly.

He shrugged. "I don't know. You go ahead. I'll wait here."

A long, breathless tension crackled in the small room. Ward remained standing at the window. At last he heard movement, and knew they were gone. When he was certain they were out of the hospital, he went to the desk. "I am Ward Hamilton," he said. "My wife—and baby—are in the maternity ward. I want to see her as soon as I can."

He returned to the alcove, the window, the chair that was like a torture rack, the hoary, unintelligible magazines. The hospital grew quieter as time plodded into the sullen hours before dawn. Lights were dimmed, voices unconsciously lowered, steps slowed. A chill settled, pervading the building. Sometime in the early morning, after daybreak, a nurse led him through the corridors to Lily's room.

She lay pale and enervated, her wan cheeks freshly scrubbed, her dark hair damp and brushed back from her face. She did not flinch under his gaze. She watched him idly, in almost euphoric serenity, detached, obdurate. Whatever he had wanted to say, he saw as useless words. He said only, "Why, Lily? Why? You knew it was Robert's baby."

"Yes."

"You knew you were pregnant—when you married me."

"Yes."

"Why me, Lily? Did you hate me that much?"

"I didn't hate you. I knew what you had done to Robert, but I didn't hate you."

"Then why such a cold and calculating decision?"

Her pale eyes did not blink. He saw the steel structure reinforcing that gentle exterior, the innocent and fragile face, the unyielding spine in that delicate form, the gall boiling beneath that shy smile and honeyed voice. "I knew

224

. . . you were Robert's brother. I knew . . . you'd be very rich. . . ."

"But you didn't give a goddamn what you did to me?"

"I couldn't care." She stared up at him. "I did only what I had to do." Her gaze did not falter. "For the same reason you do all the things you do . . . the very same reason . . . self-preservation. . . ."

BOOK TWO:

BELLE, 1877-1890

Chapter Seventeen

FLORIDA'S RETIRING GOVERNOR, Marcellus L. Stearns, called it, "the most progressive legislative action taken by your government and your legislature since Florida's statehood in 1845."

As soon as the legislature passed, early in its 1877 session, the authorization for leasing of convicts to private enterprise as laborers, Ward made further history by being the first businessman in the state to contract for convict labor.

Neither the people nor the newspaper editors around the state were convinced that putting convicted felons out to work on roads, rails, fields, farms, groves, or in mines was progressive, safe, or in the best interests of the common citizen. Jacksonville *Union* editorials proclaimed: "We'll be watching this latest experiment closely. So closely, in fact, that we may sleep with one eye open from now on, if we're able to sleep at all. By any yardstick, none of us can be safe in our beds. A few guards with guns can easily be overpowered by violent convicts set free in open places, tempted to freedom, with nothing to lose but lives already forfeit by their own heinous crimes against man and property."

In late January, the first freight car departed Tallahassee with a company of prisoners bound to Lake City, to begin work repairing the gradings, creek bridges, roadbeds and railjoints of the New East Florida & Gulf Central Railroad. The editor of the *Ocala Banner* wrote: "This man Hamilton is risking the peace, tranquility, and constitutional rights to security and freedom of all the rest of us in order to harvest the fruits of cheap prison labor. Like so many 'outlanders'—those quick-buck adventurers who invade our lovely homeland seeking fortunes, without that vital obligation to our soil felt by us natives—Hamilton is recklessly thinking only of one thing: profit. The day they set the convicts free in north Florida, at the whim of this Yankee plunderer, may well be the blackest day of infamy in Florida's history."

People stood in sullen silence along the station platforms and trackbeds, watching the first convict train roll slowly east. Each prisoner was wrist-shackled, his chain run through large metal eyebolts embedded in two-by-fours set around the walls. The inmates could sit down on the flooring or stand up, but they had little space to move around, crowded in the cars like cattle.

Most of the prisoners ignored the silent crowds lining the tracks. These men slouched against walls, slumped on the flooring, or stared, through the barred windows in the doorways at the wild country stretching empty and inviting toward the free horizons, looking ahead to the moment when their shackles would be removed at Lake City.

Ward arrived in Lake City a day ahead of the convicts. He was in the station work yard with his employees—flagmen, track walkers, switch tenders, engineers, firemen, brakemen, and dispatchers. Despite the fact that he was delivering thousands of feet of lumber and logs, and tons of naval stores and other materials east to the Third Army construction at Jacksonville, his trains had been set on a new and precisely observed schedule. While the railbeds were being repaired, most trains would run early morning, noon, and late afternoon, with some night trains. The other hours were held open as much as possible, for repair work.

Soon after Governor Stearns assured Ward that the state legislature had agreed that labor might be the physical outlet needed for the pent-up energies of the convicts, Ward began to consider a guard corps of his own to augment the state- and army-furnished prison guards. He wanted a command with the interests of the railroad first in its priorities.

He had only to be reviled, cursed, and otherwise verbally assaulted on Forsythe, Monroe, or Adams Streets in downtown Jacksonville to realize that the convict-leasing program—like all unknown quantities—aroused fear and dread in the minds of the populace: what they didn't know, they feared. What they feared, they opposed.

He found Uzziah Giddings at the same bedraggled fish camp on the St. Johns River where he'd located him a year earlier when he had come south, searching for Robert.

Uzziah smiled and leaped to his feet on the end of the rickety wooden dock where he pole-fished for brim and stumpknockers. "Masta Hamilton. Hit's good to see you, suh."

"You still hiring out as guide, Uzziah?"

"Huntin' guide, fishin' guide, manhunter—it's all the same to me, Masta Hamilton."

"How'd you like to come work for me?"

"What's the mattah, Masta Hamilton? Yore brother broke loose again?"

Ward smiled. "No. He's still in prison. He lost his leg."

"Pore devil." Uzziah shook his head, recalling. "I knowed he'd lose it or die. That leg purely stunk."

"I want to hire you permanently," Ward said.

"I'll take it." Uzziah nodded emphatically.

Ward laughed. "Don't you want to know what the work is?"

Uzziah stood tall, lean, barefooted, squinting against the sun. "Don't matter. Permanent job. I'd likes to try that. Never had one of those in my life, a job where you eat regular and git paid countin' money. Masta Hamilton, you got yourself your man."

Uzziah was with Ward when the convict train pulled into the freight yards at Lake City. Uzziah wore new snakeskin boots, lightweight pants, a denim shirt, and a slouch hat. But most remarkable were the handgun—a Colt .38 holstered at his belt—and the shotgun slung in the crook of his arm. He carried them easily, with an air of authority, a cold sense of danger about him.

Uzziah's presence caused almost as much excitement, dissension, and uneasiness as the arrival of the convicts.

This arrival was an historic moment. Much to Ward's rage, politicians, photographers, reporters, and bleeding hearts from all over the country—people who didn't believe poor convicts should have to work—crowded the area. Only Ward's refusal to permit them aboard the work train kept the large audience from accompanying the prisoners to the labor site. Flash powder exploded as bulky cameras recorded the moment for posterity. Ward moved the convicts quickly aboard the work train, assembling and loading them while cameras clicked, magnesium powder flashed, and politicians pontificated. These people still assembled on the tracks as the train pulled out of the station.

Ward, wearing a wide, flat-brimmed planter's hat against the tyranny of the sun, a denim shirt open at the collar, Levi's, and snake boots, watched nervously as the convicts were unshackled at the specially equipped freight cars and led through the milling crowds to be placed aboard the flatcars for the run to the work site. Two army guards stood at each end of the flatcars, a prison guard on the coal tender, and Uzziah, with Ward, on the caboose.

"Who is this nigger?" The prison official jerked his head toward Uzziah.

"Uzziah is my superintendent of guards," Ward said. "He represents me and the railroad. He'll be in charge of all guards."

"The hell he will. You think my *white* men are gonna take orders from a nigger?"

"They'd better, if they're smart. Maybe they'd like it better if you called Uzziah an Indian—"

"Blackest looking Indian I ever saw."

Ward shrugged. "That's up to you. Uzziah is in charge. I trust Uzziah with my life, my reputation, and my future. I don't know what your guards might do in case of trouble. I *do* know what Uzziah will do."

"Yeah? What's that?"

"What I want him to do."

*　　*　　*

232

Tension crackled in the atmosphere like static electricity
from the moment the yard locomotive halted outside Lake
City and the guards ordered the prisoner work party off
the flatcars.

Uzziah sat implacably atop the caboose, his legs crossed,
his shotgun across his lap. Few of the convicts glanced
toward him. They eyed the nearest guards, sizing them up,
weighing them, considering the firepower and accuracy of
their guns. There was only one thought in the minds of the
prisoners: escape. They saw this as their single opportunity
to lunge into the jungle growth beside the tracks, to run
and keep running. This was their sole chance because this
"noble experiment" was doomed to fail, in this place, at
this time. It would never be repeated.

Picks, shovels, and sledgehammers were handed out.
The prisoners sullenly accepted the work equipment, grinning coldly and knowingly at each other. A heavy pick
driven into the skull of a guard would create diversionary
panic enough to open the way for a total exodus, every
man for himself, running, all in different directions. They
were pleased to see that the prison had not provided a
kennel of bloodhounds.

But the break didn't come off that easily. Ward and his
people had worked out the repair plan carefully, with two
considerations: the work that needed to be done, and the
best way to control the convicts making those repairs.

The work crews were broken down into small squads.
Each squad had its own guards, one on each side of the
rails, standing well aside at the very brink of the swampy
undergrowth, gun across their arms, waiting.

There was no large concentration of prisoners. The convicts swore and worked desultorily, watching each other,
the guards, and the implacable "Indian" perched on the
train caboose.

The Florida sun blazed pitilessly. Two men were felled
by sunstroke and dragged into the shade of the caboose
where they lay only half-conscious. Younger, slighter
prisoners were assigned as waterboys. They ran, water
from creek beds sloshing in their buckets, tin ladles rattling.

It was three hours before the first break came. The convict who broke from the ranks and ran was a black youth,
under twenty. He was lithely built, his sinews corded and

233

glistening in the sun. He dove directly at the nearest guard, grown careless in the enervating, unrelenting heat.

Using his shovel as a staff, the boy caught the guard as he turned and before he could bring the gun up. The shovel's handle caught the guard under the chin, driving him backward and down the embankment. Following the guard, using that momentum, the boy dove outward into the matted morass.

Before the other guard could react, Uzziah leaped up and fired from the top of the caboose. The second guard jerked his gun up, fixed it on the squad, and yelled, "Hold it!"

The squad of prisoners froze. A couple of them had flung their shovels aside. Slowly they retrieved them, making no move that could be misinterpreted.

The young escapee was a flash of glistening brown against the massed elders, willows, bay brush, and vines. Then he was gone, splashing loudly for a moment as he forded a creek. Then there was silence. The convicts all along the tracks howled exultantly. They hadn't executed the mass break they'd envisioned, but one of their kind—the first of them—had made it.

Ward jerked his head and Uzziah descended from the caboose. "Can we trail him?"

Uzziah only nodded. Ward said, "Come on."

They enlisted one army guard and entered the swampy undergrowth. Uzziah, who moved like a panther through the thickening jungle, seemed not to hurry. He found the place where the prisoner had clawed his way out of the creek. Uzziah stood a moment, then strode deeper into the bog. Ward and the guard followed.

They moved steadily into the rain forest. It was breathlessly hot among the scrub trees and vine webbing. Mosquitoes swarmed up around their heads. Wild animals, disturbed, raced in panic across the leaf-piled ground. Birds chattered, screaming from bush and tree.

The three pursuers were less than forty minutes into the sweltering marsh when Uzziah paused and held up his hand, signaling them to stop and remain silent. Holding their breath, they waited.

Uzziah inclined his head toward a spongy hummock. Ward spotted movement, thinking at first it was a cautious, frightened animal. Then the convict limped out, panting. He held both hands high above his head. He was lathered with sweat, mud, and grime, streaked with briar cuts and already swollen about the face and neck with insect bites.

"Don't shoot," he said. His face was contorted with agony, his black eyes white-rimmed with terror. "I was on my way back."

"Rattler got him," Uzziah said over his shoulder. The boy's foot was already swelling badly, turning purple and gray, discolored with poison and crippling with pain.

"All right," Ward said. "We'll take him back. Let's go."

They marched the boy out of the marsh up the side of the rail grading to the rails. The prisoners fell silent and sagged, defeated. They saw the agony, terror, and hopelessness swirling in the captive's face and eyes.

Ward let the whole company see the escapee. He forced them to look, marching the crippled boy along the tracks so they had to observe him. Then he spoke coldly to the guard who'd accompanied him and Uzziah into the morass: "Shoot him."

The guard stared at Ward a moment unbelievingly, then shook his head, retreating a step. "Hell, Mr. Hamilton, we got him back."

Ward's look of contempt raked the guard. "Uzziah," Ward said over his shoulder, "kill him."

"Yes, Masta." Uzziah nodded. The terrorized boy had heard Ward. He shook his head, retreating along the tracks, stumbling, vomitus seeping from the corners of his mouth. Uzziah said to him in a low tone, "You got one chance, boy. Run."

The boy looked around wildly. There was no help for him. He knew he could not escape, but he could not face that gun in the Indian's hands, either. As Uzziah brought the gun up, the youth wheeled around, hobbling, stumbling toward the incline.

Uzziah fired. The sound rattled and reverberated through the swamp. The bullet struck the convict between the shoulder blades, as if his heart were the bright center of a target painted on his bare back. The boy plunged forward on his face. He twitched only once, his whole body wracked in a spasm, then he sagged face-down, arms outflung, dead.

Guards and convicts stood immobile, sick. Far above them, a buzzard circled in the cloudless sky. Within seconds, another black scavenger joined it, circling on the updrafts.

Ward got up on a flatcar.

"All right, you men." He stared unblinkingly down into their faces, raking his gaze across them. "I'm going to tell you now what you can expect. I know you each saw this work party as a chance to run. You've still got that chance. You'll have it every day you work out here. But first, you'd better be warned what you can expect.

"If you run, we'll trail you. If we find you, we'll kill you on the spot. There'll be no trial, no questions, no answers, no chances. We've got only one way to keep order here as we move deeper into unsettled country, and that's by meeting violence with violence. We brought this boy back for one reason—so you men can see what your chances are out there.

"Any one of you who attacks a guard—for any reason—will be shot. We can't take any chances arguing with you about it, and we won't.

"Now that's as straight as I can give it to you. You're all here because you committed some felony. You've forfeited your rights as citizens, but not as human beings. Act like men, and we'll treat you like men.

"If you want to work, you'll be paid ten cents an hour, a dollar a day. That's not much, but it's a hell of a lot more than the nothing you'd collect for sitting cramped in your cells at the state pen. That dollar a day will be credited to your prison account. It'll be there to help you when you've served your time.

"If you work out here, you'll be treated the way you force our guards to treat you. If you decide to work, we're going to feed you well, because we want you healthy. We want you healthy for one reason: so you can work better.

"You'll sleep nights in barred boxcars, on cots, twelve men to a car.

"So that's your choice. You can work well, sleep well, eat well, and get paid, or you can go back to the state pen and rot in a cell. I don't give a damn. The choice is yours."

By now, half a dozen buzzards circled slowly overhead.

* * *

The record-breaking repair of the sixty-odd-mile right-of-way between Lake City and the East Coast made headlines in the state newspapers.

Over the weeks of work, there was a second break. Two men ran while the company of convicts was being shackled after supper for the night. One was found dead, drowned; the other either escaped by swimming the St. Johns River, or he drowned in it. He was never found.

These incidents made headlines too. Ward Hamilton was reviled almost daily in the press, rapidly becoming one of the most despised "outlanders" known to be exploiting, robbing, and endangering the public safety of the state. In Live Oak, he was hanged in effigy.

When the right-of-way was repaired, time remained on his work-lease contract with the state penal system. He kept the company of convicts for another month. These men were put to work sandblasting, scraping, chipping, and finally repainting every piece of NEF&GC rolling stock.

He was alone in his office when Clifford Stone, his male secretary, announced a caller: "A Mr. Gilman Rich, sir."

Ward stared at Gilman Rich as he might gaze for the first time at a sideshow pitchman. In his late forties, Gilman Rich had pinkish-red hair, a sun-leathered face, and the most incredibly brazen and cruel blue eyes Ward had ever encountered. Rich was meticulously dressed in highly polished light tan button shoes, tight-ankled brown trousers, and a hip-length brown jacket sprouting a handkerchief like a wilted flower from its breast pocket. He wore a soiled celluloid collar with a string tie, and carried a brown derby.

"Come to you, Brother Hamilton," Rich said in a sly, boisterous tone, "because I knowed you need me."

Ward smiled, watching the man make himself at home, inspecting the office, taking a cigar from a desk humidor, sitting in a comfortable chair, and pinking his trousers up at his knees. Rich truly looked like a carnival barker.

"What I am is a rumormonger," Rich said, smiling with pride. "I am, sir, a professional slanderer. I slander you and your company for pay. Now, lately, many companies, corporations, and rich individuals like Vanderbilt and Morgan, they've been hiring representatives who improve

237

their shabby images, get them praised and approved in newspapers, and the like."

Rich laughed, nodding. "Well, sir, I don't work like that. I travel about where I think I can do you the most good. Hotels, taverns, barbershops, wherever men gather in towns and cities around the state. At your expense, of course. But my expense account is carefully itemized, every month. And in these places I peddle slighting remarks about you—slander about your company."

"You mean against other competitors, don't you?"

"No, sir. That's the last thing I mean. I never slander no competitor of your'n—'less he pays me better than you do. But whilst I'm in your employ, I'm loyal to you. I peddle rumors and lies only about you. I run you down. I remark how you and your company are in trouble, about to be swallowed up by a competitor who is a lot smarter and a lot richer and a lot sharper in his practices than you. Or maybe I hint how some 'community-minded' huge corporation is going to take you over, merge you right out of business."

"Why would I pay you to do that?"

"To prove you're smart. It's the way business is done these days. 'Specially down here in the South. This here is the land of the underdog, the defeated, the loser. Every man jack you meet is suffering oppression from somebody higher up—the government, the army, the rich, the unfair competition. You know why folks here in Florida hate your guts?"

"Because I'm an outlander."

"No. Because you ain't won their pity, their sympathy. Hell, you ain't even tried. But if I got out and slandered you—first, they'd figure you're gittin' what you deserve. Then they'd feel like maybe you're gittin' a raw deal. That's when I bear down against you. You're all of a sudden just like them, in the same leaky boat. Hell, you ain't a rich outlander no more, you're one of *them*. One of the people. It'll cost you, brother Hamilton, but it'll be the best public relations money you ever spent."

The scraping, cleaning, and repainting of the NEF&GC rolling stock brought Ward directly into confrontation with General Maitland O. White again.

The general glared around Ward's office, overlooking

238

the Jacksonville railyards. "So this is where you hide out?" His voice struck abrasively, clawing like talons.

Ward shrugged. "Functional if not gaudy, General."

"I sent for you, Hamilton. Three times."

"I've been busy."

"You must have known I could have put you under military arrest and had you brought to me in cuffs."

"I knew you *could*. But I didn't think you would. I know you're smarter than that."

"Still an arrogant young bastard, aren't you? Sure of yourself, pulling sharp deals on me and your government, your brother languishing in a federal penitentiary for theft, and you dare to go on brazening out your crimes."

"General, we can spend the rest of the day reviling each other, or we can get down to whatever business you have with me."

"So you didn't think I'd arrest you, eh?"

Ward shrugged the question off. "Why are you here?"

"You damned well know why I am here. First, you compromised the army into allowing you to use its rolling stock. And now I am in the embarrassing and degrading position of looking for almost a hundred missing army flatcars, government property signed out to you. Oh, I could have arrested you, and I warn you—"

"No, General. I warn you. This is March, 1877. The days when the military could arrest, imprison, and execute civilians on whim, prejudice, rumor, suspicion, or lies, are past. Your reign of terror down here is over, and you know it. The whole south is belly-sick of this army of occupation and its rapes and excesses. The stench floats north on every wind. Reaction has set in even among the most rabid rebel-haters up North. You people have gone too far. Old Rutherford Hayes won the election and took office in January because he promised that if the courts awarded him this election, he'd pull you bully-boys out of here. Now he's president, and it's only a matter of time. Meanwhile, you're smart enough to be on your good behavior. No, General, I wasn't worried about your arresting me. Before you came here to my office, or after."

General Maitland White got up and prowled the room, frustrated. "My God, you are *arrogant!* Do you think my weakened position—which is not as weak as you think—

239

would keep from prosecuting your heinous crime against my country?"

"What crime is that, General?"

"Theft of government property."

Ward laughed at him. "Come now, General White. If you even *suspected* me of stealing government property, nothing would stop you from arresting me or even ordering me shot on sight, if I know you as well as I think I do."

"I'm gratified you understand me. I think you also understand why I've delayed arresting you."

"Because I'm the best carrier, at the best rates, the government has dealt with down here? Because you're grateful for the way I've fulfilled my contract for delivery of stores and materials to the new army base, to the letter and well ahead of schedule?"

"You cool son of a bitch. No, I feel no gratitude because you lived up to your contract with the federal government. I expect every contractor to do that. It's part of my job to see that they do."

"Then you feel a warmth toward me for the way I have served—"

"Shit. I feel nothing for you—except outrage. Man, you've stolen almost a hundred flatcars from the U.S. Government. I want them back. I want them back now."

"General, these are serious allegations. And I'll tell you why you haven't arrested me. You could get your beribboned tail in a sling for arresting me falsely. You could get yourself a trial—in civilian court—for false arrest and slander."

"There's almost no way a man could slander a slick operator like you, Hamilton. I didn't arrest you for one reason: I can't find those flatcars."

Ward put his head back laughing. "Now, General. I own seventy-two miles of rail line, sidings, switches, and roadbed. Where in hell could I hide a hundred army-painted, army-serial-numbered, army-stamped flat cars?"

"I don't know. I've had my people and detectives hired by the War Department out looking. We've covered every mile of track controlled by your line. And don't look so goddamn smug. We found flatcars—*more* than a hundred—and almost a hundred have been sanded, painted and any identification marks evidently removed. We

240

know what you've done. But I've been warned that until we can match car serial numbers, we'll have to move slowly against you. But the operative word is 'move,' Hamilton. We will move; we are moving against you. We'll continue to move against you until you're sitting in the cell next to your brother's."

"I appreciate your concern for my comfort and convenience, General. But of the two of us, I think you'll end in prison well ahead of me."

Maitland O. White's face flushed a violent red to the sandy roots of his graying hair. Then his face paled. His eyes glittered and he ground his teeth. "By God, what kind of accusation is this?"

"No accusation at all, General White. A polite and well-intentioned admonition, sir. Perhaps your unfounded suspicions of me are based in your own fears. Eleven years ago, when the army of occupation came in here to the Third Military District, graft, confiscation, and outright theft were recognized as part of the spoils of war. Seizing ten thousand bales of Confederate cotton and disposing of it privately; what the hell, everybody was doing it, eh, General? This was merely a military prerogative. eh, General? And what the hell, even if the government does decide in a different political climate to prosecute, probably the statute of limitations will mitigate in your favor, or maybe the government will allow you to retire quietly, considering its gratitude for your years of service—"

"You young bastard. You can't prove these charges—"

"I *can* prove them, General—with as much ease as you'll ever prove I stole a hundred army flatcars, or even one army flatcar." As if suddenly tiring of this conversation, Ward thumbed through papers carefully filed in a manila folder. He selected a sheet of paper and carelessly flicked it across the desk.

General White hesitated, then took up the paper. He read it slowly, rage boiling up through him. "I've seen this thing, you son of a bitch."

"General, I show you that receipt only as a gesture of friendship. I returned your flatcars. I have your signature on that receipt. You can read it there: 'Maitland O. White, General, U.S.A., per RNK, Major, U.S.A.' Randolph Nye Killian, I believe, your new executive officer

241

succeeding Major Milner, with every privilege to sign receipts and requisitions in your name."

"You've done it again, haven't you?"

"I returned your flatcars, General. There's all the proof I need."

"Where in hell are they?"

"General, you're being facetious, aren't you? You don't really expect me to keep track of army rolling stock after I've returned it and been relieved of responsibility by a receipt over your own authorized signature."

"You're not going to get away with this."

"You should be wondering if *you'll* get away with it, General. This receipt absolves me of all responsibility in the matter. I do suggest, however, that the cars *may* have been shunted onto sidings somewhere in south Georgia. That's where they were—rusting—when I borrowed them over your signature. That's where they'll rust and rot, abandoned when the army pulls out of Georgia. You know the government won't move that rolling stock; it would cost too much. It's not worth it. Abandon it, that's what they did after the war, what they'll do after every war. I can tell you another reason the army won't recover and move those aged flatcars: the gauge on too many railroads is narrow, not standard. There are thousands of miles of less-than-standard-gauge tracks these cars couldn't move on at all; they'll rust and fall apart right where they're abandoned in Georgia."

General White stood up abruptly. "You've got it all figured out, haven't you, Hamilton? I can put through a copy of this receipt. No count will ever be made against it, and you've stolen yourself one hundred army flatcars. That's the way you figure to get away with your theft, isn't it?"

"Accuse me of theft one more time, General, and I'll forget all my respect and admiration for you and your rank. Bring charges against me on the stolen cars in the face of that receipt, and you and Major Killian will sure as hell face trial with me. Only you'll face countercharges of slander, and your credibility is going to be destroyed when you're forced to answer—under oath, General— about ten thousand bales of Confederate cotton diverted—"

"You said it yourself, boy. Even if such charges were

242

ever pressed against me, there would be the statute of limitations. Those charges wouldn't stand up in court."

"Maybe not. But call my bluff, and we'll see. I think we understand each other, sir. My charges may well not stand up in court, but if you're smart enough to be a general, I don't believe you'll want to put it to the test."

Chapter Eighteen

HE RETURNED TO Errigal in April. He had not been back
to the Harkness plantation since Lily's baby was born at
Christmas. He had not wanted to go back there. He was
not ready to face Lily, her family, or himself in that place.
He worked at a feverish pace, trying to stay too tired to
think. He could not look ahead because he could not confront the future yet. He suffered, but his railroad did not.
He invested eighteen and twenty hours a day in the rail
system, and results accrued beyond his wildest hopes. He
found that by working with the farms, industries,
businesses, and communities along the route of his railroad, he could increase traffic, both passenger and freight.
Because the coach road was so poor between Jacksonville
and the Panhandle, most people preferred the trains; they
had ridden them even when, under the old Baxter Marsh
regime, they had been tiring, uncomfortable, off schedule
by hours, and unpleasant. He hired crews of blacks to
wash down his coaches with oversized mops at the end of
each run. All soot, trash, oil, and dirt were polished away
by women working with brooms, strong detergents, and
pine-scented polish. His passenger coaches glowed, the
metalwork shone, and he deepened the padding of all
seats. He avidly sought new ways to improve and upgrade

his cars and service. He poured income from the company back into it.

He found that by encouraging farmers and fruit growers to build and plant along his lines, he insured a growing income. He learned from analysis of traffic that each family lured to his service area was worth two hundred dollars to the company. All of them had to transport worldly belongings on his freight cars; they traveled on his passenger coaches; they shipped via his carriers. He set his people to surveying the land that had been granted to the company for rail extension. He learned that the best packet of land was almost a million acres in the Indian River region along the East Coast. The area itself was swampy in places; sparsely settled, and nowhere near his north central lines. He did hold title to property bordering his railbeds, though not in such vast sections as the Indian River property. Still, he had Phillips Clark incorporate a land development company. He advertised in state and Northern newspapers that he would give one acre free with every five acres of farm, grazing, or grove land bought at two dollars an acre. People arrived with money in their fists and dreams lighting their eyes.

His enthusiasm for opening up new territory was shared by developers all over the state: a Russian named Demens, down in the Tampa area; Henry Plant, who had been developing Florida since his arrival at the end of the Civil War; Dayton Fredrick; Disston; Samuel Swann. The state government entered into these schemes with such alacrity, zeal, and lack of foresight that the state was pushed to the verge of bankruptcy through its unwise guarantees of rail, canal, and ship traffic bonds. Still, it was the government's most pretentious plan of all for developing inland water commerce to save Florida from financial ruin. Hamilton Disston, a Philadelphia saw manufacturer, purchased four million acres of so-called swamp and overflow land at twenty-five cents an acre, and the state, with the million dollars realized in cash from the sale, was able to liquidate the most pressing of its bond defaults. This won release of all public funds tied up in the courts.

Disston's purchase extended from the Gulf across central Florida. Here he dug a network of canals that connected Kissimmee, a railhead in the middle of the state, with the Gulf by way of the Kissimmee River, Lake Okechobee, and the Caloosahatchee River. He was able to bring boats from the Great Lakes via the Mississippi and the Gulf to Kissimmee, which was to be the hub of his waterway empire. He built shipyards and a boiler factory at Kissimmee, but at the same time, Plant was extending his rail lines south across west Florida, so Disston's waterways sagged into abandoned drainage canals.

Plant, the principal owner of the Southern Express Company at Atlanta, purchased small Georgia rail lines gone bankrupt after the war, and extended them like spreading tendrils south across Florida to the Gulf coast. It was Plant's competition that was strangling Dayton Fredrick in the north, and Disston's in the south. But Plant continued to extend lines as long as five thousand acres of land were granted for each mile of railway.

Land bonuses were easily acquired, and traffic in railroad charters enjoying these grants became profitable and competitive. Plant purchased a charter for thirty thousand dollars and, under it, completed his cross-state line from Kissimmee to Tampa, effectively breaking Demens's control and bankrupting Disston. The charter carried a grant of five thousand acres. When Demens's lines failed, Plant acquired them.

Railroad construction effectively discouraged and stalled inland waterways, for a time. But steamboat travel had always been popular in Florida, and after a depressed period, the steamship companies flourished again, becoming formidable freight- and passenger-carrying foes for Ward and other railroaders.

He was driven, with little time to agonize, grieve, regret, lament, or even to plan his personal future beyond what tie to wear with what suit, what to eat for dinner, or what newspaper to bother reading, since most of them had chosen him as a prime target for their spleen and venom. He didn't know why this was. They despised him for coming into Florida, hated him for building a successful line, and could not forgive him a profit. He was no more an outlander than Demens, Plant, or Disston, or even Dayton Fredrick. Yet every progressive action he instituted was labeled further rape by a conscienceless freebooter—and this was on good days. He decided they reviled him because he

246

was only twenty-one. A man could be forgiven many trespasses if only he were too old to enjoy them.

Time worked like aloe on his wounds. He admitted at last that Lily had been as honest in her dealings with him as he had been with her. When he had married her, he had not really loved her—not in the way that love allegedly sanctifies and, as much as possible, secures a marriage. He'd had his own hidden reasons for marrying her, and, as it developed, she had hers for marrying him! He had been stunned and entranced by her frail, unearthly beauty—only to find that she was as untouchable as rare and fragile china. He had wanted her fiercely, but whether he'd honestly loved her or not, he could not say. He had believed she held the key to Robert's stolen money, and this, as much as rampant passion, had convinced him he should marry her without delay.

Robert had stood there between them from the first, and he was still there, like some unseen, unmovable apparition. And now Robert's son was there. Lily had lied to him, deceived him, almost destroyed his manhood. But in many ways, she'd been far more forthright in their relationship than he. She had warned him she was dead inside, but he had not listened, not believed her, not cared. He would bring her alive, make her want him as he wanted her. She had told him she hated the rough and aggressive way he touched her, but he had laughed, thinking it was only part of her coy, Southern belle routine. Well, it hadn't been an act; she had not lied; she had not wanted him to touch her. She had not wanted him to love her at all, physically, and she had told him this. It was only the packaging and the atmosphere that convinced him she was merely tantalizing him.

He felt deceived, betrayed, almost castrated, but it was in his pride where he hurt. She had not dissembled. Lying pallid and exhausted after her baby's birth, she admitted truthfully that she'd acted from one motive, and one alone: self-preservation. She had acted as coldly and deliberately and premeditately to save herself as she believed he behaved in all his relationships with others.

There was one fact that could not be denied, however: they could not go on like this. A decision of some kind had to be resolved, a determination made, a conclusion reached between them. He bought a ticket to Atlanta.

He found a changing world in the Georgia capital. The army of occupation was withdrawing from the South. Rutherford B. Hayes had honored his pre-election vow. The departure of the huge blue army altered and restructured the very face of the city. One would not have believed that so many departments, agencies, branches, offices, and shops could have spread in every direction across the town. As these ancillary stations closed, buildings that had bustled and bristled with activity stood suddenly without tenants. Guards patrolling the streets abruptly vanished and were seen no more. Heavy equipment was convoyed out in mule trains several miles long in brown, unbroken passage, headed north. Everywhere sprouted dunes and hillocks of abandoned equipment and supplies, the ugly residue of conquest. Here and there along the routes of exit, defiant rebel flags appeared and people threw open their windows and banged out "Dixie" on their pianos. On every street corner, blacks stood confused, desolated, lost, betrayed, hungry, and without hope.

No one ran out to meet Ward's rented carriage when he drove into the yard at Errigal. The family appeared silently on the veranda, sedate and somehow tense and warily watchful.

He swung down from the carriage and crossed the veranda, aware that he looked successful in his tailored suit and polished boots. He was still coyote-thin, but he wore the arrogance of authority well.

They greeted him warmly; he was still the son-in-law before the world. And to the Harknesses, this was of utmost importance. Lavinia kissed him lightly, pressing her full breast for an instant against his rigid bicep. Beatrice hugged him briefly and bussed his cheeks with chaste, chilly lips, carefully closed; she may still have believed women became pregnant from kissing with their mouths open, though she was the oldest daughter. Charles Henry appeared genuinely pleased to see him. Harkness's pale eyes filled with tears. By now, Ward knew the aging man was sentimental and wept at poker. Miz Marcy held him tightly in her arms, which, as she did it, was somehow more formal than a handshake. She neither kissed him nor smiled, nor said she was pleased to see him. She did say in a noncommital tone, "You've stayed away so long."

Lily came smiling into his arms. She enclosed him in an embrace, slipping her arms up his back to his shoulders and pulling him down to her as if she had longed hungrily for him. If one hadn't known her better, one might have believed her a sexy little baggage. Ward was neither heartened nor dejected by her welcome. Whatever she did here on the veranda was for public consumption; it had nothing to do with what went on between them in privacy.

Lily took his hand and led him up the wide staircase to the upper floor. Errigal looked brighter and more affluent. He had been sending five hundred dollars a month regularly. The Harkness family had used the money prudently.

Lily did not say she had missed him. For this he was thankful. He didn't want them to start lying, even politely, to each other again. Not now, in the face of all they knew. Once they were alone, she spoke blandly of the things she had been doing, the baby clothes she had sewn, the people who had visited Errigal over the past four months, the parties she'd attended.

"Sounds like you've been quite busy."

"Yes. I try."

One of the many guest rooms had been converted into a nursery, the new center of the house. Aged baby beds and youth furniture had been stripped, restained, and polished. It looked as if the infant received the total attention of every adult on the farm.

Lily stood beside Ward at the baby's bed. She was inches from him, but carefully did not touch him. Ward stared down at the child that might have been his son. The baby looked healthy, if less than robust in coloring. Three new black teenage girls from the sharecropper families had been recruited into the house as full-time servants for the baby.

Smiling proudly, Lily turned back the covers. "He's four months old. Hasn't he grown?" She hesitated. "Well, he has grown. He's gained several pounds. He eats like a little starving rebel soldier."

"He's a beautiful baby."

"Everyone says he has my eyes."

"And my name."

Lily's head came up. Her face taut, she met his gaze, an

odd look shadowing her pale eyes, but without the least display of trepidation or apology. "I've named him Robin."

He winced. Robert was between them as always, more now than ever as Lily cooed over Robert's son. "Robin?"

"Yes. Robin Evan Hamilton. Evan is my mother's family name. Don't you think it's pretty? It fits him exactly. Everybody says that. He just looks like a little Robin Evan Hamilton."

He exhaled, staring down at the baby because there was nowhere else to look. "Have you thought of coming to Jacksonville with me? Or of getting a divorce?"

Her head tilted, erect. "A divorce? Of course I haven't thought of a divorce."

"You might. We do live apart. You have borne another man's child."

"Your brother's son," she replied quietly. "Your brother is in prison, where *you* helped to put him. No, I haven't considered divorce. Robin deserves to live well, cared for as he might have been if Robert had not gone to prison."

"Robert *did* go to prison. You were pregnant when you married me."

She shrugged. "If you wish a divorce, you'll have to get it."

"It isn't done that way—for many reasons. Women get divorces."

"Well, I never will. Never. If you want a divorce, you'll have to sue for it."

"You could end up with nothing."

She shrugged. "That's up to you."

"I might do it. I have grounds—even if I agreed to pay for Robin's support."

She met his gaze unblinkingly. "Try it. You'll have to prove Robin isn't your own son. I won't get a divorce, but I'll contest your getting one. I'll fight you if you try it. You may get it, but I won't help you and I won't stand idly by. You'll have to prove Robin isn't your son. You'll have to destroy him."

"He's a child. He'll live it down, whatever happens. But you'd be truly harmed if you took such action, Lily, have you thought of that? None of your hypocritical friends would even receive you anymore. You'd be a scorned woman."

"Perhaps. But you're the one they'd laugh at."

"What?"

"Do you think they won't laugh at you? The big, masculine, he-man railroad owner. Maybe you're right. I may be reviled in polite society, but you would be ridiculed where it would hurt you most—in your beloved business world."

"You've thought it all out, haven't you?"

"I learned from you. Plan ahead; think of all that might happen, before it can happen."

"And you think I'll go on like this, rather than face ridicule?"

She shrugged again. "That's up to you."

"You're really as hard as nails under that pretty, frail little exterior, aren't you? Don't you love anybody but yourself?"

"Yes. But you put him beyond my reach."

"And I'm to go on paying for it for the rest of my life? Is that the way you figure it?"

"I told you, that's up to you."

"Then you may want to listen to what I have to say. You've been telling me what's to be, what's not to be. I've this to say to you: I don't give a goddamn what people say about me. If I made up my mind to be free, I could live with the ridicule of being the apparent father of another man's git. On the other hand, if I decided to let you play out your pretty little romantic game of living as my beloved wife, then you *would* live as my wife; you'd come to Jacksonville, you'd run my home, you'd be my wife, or you'd go to hell."

Lily moved her slender shoulders in a gesture of complete indifference. "I've realized I might have to come to Jacksonville sometime."

"You *will*, if you expect to remain married to me. Bring whomever you must have—whatever servants. Though I do wish to God you'd get a female maid and stop treating Thetis like one."

"Good Lord." She tossed her head. "I had no idea you cared. Thetis is good—better than any woman—with matching colors, with clothes. He can wash out the most delicate things—"

"Spare me. Just stop treating Thetis like a woman—"

251

Lily stared at him, her eyes glittering. "But poor Thetis *is*—like a woman, much more like a girl than a man."

Ward straightened as if he'd been struck viciously in the solar plexus. He stared at Lily, at the baby, at the rectangle of plantation beyond the open window. Suddenly he nodded and grimaced. Deep inside his mind where Lily couldn't hear him, he raged with abrupt, uncontrollable laughter. He'd always looked on Thetis as a fey, effeminate boy, but it took the fastidious Lily to put the truth in words: Thetis was an active, practicing, unabashed homosexual. This had been his closest tie with Robert. Thetis had loved Robert—more than his own life! Robert had never intimated that Lily shared his secret about the hidden army payroll. A person who loved him more than life itself. Not Lily. Of course, not Lily! Lily was just a woman, and females weren't the final answer to Robert. Lily would provide a shield against exposure, a marriage of convenience, a marriage to protect his reputation while he pursued his true compulsions in secret. No wonder Robert had been so gentle, respectful, and diffident toward Lily. Ward had been blind, but Lily's blindness far outstripped his. The answer to the problem of the stolen gold was so simple it was heartbreaking, and it had been there before him all along. Who had loved Robert more deeply than Thetis?

"Thetis."

Ward entered the kitchen where Thetis sat with the black girls at the pinewood kitchen table. They stopped giggling and whispering, and gaped at Ward blankly when he walked into the room.

"Why, Masta Ward." Thetis leaped to his feet and hurried around the table.

"I want to talk to you, Thetis."

"Certainly, Masta Ward. It is indeed so good to see you."

Thetis followed Ward out the rear door to the darkening yard. They walked together out to where Ward's rented carriage had been parked. Ward said, "Have you been happy here, Thetis?"

"Most happy, Masta Ward. I gits on my knees to thank you."

"Never mind."

252

"Miss Lily been most kind to me, Masta Ward."

"Would you like to go on working for her, living here, eating regularly, being taken care of?"

Thetis looked frightened. His eyes widened and he gazed around in panic. "What's wrong, Masta Ward?"

"Just this. I'm going to ask you some questions, Thetis. If you lie to me, I'm running you off the place tonight. You can fend for yourself—"

"No, Masta, please. I do anything."

"You loved Masta Robert, and Robert loved you too, didn't he?"

"I his slave."

"Yeah. You were also with him when he hid that stolen money. You want to show me where Robert hid that money?"

Thetis sat beside Ward as they drove Ward's rented carriage out of the plantation yard. Thetis motioned him to turn toward Atlanta.

Finding the hidden money was easy after that. Thetis talked softly, hesitantly, as they rode along the red clay road in the deepening dusk. Thetis said that the night Robert came out here to Errigal to see Miss Lily for the last time, Thetis had sat a few yards away in a flower bed. He heard Miss Lily beg Masta Robert to make love to her just once before he ran away. She wanted him to because she loved him so passionately and she would have him as part of her forever, no matter what happened. Thetis didn't say how ardent a lover Robert had proved to be. Obviously, Robert had accomplished the task.

After Robert had walked with Miss Lily back to her front door, it was well after midnight. Robert and Thetis had gotten back in the single-seated runabout and headed back toward Atlanta. The countryside was bristling with army personnel pursuing them. They had the gold in a chest under the seat. When they came to the tall chimney, that single remaining sentinel at the burned-out Curtis mansion, Robert had turned the carriage into the yard through the new stand of trees and abundant second growth.

Thetis helped Ward remove the bricks at the base of the chimney. They pulled out the stout box wrapped carefully

253

in oilcloth. Robert was always meticulous in everything he did. Stupid, but meticulous.

Ward hefted the strongbox, rewrapped in a tarpaulin and secured with chains, onto his desk in his office at Jacksonville. Phillips Clark stared at him incredulously. "So you found Robert's loot?"

Ward opened the box, revealing the stolen gold. "Robert was so damned stupid. Buried this stuff under an old chimney on abandoned property. Suppose kids had dug around there? Suppose somebody wanted some old bricks to build an outhouse? Suppose the land had been sold and building begun on the site—after the chimney was demolished? How many things could have happened to this money in the ten years Robert will be in prison? Hell, the Harkness family wanted me to build Lily a house on the old Curtis place."

"Well, you can afford to now." Clark put his head back, laughing.

"What's the matter with you?"

"Me? Nothing. The irony of this is just so perfect. You *knew* you'd find this money. On the strength of it, you bought a railroad, naval stores, a lumber yard. God knows what all you did, just because you knew you had that money backing you. And now you've finally found it, you don't really need it any more."

"That's why I brought it to you. I want you to buy a hundred thousand shares of NEF&GC stock at par value of one dollar—"

"It's selling right now at five."

"I know that. I have the option of buying stock at par, so I'm buying it. I want it held in Robert's name. In trust."

Now Phillips Clark looked up, staring at Ward as if he'd never seen him before. "I don't believe it. All this time I've been so comfortable, thinking what a conscienceless bastard you are."

"I don't give a damn what you think. I do what I have to do." An image of Lily's face flared behind his eyes. "I do—what*ever* I have to do."

Chapter Nineteen

WARD CROSSED THE rotunda of the Jacksonville terminal and walked down the wide steps onto the depot platform. Boys ran past him selling newspapers, sandwiches, drinks, shoeshines, pennants, and trinkets. Gusts of moist, damp steam flared across him in the hot June night. He watched the train from Atlanta roll slowly into the station. Crowds of people around him laughed and waited, standing on tiptoe, staring into the train cars expectantly. He walked through the knots of people toward the Pullman cars. He could not define his own emotions, which were a mixture of expectancy, hope, and dread. All these months he had wanted Lily with him, hopeful that they could start on a solid, honest basis at last. They could work it out now, or forget it. And he still wanted her, aware as he was of the wide chasm between them, of the constant reminder that Robert's son would be, of the truth that Lily did not love him. He had a single, forlorn hope without much substantiality: perhaps she would come to love him. He still wanted her, even though he could not say why. Perhaps he truly loved her—had loved her from the first—or maybe he hated failure and rejection and destruction of his pride and self-respect; he had to win her affection or he could not live with himself. Whatever the reasons, he perspired as he waited, and he knew this was their last chance together.

He stood outside the Pullman car. He could see Lily and her retinue within the lighted coach. She had not seen him, had not even glanced through the window toward the platform. He watched her searching for misplaced objects, giving orders to her considerate entourage, preparing to detrain. His chest felt tight, as if he had been holding his breath for a long time.

The porters emerged first with Lily's trunks, suitcases, bandboxes, and assorted other baggage, which they stacked on a dolly. Then Thetis stepped from the car, mincing, looking about, troubled. He had never been more than a few miles from Atlanta in his life. A teenaged black girl followed, carefully carrying Robin in a wicker basket. Ward felt a sharply painful twisting in his chest.

Three more black servant girls stepped gingerly onto the platform, their arms loaded, their faces contorted with expectant smiles, ecstatic at the newness of it all, the excitement. Behind them came Miz Marcy, looking gray about the mouth, travel-weary, slightly haggard in a mussed tweed traveling suit and large, velvet-trimmed picture hat. Ward stepped forward to greet her. Miz Marcy sagged against him, putting her arms around him. She did not speak.

Lavinia was next. She wore a pale green traveling suit and a saucy hat that set off her light red hair. She was exhausted, her face pale, her freckles standing in bold relief against her wan cheeks. But like the black servant girls, Lavinia smiled and looked about, interested and expectant, excited. She was not as tall as he remembered, fuller in the breasts, plumper in the hips. It was difficult to believe that a girl who looked like Lavinia, who laughed easily and possessed a wry, happy sense of humor, couldn't find a husband, even in a deprived and depleted land like Georgia.

Lavinia saw Ward standing with her mother pressed exhaustedly against him. She smiled, her face lighting, and put out her hands, running to him. He extended his arm and enclosed her within it. "Well," Lavinia said, "I've come to stay with you."

He grinned at her. "I'm glad."

Her freckled face colored faintly and she pressed closer.

At this moment, Lily stepped down from the Pullman vestibule, the conductor and porter moving to support her elbows. Walking Miz Marcy and Lavinia in his arms, Ward moved forward. Lily formed her lips into a quick kiss, gave him a glance and a brief smile, then looked around worriedly. "Is Robin all right?" she asked.

Lily had come home to Jacksonville.

Three hired hacks conveyed Lily, her servants, her family and belongings into the brightly illumined yard overlooking a bend in the St. Johns River. Ward watched Lily's face in the tonneau of the carriage they shared with Thetis and the black girl who was holding Robin.

Ward gazed in pride at the renovated mansion he had bought for Lily, and, from the corners of his eyes, checked her face for reaction. Her gaze moved across the vast expanse of live oaks, hedges, summer flowers in carefully nurtured beds, and wide, gray-floored verandas that entirely enclosed the ground floor, to the huge windows set across the front, the small balcony on the second story, the old gables, and the high-pitched black cypress roofing. "It's beautiful," Lily said. "Isn't it terribly old?"

"Just old enough to have character. That's what the realtor said."

"Well, I certainly hope so. Old houses are just so hard to keep."

He laughed. "You'll have help, I promise you."

Within the house, in the confusion of settling Robin in his nursery, finding rooms for everybody and matching them with their high-stacked luggage, Ward felt a sense of exultance and warm triumph, surrounded by easy laughter and chatter. This was his home, this was what he wanted; he would *make* it what he wanted. He would make it work.

The black man and his wife whom Ward had hired as housekeepers had the rooms brilliantly lit with gas lamps, and dinner was spread, covered to preserve its heat, on the bowlegged maplewood table in the formal dining room.

The tour of the house was disorganized, haphazard, and often interrupted. It was far less successful than Ward had hoped. Nobody seemed as impressed as he was with the recently installed bathrooms, some of the first in the city. He wanted them to share his sense of pride. He had driven

257

in hired carriages often on lonely Sunday afternoons out here among these fine old homes. He had found this one, vacant and for sale. He had wanted it the first time he saw it. It was beautiful, and held something indefinable of the old South in its graciousness. He felt sure Lily would be at home in it, after Errigal.

He led the entourage through the parlor, pointing out twelve-foot ceilings, six-foot-wide windows, screened, but opening onto the veranda almost like huge glass doors. The oak flooring, newly sanded, stained, and polished, reflected the lights as if they were hundreds of full moons. "No nails, only pegs," Ward swung his arm proudly. "Look at those thick walls, that huge fieldstone fireplace. There are fireplaces in every bedroom and dining room as well."

"Quite a lovely old place," Miz Marcy said.

"It's almost as bare as an old barn," Lily protested. "There's so much to be done."

Ward laughed, nodding. "I thought you'd want that. Decorators and furniture people having been hounding me to let them do the inside of the house for you. I wouldn't let them touch it. I thought you could have fun redecorating, doing whatever you like."

Lily glanced around and shrugged. Miz Marcy said, "Of course. It will give you something to do, Lily, something to think about."

They all heard Lily's sigh, a long, deep exhalation.

On his way to the office, Ward paused in the open doorway of the bedroom he'd shared—in a brittle truce—with Lily for a week.

She stood in front of a full-length mirror, watching the dress being lowered over her head and shoulders by a seamstress and two servant girls. Thetis stood to one side, holding swaths of matching materials draped over his arm. Lily caught a glimpse of Ward in the glass, and gave him a quick smile. "Can't find anything I like," she said. "I'll just have nothing to wear."

"It looks lovely," Ward said.

"This old thing?" Lily pouted, staring at him in the glass. The simple dress, unadorned with lace or ornament, was gathered at the waist, and flowed down over her shoe tops. It was cut daringly low at the bodice. The peach-bloom flesh at Lily's cleavage was tantalizingly suggested more than revealed. But Lily hated it and kept pulling it up. The seamstress said, "It's the latest style this summer, Miz Hamilton."

"I don't care. I won't look disgraceful and half naked just to be in fashion. You can put ruche of some kind across it."

"I'm afraid it would spoil its simplicity, Miz Hamilton."

"Then spoil it." Lily's eyes glittered. "Is this dress for you or for me?"

Ward watched Lily pirouette and preen before the tall mirror. In the week she'd been in Jacksonville, she'd done nothing about redecorating or furnishing the house. She discussed it without interest whenever Miz Marcy or Ward broached the subject. She had increased her wardrobe, keeping two seamstresses busy. Her closets bloomed radiantly with bright new gowns.

"I'll never own enough new dresses," she said. "When I think of the horrible old things I used to have to wear to parties, when I wanted to look my prettiest— I've had to go so long—too long—wearing just any old hand-me-down."

"You always outshone anybody around you," Ward said.

"Did I? Well, I don't ever know how, in those old rags. And now, since the baby, I've gained so much weight. I couldn't wear those old things, even if I wanted to."

Lily and her mother, with Lavinia sitting nearby, smiling wryly, her fingers flying in intricate needlepoint, discussed the housewarming party Lily would give, inviting neighbors from all the fine homes along the winding street. Good Southern families all, Miz Marcy was certain. Ward hoped she would carry out her plans, but she did not. They talked of the party until her mother returned to Errigal after a month, leaving Lavinia as houseguest and companion for Lily.

"I hope you find happiness here in this house," Miz Marcy said to Ward the night before her departure. "I hope you can come to love and accept Robin. He's such a beautiful baby. I'd hate to think—it would make me ill to think—you might hate him, or be cruel?"

Ward laughed, shaking his head. "Why would I hate a baby? I'm not fool enough to blame a baby for anything."

Miz Marcy exhaled and smiled. "You'll come to love Robin, if you'll let yourself. A baby brings its own love."

They saw Miz Marcy off on the Atlanta train and returned home in silence. Lily cried, her head bowed in her hands. Ward tried to comfort her as the carriage rattled through the night streets, but she withdrew just far enough to warn him she didn't want him to touch her, even in compassion. "She'll be all right," Lavinia said. "She's a Harkness. They're all weak-hearted; they cry over broken eggs and spilt milk."

"Oh, La, for heaven's sake, shut up. You rattle like a broken cup."

Lavinia laughed and shrugged. "Well, at least you stopped crying."

With spirits of camphor dampening a small kerchief pressed under her nostrils, Lily went upstairs to bed as soon as they reached home. La and Ward sat awhile in the parlor. Lavinia took up her needlework. Ward tried to concentrate on the *Times-Union*. He was aware of Lavinia's gaze falling intermittently upon him, as she glanced up under long lashes from her needlework; he noted the heightened color of her cheeks. The house settled into quiet, the silence pressing in from darkened corners. Distantly, one of the black girls sang softly to herself as she worked over an ironing board in the kitchen; the baby whimpered once and someone went running along the wide upper hallway. The stillness deepened.

In her bedroom, Lily sniffled, shook away tears, and felt her eyes brim again as she undressed and prepared for bed. She sat before her vanity mirror, brushing her hair in long, untiring strokes. She would miss her mother, but her grief went deeper even than that. Something ended and something new began with her mother's departure. As long as her mother had been here, she too had felt almost a guest, transient, not really belonging. This was her home now, her own house. Her mother's leaving underlined the fact that she had to make a new life in this strange and empty place.

Trembling, she looked back across those nostalgic terraces of her girlhood. All that was gone. She was an old married woman now, gaining weight, losing that wasplike waist she'd been so proud of. It didn't matter how little she ate—and most of the time she wanted nothing at all, subsisting on black coffee—her waist expanded. Everything was an omen, a foreshadowing, a sign that her old life had ended and she could look ahead only to emptiness.

She slipped her nightgown down over her shoulders and then removed her underthings. She saw that Thetis had left a glass of milk on her bedside table and turned back the covers on her bed. Dear Thetis! How happy she could have been if only life had not turned out so evilly for her—she and Robert, even in a cottage somewhere, perhaps with Thetis and a cook-housekeeper as their only servants. How happy she could have been!

She sat on the side of the bed and pushed off her slippers with her toes as she sipped the fresh milk. Thank God it was cold. Ice made such a difference. But she could not drink it. Her eyes filled with tears and a lump ached in her throat.

She set the milk aside and lay down, then reached out and extinguished the gas lamp. The room settled slowly into purple-misted darkness. She lay still, breathing raggedly. Sometimes, alone like this, and without hope, she hated Robert as much as she could ever hate him. He had left her to dream backward from emptiness. For this, she could not forgive him.

She could not forget him, either. Lying beside Ward at night, she dreamed of the life she might have had with Robert, a life spent in rapturous kisses and gentle, tantalizing caresses which led nowhere—because this was what they wanted. A life in which the ugly sexuality she suffered at Ward's hands was unheard of, undreamed of, unwanted, not tolerated or even considered.

She tried to recapture the sensual delight she'd known those summer evenings with Robert, the delicious sensations in her breasts, the sweet ache of her nipples, the gently rising warmth at her thighs. When Robert had touched her, she had responded, quivering with delight, satisfied with his touch, wanting no more. The anticipation was beautiful, the rest ugly and sinful and bestial. She and Robert had agreed about this. They had agreed about everything. They had been ideal together! Clean and beautiful and ideal, and ideally happy.

Lily tried to recapture those old, pleasant, lost fantasies about Robert. Once they'd been vivid, bold, exhilarating. Her mind and body had quivered in anticipation of his gentle, undemanding touch. But her images of Robert faded, the sight and physical presence of Ward came between them in a frightening way. She lay panting, trying to get a full breath of air, feeling stifled.

She gasped for breath, her lungs aching, oxygen-starved. At first she had tried to find Robert in Ward, but instead she found only the differences. Where Robert was soft and gentle and diffident, Ward was heat and fire and laughter. Where Robert was as calm and certain as the stars and moon, Ward was fierce and hard-muscled and demanding. She lay beside Ward and sought desperately for Robert, but never found a trace of him, finding only the truth that the brothers were as unlike as human beings could be— poles apart, light and dark, sunshine and rain, love and hatred, good and evil.

She rolled her head back and forth, unable to breathe naturally. Frightened, she opened her mouth wide, sucking in draughts of air. Wind rustled the live oak leaves beyond her window, but her room was breathless, stifling. She pressed her hand over her throat, biting her underlip to keep from crying out in terror.

Ward said goodnight to Lavinia. As she had done every night since her arrival, she turned up her lips to be kissed. But there was somehow an undefinable difference in the atmosphere: the silence, her mother's departure, the sense that somehow this was to be the pattern for existence in this old house. "You go on up," La said. "I'll turn off the lights. I'm not sleepy."

Ward climbed the stairs and went along the cavernous upper corridor. In the dressing room beside the master bedroom, he undressed and got ready for bed. The house sank into tomblike silence. He paused beside the bed, looking down at Lily. She was already asleep, breathing regularly. God, how he wished he could plunge into unconsciousness like that, never thinking about sex, never needing any physical or mental release from his persistent sexual hungers. Jesus, how he envied her. How he pitied her.

He lay down beside her, empty-bellied with unappeased needs. He was aware of Lily beside him—her fragile, lovely, ethereal body, the unawakened passions that he believed waited inside her. He did not touch her. He did not care to be rejected one more time.

He kept telling himself he had to give her time, but in these first weeks there had been no hint that things would ever improve between them. The hell of it was, he and Lily had no common interests outside the bedroom, and none in here at all. He felt he was drowning in the shallows of her mind.

He didn't know how long he lay there, sleepless, his mind grinding around the same old treadmill: the problems at the office, the emptiness in this house, the unchanging time stretching ahead.

Suddenly, Lily gasped aloud, as if unable to breathe. She lunged up in bed, screaming.

Ward sat up and caught her in his arms. "Lily, what is it? What's the matter?"

She could barely speak. She shook her head, stretching her neck, gasping, her mouth parted wide, almost like a fish suffocating out of water. Her eyes swirled in panic. "No. Let me alone. I can't breathe. I can't breathe in here. I'm suffocating. . . ."

Lights flared on all over the big old house. Ward got out of bed, lighted the lamp, and yelled for Thetis. Thetis dressed and ran from the house to fetch the nearest doctor.

Lavinia came into the bedroom, her red hair plaited in braids along each side of her head, her bathrobe old and ill-fitting, caught at the waist with a frayed rope belt. She poured camphor on a cloth and held it under Lily's nose. "She'll be all right," La said over her shoulder to Ward. To Lily she said in a flat, unemotional tone, "You'll be all right."

Lily clung to her sister, breathing in spasms through her open lips.

"Has she ever done this before?" Ward said.

La glanced at him across her shoulder. She shook her head, her braids flopping. "No." La smiled faintly. "No. This is new."

"Damn you, La," Lily gasped. "I'm suffocating, and you make jokes."

"You're dying," La said. "I'm not."

Lily breathed spasmodically, raspingly. Her face was deathly pale. She stared at Lavinia, hating her, her head swimming crazily. "Oh God," she whispered, wheezing. "Where is the doctor? Where is he?"

Dr. Benson Dame had dressed hurriedly, leaving his shoes unlaced, without stockings, his fly haphazardly buttoned, a mismatched jacket over his pajama shirt. He was a slender man in his forties, his graying hair thinning and mussed. Lily lay wide-eyed on her pillow, her wan cheeks rigid, breathing raggedly.

La, Thetis, and Ward stood around the bed, watching helplessly. The doctor listened for a long time at Lily's chest with a cone-shaped stethoscope. He pulled down her eyelids, checked her eyes, and took her pulse. Then he straightened, turned, and faced Ward. "In a way, Mrs. Hamilton's illness is not serious or unusual. In a way it can be quite serious. It's all in the way it is treated."

"We'll do whatever we can," Ward said.

"Of course you will." There was something odd in the doctor's face and voice, as if he were leaving much more unsaid than he put into words. His voice was quiet and serious, but a strange light twinkled in his eyes. "Of course you will."

Dr. Dame took two white pills from his black medical kit. A servant girl brought a glass of water. "Take these, Mrs. Hamilton," Dr. Dame said in a concerned, gentle tone. "These should quiet your palpitations, soothe your vapors, and help you breathe much easier. You should feel immensely improved, very soon now."

"I can't breathe. I can't get my breath in this room."

"You'll be all right, Mrs. Hamilton." Dr. Dame straightened and again faced Ward, his face oddly twisted. "I think it would be better if Mrs. Hamilton slept in another bedroom tonight, perhaps for the next few nights."

"What's the matter?" Ward said.

Dr. Dame shrugged. "There's no medical term for her malaise, not at this time. At least, none I know. Many women—many wives—suffer, as she is suffering right now. And it's quite real, I assure you. A tightness in the chest, oxygen starvation, a sense of suffocation." Again, that odd, unexplained glance. "Informally, I call the condition 'the vapors.' Your wife is suffering the vapors; she's unable to get a full breath of air in this room. She feels she is stifling, suffocated, sharing this bed. It is as if, for her, there is not enough oxygen in this room for two. Do you understand?"

Ward did not speak; he understood nothing.

Dr. Dame's voice was soothing. "You're not to worry about Mrs. Hamilton. This would be the worst thing you could do. She should soon be her old self. A room of her own will give her a sense of openness, you understand? Space to breathe, that's what she needs right now. The two of you can determine when she should move back in here, do you understand?"

Ward lifted Lily in his arms and carried her across the threshold from his bedroom. This somehow seemed far more meaningful than the night when he had carried her across the threshold into their room at the St. James Hotel.

He laid her down on a guest room bed. Dr. Dame opened a couple of windows a few inches. Flimsy curtains stirred, billowing in the night wind. Lily lay on the bed, relaxing, breathing deeply.

"There," Dr. Dame said. "She's feeling better already." He touched Lily's forehead gently with the backs of his fingers. "The medicine is taking effect already, isn't it, my dear?"

"Yes," Lily whispered. "Yes. I do feel better."

Ward and Lavinia walked down the stairs with the doctor. Ward offered him a drink of bourbon against the night air, but Dr. Dame only smiled at him and shook his head. "I wouldn't want any stimulant at this hour, my boy. My wife suffers the vapors, too. You understand?"

Puzzled, Ward heard Lavinia's appreciative laughter at his side, but he did not look at her. She insisted he return upstairs, and she went about turning off lights and the aging house settled into quiet before Ward reached the head of the stairway.

He paused, glancing toward the closed door of the guest room where Lily would spend the night. He moved toward his room, paused, then, troubled about her, turned and walked to the guest room. He touched the knob. The door was locked. He felt as if he had been struck in the groin.

He sagged for a moment against the doorjamb, wincing, seeing the image of Dr. Dame's oddly smiling face and hearing that strange, concerned, mocking voice asking, "You understand?"

Lily was still asleep when Ward left for the office the next morning. Lavinia, somehow faintly bleary-eyed, sat across the breakfast table from him. "Don't worry about Lily," La said. "We'll take care of her."

Going to work was almost an escape for Ward. Here he could plunge over his head into business problems and never come up for a breath. Things were moving at a breathless pace and he had to struggle to keep abreast of the complexities of running even a seventy-two-mile rail company. Phillips Clark had determined that NEF&GC would operate more securely if it were an incorporated entity, and he and his corps of railroad lawyers were drawing up papers of incorporation. Ward was less than certain whether he understood exactly what Clark was attempting to accomplish, but he trusted him. Clark also outlined a plan for him that would provide expansion and operating capital without endangering their personal holdings or company grosses. He was working out a bond issue he hoped Ward could present on Wall Street. "We can use other people's money much more freely," Clark told him, "and there's a hell of a lot more of it."

Several times a week, Ward took a break from his business pressures by having his shoes shined by a small black boy. While the boy worked, Ward amused himself by listening to Uzziah Gidding's simple, unadorned tales of his experiences and adventures as head of Ward's railroad detectives. Mostly, Uzziah simply heaved fugitives and hoboes off freight cars.

It was a rainy summer of hot, humid mornings followed by overwhelming thunderstorms in the afternoons and nights. Uzziah found this violent shattering of lightning a sure sign of a disastrous hurricane season. "Herons flying in from the coastline," he said, "and sea gulls in salt flats far away from the ocean. Lots of signs."

One morning, Clifford Stone announced Dayton Fredrick and his daughter. Ward stood up and came around his desk to greet them. Like Uzziah with his hurricane omens, Ward read signs of Dayton Fredrick's failing fortunes. Dayton's suits were no longer well-tailored, no longer quite impeccable, his mustache not as neatly trimmed, his hands less frequently manicured, his hair a little too long at his collar, his shoes showing scuffmarks. But the most certain sign of all was the elegant appearance of fourteen-year-old Julia. Her suit was the latest fashion from Fifth Avenue; whatever Dayton denied himself, he lavished on his daughter.

"You're looking more beautiful than ever," Julia told Ward. "Are you beating the women off with sticks? Or are you being faithful to that li'l ol' Southern belle? Did you ever get her away from Atlanta?"

Ward laughed. "Your father's going to have to send you off to finishing school to learn some manners. Either that, or a good reformatory, whichever comes first."

Julia smiled tightly. "Reformatory suggests reforming. I'm simply not interested." She held up her left hand, a diamond glittering almost vulgarly on her fourth finger.

"You? Engaged?"

"Again." Dayton laughed indulgently. "Julia is always engaged. While other girls her age are just outgrowing doll collections, Julia collects men."

"Men?"

"Vincent is thirty-five," Julia said. "I like older men; they're the best kind. They're not stupid. You don't have to teach them everything."

"Don't pay any attention to her," Dayton said, smiling. "She's only trying to shock you. I ran out of shock a long time ago. She can't impress me anymore. I keep telling her, she's still a little girl, no matter what games she plays."

"That's the trouble with you, Daddy. And with your great and good friend Mr. Hamilton. Both of you are so hopelessly old-fashioned. Neither of you can realize this is 1877. A woman of twenty can be a child, and stay a child forever, while a girl of fourteen may already be mature. I had to mature early, Mr. Hamilton. I had to look after my father. He's very choosy and intelligent about women. He won't have anything to do with them unless they're females. You know? I've had to pull *his* chestnuts out of the fire more than once, if you know what I mean."

"I hope I don't," Ward said.

Dayton sighed exaggeratedly. "Julia's on her way to Newport to spend the summer, thank God."

"I'm meeting Vincent's family. He's a multimillionaire in shipping and oil. He could save Daddy's skin, if Daddy would only let him."

"I don't trust him," Dayton said matter-of-factly.

"Yet you're going to let your daughter spend the summer with him?"

"It's far easier than opposing her. And why not? He's got a thirty-room villa on the Sound, with dozens of servants. His house is overrun with family and guests. Julia will fall in love with half of the male guests this summer. Vincent will age desperately between now and September, while I shall recover from my winter with her. Oh, I trust Vincent with my daughter, but not with my money."

"If you're not smarter than Vincent about money," Julia said, "I pity you, Daddy. I truly pity you."

"Let's not argue about this in front of Mr. Hamilton, pet. He's too busy—"

"No, I love it." Ward grinned. "Go right ahead."

"Vincent would buy into the Biltmore," Julia said. "Probably for enough to liquidate most of Daddy's pressing debts. He wants to buy into the hotel and the racetrack. His advisers have agreed. But Daddy won't let him."

"A man with as much money as Vincent has, just to speculate with, doesn't have to be smart, pet," Dayton said. "He can cover his mistakes with more money. He overwhelms you with money. I'm so damned near overwhelmed now, I don't need Vincent on my back."

"Having problems with your Lake City-St. Joe line?" Ward asked.

"Of course not," Julia said.

"Of course I am," Dayton said.

"Thanks to you, Mr. Hamilton," Julia added, her voice slashing.

Dayton sighed. "I'm being pressured by Plant to sell out to him or be run out. The Internal Improvement Fund people are on my tail. Yes, it looks like the line will go into receivership despite hell."

"Thanks to you, Mr. Hamilton," Julia repeated in that flint-hard voice.

Ward drew a deep breath. "I'd like to buy it from you. I'd like to have you go on running it for me."

"No. Thanks, but no." Dayton shook his head. "I'm getting out of railroading in Florida. I'm too young to die like this."

Julia was holding her breath. Her face flushed red. "Why don't you tell this pirate the truth?" she burst out. She shook her head and her gaze impaled him, driven into him like the spikes securing the rails of her father's line. "You've already stolen everything from my father that you're going to steal, you thief. If you hadn't stolen this line from him, he wouldn't be in any trouble now." Her face was pale. "I won't stay in this room with this son of a bitch, Daddy. You can be friendly, if you can stomach him. I never will. He robbed us. He hurt you. And he can go to hell." She strode toward the door and paused, then whirled around, her odd green eyes blazing. "But I can tell you this, Mr. Hamilton. We'll see you in hell before Daddy sells out the St. Joe line to you, you thieving bastard."

She walked out and slammed the door behind her. Dayton winced and tried to smile. "Maybe a summer among the very rich might have a tranquilizing effect on her. God knows, I hope so. I'd better go, Ward. She'll never forgive me."

"Looks like she'll never forgive me, either."

"No, it looks like she won't." Dayton hesitated and drew a deep breath. "The St. Joe line is going into receivership, Ward. I'm telling you in advance. Despite Julia's hatred, I'd rather see you get it than Henry Plant. The first thing Henry'd do is abandon the branch into St. Joe. I know that. He'd hook up the mainline with his west coast line into Tampa. Without the spur line into St. Joe, that would truly be the end—for the town and for the Biltmore."

"How was your season?"

"At the hotel? Very fair to pretty good. Sixty or seventy percent of capacity, though we claimed eighty percent. We didn't go in the red this winter. The hotel carried itself; it just couldn't carry me too. Wealthy clientele this year, for the racing season. People like Vincent Herriman. Money. Gamblers. We got by." Fredrick smiled, shook hands, and turned toward the door. Then he wheeled around and came back, and Ward learned the true motive for this visit. They had not dropped by for a courtesy call on the way north to Newport. "I need a little help, Ward. As you

269

can imagine, I'm fresh out of bank credit. They're all pushing me, all wanting their money. I've nowhere to turn. I've heard how well you're doing, and I hoped you could help me—just temporarily, of course."

"What do you need?"

"Not much." Dayton gave him that old go-to-hell grin. The man had more appeal than a roomful of stage stars. "Hell, I used to gamble away more than that in a couple of nights. But I am being pushed. If I can just pay off interest, I can hold them off. I only need enough to satisfy the wolves for the rest of the month, then I'll get a break, find some capital."

"How much?"

"I could give you a note on the St. Joe line. There are liens against it, but your note would give you some priority, some leverage in dealing with Plant and the IIF if you decide—"

"How much?"

"Hell, nothing really. Such a puny amount, I'm ashamed to have to ask for it like this, but if you could let me have forty-three thousand, Ward, it would tide me over and get me through this goddamn summer."

Ward stood at the large window and stared down at the open carriage before the building entrance. Julia stood tensely beside it, awaiting her father. After a few moments, Dayton crossed the walk to her. From where he stood, Ward could see the new spring in Dayton's step. The end had been postponed for another month. He tried to help Julia into the carriage, but she pulled away savagely. They stood arguing fiercely but quietly, two small creatures far below on the sunstruck street. Dayton put his arm about Julia and kissed her cheek gently. Julia touched his face, stroking it lightly. They got into the carriage together, holding hands like children in an unreal world. The hack rattled away along the red brick street. Ward's eyes burned and he couldn't say why. He felt a sense of emptiness, a terrible foreboding that he could not explain and that would not release him.

Ward went up to bed at ten o'clock that night. He sagged with an exhaustion which had nothing to do with physical weariness. He was emotionally fatigued, tired and empty and troubled without knowing why. He'd tried to read the *Times-Union* but found nothing to hold his attention. La sat quietly with her needlework in a club chair under a fat-shaded gas lamp. She did not attempt to make conversation, nor demand it from him. For this he blessed her. When he said good night, she reached out her hand, pulling him down for a quick, smiling kiss. Her mouth felt heated and tasted good. Jesus, he was starving. . . .

He walked tiredly up the wide staircase. Lily's bedroom door was closed. He touched the knob because he could not resist. He found it locked, as he'd known it would be. This was Lily's bedroom from now on; he could resign himself to this.

He went into his own bedroom, undressed, and put on pajamas. He turned down the lamp beside his bed, but was not sleepy. From a bookshelf he selected a book by John Locke, pulled a chair near the bedside table, and turned up the lamp. He tried to read but could not concentrate. He dropped the book to the floor, put his head back, and stared unseeingly at the remote ceiling. His eyes burned.

"Ward."

He sat up, startled. He'd heard nothing, not even the door being opened and closed and locked.

Lavinia stood in front of him, her face flushed. Looking at her, he felt his heart sink.

Lavinia wore a flannel bathrobe, pinned with an ornamental stickpin at the base of her throat. Standing before him without speaking, breathing through parted lips, she reached up and loosened the gem-studded fastener. The robe fell open. She was naked beneath it.

Ward felt excitement flare upward from his groin. He *was* starved. La's pink-fleshed, freckle-flecked body was lovely, full, and taut in the breasts, her belly round and supple above the triangle of red-tinted hair at the mound rising between her thighs.

"I waited for you to come to me," she whispered breathlessly, quivering as if chilled. "You didn't come."

"La, you know I couldn't."

"Why couldn't you?"

"You're my wife's sister."

"We both know what Lily is; she's a fool. She always has been, always will be. I know her door is locked against

271

you. I know why she has 'vapors' when she has to sleep in your bed. I know Lily is no wife to you."

La shook free of her robe, let it fall about her feet. Naked, she stood before him self-consciously, but driven by desire, her hips quivering, her hands stroking upward beneath her full, high-standing breasts, and the heat of her desire was boiling his blood, too. "I've always wanted you," she whispered, "since the first time I saw you. You walked up on that veranda and I went all weak and hot inside. I wanted you desperately, passionately; I knew you were nothing like Robert, all milk and whey inside. He was perfect for Lily—they were perfect for each other. But you were alive, vital, burning, like I was, if only I could make you know."

"La. My God. You're a guest in my house. Don't. We can't do this."

"Didn't you know how I felt? Didn't you *want* me to come and stay here with you? You asked me to come. You asked for *me*. Oh, I know what you said; you said *one* of Lily's sisters should come and stay with her, but we all knew Beatrice wouldn't come. I knew what you meant. I knew you wanted me, I knew. The moment you said it, I went all hot and wild, knowing I was coming here to you."

"Jesus, La, I'm sorry. Truly sorry."

"Why?"

He stared around helplessly, pulling his gaze away from her naked, anguished body, writhing and burning with desire for him. He could feel the fever rising from her. But they couldn't do this in the same house with Lily. God knew, he had little chance with Lily now. They might not make it under the best of conditions. They never would if he gave in now to Lavinia's fevered offering. And he felt himself weakening.

He grew rigid, knowing that La was staring down at his rigidity upthrust beneath the cotton fabric of his pajamas, massively outlined against the cloth. Breathing loudly, La sank to her knees between his legs, her gaze fixed on his brawny staff. He sat still, afraid to touch her, even to restrain her, for fear he would caress and fondle her feverish body mindlessly, as she willed him to.

He felt her faced pressed against him, her breath across her parted lips hot and moist upon his glans. "Oh no, La. God no, don't do that."

272

"I want to nurse it," she whispered, talking ͅ
throbbing hardness. "I've dreamed of it. Lying ͅ
there, I've dreamed of going down on my knees
like this, taking you in my mouth, tasting you, ͅ
you. Oh God, Ward. It's all I want, all I'll ever want.'

He caught her head in his hands, just above his tower-
ing column, her hot, wet breath enflaming his whole body.
"Let me suck it," she pleaded. "Let me show you how
wild I am for you. I'll do anything for you. Anything. I'll
be where you need me, Ward—any time—for anything.
Use me any way you like, as much as you like. I live only
to please you."

Her hands jerked away the restraining fabric and she
pressed her mouth against his inflexible erection, sucking
fiercely, her hands fondling, loving, hefting, caressing,
massaging, as she must have done in a thousand fiery fantasies. He tried to lift her away, and could not. She clung
to him, closing her mouth against him. His hands
tightened on the sides of her head, caught her ears in a
vicelike grip. She drove herself frantically upon him. But
even in his most mindless moment, thrusting himself up to
her ministrations, he knew he had to keep her away, he
could not get involved unless he wanted to throw over everything else. He had to tell her, he had to. She would not
understand. She would know only that she was rejected.
She would hate him, she would never forgive him. He put
his head back. He would tell her. But not now. Oh God,
not now.

Chapter Twenty

THE DISASTROUS HURRICANE predicted by Uzziah Giddings struck in September of that year.

The hundred-mile-an-hour winds and rain struck without logic, killing and destroying in casual passing, as insane as warfare or pestilence. There had to be some kind of cosmic reasoning behind the forces of nature, even the inhumanity of war waged by one human being against another, but Ward failed to find it.

Perhaps he could more placidly have accepted an unknown, unknowable will behind these mad and fearful forces, but his own existence seemed pointless and his rage burgeoned through a miserable summer until he felt as if he could no longer contain his inner storm; he found insanity and stupidity and mendacity everywhere, and when the hurricane struck, it was the final unspeakable outrage.

This inexplicable and uncontrollable force seemed to mirror the design and actuality of his own being. He had every reason to be exultant. He had wanted to accomplish and achieve domain in railroading; he was succeeding beyond his wildest fantasy. But he found himself far less than satisfied; his mood wavered between savage mordancy and black melancholy. He knew why he felt as he did, but what he didn't know was how to solve his problem. Like cancerous growth, it rendered him depressed and seething with inner malevolence in the face of fantastic successes with everything he touched in industry.

Perhaps it was the weather. The days vacillated between driving storms, with earth-quavering thunder and dazzling lightning, and unyieldingly sticky heat and humidity. People said they'd never seen it so hot before; it had never rained so incessantly in any summer of their memory; never had it been so humid without relief.

He searched for changes in Lily, but found none that was favorable, at least not in her attitude toward him and their deteriorating marriage. She seemed not to care where he went, when he came in, or what he did, as long as he didn't intrude into the sphere of her narrow existence. She went from hair and beauty treatments to new seamstresses who labored diligently to please her and, in the end, failed. He waited for her to express an interest in decorating the old house. She asked for a piano. When it was delivered, she ordered it set up in the music room, and spent hours playing it, lost in reverie.

Her bedroom door remained locked against him. And now there were *two* doors locked in the old house, as in some grim comedy—his and Lily's.

Locking his door against Lavinia's mouth and nakedness and flailing hips and soft hands was the single most difficult discipline he ever accomplished. That night with her when she first came to his room, naked under her robe, quivering with desire, had ended at eight o'clock the next morning when he had reluctantly forced himself to leave Lavinia's arms and lips and thighs after an incredible, wanton, and memorable adventure that aroused him even in recall. La had not lied. She had wanted whatever he wanted, often before he knew he wanted it; she had lain herself out to be used in every conceivable fashion. He could not believe that Lily's sister, reared on the same farm, could know or even suspect the sensual patterns of behavior she displayed for him. How could she even know of them? The soft, shy laughter, the lowered eyes, the direct, bared glance meeting his gaze, movements that in themselves were aphrodisiacs—she had listened, in the whispered gossip of women, to all the forbidden "crimes" committed against females by their lovers or husbands,

275

and in those "crimes" she found her passions, her fantasies, and her orgiastic dreams.

Her very vulnerability, her inner desire to be pleasurably misused, was a challenge in itself; he found himself putting into practice the wild sensual exercises Phillips Clark related after his visits to Bay Street. Whatever he did to her, La accepted heatedly. Possessing her fevered body was like acting out all the repressed fantasies that wheeled in delicious depravity in the back rooms of his mind, but which he had stored away as fantasy. It all became fevered, mind-boggling reality with La. It was like having all the wonders of Phillips Clark's Bay Street brothels in the privacy and convenience of his own home.

It had been too good to be true; and yet it was true. He did not know what gods he had pleased with what actions in his life, but he would gladly have burned incense in thanksgiving to those deities of forbidden pleasures.

But it could not be. The next day, he invited La downtown to have lunch with him. He wanted her in a public place where she would have to restrain her impulses. He would have to talk quietly and sensibly to her, and she would have to listen. But she didn't listen. She didn't hear him. She believed that whatever he was saying, he was saying from a sense of duty, and didn't really mean it. Sitting across the table from him in the St. James Hotel dining room, her breath quickened; she kept dampening her lips in a most upsetting way; her eyes danced and glazed over and danced again, and her whole body delivered its own message: wait until we are alone together in bed tonight.

After he had locked his bedroom door, he had lain, his throat taut, his body drawn in a knot, his belly empty with longing, his sheathed sword bristling, his agonizing needs boiling inside him. He heard the house grow quiet, and then he heard La turn the knob and discover his door locked against her.

She whispered his name. Feeling like a clown, a stupid moron, an ungrateful clod, he lay silent until she went away. God forgive him. He couldn't forgive himself and he knew La would never forgive or forget this terrible rejection.

He lay sleepless all night. He knew she was as sleepless and fevered in her own bed. He could still go to her. With

276

a simple lie she would want to accept, things would be smooth between them again. He tried to rationalize his going to her bed in the night. If God found reasons for plagues and earthquakes, perhaps there was some cosmic adjustment in Ward's being provided with a concubine in a house where his wife lay as cold and remote to him as some stranger.

He forced himself to remain behind that locked door, and he swore that somehow that door would be locked tomorrow night. As much as he needed Lavinia's fevered body, he didn't want *her*, and all the obligations such an involvement might entail. She wasn't what he wanted, and he had to keep that fact in the forefront of his mind.

He looked forward in dread to meeting La in the morning. Would she rage in anger? Would she make a scene, leave the house? She had offered her body and he had rejected her. Would she go back home?

When he came down to breakfast, La was at her place at the table, pale, gray, taut about the mouth. She said nothing. She did nothing. She was polite. She answered when he spoke to her. She remained deadly civil, cold, distant, unapproachable.

He regretted the loss. He could not erase the heated memory of that long night with her in his bed. He knew that had been but a preliminary. Only the gods of sensual pleasure knew what might lie ahead for them—how he might have used her, limited only by the reaches of his own imagination, or hers.

Now she went about the house silent and chilled and diffident. He saw in her face that La would hate him forever. She would never forgive him. Hell, maybe the gods themselves wouldn't forgive him his stupidity. But now she *did* hate him; she despised him with an icy contempt. So be it. He *was* hated. The list grew longer and longer.

The activity of September's hurricane took priority in the newspapers. Florida and the Gulf Coast states lay vulnerable in the path of these tropical storms, which were spawned in the Caribbean or east of the Lesser Antilles to blast in from the Atlantic, three-headed killers with their tidal waves, wind, and rain. Winds rushing into low pressure areas revolved counter-clockwise about the storm's eye. Maximum wind speed could not be accurately

277

measured because measuring equipment was always destroyed well before the storm peaked. Rainfall in a hurricane could exceed four feet. The most fearful force of all—the tidal wave—could destroy everything before it. There existed no meteorological stations to provide adequate warning. Tracking a hurricane was unheard of. In 1848, winds, walls of water, and sheets of rain destroyed the military post on Tampa Bay. Towns were wiped out and shipping fleets sunk with all hands drowned. As skies blackened and the storm neared, likely to strike from any direction, people set themselves against its fury as best they could, and prayed.

Ward read with relief that the hurricane, reported in the open waters of the Gulf, was headed directly on a line with Galveston on the Texas coast.

He was stunned when the very next government information reported that sometime during the night, the storm had veered eastward and struck full-force, the eye crossing the coastline near Port St. Joe and Appalachicola. Later reports confirmed that Port St. Joe had taken the brunt of the storm, inundated by a twenty-foot wall of water that had claimed at least fifty lives and left few buildings standing in its wake. Later, among the structures reported totally demolished, were the Biltmore Hotel, its gambling casino and race track. The report stated that the hotel, undermined by water and torn from its foundations, crumbled, demolished beyond repair.

Sick, Ward felt a need to rush out there. All he could think was that he had to know if Julia were safe. All summer she'd been out of his thoughts. Suddenly, he was ill with fear that she might have been killed in the tidal wave. But he had not gone to St. Joe. There was no need. He stood at his office window, watching the dark sky swirl with smoke-thick clouds and lightning cracking brilliantly white, as Jacksonville felt the rough edges of the storm's fury. On his desk lay a newspaper. From its society page, Julia Fredrick smiled up at him at a horse show in Newport.

He rode home in a tightly curtained hack. The carriage rocked on its thoroughbraces, battered casually by the whirling gusts. He was consumed with hatred for everything and everybody in God's world, including the gods

278

themselves. Dayton Fredrick had been battered and beaten by human foes; what chance had he against nature itself? The world seemed steeped, wheeling and whirling, in cruelty, injustice, and the mindless buffeting of insensate forces of cosmic inhumanity.

He sat silently at the dinner table. Lavinia sat unspeaking, her eyes lowered, across from him. Lily did not eat with them. She sent word by Thetis from the music room that she was not hungry. Until ten o'clock that night she played the same shallow love song over and over:

> "I shed a tear for you,
> And for the happiness we knew,
> I shed a tear or two."

He tried to ignore the repetitive music. The melody lodged inside his brain and wheeled and skittered there like bats in flight. He tried to talk to La about the hurricane, the destruction of property, the loss of life, the demolished hotel owned by a friend. La was polite but distant. The storm and its havoc were remote to her, as unreal as death, ruin, devastation, in some faraway land. She knew about inner agony, in her own life. This alone held urgency for her, and she did not discuss this with him.

At ten o'clock, he managed to draw Lily away from the piano. She displayed a total lack of interest in the hurricane or its destruction. She chatted with La about the new dresses she'd expected to be delivered today but which had been inexplicably and inexcusably delayed. She wondered if she should alter the style of her hair. The latest fashion featured large rolls of curls across the crown, swept back from the face, and carried to the nape of the neck in a looping effect, like a fall. In pictures, the style looked smart; it might be effective, but perhaps it was wrong for her face structure. And then there was her complexion. She was looking absolutely sallow and hollow-eyed lately.

"Maybe you need to get away somewhere," Ward said, but his irony was entirely lost on her and hardly appreciated by Lavinia, wound in her own tight skein of frustration and repression. Jesus, another happy evening at home with the Hamilton family.

Lily went up to bed, yawning. The room grew silent, the rattle of thunder loud, bristling against the walls. There

279

was no longer any sense of shared silence between Ward and Lily's sister. Lavinia seemed waiting uncomfortably for him to leave. She had nothing to say to him.

Rage bubbled like a cauldron inside him, anger too violent to be contained. Somewhere in this meaningless existence, there had to be some reason for living.

He paused at the head of the stairs, offended by Lily's closed bedroom door, incensed by the sure knowledge that it was locked against him.

He strode along the corridor. He hesitated outside the door, then raised his bootheel and struck the framing just beneath the knob. The door swung back like a broken wing.

He stepped inside the room, his face gaunt and pallid. "I just wanted you to know how easily I can get in when I want to."

She lay taut, staring at him. It was as if she were caught in *flagrante delicto*. Actually, she was—as nearly as she would ever be. Her sheer gown was folded up over her hips. She lay with her legs apart, her hand pressed onto her pudendum.

She did not move. Like a mesmerized bird, she lay watching him, immobile, unable to move. "What in hell are you doing?" he said. He did not need to ask.

He kicked the door closed behind him. When it swung open again lamely, he threw a chair against it.

Face stricken, eyes wide, Lily lay and watched him. "Is that the way you dream about him?" Ward demanded.

Breathing raggedly, she tried to brush her gown down over her bared thighs. "You've no right," she whispered. "Barging in here."

"You're wrong. I've every right. More right than you have to deny me while you lie here and *masturbate*, thinking about my brother."

She closed her eyes as if trying to shut out the sight, the sound, the physical presence of him.

"I'll teach you what love really is," he said. "Man and woman. The way God meant it."

"No." Her head rolled back and forth on the pillow. She kept her eyes tightly closed.

"Yes. Love is exalting. It *can* be. Shared love, not secret, hidden—trying to bring back someone who is gone—and who would be no good to you if he was here."

280

He loosened his belt and unbuttoned his trousers. His throbbing erection burst free. He walked toward her. "Look at me, damn it," he said. "A man. A man, damn it, Lily. Look at my *cock*, damn you."

She turned her head away, chewing at her lip, refusing to open her eyes. He caught her sheer gown and ripped it away. He threw it behind him on the floor. She was afraid to oppose him. She simply lay unmoving, breathless, tense.

Ward came down between her legs, which were still spread wide. He caught up one of her pillows and thrust it beneath her hips. "If you've got sensations inside you," he raged, "I'll reach them, so help me God. You *will* care. You *will* want it."

"No." She barely spoke the word between clenched teeth.

He winced, wavering inwardly, but refused to surrender. She had to be made to care. He caught her hips in his hands and manipulated her easily, drawing her thighs up to him, pushing her legs wider so she lay open to receive him. He thrust himself into her. Words poured from his mouth as he worked against her body, trying with everything in him to arouse her. He tried to make her say aloud what he was doing to her, to make her say the word. "I'm fucking you," he told her savagely. "Say it. Say it. Say it."

He drove himself deeply into her, worked her crotch against him, felt the spasms surge upward so he bucked mindlessly, buckled, and fell upon her, exhausted.

She lay for a long time, unmoving. Finally she pulled away from him. "Well, I don't like it," she said, her voice a tense, flat whisper of despair. "I hate it. I hate you. I hate your wallowing in filth, trying to drag me down with you. I hate the vulgar things you say, the nasty things you do, the rotten things you want me to do. I hate you more than I've ever hated you. You could never make me want to wallow in filth with you. Never. No matter what you do to me. Kill me . . . kill me . . . go ahead, kill me, because you'll never make me love you."

He staggered in defeat to his own room. Whatever the achievements in his life, whatever other accomplishments, he could never reach Lily. He could reinforce her hatreds, but he was powerless to stir her love, to make her love him. He felt dirty, demeaned, rejected, castrated, destroyed. He felt lost.

He left his bedroom door unlocked that night. He'd leave it unlocked as long as he lived. La might not discover it tonight, or soon, or ever. But if she ever did come back to him—she or any other woman—by God, she'd find his door open to her.

Chapter Twenty-One

SOMETIMES A SIMPLE lack of firewood knocked the Jacksonville-Lake City trains off schedule. The engines burned wood; within a year, each one consumed over fifteen thousand cords of fuel, averaging fifty miles or less per cord. Trains carried as much of the fat pine as possible. Along the route, woodcutters, under contract, stacked up cords of sawn logs. When the demand exceeded the supply, or the supplier was late, the train crew—including the engineer himself and any willing male passengers—would get out with axes and crosscut saws to haul in enough fuel to reach the next wood station. When this happened, schedules were destroyed. Ward wanted a complete conversion to coal-burners, and this was the goal toward which he headed. Once loaded, a coal car could supply a train to its destination easily. Consumption of coal, for as many freight cars as a heavy locomotive could draw, averaged three to five pounds per car per mile if the engine were carefully tended. Coal was the way of the future.

Further, the need for additional rail miles drove him relentlessly too. More and larger corporations, with unlimited capital, were entering railroading. Independents were being absorbed or frozen out. He didn't intend to allow this fate to befall him, but he was being hemmed in and pressured from all sides. It was like being boxed in and finding a way out, or perishing.

"We didn't come this far to die," he told Phillips when the attorney grew restive about their status among the surviving companies.

"You're up against some real bastards," Clark warned him. "Cutthroat is the mildest game the boys are playing."

Ward's first real opportunity to expand came with the sad but less-than-astonishing report that the Lake City-St. Joe Railroad, owned by Dayton Fredrick, was in receivership and up for auction.

Ward sent Bracussi and Phillips Clark to Tallahassee to investigate the circumstances of the bidding: procedures, a likely bidding-floor, competition, keenness of interest. He didn't have to spell out, either for his auditor or his counsel, what he wanted.

They returned in four days, smiling, confident, and enthusiastic. Even though it was narrow-gauge and would have to be upgraded to standard-gauge at once, the line offered great potential for the Jacksonville-Lake City company. The St. Joe line would hand Ward dominance in the northeast, central, and coastal regions of the west. It would get him safely out of the narrowing box.

For this reason, he, Phillips, and Bracussi went beyond mere consideration of top bid and competitive bidders to the price they'd have to pay to wrap up the deal. Because Henry Plant was actively involved and confident that he would take over the St. Joe line, they decided against the risk of a competitive bid. Plant was too rich for their blood.

Bracussi had learned, for a price, the ceiling bid being presented by the Plant people. Plant was determined to own the St. Joe company, but because he held his competition in something less than awe, he was bidding only slightly above the actual demand price.

"We want that St. Joe line," Ward said. "Let's get it."

They figured the actual dollar value of the entire system, including rolling stock and rails, all of which would have to be peddled on the market, but which would provide some return. "We'll up Mr. Plant a hundred thousand," Ward said, when all figures were in. "We don't have to, but it's the only way to be safe."

When the bids were opened, Plant had bought the St. Joe line—topping Ward's bid by one hundred dollars.

Ward was stunned. "The son of a bitch," he said. "He's even a bigger crook than I am. You know damned well there had to be collusion somewhere for him to outbid us by a hundred dollars."

He was still recovering from the staggering blow of losing a rail line which, in the past weeks, had come to be vitally important to him and to the existence of his own company in the toughening competition, when he received a second heart-stopping shock: word came that Dayton Fredrick was dead.

Less than a dozen people attended Dayton Fredrick's last rites. Remembering the charismatic, extroverted, generous, and open-hearted man, Ward found it incredible and sad to find that Dayton was so quickly abandoned by the hundreds of people who had known him, loved him, and profited from his laughter and his largesse.

Ward·walked into the funeral parlor where Dayton's body rested in a rich metal casket with brass fittings. The coffin was closed. A few expensive but forlorn wreaths, underlining how forgotten and forsaken Dayton was in death, wilted near the bier.

Whitney Cushing related to Ward the circumstances of Dayton's death. Cushing had remained friendly toward Ward since their earliest poker matches at Dayton's Biltmore. Cushing and Byers handled the bond issue floated for Ward's railroad. When Ward was in New York, Cushing always arranged a marathon stud poker party for his "Florida pigeon."

"Dayton commtited suicide, you know."

Ward winced. "No. I didn't know."

"He'd been depressed, melancholy, defeated, for a long time. Worried about his daughter, though he very carefully never let her guess how concerned he was. That little baggage is still topic number one with all the gossips between here and Boston. I don't know what will happen to her now that Dayton is gone. She was his whole life. Whatever he tried to accomplish—and God knows, we all warned him that he was getting in ninety miles over his head—it was to secure Julia's future. I think his whole aim was that she be rich so she could *marry* rich, you know. That 'money marrying money' is a lot more than potboiler fiction. Money is marrying money more and more these days. Maybe it always did, but that's what he wanted for Julia."

"She's only fourteen."

"Going on twenty-eight." Cushing smiled ruefully.

"Still, planning marriage for her, like a stock merger?"

Cushing nodded. "It's done. Even the long-range planning. There are a hell of a lot of multimillionaires in this country now—an elite that controls money as well as society and government. That's what Dayton had in mind for Julia. He was planning for her future. He knew Julia would be married by the time she was seventeen—eighteen at the latest—for one reason or another. He wanted a real fiscal merger for her. He certainly encouraged her to travel among the very wealthy, no matter what it cost him. And in the end, I guess it cost him his life."

Ward's face contorted with revulsion. "Did he shoot himself?"

Cushing smiled wryly and shook his head. "I can see that the very idea of blowing one's brains out is almost as abhorrent and foreign to you as it is to me. I haven't the guts for it. Well, it was alien to Dayton's nature, too. It was far too lacking in drama—or even melodrama—for old Dayton. He sent Julia up to wealthy friends in Connecticut, promising to follow as soon as he wound up transfer of the St. Joe line.

"Dayton hung around Lake City. You know he was totally wiped out in Port St. Joe; nothing left there, not even salvage. That beautiful hotel and its furnishings are rubble and craters in the ground. Nothing. They say, though, even that last night in Lake City, Dayton was still hosting parties, celebrating with Plant and others—"

"Celebrating?"

"You know Dayton. Said he was celebrating his liberation. He was free of railroading and, incidentally, worse than broke, deeply in debt. But free."

"Jesus. It sounds like Dayton."

"It *was* Dayton. Down to the last manicure, the last fifty-dollar gold piece tip for the waiter. He threw big champagne parties and beef barbecues to celebrate his new-won freedom. Bankruptcy." Cushing shook his head. "He had flair, you have to say that for him. And there he was at the station the morning the first train left for St. Joe, with all pomp and circumstance, under Plant's new ownership."

Cushing stared at the backs of his hands. "The governor was there, Plant, state legislators, railroad dignitaries. All of them had been at Dayton's party the night before. They said Dayton was in high good humor. Told somebody he was on his way that day to join Julia—and they'd tour Europe before he announced any new plans. Then he showed the only anger anyone detected the whole time. He was laughing, but he told Henry Plant that Plant could take over the St. Joe line, but Dayton didn't have to watch it. Before the train pulled out, Dayton got in a carriage and drove away from the station, still laughing. He shook hands all around, joked with everybody. People figured what the hell, maybe Dayton really didn't want to watch the new era begin.

"He drove maybe five miles out of Lake City to a crossing. He hid along the side of the tracks until the train was almost on him, too late for the engineer to stop the engine. Dayton just stepped out in front of the locomotive. Thank God, the engineer said he was killed instantly."

Ward felt deeply depressed and melancholy. He needed a drink. His eyes burned. He was aware of a man who approached him smiling, his hand extended. Ward managed to smile in return. "Mr. Hamilton?"

"Yes."

"By gad. Glad I was able to get here today. Been hoping to meet you, sir." He laughed. "Yes, sir, looking forward to the honor. Sorry it had to be under these here conditions, of course."

Ward glanced around. The smiling man seemed representative of the other attendees. They stood in small, animated groups, chatting as if this were a cocktail party or an Irish wake, the man in the closed coffin forgotten.

He hadn't had experience enough with death or funerals to accept this convivial atmosphere as normal. "Yes," he said. "It's very sad."

"Did you know the deceased well?"

"No, I guess not. Not too well."

The man winked. "Hope you didn't lend him any money." He nudged Ward with his elbow.

"As a matter of fact, I did."

287

"Well, we all got to learn, I reckon. Didn't know him too well myself. Did him a few favors up in Tallahassee. Oh, let me introduce myself. Name's Gates McCall, Mr. Hamilton. State Senator Gates McCall. Just wanted to say to you, no matter that we Democrats have regained control of the state government, we don't want you to think you don't have friends in Tallahassee. We want to build this state, and we know we can't do that without making concessions to money and railroad people. Well, sir, you can count on it. We want to help our friends."

Ward nodded, forcing himself to go on smiling. He felt nothing but contempt for the man, but he recognized him as the wave of the future. Before they parted, Ward signed a gold-embossed permanent pass on NEF&GC trains. He presented it to McCall. "Just show this at any ticket window or simply board our trains at any time and show your pass to the conductor, Mr. McCall. You and your party will be extended every courtesy possible. We don't want you folks at Tallahassee to think you don't have friends at NEF&GC, either."

McCall winked and laughed, effusive in his appreciation. Ward watched him tuck the card in among half a dozen other similarly gold-embossed cards. Ward regarded McCall with interest. He'd just made a down payment on a mean and petty little soul.

Someone touched Ward's elbow and he turned, looking down into the grief-strained face of Dolly Marsh. His heart seemed to hesitate for a moment. He had not seen her since their visit to the Biltmore. It seemed another age, another couple who had sneaked away to that hotel in Atlanta. Dolly looked lovely, if bitterly melancholy with loss.

"I'm sorry about Dayton," he said.

"Are you?" She swallowed at the lump choking her. "Why? He's been dead for a long time, I think. Certainly since the storm demolished the Biltmore. He knew then that he had no life left, nothing, there was no second chance for him. There's no second chance for anybody; Dayton faced that. I think all he looked for was a graceful exit—he had to find his own way out."

"I thought there'd be more people here. Hundreds. Flowers beyond belief—"

"Why? Dayton's dead. He can't help them or hurt them.

288

Not anymore. He's just a poor son of a bitch who stepped in front of a train—on purpose."

"Is—Baxter with you?" Ward asked hesitantly.

"No. Probably one of his spies is. Or maybe Baxter has finally given up; I don't know. By the way, I'm sorry about the way he threatened you. He's a bully where money is concerned. He knew he could frighten you. That's one of the ways he gets his thrills. The other is by spying on me—watching me in bed with some other man, if he can arrange it. It's the only sexual pleasure he is capable of."

"He has spies in business, as well as on you?"

"Not in business so much anymore, since he's retired from Wall Street. He doesn't care what goes on in industry anymore, but he learns what he needs to learn for his sexual stimulation. It's the only excitement that stirs him. Pornography. Watching sex acts. He's like a sparrow gorging on horse shit. He wallows in it."

Ward started to speak, but hesitated. Dolly smiled. "You wonder if Baxter has known all these years about Dayton and me?"

"He must have known."

"He must have."

"But he's never confronted you—about Dayton?"

Her laugh was a rasping, aching sound. "He knew better. He knows better. If he'd ever even once mentioned Dayton's name, I'd have left him, and he knew it."

"He knew, but he didn't want you to leave him?"

"He'd have been robbed of his voyeuristic pleasures if I'd left him. I've loved Dayton a long time—maybe for more years than you've lived."

"Why did you stay with Baxter Marsh?"

"Very simple, child. Because Baxter Marsh was richer than God. And Dayton owed millions. Oh, it would take too long to tell you all the reasons why I stayed with Baxter. Besides, some of those reasons turn my stomach, and some of them break my heart when I try to talk about them. And crying ruins my makeup. If you marry money, you earn every penny of it. I guess I was willing to pay the price."

He gazed at her. "Even when you knew what Baxter Marsh was?"

"Even then. Millions of reasons, my naive and idealistic

289

darling, all of them either green or gold. Baxter is a very vile person in many ways. But in many other ways he's nicer than some of his peers. He has many good qualities. You'll learn, child, as you associate with people like Baxter and Cushing and Byers and the others, that a lot of men—and women—when they have too much money, too much education, too much leisure, too much authority, too much of everything, let their minds become cesspools. They collect filth, pornography, perverted hangers-on. You'd be amazed how many of the greatest philanthropists and religious benefactors have secret collections of dirt of some kind. Behind their public image of scrubbed-clean, handwashing do-gooders, there's dirt. They're no better than Baxter, no different. In many ways they are uglier, because the sense of secrecy is their real thrill, the only one they're truly capable of experiencing. So their orgies become onanism too, even if six people are involved. I know you think you're working your way into a wonderland, my poor baby. I just want you to be prepared for the truth."

Ward stood in the short line to express his condolences after the graveside funeral services. Julia pointedly turned and walked away when he approached. He caught her arm.

She turned and he felt her body trembling. She wore black, with a black veil concealing her face. She was slumped inward, round-shouldered with grief. She tried to push past him. The few onlookers paused, watching tautly.

"I just want to say I'm sorry, Julia."

"Why? Sorry that Daddy is dead? Why should you be sorry? You killed him. Isn't that enough for you? Must you come here and gloat over it, too?"

He felt as if he'd been hit physically. He retreated a step, wincing. Julia thrust past him, shaken with ill-controlled sobs. He shivered, sick at his stomach. He remained standing where he was near the raw, open grave until only the gravediggers were left, waiting to cover the open hole. He crossed the grassy knoll to the waiting carriage, and returned to his hotel and bought a fifth of bourbon. He went up to his room and locked the door.

His sense of cosmic sadness, of loss that he couldn't

contain, baffled and troubled him. He wanted to weep, not for Dayton Fredrick, but for himself.

He poured whiskey over ice and sat at a window, drinking. He stared across the city as the sky darkened and the room grayed, purpling with dark. He did not move except to pour himself a fresh drink infrequently. Not even the liquor helped; he may as well have been drinking iced water. He remained coldly sober, melancholy and empty.

He became aware someone was knocking on the corridor door, sharply and insistently. Whoever was out there may have been there for a long time; the sound had only gradually rattled into his consciousness.

He got up, astonished at his own sobriety, and crossed the room. He set the glass down, turned up the lamp, and opened the door.

Julia stood there.

For a silent moment they faced each other. Julia was in mourning, but dressed smartly. Her hat, a black velvet Windsor, with jet edge and fancy jet crown, was years too old for her, and yet it looked somehow right on Julia—trimmed with fancy black brocaded ribbon and a rosette of satin, with black, jetted tips and aigrettes. A black half-veil laid a shadow across the bridge of her nose. Her dress was eight or nine yards of albatross material, with a single, deep-kilted, flounced skirt, tunic-edged with lace and tapped with a long, close-fitting basque. She looked old beyond her years, lovely in a sad, sophisticated way. She said, "May I come in?" But she did not wait for him to reply.

She stood in the center of the room. He closed the door and leaned heavily against it, feeling faintly giddy after all. She said, "I'm sorry you felt compelled to come to Daddy's funeral. You somehow spoiled it. I hate people who make hypocritical appearances, for appearances' sake. Do you think you fooled anybody?"

"Did you come all the way up here just to say that?"

"Don't you think somebody ought to speak the truth to people like you?"

"If people are really like me, the truth won't touch them, sweetheart."

"You did kill him, damn you." She spoke coldly, as if he had robbed her and her father of some substantial heritage, birthright, and bright honor. He could not believe

291

that he was the first man to bid successfully against Dayton Fredrick in his forty-odd years. Nor did he bother to tell her that her father had been hanging on by his nails, frustrated, already defeated. But he realized she had idealized him from the first moment they had met; his defying and defeating her father had hurt her savagely, as nothing else ever had. "I'll take his place," she was saying. "You won't find me as easy to defraud."

Julia stared at him in the deep saffron light of the room. They were two strangers together for a moment in a strange place. She felt sadness wash down through her. She felt chilled with that cold which marks the end of something vital and even precious. She could look forward to being as good as her father had wanted her to be. She didn't have to bother with boys anymore, thank God. They bored her more now than ever. With her father dead, she felt as if the whole cosmos had fragmented and spun and sparkled and showered in bits and pieces about her head. She gazed at Ward Hamilton where he slouched against the door, and wanted to cry out in protest. She was bereft. Her father was gone, and she could never have the one man she wanted. She refused to settle for less. She would achieve, for her father's sake. But all she could really see ahead for herself was a succession of empty, cold nights. Her eyes filled with tears—carefully concealed beneath her veil. It is never easy to accept the fact that one's life is ended before it has even truly begun. Then, with the perversity that drove her, she shook her head, drying her tears. Her voice cut at Ward like a surgeon's scalpel. "Did you really think I'd let you bid-in Daddy's railroad?"

Ward drew a deep breath and shrugged. "I only knew someone had gotten word to Plant."

She smiled coldly. "He was very grateful."

"I'm sure he must have been."

"You may also be sure that any time I can stop you, I will."

"Is *that* what you came here to say?"

"Are you in a hurry?" She glanced about. "Am I detaining you?"

"You may be enjoying this scene, Julia, but I'm not. It's childish and vengeful."

"And it hurts you because you have to face the truth about yourself and what you are."

He straightened, grinning tautly. "Don't be too sure, Julia. In one way, you and I are very much alike. I faced the truth about myself—as you have about yourself. I faced it a long time ago, when I decided what I wanted, what I might have to do to get it, and what it might cost. I made up my mind to pay that cost. If part of that price is your hatred, I'm sorry, but—" He bowed. "You've called me a thief, a pirate, a son of a bitch, and I've not even protested. Someone said if you tell a man the truth about himself, he may kill you. So be careful, Julia. You may strike an exposed nerve yet."

"Stop laughing at me."

"I'm not laughing, I assure you. I stand too much in awe of you to laugh. I love you too much to laugh at you. I'm too troubled about you and what's to become of you to laugh at you."

"Don't trouble yourself about me." Her head tilted. Pride underscored her words. "Daddy left me property and money—put away well ahead. And that brings me to the reason why I'm here."

"You mean it wasn't my pretty face after all?"

She straightened slightly. "I found among some papers that Daddy borrowed forty-three thousand dollars from you."

"That was between Dayton and me. Don't worry about it."

"But I do. I'm sick about it. That he would borrow from an enemy such as you. I refuse to be obligated to you in any way. Any way at all." From her black handbag she withrew a draft on the Stockmen's and Farmers' Bank of Atlanta, made out to him in the full amount of her father's debt.

"Julia, don't do this, not now. You'll need it."

Her mouth twisted. "I couldn't stand to use it, knowing it belonged to you."

"Not even as a loan?"

"Certainly not as a loan."

"I'm sorry you hate me so deeply."

She bit her lip, looking for a moment like a forlorn little girl. "I don't hate you at all. I wish to God I did. It's just that I know I *should* hate you."

293

"Julia, listen to me."

"Don't you touch me."

He stopped, dropping his hands to his sides, and laughed helplessly.

"My God, Julia. How can I deal with you?"

"You can't. Just take your money and we're quits." She placed the draft on the table beside the half-empty glass.

"I'll worry about you, Julia. Where are you going? What are you going to do?"

His concern armed her against him. Her body stiffened. She shook her head, staring along her nose at him. "Well, don't worry about me. I'll get along well. I assure you, as long as there are rich men in this world, I'll be fine."

Chapter Twenty-Two

WARD RETURNED TO JACKSONVILLE, haunted by Dayton Fredrick's death, wholly dissatisfied with the pattern and texture of his own existence, and coldly determined to break at once out of the closing box in which he found himself daily more constricted.

"We can't go west," Clark said. "Plant has stopped us out there. The center of the state is pretty well open, but for a good reason—there are fewer than two inhabitants per square mile."

They made the decision to go south along the East Coast. The determining factor was that this was the only route open. A Wall Street financier named White had provided the capital to build a narrow-gauge line from a terminal at South Jacksonville to Tocoi on the St. Johns River. For many reasons the line languished. The wood-burning locomotives were slow, the coaches uncomfortable; it took a man with a strong stomach to brazen out the entire run by rail. But a market was slowly emerging. Men were clearing land for citrus groves, farms were appearing, and hardy optimists built "boardinghouses" for seasonal tourists along the wide, sugary white beaches at Daytona. Presently, travelers reached these points from Jacksonville only by boat. Coastwise sailing pockets enjoyed handsome profits. Steam rapidly replaced sails. By now, steamboat traffic on the St. Johns, Halifax, and Oklawaha rivers prospered as never before—and water travel had always been the preferred mode of travel in Florida. Large and luxurious side-wheelers offered top-quality accomodations for excursions south on the major waterways. Registry of the St. Johns River traffic showed a total of fifty vessels, aggregating six thousand tons. The DeBarry-Baya Line ran between Jacksonville and all points on the St. Johns, held mail contracts, and toted holds crammed with freight. For all these reasons, rail traffic faltered in the area. And added to to all the other circumstances militating against rail traffic south of Jacksonville, there was no bridge across the St. Johns. Even that hardy soul willing to subject his cast-iron stomach to the discomforts and delays of the narrow-gauge line had to cross the river from Jacksonville to South Jacksonville via boat.

Ward found the Stockmen's and Farmers' Bank at Atlanta reflecting that growth and affluence which had accelerated and blossomed when NEF&GC expanded. Hobart Bayard greeted Ward warmly. He and the other bank executives were willing—anxious—to believe Ward could weather, if not overcome, the fierce and established steamboat competition south of Jacksonville. They agreed to finance his attempt, and he took over the Jacksonville-Tocoi Railroad.

Like a faint cloud boiling on his horizon, a forewarning of dangers ahead, Ward was able to have the charter and land grants approved by the state legislature only with restrictive stipulations. He found legislators, Gates McCall among them, affable and even obsequious, but also wary; Tallahassee was clearly dominated by the huge rail corporations proliferating across the state. The Jacksonville-Tocoi charter assumed an expansion south as population increases dictated. This franchise, covering a total of approximately fifty rail miles, carried a grant of five thousand acres per mile, but this proved to be a coveted prize. The IIF refused to extend the unexpired term for improving and upgrading the line or losing the franchise. This period, which had been allowed to approach lapse-date by the former owners, who saw little profit in upgrading or expanding, covered only seven months. Within this time, the Internal Improvement Fund people warned Ward, the narrow-gauge line had to be upgraded to wide-gauge standards as far as Tocoi, and all right-of-way cleared for extensions an additional twenty miles to Palatka.

Ward had planned to use convict labor to improve his new roadbed, but the time element precluded this; convict labor was unskilled labor. He advertised, in newspapers across the South and as far north as Baltimore, for skilled rail workers. Construction was undertaken and pushed forward as swiftly as the miles could be covered. Crews worked in one shift ripping out the thirty-pound, narrow-gauge track, and the second shift came in behind them, laying new crossties and sixty-pound, wide-gauge rails.

Uzziah Giddings was placed in command of railroad security. Originally, Ward had intended that Uzziah would oversee the work crews, check on employee theft, waste and destruction, and keep work moving in two shifts. By the end of the first week, Uzziah was back in Jacksonville. He and Phillips Clark joined Bracussi in Ward's office. "We keep going, Masta," Uzziah said, "we have to fight."

Ward stared at the mustee. "Fight? For God's sake, fight who, Uzziah? Indians?"

Uzziah smiled and shook his head. "Fight white man."

"What you're up against is the Florida Homestead law of 1862." Clark told Ward. "That year, in order to spur growth, the Florida legislature passed a law deeding land to homesteaders who simply claimed and proved it up. They only had to move in, build a shack, and register the acreage they could prove up, and it was their land. The law is old, but the squatters are new. They're coming in by the hundreds."

"They squat on rail property." Uzziah swung his arm, troubled by words. "A house on the rail right-of-way—rails want to cross their land—they say no, they refuse to move. We stop or we fight."

"Well, we sure as hell don't stop," Ward said.

"We may have to go to court to settle this," Clark told him.

"Court? And settle it after maybe three years of delays—if we're lucky?" Ward got up and paced the office. "I've got six months, not six years. We'll run the bastards off, and go to court later."

"You're really asking for trouble."

Uzziah nodded. "Bad trouble."

*   *   *

Ward not only had bad trouble at the rail company, his life at home was not brightly felicitous.

Robin was less than a year old. He'd learned to crawl and to totter around the house holding someone's finger. But the lesson he'd learned best was to win his own way in every battle of wills. At every meal, he cried until he almost went into convulsions, his mouth gray and teeth chattering, when servant girls tried to get him to eat. His screaming managed to tie in knots everyone's nerves except Lily's.

She refused to believe he was simply screaming to regain the attention turned away from him for that brief interval. He was totally spoiled because Lily refused to allow him to be corrected or curbed in any manner. "He'll find unhappiness enough in this life," she said. "He'll have his own way as long as he is in my house. We won't break his little spirit."

Nobody broke his little spirit. Daily he became more despotic. He whined and cried continually unless some adult was in constant attendance. When he broke every piece of glassware set on any table within his reach, Ward and Lily clashed. "The answer is very simple." Lily said in a soft and patient tone. "If we don't want Robin to break anything, we'll put it up out of his reach."

"The hell with that," Ward said. "Teach him now that *he* has *his* toys and *we* have *ours*. We keep our cotton-picking hands off his, and he lets everything on every table alone—or gets his hands blistered."

Lily looked as if she'd faint. "You *would* hit him, wouldn't you?"

"If you don't hit him once in a while now, Lily, somebody's going to be hitting him all the rest of his life. That's why they put red and green signals on rail lines; you've got to obey rules or there's chaos."

"I don't see that running a stupid railroad has anything to do with breaking a little boy's heart," Lily said. She tilted her chin, her eyes glittering. "Why don't you just admit the truth?" Her fists were knotted at her sides, white-knuckled. "You hate the poor little thing. You despise him. You'd be cruel to him every chance you got, if I let you."

"The question, Lily, is which one of us is really being cruel to him? Me, for wanting him to know his rights end

298

at the tip of my nose, or you, for letting him think the world is his to walk over."

"The world *is* his to walk over. It will be. Your hatred won't stop him."

"I don't hate Robin. I don't have any reason for hating him—yet."

"Oh yes, you do. Don't lie. You've hated this baby since the day he was born. You'll always hate him. But you won't hurt him, or curb him, or break his beautiful little spirit, because I won't let you."

Charles Henry Harkness, Miz Marcy, and Beatrice, with a retinue of black servants, arrived in September, planning to visit through New Year's. Ward was pleased to have his father-in-law in the big old house. Charles Henry found Jacksonville a place of unceasing wonder. He drove downtown with Ward and wandered the streets, returning home with Ward in the evening. He found the energy and movement in the town incredible; it was more like a northern industrial hub than a slow-moving Southern parish.

Ward and Charles Henry resumed an old pleasant habit, spending an hour or two each twilight out at the carriage house behind the mansion. Ward had by now bought a couple of carriage horses and a phaeton, and hired a black man to live in the carriage house above the stables to care for the animals. The black man's name was Luke and, after the first few days, he joined Ward and Harkness in the shadows outside the stables. Because it would be unseemly for a black man—at that time and place—to sit on a chair in the presence of white men, Luke hunkered on the ground, his back against the wall, saying he preferred it. Luke was in his late forties, a philosopher of sorts. Like Harkness, he loved straight bourbon sipped from a cup. He liked to reminisce with Masta Charlie about when times were different.

Harkness was deeply troubled by the schism he detected between Lily and Ward. It required no particular sensitivity to see that Ward and Lily lived together under a strange, tense truce, a terrible mutual politeness, a strained and unnatural civility that threatened to shatter at any moment. Harkness liked Ward and found dozens of small opportunities to point out and underscore Lily's virtues.

299

"She'll be a good mother," Harkness said over bourbon. "As soon as she realizes Robin isn't the first human child born unto woman on this earth."

"A parent ain't kind or fair to his child that lets that child run wild," Luke observed from where he leaned against the barn, sipping his drink. "A child what don't learn the rules the easy way at home is shore doomed to learn them the hard way outside his house."

Harkness nodded and sighed. "Lily is trying to raise Robin right, you'll see. Already she's started taking him to church. When he's big enough, churchgoing will be right natural with him."

Ward winced. In his catalogue, Lily's churchgoing was less than a virtue; it had become a kind of obsession. She attended three services at the Magdalena Baptist Church on Sundays, went once on Wednesday night for prayer meeting, and held special prayer services, conducted by the assistant pastor, in her parlor on other days.

"One good thing has come from Lily's churchgoing and her insisting that the whole family accompany her," Harkness said. "Lavinia has attracted the very favorable notice of the young assistant pastor. Have you noticed?"

Ward sighed. "No, I hadn't noticed. I did see that young Williams is around most of the time, but I thought it was church business."

Harkness smiled. "Part of it is. Andrew is a hard person to cotton to, right off. I don't think I ever met a more stiff-necked, inflexibly righteous young man in my life. He knows the true way, the true religion, and that's the way it is, there ain't a doubt in his mind. But underneath, I suppose he's a good man at heart. And he does think the sun rises and sets in Lavinia."

Harkness felt with strong conviction that if Lily searched the nation, North and South, she wouldn't find a better husband than Ward Hamilton. It distressed Lily's father that Lily did not even share a bedroom with her husband. Though he himself had not approached Miz Marcy in ardor in God knew how many years, at least she shared his bed if none of his long-suppressed animalistic desires.

He mentioned this to Lily, alone with her one morning on the screened sun porch overlooking a sparkling slice of river. "A man and woman ought to sleep together, Lily."

"Don't speak in such a vulgar manner, Papa," Lily said.

"There's nothing vulgar about married folks sleeping together, Lily."

"There is in your tone. This is a matter Ward and I can settle."

"I'm afraid not. Ward lets you do about what pleases you, Lily, but that don't mean he's always partial to what you do. You might think about that sometime. He's a good man—a good, strong, and kindly man—and I'd hate to see you lose him, Lily."

"You don't have to worry. Ward and I understand each other."

"Do you, Lily? Or do you simply make no effort to understand him, or to appreciate him, or to try to please him at all? Are you just taking him for granted while you're existing in a dream world, where things are always as only *you* want them?"

"Things *are* as I want them, as nearly as they can be. And I don't want to talk about it."

"Lily, you know I love you, girl, more than life itself. It hurts me to see you existing in an unreal world while your husband is neglected—a real man, of flesh and blood and reality."

"I don't know what you're talking about. I don't want to know what you're talking about."

"Lily, Lily. Don't you think I can see? You used to dream about Ward's brother, back at Errigal. Even when he was imprisoned, you went on dreaming about him. Unreal dreams. I didn't think it was too important then. A young girl in her dream world. But good Lord, Lily, you're still doing it."

Lily lunged upward from her chair, but her father caught her arm, gently but firmly restraining her. "Let me go, Papa."

"Listen to me, Lily. What's the sense of mooning and dreaming and yearning over a man you can never have, and may never even see again? Robert is gone. It's like he's dead. We are all sorry, but we accept it. He's a prisoner, and worse than that, a prisoner with one leg and no hope for the future. You have everything here, Lily. But you ought to be willing to work, to make just a little effort to keep it."

* * *

That night when Ward returned from the office, he found that Miz Marcy and Charles Henry Harkness had returned abruptly to Errigal. Lily refused to discuss their departure. She said simply that something had happened at Errigal, and her father had been called home unexpectedly. No, she had no idea when he might return, if ever.

The party Miz Marcy and Lily had been planning during Miz Marcy's brief and abruptly terminated visit, was carried out to reality. Once Lily dedicated herself to the affair, no expense was spared, and she worked obsessively to make her soiree an event Jacksonville would long remember.

Her guest list read like pages torn from the local blue book of social, religious, business, and professional leaders of the community. She hired caterers to augment her own staff of servants. She dressed Uzziah Giddings in kneepants, a ruffled shirt, and a tight-fitting rust jacket. He merely glided silently about the house, insuring its security. She brought in an ensemble of black musicians to play for dancing.

The old mansion glowed, brilliantly illumined, decorated, and ornamented. Though Robin screamed to be permitted to attend the party, Lily did finally insist that he be bodily removed, blue in the face, wailing and kicking, to the nursery. She sat there with him until well after the first guests had arrived. When Robin finally fell asleep, sobbing, she came down to the party.

Andrew Williams, the young assistant pastor of the Magdalena Baptist Church, was among the guests, along with the pastor and his wife. Williams proved to be just about as Harkness had described him. Handsome, with soft blond curls brushed back from his severe, seldom-smiling face, he had the look of the fanatic or the starving poet. There were, in woodcuts of the witch-burners of Salem, men with the same intensity swirling in their eyes.

Lavinia introduced Williams to Ward and left them alone, saying she was certain they would have much in common. Ward wondered what in hell that might mean. If he hadn't known better, he'd have believed Lavinia was playing a joke on him. But Lavinia did not like him well enough anymore to tease or torment him.

In five minutes, Ward had had more of Andrew Williams's cold-hearted fervor than he could stomach. He found the assistant pastor, who was about his age, officious—a religious zealot without concern for any but the positive, insular, dogmatic precepts of his own true way. With a tight smile, he admitted to being arrogant in his confidence. His narrow views admitted no opposition, no possibility of error or uncertainty. Ward found him rigid, sanctimonious, and intolerable. When Andrew began to denigrate those couples who actually went out on the polished dance floor, Ward excused himself and escaped as quickly as possible.

He found Lily at the piano. The ensemble had taken a break, and the guests were gathered, at Lily's request, but without apparent enthusiasm, in small groups about the dance floor. He felt his face burn. Lily knew dozens of songs, and had entertained for hours at Errigal with her playing, but tonight she had chosen the song she played, hour by unbroken hour, when there were no guests in the house:

> "I know you've found a love that's new,
> And I am so glad for you,
> But for that happiness we knew,
> I shed a tear or two."

Lily sang through the complete chorus twice. People stirred and glanced at each other restively and questioningly.

> "I try so hard to hide my broken heart
> And yet the teardrops start
> When someone speaks your name."

Ward sweated through the melody a third time. It was, for him, as if Lily sang it for Robert, summoning him because he could not be present, because she could evoke, for herself, his presence in this way. He admitted this may have been pure imagination, and yet, after the brief, half-hearted applause of her captive audience, Lily once again smiled around at them, and lifted her voice in the same plaintive tune. By now, the guests were growing noticeably agitated.

Ward retreated, aware of the glances exchanged among

303

the guests—almost all of whom were strangers to him. He turned on his heel and went as unobtrusively as possible into the dining room and asked a servant to bring him whiskey in a punch glass. The melody trailed him relentlessly.

Andrew Williams spoke disapprovingly at his elbow. "Whiskey is the wine of hell, the liquor of the devil, brother Ward. Whiskey would never stain my lips."

"Yes, well, maybe you've never been really thirsty."

"Oh, I've experienced temptation, brother. I've known the powerful, ugly pull of temptation. I am only a poor, weak vessel—" his chilled smile denied this, of course— "and even our dear Jesus, perfect as human flesh ever can be, knew the agony of temptation. The sin is not in being tempted, brother Ward, but in capitulation. We must resist sin; we're all strong enough to do that. Certainly, I would like a drink of strong spirits. Perhaps there would be a delightful excitement in it, an arousal of the mind and body, a transient freedom of the spirit. I don't know. I shall never know. Just as there may be lustful pleasure in holding another man's woman—another man's holy wife, mind you—in your arms while you waltz to the devil's music, but I'll never know the sinful pleasures of dancing, either. I am made strong by my resistance to temptation, my refusal to capitulate to sin. I am made whole in God's sight. That price is small enough to pay, brother."

"Good for you." Ward took a long drink, shuddering. The worst aspect of Williams's diatribe was that it didn't drown out the sound of Lily's singing, the sense of growing tension in the ballroom. From that lighted arena, he heard Lily begin, after a brief pause, to sing that same tune one more time. He tossed off another long drink.

Suddenly the music stopped. Discord blared as Lily's hands struck the keys. She cried out, enraged, "Let me alone, La. I am playing to entertain my guests."

"Our guests want to dance again, Lily," Lavinia was saying. Ward strode across the dining room and stood in the doorway, staring across the brilliantly lit room. Lavinia bent over Lily, catching Lily's wrists in her hands. Andrew Williams paused at Ward's shoulder, rigid and unbending. "They all loved your song, Lily," Lavinia said. "But the musicians are back now to play for dancing."

"Let me alone, you slut." Lily fought to free herself.

Some guests stared at each other oddly, while others edged toward the cloakroom and the exits.

"Please, Lily," Lavinia said, "don't make a scene like this."

"Why shouldn't I make a scene, you slut? Are you the only one permitted to make a scene, carrying on like a cheap whore in my own house—in my own bedroom—with my husband?"

Speechless, Lavinia released Lily's arms and retreated, shaking her head. Lily's face went pallid, her cheeks rigid, her pale eyes blazing. "Don't try to tell me what to do in my house. Don't ever try to tell me what to do, you slut."

Ward stood unmoving. Guests walked past him on both sides, leaving. A few even remembered to say good night to him. He nodded without bothering to look at them. Lavinia wheeled around and ran across the room. Andrew Williams caught at her arm, but she struggled free and ran up the stairs, her hand pressed over her mouth.

In less than twenty minutes, the last of the guests had departed the premises. Williams bowed stiffly toward Ward, and strode from the house. He forgot his beaver hat and coat, and had to return. Again he retreated, without speaking.

At the piano, Lily seated herself again. She sat for a long minute, letting her nerves calm, then she moved her fingers across the keys and sang in her sweet, untroubled contralto:

> "For all that time which slowly goes,
> Like the lonely river flows
> Down to the sea,
> I shed a tear.
> And for the love that will ever be,
> As long as mem'ries cling
> To everything,
> I'll shed a tear or two."

Ward sat at breakfast the next morning when Lavinia came down, her face gray, her eyes irreparably damaged. She wore the pale green traveling suit and tiny matching hat she had worn when she arrived from Errigal.

"I just want to say goodbye," she said. "I'm going home to Errigal this morning. I won't see you again."

Ward nodded. He stood awkwardly with his napkin in his fist. He did not know what to say; there seemed no words.

"Well, what's the matter with you two this morning?" Lily walked in and gazed at them along her nose. "You look as if you'd just been caught stealing watermelons, I declare."

Ward stared at Lily incredulously. She had never looked more refreshed, brighter, or as cheerfully unconcerned. He had lain awake until five o'clock this morning. Jacksonville roosters were crowing before he slept. He had felt sick all night. He'd had a bellyful of this marriage. There was neither reason nor purpose in it for him. He had made a mistake; there was no sense in prolonging it. He wanted just one thing from Lily, a divorce. But this was not the time to discuss it. Somehow they had to deal with Lavinia's grief.

Lily sat down at the end of the table. She looked up at Lavinia and laughed. "Why are you standing there like a ninny, La? Sit down. Eat your breakfast."

"I'm not hungry, Lily."

"Stop being childish, La. I declare, you're acting like a silly fool."

"Am I? I'm going home this morning, Lily."

"Home? To Errigal? Why? What about Mr. Andrew Williams? He's your one chance on this earth of ever catching yourself a husband. He's not going to chase after you to Errigal, I can promise you. You'll certainly lose him if you run away like a little fool."

"I'm sure I've already lost Andrew," Lavinia said. She shrugged. "We don't have to talk about it, Lily."

Lily's mouth twisted. "Well, we certainly do have to talk about it. I need you here. You certainly will never find a man to marry at Errigal. If you act like a fool, you'll just throw away a perfectly handsome man who is willing to marry you."

"I don't want to talk about it. I am going, Lily."

"No." Lily shook her head. Her face went deathly pale. "I told you, I won't let you go. I need you here. Stop acting like a child, do you hear me? Stop it. Stop it. Stop it."

Suddenly, Lily buckled forward over the table. Her hands clasped at her solar plexus. Her mouth parted wide and she threw up, the vomit gushing across her lips and splattering over the table. Both Lavinia and Ward ran around the table to her. Sobbing, Lily sank back against her chair.

"What's the matter, Lily?" Ward bent over her. He touched her shoulder compassionately, but she shook his hand away.

She stared up at him, her eyes livid, her lips stretched taut across her teeth. "What do you think is wrong?" her voice rasped, each word hard and slashing. "I'm pregnant, damn you, that's what's wrong."

Chapter Twenty-Three

THE OLD GRANDFATHER CLOCK in the downstairs foyer
gasped and then chimed midnight, twelve musical strokes.
Ward closed the thick magnolia-wood front door and
leaned against it for a moment, exhausted. He had survived the longest day in his life, the sort which threatened
to be the norm for his future.

A low-trimmed gas lamp with a tulip-shaped, spun-glass
shade had been left burning for him in the foyer. The rest
of the house was silent, with that stunned silence of a deep
slumber. He yawned almost helplessly. It seemed an
eternity since he had walked out of this house this morning,
leaving Lily ill and Lavinia holding back tears as she
tended to her sister.

Lily's pregnancy was on his mind all the way to the office.
He wanted to revel in exultance; he was going to be a father; but Lily hadn't left much to cheer about in her announcement. She looked on it as almost criminal, a curse
against her, a hated confinement. But she *was* pregnant.
With his child.

He exhaled heavily. This altered his determination to
seek an immediate divorce. He continued to hope against
the reality of his existence. Perhaps if they had a child of

their own, they might still make their flawed marriage work. He did not know that he wanted to, and yet there was the obligation—to his unborn child, to Lily, even to Robin. No matter what he wanted, everything was tossed into abeyance. He could not endure to go on in this monk-like existence. This looked like a sure route to insanity. Yet he did not even consider walking out on Lily and the children. A man made his bed. . . .

His problems at home were driven from his mind almost as soon as he entered his office. Uzziah Giddings awaited orders before returning to the work site along the St. Johns. Phillips Clark stood by, cautioning Ward to go slowly against the homesteaders. To Ward, it seemed a problem requiring immediate action. He expected to go out and solve it. Nothing but settlement in court would satisfy Clark.

The controversy was like quicksand; the more one struggled, the deeper into the unknown, unseen morass one sank. Ward had thought it a conclave of disgruntled squatters who had appropriated railroad property for their subsistence farms. Before ten o'clock that morning, he was disabused of this mistaken view.

A muster of cattlemen, land developers, and railroaders marched in about nine. News of his confrontation with the homesteaders had spread rapidly across the state, polarizing the haves against the have-nots. This group of angered men blamed the Democratic regime at Tallahassee, where Governor Drew had appointed a Railroad Commission.

"Since that body convened, things have rapidly deteriorated from impossible to incredible."

"You know what the Railroad Commission is? That's three men, empowered by the state to bankrupt railroads at their pleasure."

The man most reviled at this meeting was a state senator named Wilkinson Call. It was Call's resolution that had led directly to Ward's confrontation with squatters along his right-of-way.

"Wilkinson Call, there's the varmint sucking our eggs. Call introduced and managed to get passed in the legislature a law stipulating that all land grants to railroads—regardless of how far back into antiquity these grants extend—should be forfeited unless the railroads complete

309

their building contracts in a time stipulated by the Internal Improvement Fund and/or the Railroad Commission."

Ward nodded. "They gave me only seven months to open rights-of-way between here and Palatka or lose our grants and the franchise."

"Yeah, but that's your problem; it ain't the point that's got them squatters all riled up. There's another line in that law that them squatters live by. That's the line in Call's resolution that can wipe us all out, cattlemen, land developers, or railroaders. That line says any lands redeemed by the state through failure of railroaders to complete their contracts are to be opened to homesteaders in small lots."

"That's right. That means all these patch-pants squatters have to do is delay and harass you long enough, and they got improved land to cut up among themselves."

"And anybody that don't want you to finish your line on time just foments enough hate talk among the rabble, and they'll stop you for him. He's got himself a franchise and land grants. The rabble get a few acres in payment."

"It's a hate-the-railroads idea. Florida crackers thrive on it. To them it's better'n grits and red-eye gravy."

"It's a populist play. Call calls it 'rescuing of Florida's lands from the railroads."

"That son of a bitch," Ward said. "If we hadn't built railroads, he wouldn't have a state to screw up."

Another man laughed sourly. "Have you seen the Ocala *Banner*? The editor down there calls Wilkinson Call 'a man the common people love and the corporations fear'."

"Most of the railroads in Florida will be in receivership in another year unless somebody stops this stupid mule-head."

This knot of men seethed with impotent rage. They ranted in Ward's office; they cursed and vowed vengeance, but none of them had any concrete ideas for dealing with the immediate problem immediately. Ward had no time for generalizations or vague threats about future retribution. Because few of them faced disaster as Ward did that morning, they agreed with Phillips Clark that the controversy should be carried to the courts for final resolution. Even the cattlemen, with millions of acres of unfenced and unmarked grazing land among them, upon which nesters encroached overnight, were afraid of overt action.

This time the ragtag nesters had the state and the law behind them.

Ward thanked them for coming and promised cooperation in any solution they found for their mutual problem.

He waited only until the door closed on them before he exploded in anger. "Those lily-livered bastards. They're running scared. They know they're being robbed, but they don't know what to do about it. They can't call the police because it's the police who are robbing them. Well, I'm damned if I'll stand by and be robbed—even by the State of Florida."

"Smells like bad trouble," Giddings said. "I do what you say, Masta."

"I want you to hire some help. Big boys, tough, with big muscles. I don't give a damn about the size of their brains, just so they can wield pickax handles or shoot straight."

"For God's sake, Ward," Clark broke in. "If you do this, you're going outside the law, just as the nesters are—only worse. They haven't killed anybody yet."

"Neither have I. And I won't, unless I have to kill to protect my property. And protecting my property means protecting the right to build *my* lines on *my* land. And don't forget, it is my land."

"This hasn't been determined in court." Clark shook his head. "You can't push squatters, Negroes, and Indians ahead of you into the Everglades, just to build your railroad."

"The hell I can't. If they get in my way, I will. That land was granted to me with the railroad franchise. If it was to be land that I could use *unless* some patch-assed nester was squatting on it, they should have put that in the charter."

"It's just that times are changing, Ward. Everything isn't just for the railroads any more. The state is growing. So the Homestead Law is a bad law, not needed any more, obsolete. Still, it *is* the law. People are settling open lands. The law says it's land they can claim and prove up."

"Not my land, they can't. They can't squat on it, claim it, or prove it up. If the state won't move the beggars, I will."

"Smells like bad trouble," Uzziah repeated.

"That's what I love about you, Uzziah," Ward said. "Understatement."

311

Ward climbed the wide stairs slowly, supporting himself with his hand on the polished bannister. It seemed a long way up to the landing. He yawned again. He should feel better. He and Uzziah had recruited and armed a small force to protect the railway workers. He was going to the site in the morning and remain there until his right-of-way reached Palatka. But he felt no pumping adrenalin, no sense of accomplishment or purpose. He felt only exhaustion.

In his room, he undressed and stepped into his cotton pajama pants, too tired to slip his arms into the tops. As he reached out to turn off the lamp, a faint knock sounded at his door. He turned as the door swung slowly open under the light touch of Lavinia's fist.

"Come in," he said. The supple symmetry of her body was accented by lights and shadows gleaming along her robe. Her red hair was braided on each side of her head. He felt that hot surge of desire flare like liquid fire in his loins. There was no better antidote for exhaustion than passion. But he knew better; he could never touch his sister-in-law again. Lily had effectively killed anything between him and Lavinia; Lily's self-righteous contempt for sex could render filthy any human contact. Poor La. He was astonished to see her still in this house where she had been so publicly maligned.

For a moment Lavinia stood hesitating in the doorway. Then she stepped inside, and closed the door behind her. She did not lock it this time. She said, "Your door—it wasn't locked."

"It hasn't been locked for almost a year, La."

She sighed heavily and bit her lip, then smiled. "At least, knowing that, I don't feel so much like a bitch in heat, chasing after you when you didn't want me."

He spread his hands. "There never was a time—after that first night—when I didn't want you, La. You've got to be smart enough to know that."

"It's hard to be objective and intelligent when you're hurt, I guess."

He tried to smile. "Yes. I've found that to be true—more than once."

She gazed at the backs of her hands. "I came in to tell you I'm going to stay on. I didn't want you to have to

312

worry about Lily having no one with her. I will stay; Lily does need me. I can tell you the truth. It's funny, but you are one of the only people I can be wholly truthful with. I didn't want to stay here. I don't want to stay here."

"I don't want you to go on being hurt, La."

"I don't think that would change much. Here or Errigal. I am hurt. I have been hurt. I shall be hurt. The conjugation of my life, I guess." She tried to smile. "What I want you to know is I am staying only because of you."

He winced, but Lavinia smiled and shook her head. "Oh, I don't hope—for that. I gave up that hope—back about the time you started leaving your door unlocked again. No. It's because you are a good person, Ward. Maybe the kindest, dearest, best person I've ever known. Because Lily needs me, *you* need me. And because you need me, I am going to stay. That's all—I wanted to say."

He laughed and walked across the room to her. "That's enough. You just gave my sagging ego the shot it needed. You just made my day—or night." He put his arms about her and drew her to him to comfort her, to thank her. But her face and hands against his bare flesh inflamed her. Suddenly a quiver wracked her body. She clutched her arms about his bared waist, kissing and nuzzling at his chest muscles, his paps.

"Oh God, Ward, I never intended this," she whispered, anguished. "Let me stay with you. Tonight. Just tonight. I swear I'll never bother you again. I swear it."

Her fevered, trembling hands were already moving, sliding across the hard-muscled planes of his belly, closing on him. She sank downward slowly, drawing her heated tongue across his stomach.

He reached behind her and locked the door. "What the hell?" he said. "You get the name, you might as well get the game . . . ."

Ward rode south on the work train the next morning, with Uzziah Giddings and the small army they had recruited and supplied.

On the ferry, crossing from Jacksonville to the terminal in South Jacksonville, Ward stood gazing back across the St. Johns. There was only one answer to a successful railroad operation along the East Coast below Jacksonville—providing he was able to build his line. He saw in his mind

313

a drawbridge across the river at the old cow ford. Jacksonville would then be just another way station and not a roadblock or dead end. Things were changing swiftly. Because Plant had opened a Waycross-to-Jacksonville spur of his South Georgia railroad, travelers and freight could come directly into Jacksonville without crossing Ward's Lake City lines. Plant had also opened a line from Atlanta to Lake City that bypassed Jacksonville. Where a rail traveler formerly had to go west across Georgia and into Florida to Live Oak and return ninety miles to Jacksonville—making the short trip from Savannah to Jacksonville a matter of a day and a half of travel—ten hours had now been chopped off that travel time. Also chopped off was the revenue accruing to Ward's Lake City-Jacksonville road.

Ward gazed at the receding skyline of the town. If he were to exist, he had to find and serve new markets, new outlets, and make new improvements in rail service. Building this line against the opposition of settlers came first, but, beyond that, there had to be a railroad bridge across this river.

With the fight directly before him, Ward was already looking far ahead, beyond this battle to the one for permission and capital to span the St. Johns. He grinned as he thought about La. He should have been tired, but he wasn't tired at all. Anyone who said sex was tiring just never had really enjoyed it. He looked ahead to a good fight.

As the train slowed, approaching the work site, Ward saw the first of the sullen nesters lining the roadway. The men, and a few of the hard-faced women, were armed with shotguns and rifles.

Ward warned his men against firing at anyone, unless they were fired upon first. "We won't stand for destruction of railroad property," Ward told them. "We won't stand for work stoppages."

The people pointed at him, recognizing him as the "head varmit," even though he wore Levis', a denim shirt, and a flat-crowned hat. They cursed and shook their fists, but they were disorganized, without a leader. Work continued along the roadbed.

Ward sent Phillips Clark to Tallahassee. He himself, in the next weeks, traveled by steamship, power boat, log train, coach, and saddle horse. He visited every cattleman and land developer he could find. To each he posed the same question: "Have you lost land to squatters?"

The organized cattlemen and land developers joined him. They visited Tallahassee and lobbied for the repeal of the 1862 Homesteaders' Law. They argued that Florida land was now far too valuable to be opened to squatters. Nesters encroached on lands owned by cattlemen and land developers, or so long ago appropriated that possession was assumed under common law. Because of nesters, railroads were being stalled by threat, force and lawsuit, and penalized when they could not fulfill building contracts. Land granted to railroads was being stolen by squatters who moved in, built shacks, and refused to budge.

The legislators were sympathetic but wary. Representatives of people who had legally homesteaded farms and even huge groves under the terms of the 1862 law charged that railroaders like Plant, Demens, White, Hamilton, and others were driving them, along with helpless, disenfranchised blacks and Indians, into the swamps in their landgrabbing drives forward in the name of "progress." They insisted that the cattlemen, land developers, and rail owners represented money and brutal power. The growing numbers of settlers represented a sizable block of votes, and this didn't even count the Negroes, who by now had been almost totally dispossessed by white-supremacy laws passed in the legislature. Legislators promised action, and then did nothing.

Clark returned to the work site and reported to Ward that Plant's people were in Tallahassee arguing for injunctions to halt further progress of the Jacksonville-Palatka line until the matter was examined and adjudicated in the courts. One of the most vocal anti-Jacksonville-Palatka lobbyists was a young girl reputedly in the employ of Plant's Southern Express Company. "That girl is Dayton Fredrick's daughter. Julia Fredrick is as loudly against you as anybody." Clark shook his head. "She makes an impressive witness for the downtrodden nesters."

Ward grinned tautly. Julia Fredrick, prominent in the camp of the enemy. It was almost as if he could hear her saying, that day in his office: "The Fredricks are fierce in their emotions—love or hate—and singleminded in their devotions . . . and they're all the same. Violent . . ."

*   *   *

The line reached Tocoi, and moved southward toward
Palatka. For each mile of new rails laid, a dozen new hot-
eyed, sullen faces of armed backwoodsmen and their
women appeared.

The showdown came ten miles outside of Palatka. There
was a change in the atmosphere, a sense of solidarity
among the nesters. Somebody was organizing and leading
them. They appeared at nine o'clock in the morning, and
retreated to prepared meals at some distance from the
tracks, at noon. They reappeared at one, seething with unspoken rage, sitting or walking in the path of working men
and heavy equipment.

Three days before Ward's time limit expired, the settlers
barricaded themselves behind log ties and barbed wire
fencing. For a long time they were exhorted by a tall,
gaunt, man, shirtless in stained overalls. The man's name
was Marve Pooser. He was the recognized leader of the
displaced settlers. Ward's men were unable to learn from
where Pooser had appeared, whenever he had lost property, or whether he'd ever even held any. With Pooser
leading them, the nesters squatted implacably in the blazing
sun, their guns fixed on the work party.

Ward called up his largest steam-driven tractor. He
climbed aboard and ordered it driven toward the barricade. The great engine struggled forward, turtle-like, on
the newly cleared ground.

Ward held up his arm, signaling the operator to halt the
rig a few yards from the log battlements. "Pooser," he
called, "we're coming through. You people are on railroad
property. You can't stop us. Somebody's going to get
hurt."

"It's you, you outlander son of a bitch." Pooser leaped
up on the log structure, holding a rifle.

Uzziah and his men came running. Before they reached
the grader, Pooser fired.

Ward felt as if someone had struck him just inside the
left shoulder with a dull axe. He staggered under the impact of the bullet. He braced himself and hung on.

Uzziah yelled at his men, "Shoot the bastards. If they
don't move, shoot."

Pooser stood atop the logs and stared at Ward on the
tractor. Behind Pooser, silence rose like heat waves, in-

credible tensions growing in the blazing heat. The nesters waited for Ward to fall. He leaned against a fire-hot metal upright, but he did not fall. They waited for him to order the machine to stop.

He did not. His hand pressed against his bleeding, broken shoulder, and he jerked his head, ordering the iron-wheeled juggernaut forward.

He stood where he was, his knees threatening to buckle. He saw nothing clearly. Through a gathering and occluding haze, he saw Uzziah and his men walking beside the grader. Uzziah gave a signal, and his men began to fire over the heads of the settlers. Pooser stood atop the barricade until the last minute, then leaped to safety. His retreat broke the back and spirit of the nesters.

As the log barricade was uprooted and hurled aside, Uzziah's men broke through, pursuing the backwoodsmen, who wheeled around and retreated into the thick cover of the swamps.

Uzziah ran to the tractor and climbed up beside Ward. "You all right, Masta?"

Ward tried to grin. He could see Uzziah only as a distantly removed blur on some undefined horizon. "Are you St. Peter? Or Satan?"

Uzziah smiled. "Get you to doctor."

"The hell with that. Keep this road moving."

Three men carried Ward into Dr. Branford Wynn's office in the village of Palatka. Ward was barely conscious, weak from loss of blood, and almost mindless from the pain in his shoulder.

Dr. Wynn, a thin, sun-leathered man in his forties, showed little compassion. He examined the wound. "Looks like you got what you asked for, mister. Coming in here, walking over people, running them out of their homes."

Ward stared up at the doctor, barely able to discern his features in the pink fog. "I don't need a sermon, doctor; I need help. Do you want a real railroad into this godforsaken backwater dump? Or do you want to turn the place over to the squatters? Do you want freight and people hauled over your mud roads by oxen? If you do, just leave that bullet where it is."

The doctor laughed. "By God, boy, you got guts! With that bullet tearing you up, you're still full of sass. I like

317

you, boy, I like your style. I ain't one to take to strangers; us backwoods crackers don't, but I like you."

"I don't give a damn whether you like me or not. Just patch me up. I've got work to do."

Chapter Twenty-Four

WARD SLUMPED ON his spine in an easy chair on his sun porch and ordered a servant to bring him another bourbon over ice. "And take it easy on the ice," he said.

Enforced idleness chafed him. His left shoulder was wrapped like a cheap salami. He had been brought home, on his back, via train and horsedrawn ambulance. He had fainted in Dr. Wynn's Palatka office. The doctor was probing none too dexterously for the bullet, and suddenly Ward felt as if something flashed in his brain and he could feel himself spinning outward from reality into warm and soothing silence. The last thing he heard was Dr. Wynn's terse, "Well, it'll be easier digging with him out like that."

He was out. Once he was helpless, underlings assumed command. Dr. Wynn ordered him returned to Jacksonville for at least a month of rest and recuperation. The employees had him aboard a train and on the way north before he had strength to protest.

Inwardly, he had been protesting ever since. He found this quiet almost intolerable. At first, lounging on the sun porch, his shoulder propped among pillows, his feet up on an ottoman, he had relaxed as much as possible. But he was unable to forget that he'd left a job incomplete—a project that could ruin him if it failed. His was no well-financed corporation that could assimilate its losses. He could afford no failures.

He stared at the river, enjoying briefly the carefully tended gardens and the wild trees that had been manicured if not domesticated: the linden, the flowering dogwood, the massive live oaks, the rows of clipped cedars, the waxy-leafed magnolia. He surveyed the beds of hydrangea, yellow alamanda, ligustrum, hibiscus, marigolds, and petunias. He was reduced at last to counting the flowers.

Servant girls brought Robin out to the sun porch in the morning. At first, Ward was a stranger to him and Robin was wary, but finally he played contentedly around Ward's chair and, exhausted, slept in his arms.

The house was quiet. Lily was often at the piano. He tried to ignore her absorption with the same simple tunes, endlessly repeated.

He looked up with some pleasure when Bracussi hurried across the parlor toward him. Bracussi shouted the news as he entered the sun porch. "We made it, Mr. Hamilton. We finished the contract to Palatka—with sixty-three hours to spare."

"Call me Ward, Ralph."

Bracussi nodded happily, pumping Ward's hand. "The whole company is celebrating right now, Mr.—" he caught himself— "Ward. They're sorry you can't be there with them."

"Have a drink, Ralph."

"Thank you, sir." Ralph poured bourbon into a glass of ice.

Ward grinned expansively. "I suppose Clark is celebrating on Bay Street?"

Bracussi grinned and winked. "I think so. But we're celebrating, too. We're all celebrating."

Bracussi opened his briefcase and placed dozens of letters, most of them poorly written, scrawled, with misspellings, but all delivering the same undeviating message: hate.

Ward glanced through the stack of letters. There were threats in each of them, like something orchestrated. If Ward Hamilton appeared in the town of the writer, he would be slain on sight. The writer was a better shot than Marve Pooser. He wouldn't miss next time.

Ward sent for Gilman Rich. His hired rumormonger entered the room, shaking his head. Ward said, "You're not doing me a lot of good in the redneck country, Rich."

"Lord, Mr. Hamilton, don't say that. You don't understand how bad things *could* be. I know you're hated. Lord, you'd think you'd personally burned half the people in Florida out of their homes. I know there have been threats on your life. But it could be worse. Oh my, yes. I'm out there doing my best, slandering you every day. Only, in your case, you're my first failure. It just ain't working, Mr. Hamilton. Still, we don't know how much worse it could be if I hadn't been out there working, talking against you."

Ward waved his arm toward the letters. "Are those threats real?"

"I'd take them seriously, Mr. Hamilton."

Ward took the threats seriously enough to call Uzziah Giddings in from the work site. He explained to the halfbreed what he wanted. Uzziah would live in the house, ride to and from work with him every day, and accompany him whenever he traveled into the interior of the state, even to Tallahassee.

Ward then sent Uzziah to his clothier on Adams Street with a message to fit Uzziah in business suits, soft-collared white shirts, and coltskin button-shoes with military heels and welted soles. Uzziah returned home in a three-button, semi-form-fitting, single-breasted sack style with long roll lapels and tight cuffs.

Even Lily smiled and told Uzziah how elegant he looked in his new black derby. Ward had a full-length mirror moved into the third floor bedroom where Uzziah would sleep.

Ward was forced to remain idle, physically. But gradually he directed the affairs of the company from his sun room command post. He ordered the work crews to continue from Palatka. He had never intended ending his line at the fishing, lumber, and farm town. He found himself short on cash due to the problems the company encountered, but he extended his rail lines fifty-one miles across from the St. Johns River to Ormond and Daytona. In the process, he ran into construction troubles. Extension was delayed because of boggy, seemingly bottomless marshes. When this pulpy morass was finally filled and roadbeds graded well above the high-water mark, the workers had to cut through layers of rock. His engineers advised against blasting. Workers had to hack their way, using tools, through this time-and-weather-set rock in order to lay the roadbed. A bridge was built across the Halifax River. Ward saw this construction feat as preliminary to spanning the St. Johns at Jacksonville.

He sent Phillips Clark to Tallahassee to make the necessary arrangements for building the first railroad bridge across the St. Johns. Clark stayed for weeks, reporting only sporadic progress. There were many palms to grease. There was not a legislator in Tallahassee who did not believe that the bridge across the St. Johns would be the most important progressive step in Florida's history to date. And each was less than loath to profit personally from its construction. Ward raged, threatening to go to Tallahassee personally, but Clark insisted that discussion had reached a delicate stage and required only diplomacy, patience, and a little more money.

That winter, Ward met Henry Flagler for the first time. The retired Standard Oil corporator found Florida attractive but rough, almost like the frontiers west of the Mississippi. Not even the electrically lighted St. James Hotel, with its bowling alleys, billiard rooms, and sun parlors, impressed the tycoon. His new wife found fault with everything. They were less than enchanted with Jacksonville; there was neither the sunshine nor the languorous atmosphere they'd anticipated. Flagler, at fifty-three, admitted to Ward that he was probably prejudiced against the city because of the sorry state of rail travel from Savannah southward. From New York to Savannah, schedules and accommodations had been excellent. Suddenly, from Savannah, he and his party, in his private car, had been connected to a night train for a roundabout sixteen-hour trip to Jacksonville. "To get here, it's either a train that goes more than a hundred miles west and south to Live Oak and then back ninety miles east to cover what should be a hundred-and-twenty-mile trip, or you take an inland steamer that makes the trip in a day—unless it runs aground. Then you'll remain aboard a week or more." Flagler and his wife, eighteen years younger than he, departed at once for St. Augustine, via the St. Johns River steamboat to Tocoi, and then aboard Ward's upgraded line to the ancient village on Mantanzas Bay. Before that winter ended, rumor came to Ward that Flagler was deeply interested in Florida development. But Ward was too involved in his own affairs to heed the warning. At the time, it seemed less than a cloud on his busy horizon.

Ward was sitting alone having grapefruit and coffee for a midmorning snack when a servant announced the Reverend Andrew Williams.

Ward winced and took a long drink of coffee, keeping the cup over his face to conceal his displeasure. God knew he was lonely and bored, but not miserable enough to welcome the assistant pastor of Lily's church.

Andrew told the servant to close and lock the glass-paned double doors between the sun room and the parlor.

"I hope you haven't come to pray for me," Ward said, mildly mocking.

Andrew didn't smile. "I'm sure God forgives your prideful lack of faith; I hope He can forgive your fleshy sins as well. I am trying to. I had believed myself a forgiving Christian man, Mr. Hamilton, but I find it hard to forgive you."

"Oh?" Faintly angry, Ward wondered when he'd asked his forgiveness.

Andrew stood glaring down at Ward like an avenging angel. "I have prayed almost constantly since that night, Mr. Hamilton, but I still find my rages murderous—against you."

"What night is that, Andrew?"

"You very well know, sir. The night your wife—Miss Lily—accused you before your guests of adulterous conduct with—" his voice broke— "with Miss Lavinia."

"Miss Lily isn't well. Have you considered that?"

"I've considered every aspect of this tragic affair, sir. I've tried to tell myself her accusations could not be true. I know Miss Lavinia had seemed to me the incarnation of an angel—until that terrible moment. I was mortified, anguished, and heartbroken."

"I'm sorry about that."

"Are you? The only reason I am here is your godlessness. You are the godless kind of lecher who would take advantage of a helpless young girl's innocence and virtue."

"Have you talked to Lavinia about this?" Ward's voice

323

was strained; he had reached the raw edge of his patience.

"I have talked to *Miss* Lavinia. She says her sister does become hysterical at times, and doesn't know what she's saying. Miss Lavinia vows that nothing has happened between her and you."

"Then that's the truth."

"God knows, I wish I could believe that."

"If you were smart, you could. If you hope to marry Lavinia, to live in peace with her or yourself, you'd better start by believing her, trusting her."

"I don't need you to advise me on my relations with Miss Lavinia. I prefer you not even to speak her name. I could trust her, except—"

"Except for me."

"I can't get it out of my mind that you must have broken into Miss Lavinia's room. Miss Lily did accuse you of scandalous conduct. Where there's smoke, there's fire. You must have attacked Miss Lavinia, torn away her dress and her undergarments, exposing her naked flesh to your lascivious eyes. You must have ravaged her helpless body, forcing her to unnatural—"

"Are you enjoying this graphic description, Andrew?" Ward inquired.

Andrew paused, white-faced and trembling, and caught his breath. "You are a carnal cad, sir, a low, vile creature for daring to suggest that I—a man of the cloth—could draw pleasure from evil acts of adultery."

"You sounded pretty excited."

"Outraged, sir. Outraged."

"Oh."

"You have a poisoned mind."

"One of us has."

"You're laughing at me in my anguish. I should horsewhip you."

"Why? For laughing at you?"

"For destroying any hope of marriage between Miss Lavinia Harkness and me."

"If nothing has happened, I don't see why your romance is destroyed, or even affected—if you care for her."

"I told you my holy feelings toward Miss Lavinia are none of your concern. You sully them by talking about them. I have cared deeply for her. But she has been accused of adultery before members of my own congregation! My pastor! His wife! How could Miss Lavinia and I have any life together now? How could I hope to rise, respected and venerated in my church, with this ugly stain on us?"

"Your *Miss* Lavinia told you nothing happened between her and me, boy. Either believe her, or get out of here and forget her. There's nothing I can tell you."

"There *is* something you can tell me. I want your vow that nothing happened. I want you to swear you never touched her, never went near her, never *will* go near her again. Only then can I start to build my life again. There is no chance for Miss Lavinia and me, as long as that ugly stigma remains against her."

"What you really mean is, as long as you doubt her."

"I'm torn apart by doubt. I believe her. I want to believe her. And yet—"

"Why are you here? You've just said you're not going to marry La."

"How can I? She has been disgraced—by you—before my congregation."

"Go to another church, away from here."

"It's not that easy. Rumors follow one. If you are found to have run away from some scandalous situation— No. I'll have to stay and face my congregation without Miss Lavinia."

Ward shrugged. "If that's what you want."

"What I *want*?" Andrew stared toward heaven. "It's all you've left me in your lust."

Ward sat in silence for some moments. At last he said, "I don't know what you want of me. Some public gesture?"

"You? What could you do?"

"I don't know. Lily and your pastor have been hounding me about the need for a new church building; suppose I were to donate the land and build the empty edifice? Your parishioners should be able to furnish it."

Andrew stared at him. "Why would you do that?"

Ward shrugged. "I'd do it as a wedding gift for Lavinia and you, of course. If Lavinia wants to marry you, and you agree, I'll do it. But I'd do it in honor and as a living memorial to my dear wife. There would be a large brass plaque stating this—in Lily's honor, with all my love and faithful devotion."

Andrew swallowed hard. Ward could almost see the wheels grinding in the pastor's inflexible mind. Ward's unprecedented offer had convinced Andrew that Miss Lavinia's brother-in-law *was* guilty of adulterous behavior. Andrew was sick at his stomach. He wanted to howl out his rage and hatred for this adulterer. But if he did this, he not only lost Miss Lavinia, but he lost a gift to the church that might redound to his benefit. He knew now that something *had* happened between Miss Lavinia and her lecherous brother-in-law. He could strike this blackguard across the face and walk out, but if he did, he walked out with nothing except his cold pride and empty hands. He could accept this knave's proposition, but if he did, he was forever silenced on the sin between this rogue and Miss Lavinia. He swallowed back the tears that welled up in his throat.

Ward watched Andrew coolly. He continued in a mild voice that in itself was taunting and insulting, "That new church would be *your* wedding gift. The church hierarchy would be so informed, in so many words. It would be bestowed with the understanding that your future promotions should take in consideration that this gift came to the church only through your good offices. It could not hurt you if the church deaconry knew that building will never be erected or the land donated by me, except as you are favorably considered, and that church building would be erected when and if Lavinia agrees to marry you. If she wants you, you can have a church building that will knock their eyes out. If she doesn't want you—the hell with you."

Andrew exhaled heavily. He put guilt out of his heart, wounded pride and doubt from his mind. He nodded.

Ward summoned young Quincy Duval, an archictect who had worked with NEF&GC, designing its depots, shops, and freight buildings. "I'm going to endow a church building to the Magdalena Baptist Church," Ward said. "I'm also endowing the land. I'm doing it as a living monument to my wife. I'll try to picture for you what I want. I hope I can make you understand me."

He described a huge stucco cathedral, ornate, gaudy, with pink figurines and ornamental designs along the eaves and cornices. He envisioned the interior of the temple with cake-icing-white plaster walls, extending upward to the highest reaches of the transept. The chapel must be left totally bare. In his mind, he saw a huge vault as empty as the hearts and minds of the intolerant people who would congregate inside it.

Duval promised to deliver precisely the design he requested. Ward added, "Beside the entrance, spectacularly large, I want a bronze plaque which should read something like: 'In honor of the devotion and love and sensitivity of my wife, Lily Harkness Hamilton, and of her friends, associates, and members of her congregation who feel, see, and worship as she does.' "

Lily's pregnancy was nine months of waking nightmare. She awoke crying out in the night, with flaring headaches and paralyzing pains in her lower back, as well as a total lack of sensation in her legs and ankles. Thetis was sent racing night after night to bring Dr. Benson Dame. Finally the harassed physician refused to come, saying each time that Lily's agony had no physical basis that he could find. He told Ward, "It's all in her mind, all in her imagination." To Lily he said, "I'm leaving a bottle of the same tablets I prescribed the first time I called on you. These pills will relieve your pain in exactly the same way they cured your suffocation." To the druggist, he wrote a prescription, to be filled as often as needed, for a placebo.

To Ward's astonishment, Lily's odd behavior at her first formal party did not stop visitors from appearing at her door each afternoon. Finally he realized that most came, not from any sense of compassion or concern for Lily, but from curiosity. She had become an object of morbid interest. No one knew what she might do next. These women came as sympathetic intimates, but they went away clucking like hens, smiling behind their hands and eyeing each other knowingly.

He learned by accident that one of Lily's most consistent topics of conversation was Ward's physical cruelty to her, the way he mistreated her. She won unmeasured attention, pity, and avid interest with her revelations. She was totally and completely the center of attention.

"And he's unfaithful," she said, sniffling into a lace handkerchief. "Flagrantly unfaithful, with some of the

327

most socially respected women in this town. I could shock you if I told you their names."

At first, Ward quivered with rage. He wanted to confront Lily, demanding to know the names of his blue-book concubines. But then he laughed at himself. He was damned if he would play Lily's games with her. He didn't give a damn what she said to her empty-minded friends. To hell with her and to hell with them. Lily was happy when she was whispering scandalous accusations over her fragile teacups, behind closed doors. Alone, she wandered the house miserably like a trapped animal, or sat for hours playing the same tune at the piano. He encouraged her teatime acquaintances to visit her as often as possible; at least her mind was diverted. "Lily depends on your love," he told these women with a straight face. "She's only really well and happy when you wonderful ladies are visiting with her."

As the months passed, Lily's terror grew; she became obsessed with the idea that she would die in childbirth. She'd first fastened upon this notion after a visit to a fortune-teller with a group of her friends. The woman, who claimed to be a gypsy born with a caul, laid out cards, and revealed glibly: "I see you in a hospital. An illness. No. Something. A delivery." The ladies with Lily snickered knowingly and approvingly. The woman nodded solemnly. "A baby. You are going to have a baby." Lily asked if she would have a boy or a girl. More cards were placed face-up on the table. The woman's swarthy face darkened. "I see—I see . . ." She refused to go on. Only when Lily pleaded and had paid an extra ten dollars and agreed to accept calmly the woman's revelation did the Gypsy whisper, "I see . . . *death.*"

From that afternoon, Lily grew morbidly fascinated by the occult, black magic, witchcraft, second sight, and crystal gazing. Wherever she heard of a new sorcerer—astrologer, palmist, clairvoyant—she gathered a coterie of friends and visited the practitioner. She had dozens of bosom friends now; she was one of the most popular young matrons in the town; young and middle-aged women found Lily totally unusual, odd, different, one of a kind—fascinating. Lily sought answers feverishly, but never found the replies she wanted. What was the name of her husband's latest mistress? Was a second marriage in the cards for her? What sort of man could be discerned in her tea leaves? Could the crystal ball foretell a time of happiness for her?

Once, after midnight, she sent Thetis for Dr. Benson Dame. She had been thus instructed by a black practitioner of voodoo. Dr. Dame refused to come to the Hamilton house. He told Thetis coldly that he could accept only one call from Mrs. Hamilton—when she went definitely into labor.

But Thetis had been coached well by Lily. He gave the doctor an envelope containing a one hundred-dollar bill and a note: *Please come. Urgent.* The doctor pocketed the bill and agreed to make this one last house call.

When he arrived at the Hamilton house, he found Lily in the dimly lit parlor. She waited until they were alone. Then she bent toward him and whispered, "I have something that will protect us. Both of us."

"Protect, Miss Lily?" The doctor frowned, sighed, and yawned.

She handed him a small round creek pebble, highly polished. "Keep this with you all the time," she said. "I have one exactly like it." She showed him a similar river rock. "This will insure a safe delivery for me. It will protect you."

He bit his lip, wanting to tell her the only real protection he needed was from her late-night summonses, from his own loss of sleep.

"I am not afraid now. Not anymore," she confided.

"Have you been afraid?"

"Haven't you? I've lived in terror. Until now. Until today when Madame Estelle gave me these sacred stones blessed by the voodoo god of fertility. Damballah, she said. Damballah will protect us—"

"I don't believe this," the doctor said, mostly to himself.

"—even from Ward."

"From Ward? From your husband?"

"Ward wants me to die. You are in danger, too. He's willing to let you die to be certain I don't survive this—this ordeal; you must know that by now, as often as you've come to this house. He's said he wants me dead. You must see the way he watches me."

The doctor exhaled. "I'll keep the stone, Miss Lily. You

329

have nothing to worry about. From your husband, from Damballah, or from me. You're going to be all right."

"I know." She smiled secretively and smugly, closing her fist tightly over her polished pebble.

The eighth and ninth months of Lily's confinement were particularly anguishing for her. She was too bulky and awkward to travel around the town to her seances. Her company came less frequently, and she developed excruciating headaches. She screamed in pain, waking up at night, swearing she was being systematically poisoned. People in this house who wanted her dead were slowly poisoning her.

Ward dispatched clerks from Jacksonville's most exclusive stores with the latest fashions in gowns, dresses, and delicate underthings. He paid stylists to visit the house, to design and display clothes, hats, hair styles, shoe modes, and cosmetic effects. As long as Lily was thus engaged, she was free of those debilitating and agonizing head pains.

He did not know that each visitor to the house departed with the whispered information that Lily's husband physically maltreated her and offered these diversions merely to keep her quiet. He did not know this, but even if he had known, he no longer cared.

He returned to work at his office. Though his company had no real assets, its credit was excellent; business was good and the outlook promising. It was his own decision to push farther south and to spread himself and the company, as Phillips Clark continually warned, "thin, thinner, thinnest."

Andrew Williams had resumed his courtship of Lavinia, calling on her formally each evening at seven and departing precisely at nine. One night when Lavinia came into the living room after saying goodnight to Andrew on the dark veranda, Ward asked if she really cared for Andrew. Lavinia replied that she could, in time, learn to care for him. "That seems a hell of a prospect," he said.

"All my prospects seem like hell," La said. "A girl must marry. The worst thing that can happen to her is not that she be raped, but that she not be asked to wed. At least Andrew has asked me."

* * *

Lily's screams at two o'clock one morning awoke the household. Her pains were excruciating, she wailed. Thetis was dispatched to fetch Dr. Dame. Luke was ordered to harness the horses to the phaeton and stand ready at the front doorway. Thetis had to weep to convince Dr. Dame that Miss Lily's pains were not in her lower back, but in her abdomen. Thetis resorted to the lie that finally convinced the physician that this was not another false alarm. "I do believe, Masta Doctuh, suh, Miss Lily's watuh has broke. Yas, Masta Doctuh, I distinctly heard Miss Lavinia say that."

The doctor surrendered. "Tell Mr. Hamilton to get her to the hospital. I will meet them there."

Lily's labor was protracted, difficult, and almost fatal. Lily was in the labor room for thirty hours. She simply did not dilate properly. One might almost believe that subconsciously her whole body resisted the delivery of this child. She was deathly pale, sobbing, and debilitated by the time the nurses wheeled her into the delivery room.

Ward and Lavinia waited in the corridor as the hours dragged away. They could learn nothing from the staff about Lily's condition. Dr. Dame did not come near them. Somebody said he was sleeping on another floor. At one time, the entire obstetrics ward was in fevered activity, with nurses, orderlies, and residents hurrying, their faces grimly set, into the delivery room where Lily lay, a breath away from death.

When Dr. Dame came out at last, he was quivering with exhaustion. "It's a little girl," he said, his voice hoarse. "She had a hell of a time. They both did. But—" he tried unsuccessfully to smile— "there was nothing to worry about. Lily was gripping this in her fist the whole time."

He opened his palm, holding up the polished pebble. The small stone gleamed dully in the corridor lights.

At ten o'clock that morning, Lavinia was allowed to visit Lily. When Ward would have accompanied her, the nurse shook her head. "I'm sorry, sir. Mrs. Hamilton doesn't want to see you, sir. I am sorry. Dr. Dame left orders. You're not to go in until Mrs. Hamilton sends for you. Dr. Dame said you would understand."

* * *

Lavinia returned from Lily's private room, her face swollen from crying.

"The baby?" Ward gripped Lavinia's arm. "Is she all right?"

"Beautiful, Ward. She's beautiful. The most beautiful little girl anyone ever saw."

"I want to see her."

"Not now, not yet . . ." Lavinia bit her lip, and her eyes brimmed with tears. She clutched his hand fiercely in hers. "Lily blames you for the terrible ordeal she suffered. All she talked about, the whole time, was how you tried to kill her."

Finally, on the fourth day, after Miz Marcy, Beatrice, and Charles Henry Harkness had arrived from Errigal, Lily agreed to let Ward visit her and the baby.

When Ward walked into the room, the infant was lying on the bed beside Lily. Lily watched him without smiling.

He sat on a straight chair at the side of the bed. His heart lurched. Lavinia had not exaggerated. His daughter was the loveliest child born to man.

"Oh God, Lily," he whispered. "She's so beautiful."

"Well," she said. "You got what you wanted, didn't you?"

He barely heard her. He touched the infant's hand. The tiny fingers opened and then closed tightly upon his thumb.

Looking down at her, exultant, Ward knew it was worth it. All of it. She had caught him in her tiny hand and he knew she would never let go, as long as he lived. He was enslaved. He did not want her to let go.

Chapter Twenty-Five

THE NEXT YEARS of Ward's life belonged first to his daughter. After her, the railroad remained his consuming passion, but never again did his company and his battle for corporate existence dominate his heart and mind as Belle did. From the moment Belle closed her fingers on his thumb in that hospital, Ward was enslaved.

Ward named his daughter Belle. Lily wanted to name her Beatrice Marcia, for Lily's beloved spinster sister and her mother, but Ward was adamant. "Look at her, Lily. She looks like a Belle, a little Southern belle."

Lily protested violently, but then suddenly capitulated. She shrugged, staring at Ward, her face twisted with contempt.

After Belle was born, Lily's delicate health deteriorated. She lost weight until she weighed no more than a hundred pounds. Dr. Dame was unable to find a physiological cause for her malady. Lily wanted her mother with her, so Ward invited her family to come from Errigal, to stay as long as possible. For the next fifteen years, the Harknesses spent the six winter months in the Jacksonville house. When the family arrived, Lily improved noticeably for the first few weeks, becoming renewed and revived, and even gaining weight. Then, gradually, she weakened, seeming to

333

wither physically; even her eyes faded, and lost their luster.

Because of the delicacy of her health, she stayed more and more upstairs. She converted three second-floor bedrooms into a parlor suite where she entertained her guests and spent most of her days.

Only Ward was unwelcome in her sanctuary. The first time he came into her rooms to inquire about her health after she'd returned from a month of recuperation in the hospital, she greeted him cuttingly: "Please leave that corridor door open when you are in my room."

He shrugged and left it open. "How are you, Lily?"

"I'm going to live." She spoke coldly, gazing at him unblinkingly. "Despite everything you can do."

He nodded. "Is there anything I can do for you?"

"Yes. Stop pretending you care about me or my health. We both know that unless you can use my body in your filthy sexual attacks, unless you can treat me like a whore while you mouth filthy words, you have no interest in me. Stop being a hypocrite."

He shrugged again. "Well, we can say you are well enough to spit venom, eh?"

"I have nothing for you but venom. You've left me nothing but venom. There is no sense in your thinking you can come in here and force yourself on me. I'll kill you first. I'll kill myself first."

"I don't think you'll need to be so drastic. It's been nearly a year, Lily, since I've touched you. I've managed to restrain my violent passions. I can go on restraining myself."

"Oh, don't lie. You'd be in here at me every day—twice a day, like some dog with the scent—if I'd let you. Well, I won't. I'll never endure that torment again. There'll be no more confinement, no more labor, no more children."

He shrugged. "All right."

"I just want you to understand me."

"I think I *do* understand you, Lily. I truly think I do."

The Ouija board became the essential interest of Lily's existence. She bought the instrument initially to learn from it when she might expect to recover her vitality. She sat mesmerized for hours at a time with her slender fingers resting lightly upon the planchette as it zipped madly across the face of the board. She could not direct the heart-shaped pointer alone, but needed the strength added mysteriously by some congenial partner. This cooperative touching stirred the unknown forces which, without conscious volition, moved the small, paddle-like planchette on its casters across the letters and figures of the large board to draw out its fascinating mediumistic messages.

Ward was pleased that Lily had developed a new interest. As always, though, she plunged into this latest fad with total involvement and to the exclusion of everything else. "Lily always has put her whole heart, mind, and soul into everything she did," Miz Marcy said.

One evening, with family and guests present, Lily announced in breathless pride that she'd had a new message of affection and attachment from Prince Edward.

"From the Prince of Wales?" someone said, astounded. "Do you know him? Does he write to you?"

"We correspond," Lily said archly, "through the Ouija board."

Those less than intimate with Lily glanced at each other, faintly troubled. Ward felt a shaking his his solar plexus, as if his heart had somehow shifted heavily.

"Oh, you'd be surprised at the messages I get through Ouija," Lily said. "Those from Prince Edward are always so lovely." She tilted her head and stared unblinkingly at Ward. "Some messages contain the names of Ward's latest mistresses."

"Good." Ward managed to smile. "Could you get me their addresses too?"

The next day Ward came home early from the office, deeply disturbed. He asked Lily if she would like to attend a performance of *The Second Mrs. Tanqueray* at the Jacksonville Opera House. She refused. He suggested she take afternoon drives in the phaeton. "It would do you and the children good," he suggested. She grew nervous and excited, refusing.

"Let me alone," she cried out. "I don't need you telling me what to do."

"You're spending too much time with that Ouija board, Lily. Even Dr. Dame says so."

"Damn Dr. Dame, and damn you. Dr. Dame says what you want him to say. You don't deceive me, either of you. Are you afraid for me to listen to Ouija? Are you afraid of what I'll find about you?" She screamed at him to leave. She grabbed up a book and an open box of chocolates and threw them at him. "Get out of here. Get out of my room."

She wept, crying at the top of her voice, beating at him with clenched fists until he finally retreated. She locked herself in the room and barricaded the door.

Lavinia, Beatrice, and Miz Marcy tried to get in with promises, threats, pleading. Lily refused to allow anyone in her room but Thetis. They sat beside a bay window overlooking the gardens and the river, their hands lightly touching the planchette. That afternoon Lily received her first proposal of marriage from Edward, Prince of Wales. The message was spelled out quite clearly, the planchette racing so their hands could barely ride it.

Ward sent for Dr. Dame. At first, Lily said it was a ruse to trap her and refused to permit the doctor inside her room. She knew what Ward wanted: to take away her Ouija board. He wanted to punish her, to hurt her. Only when Ward left the house and she saw him from her window, walking through the formal gardens out to the street, would she allow Dr. Dame into her room.

The doctor emerged from the house after an hour. He met Ward at the stone hitching block at the curb where he sat, and they walked together to the river. "It's a very sad thing," Dr. Dame said. "Her hatred of you is an obsession; it is the motivation of her life. The very sight of you disturbs and arouses her, driving her past reason into a frenzy."

"What can I do?"

"My only suggestion to you is that—for the present, at least—you stay away from Lily as much as possible. Don't go unasked into her rooms. I could have suggested this the first time she could not breathe when she was forced to share your bedroom, but I hoped the condition would be temporary. It hasn't been. Your presence upsets her, triggers her tantrums and violences." Dr. Dame shook his head and they walked for a few moments in silence. "We medical men don't know very much—nothing really—about the human mind. To Lily, this seems to be a grim game she is playing with you. The contest seems to be whether she'll kill you off first—with a heart attack or brain hemorrhage—or whether she'll escape you—"

"Escape me?"

"Into insanity. Insanity is an escape. When the mind can't endure the rigors and traumas of sanity—the unbearable agony the rest of us accept as the everyday world—it retreats, or escapes, into insanity. That's the game, I'm afraid, that Lily is playing with you."

"Good God."

"It's not too difficult to understand if you consider that Lily is entirely self-centered. For each of us, the whole outside world revolves about ourselves at its core. It could not be any other way. We *must* be the center of our own universe, but with Lily it has gone far beyond that. She is at the core of a world that must conform to her desires, or she will destroy it, although that may mean destroying herself."

"Will she—recover?"

Dr. Dame shrugged. "It would take a smarter man than I am to answer that, Ward. The prognosis, at present, is not very promising. You can be kindly, understanding, and more patient than Job. This may not help, because it is not what you do that is important, but how she responds to and interprets what you do. Whether or not she will respond, I can't say. But you can begin by going near her only when she sends for you."

Lavinia's marriage to Andrew Williams was celebrated Christmas week. The house was overrun with relatives of the bride and guests. Although the new, gaudy structure of the Magdalena Baptist Church was well on its way to completion—having been started the day Lavinia announced her engagement to the young assistant pastor—as a further wedding gift to Lavinia and Andrew, Ward also paid for the wedding, the parties, the dinners, and the elaborate, flower-bedecked nupitals in the old church.

Lily came out of seclusion, vibrant, warm, radiant. She drove every afternoon in the phaeton with Robin, Thetis, and Luke, to look at "her church."

She was a gracious hostess, pleasant and interested, making every effort to see that everything went off smoothly and without flaw. The only sour note came when

Lily wanted to read, during the wedding ceremony, a message of congratulations from Prince Edward.

The night before the wedding, Lavinia came stealthily into Ward's bedroom, long after midnight. He was awake, sitting at a window in the darkness. Lavinia tried to speak normally, but suddenly broke into sobs and sagged against him.

He sat in the chair, holding her curled in his lap as if she were a child only a little older than Belle. Like Belle, she was contented in his arms, secure there and reassured. "It's all so wrong, Ward. I've got to—to ask you if Andrew and I can live here—in this house with you—after we're married. I've put off asking you as long as I can."

"Does Andrew want to live here?"

She bit her lip. "He suggested it. His salary *is* very low, Ward, hardly enough for him to exist on alone. That's the truth. Even the head pastor lives practically on the donations and charity of the congregation. Andrew says that this house is so large and you have so much that he wanted me to ask you—to beg you—to take us in."

"And what do *you* want?"

She wept, clinging to him. "What difference does it make what I want? I begin to think perhaps I can learn to live in peace with Andrew, then he does something like this, sending me to you to *tell* you we're going to live under your roof, on your charity. Oh God, how can I respect him or love him, after that?"

"You do need a place to live."

"Yes. I suppose that's all Andrew is thinking about. But I know how Andrew vilified you, accused you of raping me. Rape, oh God, rape, when you could have me only by speaking my name, or looking at me across a room. He threatened to horsewhip you. And now . . ."

Ward caressed her tear-streaked cheek with the backs of his fingers. "I want you to stay, La. If that means Andrew will be here too, so be it. We can prepare a suite like Lily's for you. It is a big old barn of a place; Andrew is right about that."

"Oh, Ward, my dearest Ward. God knows, I can't ever thank you. But God also knows I'm going to try."

He laughed. "I think you're trying to seduce me now."

She pressed closer against him, her voice hollow. "I'm

338

trying to put some sanity back in my life, to wash out the hypocrisy, the lying, the pretending. Andrew will live here in your house like a parasite on you, but I won't. Whatever you want, whenever you want it, as long as I live, Ward, I'm yours to use."

"Listen to me. I won't have you sick or torn up inside about this. I do want you to stay, until Belle is grown. By that time, Andrew should have his own parish, and an income of some size. I want you to take care of Belle for me. I vow right now that Belle will never grow up confused and afflicted like her mother. I won't let Belle be force-fed false, straitlaced, hypocritical notions of life; I won't have her going to Lily's church. Maybe some people can remain mentally stable and absorb the hypocritical laws forbidding sex and pleasure and human existence itself. I won't let Belle be subjected to it. If she's taught anything, it will be the truth."

"Oh God, Ward. What is the truth?"

He laughed sourly. "Hell, I don't know. Your tits are the truth. The fever at your thighs is the truth. Other people can do what they want with their lives; I don't care. If they get spiritual gratification from conflicting lies imposed upon their most natural instincts—good. But not my daughter. She'll grow up free. And I want you to help me see that she does, La."

For every mile of road Ward's men laid south of Palatka, two miles were destroyed during the night by vandals. He was forced to employ a full-time army of gun-carrying mercenaries to protect railroad property. He delegated authority for hiring the guards to Uzziah Giddings. The half-breed hired many blacks, some half-breeds like himself, and a couple of Indians. That Indians and blacks opposing them aroused the redneck squatters as nothing else had. In their eyes, this eptiomized Ward Hamilton's total contempt for them as homeowners, as human beings, as white people.

Phillips Clark returned from Tallahassee bearing all necessary clearances for spanning the St. Johns with the first railroad drawbridge—a creosoted piling-and-concrete truss. Construction got under way that spring.

Finding that he was short of operating capital, Ward

made a trip to Atlanta. The Stockmen's and Farmers' Bank had expanded, and was now housed in a six-floor corner building in the center of downtown Atlanta. Hobart Bayard occupied his own suite of offices, with two male secretaries to serve him, as a senior vice-president. Neither of them put it in words, but both realized that the affluence of the Stockmen's and Farmers' Bank reflected the strength and growth of NEF&GC. Hobart almost offhandedly arranged a new half-million dollar line of credit for Ward, congratulating him on the latest financial statement from the railroad. Hobart inquired about the health of the entire Harkness family but appeared to listen only when Ward talked about Lily.

As Ward was leaving, Hobart said smilingly, "By the way, I had lunch the other day in the company of a young friend of yours, a most remarkable young woman: Miss Julia Fredrick. She's just this year out of finishing school in New England, but she is—and this I could hardly believe—a junior executive with Henry Plant's Southern Express Company. She has her offices right down here in the business district."

"I believe it," Ward said.

"Do you? I was shocked at first. Wasn't sure I approved of the idea. She is the first woman in the business world of Atlanta. A few years ago, no respectable lady would even enter the business district for a visit. It was solely a male's world. Now here, suddenly, is Miss Julia Fredrick—an executive working right along with men. It has the industrial people turned upside down, I can tell you."

Ward grinned, thinking about Julia as he had seen her last. God, how many years had it been? He sighed. "I would have been astonished at anything less."

The switch-throwing ceremony for the first electric illumination in Jacksonville created the sensation of 1883. Everyone turned out, lining the streets outside the St. James Hotel. As soon as dusk settled, hotel officials closed the starting mechanism.

Lights flared on abruptly and simultaneously inside and outside the luxury hotel. Every room on every floor boasted an electric bulb suspended on a cord from the ceiling, and a fan operated by electricity with varying speeds. All this in addition to the newly installed telephones on every corridor wall throughout.

As thrilling as was the electrification of the interior, the illumination of the exterior—the marquee, the canopy, the new four-story-high sign—was breathtaking. People thought they were witnessing miracles. It was as if God Himself were close at hand, they said. Perhaps the end of the world, by fire, was near. Dozens of sermons that next Sunday were based on the miracle of light at the St. James.

People stood in silent awe around Ward, but he was too enthralled even to be aware of the crush of human beings. He remembered how in Lumberwood, Ohio, he'd watched his first trains roll past. He'd been exalted, uplifted, confronting wonders too magnificent to credit. Locomotives racing past, their wheels igniting small false flares in friction against the rails, had been wondrous, but the sight of electric lights, turning the Jacksonville night as bright as high noon, inspired and overwhelmed him.

He stood unmoving after everyone else had departed. Only when the huge electric sign was darkened was he freed to walk away. The next day he ordered engineers to install a generator in his carriage house and begin the wiring of his property for electricity. When the work had been accomplished, he held his own miniature ceremony. He strode through the house with Belle in his arms, turning on all the lights, starting the electric water pump that would supply the kitchen and all the bathrooms, lighting the stables, the barn, the carriage house, the gardens. He brightened the night until the curious came racing in on horses, in carriages, afoot, to stand gaping at the miracle.

Lily stared, silent, pale. She clutched Robin in her arms and covered his eyes with her hands. Ward believed she was as awed as he had been, but she was enraged and terrified. They would all be burned to a crisp by his latest contraption. She was not pleased when he revealed that he planned for the new Magdalena Baptist Church to be the first electrified chapel in the area. For months, she refused to allow an electric light turned on in a room where she was.

Meanwhile, Ward ordered all NEF&GC passenger trains equipped with power plants for generating electricity. His coaches raced through the backwoods night, glowing yellowly, stampeding cattle, frightening horses, creating a sensation every mile they traveled. His illumined night coaches were the most talked-about vehicles in the state. People knew Ward Hamilton now, and they lined up to ride his lighted night coaches.

Robin was seven, spoiled by every black servant and all the Harknesses. A thin, pale child who wore ruffled shirts, skirtlike short pants, huge bow ties, knee-length stockings, and his hair in shoulder-length curls. Even at seven, he could do the intricate tatting and lace knitting taught him by his Aunt Beatrice, which Miz Marcy praised extravagantly.

Robin still ate his meals only under the most favorable conditions. Certain foods—cream puffs and eclairs—he devoured gluttonously. With one hand he stuffed the confections into his mouth, and held them in with the other. He ate until his stomach, distended and drum-tight, sent him into screaming tantrums. But he never learned. He continued to eat until he was ill, or he ate nothing.

Ordinary foods like meat and vegetables, he refused to eat unless he was bribed with money, gifts, or treats. He enjoyed being begged to eat and had tantrums when he was told to join the others at the table.

When Ward tried to correct him, Robin screeched at him, raging, "Don't you tell me what to do! Don't you dare tell me what to do. My mother says you don't tell me what to do."

Robin ran to Lily, and buried his face in her lap, sobbing. Lily soothed his curls, whispering comfortingly to him. No one would hurt him, she promised, as long as she was near. She looked up, her pale eyes glittering and fixed on Ward across the table. Her voice cracked with chill. "You hate this child, Ward. It's quite obvious to all of us, even to the poor little child himself. Do you have to destroy him?"

Ward stood up, threw his napkin on the table, and walked out. That night, and many nights like it, neither he nor Robin ate in that house. He realized that Robin hated and feared him, and why shouldn't he, told all day long that he had only one thing on earth to fear: that moment when his father came home?

* * *

By the time Belle was five, there was no person of importance on earth but her daddy. "Take me where my daddy are!" was her battle cry.

She rode, standing at Ward's shoulder, in their carriage. She spent whole days playing contentedly in his office. Ward tried to include Robin in their outings, but the boy wouldn't respond.

Belle was possessive and demanding. Everything she did or said seemed miraculous to Ward. That she loved him was all he asked of his gods anymore.

She loved trains from the time she was two years old. Ward had to sit with her in his runabout at crossings when trains rumbled past. She sat silently, fascinated.

He took her to Lake City on his train. She wanted to ride in the engine with the fireman and the engineer. With Ward beside her in the cab, she was happy, covered with soot, her knees skinned, her eyes brilliant with happiness. She loved the rhythm of the wheels on the rails just as Ward always had. She could sit listening to the music for only a few minutes at a time before she fell asleep in his arms.

Ward gave her everything he could lavish on her; toys, gifts dresses, coats, shoes. He wondered only if he were giving her enough. So did Belle. . . .

He brought Belle home in his arms one night after one o'clock, from a trip, with Uzziah Giddings along, on his train as far south as St. Augustine. Belle babbled strangely, burning with fever, sprawling limply, a dead weight.

Cold had settled over the area that morning. He'd been too busy getting Belle ready for the trip south to notice. The train was cool but not unpleasant and Belle played happily with Uzziah and Ward as her attentive slaves.

At noon, they walked in groves seeded and tended and budded by the Chinese horticulturist from the university at Deland, Dr. Lue Gim Gong. Known as the Luther Burbank of Florida, the Oriental citrus culturist had introduced a new variety of orange. A small, retiring man, he told them he was glad it was cold. His fruit would show no damage. His orange would withstand ten degrees greater cold than other varieties.

Belle was sniffling and wiping her nose on the back of
343

her hand as she skipped between the rows of orange trees. She had difficulty breathing on the train north to Jacksonville. Her fever was a hundred and three by the time Ward got her to Dr. Dame.

Ward crouched stricken beside Belle's bed all right. He did not even acknowledge Lily's angered accusation, "You've dragged her around until you've killed her. I hope you're satisfied." Ward did not look up. He did not know when Lily finally left the room.

Ward slouched in his chair, tears burning his eyes. He spoke only when, during the night until just before dawn, Belle would whisper his name. "I'm here, baby. I'm right here." She would smile and sink into that fevered state of half-sleep.

Inside his mind, Ward said, "If you take her, God, You'd better plan to take me, I won't live without her; I'm damned if I'll live without her."

He did not move from Belle's bedside until, at dawn, her fever broke. She sweated until her night clothes and covers were wet. Dr. Dame smiled and nodded. "Well, we can all get some sleep now."

But Ward shook his head. He could not sleep. He would stay there in case Belle woke, calling him. The servants changed her gown and her bed things. She slept deeply, breathing loudly but freely.

It was not until he reached the office late that afternoon that he learned that a freeze had gripped north and central Florida. Tallahassee reported a low of ten degrees. The mercury fell to seven degrees below zero at Jacksonville. A crust of ice covered the St. Johns River for the first time in living memory. Orange groves were destroyed, trees blackened and killed by the cold. No farm or grove had been spared west to Pensacola or south to Palatka.

The farmers and citrus growers of north Florida were ruined overnight. This meant Ward's freight cars were idle between Jacksonville and Lake City. People stared at each other, numbed with defeat. In Florida, where it never snowed, cold had wiped out agriculture and, with it, the economy of the state.

Chapter Twenty-Six

THEY CROWDED INTO Ward's conference room overlooking the Jacksonville train yards. Men had arrived from as far south as Hawthorne and Gainesville. Not a single grove north of Ocala had survived that freeze. These growers faced ruin.

"The expense of clearing away dead trees and planting seedlings might still be borne by some of us—those with any financial backlog," one grower told Ward. "But it's a matter of four or five years before we can hope for a return from our groves. Few of us—none of us!—can sit it out that long. Even if we could, what guarantee have we that another freeze next year, or two, three, or five years from now, wouldn't wipe us out again? I think I speak for most of the growers here. We appreciate your calling us together and offering to help. But we don't see what help, short of a miracle, could save us. We simply can't make it. We gambled. We lost. We came here to Florida hoping to make money in citrus. We sank every dollar we could beg, borrow, or steal into our groves. Most of us know better now. It was a hard lesson because it ruined us."

Ward introduced Dr. Lue Gim Gong. The citrus culturist displayed his new, hardier variety of orange. The growers, even those who had no resources left, no way to start

345

over, were impressed. They were citrus men. Lue Gim Gong's orange trees had withstood the cold and produced a larger, juicier, sweeter fruit. It looked like a miracle, but not enough of a miracle to save them.

"We want you people to know that the night of the big freeze, the temperature got down to freezing in Deland where these oranges were grown," Ward said. "That's admittedly not nearly as cold as it got up this way. Even Lue Gim Gong's oranges would have perished in our freeze. But with smudge pots, these trees would have withstood another fifteen- or twenty-degree drop. But that's only part of the good news."

Haltingly, the Chinese horticulturist stated that below Deland, in the Indian River section, temperatures during the night of the freeze never fell below fifty degrees, even at dawn. "It's down there around Indian River that I believe, with a hardier variety of orange, that the future lies for the citrus industry."

A sound like a growl of anguish arose among the men. This was like telling them—ten years too late—that they had made a wrong turn and missed Paradise by a hundred miles. "What good does that do us now?" they wanted to know.

"Suppose I could offer you cleared land in the Indian River country?" Ward said. "Acre-for-acre exchange for land and improvements you hold now in these northern counties?"

"Why would you do that?"

"Because I own land down there, because my trains run south. I would extend my lines through this orange-growing country, as far south at least as Melbourne. I would take your old holdings as security. I would expect you to agree to ship exclusively via my carriers. My company would be willing to install electric generation for pumping water for trough-type irrigation. We would advance money for planting, fertilizing, and irrigating for the first five years. We would move you, your families, your equipment and belongings, south on credit."

"By then you'd own us, body and soul."

"Nobody's forcing you to buy the whole package. You avail yourself only of the credit you need. If you can pay your way south, my conductors will gladly take your

346

money. If you can plant without our help, God bless you. You'd borrow exactly what you needed. Each of you is an individual case. Some are cases of extreme hardship who should be helped to work their way back as well as those of you with assets behind you. Those who are able may buy land from me, from the state, or from John Doe. We'll help those who want our help. And—" he grinned— "we'd still like your freight business. And I believe, with a bridge across the St. Johns here at Jacksonville, linking you with northern markets, you'll get a better deal from us than from the steamship companies."

A chattering, several degrees warmer than the gloom expressed earlier, rose through the boardroom. The atmosphere had altered. Doom had been delayed. Hope was rekindled inside these men who had been defeated by a caprice of nature. Some were nodding. Some were ready to sign mortgages and move south today; others preferred to hang on to what they had—homes and land—and discover and develop new crops.

This brought the talks to a boiling crisis again. "You're talking four or five years without a dime of income," a grower protested. "How do we live?"

"How do you plan to live as things are now?"

The man laughed ruefully. "Beats hell out of me."

Ward nodded. "Will you listen once more to Dr. Lue Gim Gong?"

Dr. Lue Gim Gong's proffered solution was simple, but untried. The growers, according to Dr. Gim Gong's plan, would set out their trees—lemon, grapefruit, and orange groves—under supervision of experts from Dr. Gim Gong's clinic at the university in Deland. The hardier fruit would guarantee an income—in time. Meanwhile, the grove owners could plant tobacco between the rows of young trees for an immediate money crop.

"You'll have an income this summer," Ward said. He smiled. "You can begin to repay me by September."

"We're citrus men, not tobacco growers."

"Then don't plant tobacco. Plant tomatoes or potatoes, whatever you feel safe with. You're not experts on any of these crops, but Dr. Gim Gong's people *are* experts. They have agreed to help you until you harvest."

The chattering rose another key. A man stood up,

347

smiling. "How do we get to this land of milk, honey, and tobacco?"

"Via Ward Hamilton's railroads," Ward said. "That's certainly the point of this whole meeting."

Phillips Clark paced Ward's office. "All you need now is money. This resettlement is like rebuilding a ravaged country. Why don't you try to get the state government or the national government to help you?"

"Because these people don't have five years to wait while Congress or some other bunch of bureaucrats argues over its merits. We'll float a new bond issue at eight percent and—"

"Hold it. I knew you weren't counting on the Stockmen's and Farmers' Bank; this kind of financing is far beyond them. But do you have any idea how much adverse publicity this big Florida freeze has had in the north? No Florida citrus shipped north this year at all? Any citrus they get is going to be expensive fruit, shipped from southern California. I see California taking over the citrus business and keeping it from now on. Every investor in the north sees it that way too. Any man who invested in Florida citrus isn't just hurt, he's completely wiped out. Grove owners are ruined. Now they are trying to move south in some harebrained scheme, abandoning homes and lands like refugees. You think they don't know all of this—well in advance—on Wall Street?"

Clark's assessment was totally accurate. A wireless request to White & Company was coldly rejected in so many words. Because Cushing and Byers had dealt with NEF&GC before, their message was wordier, but no more promising:

REGRET FLORIDA AGRICULTURE TOO RISKY STOP
NO INSURANCE AGAINST WINTER FREEZE LOSSES
STOP INVESTORS WARY STOP LOSSES IN CITRUS
ALONE THIS MONTH IN MILLIONS STOP TIMING
BAD STOP EXPERT OPINION CALLS FLORIDA WIN-
TERS MORE DANGEROUS THAN NORTHERN BECAUSE
LESS PREDICTABLE EVEN IF LESS COLD STOP
FREEZING INEVITABLE EVERY FEW YEARS STOP
THIS IS BEST EXPERT ADVICE STOP NO INTEREST IN
BOND ISSUE STOP

Clark shrugged. "I think the point is 'stop.' My advice is to call off this whole scheme or you face ruin. You'll be in receivership before you can recover a dime."

"Yes. Only if I'd stopped every time I'd been advised by experts to stop, we wouldn't be this far, would we?" Ward got up and walked across the office.

"What are you going to do now?"

"I'm going to see Dr. Lue Gim Gong."

Clark laughed deprecatingly. "He has a little prize money he's won. That's all he's got."

"I don't want money from Gim Gong. I want answers."

Dr. Lue Gim Gong supplied the answer. He displayed a grove of miles of fruit trees, with deep green leaves and healthy bark, brilliantly orange and heavy with fruit, revealing no trace of damage from cold.

When they returned from the grove, the day warm with a languorous breeze, they sat in the flower gardens. Around them, in the January sunlight, bees hummed and butterflies and hummingbirds darted, and flowers bloomed luxuriantly, as if it were spring.

"What species are all these flowers? Are they hardy winter plants?" Ward asked.

"Oh no. These are chrysanthemums, poinsettias, hibiscus, amaryllis."

Ward grinned, nodding. "If I walked into a New York boardroom carrying huge armsful of these flower blooms—and limbs loaded with ripe oranges, tangerines, and grapefruit, sweeter than any they'd ever tasted—if you had never been in this garden in January, what would *you* think?"

"I would be astounded."

"Would it be possible to carry wreaths of these flowers and bunches of fruit on limbs, and keep them fresh for a two-day, three-night winter train ride to New York?"

Dr. Gim Gong nodded. "If there were some way to keep constant the temperature of the train car, yes."

"Would ice do it?"

"Enough ice, yes, if you could replace the melting blocks."

"I'd arrange for ice at stops along the way."

"Then it can be done. I'll lend you two of my best assistants to tend the plants. We'll cut and prune carefully,

349

wrap the stems in damp cotton, and keep it damp. Yes. It can be done."

Ward's special controlled-temperature car entered the old Grand Central Station three days later. The train rumbled in under the first metal-and-glass sheds of wide span ever used in the United States. These great sheds had been used from the 1850s forward in Europe to cover entirely the tracks and platforms of a station. Railroad companies competed to build larger, more spectacular sheds. All during the last half of the nineteenth century these vast halls were the characteristic feature of the most modern train terminals. This shed was constructed under Commodore Vanderbilt's direction in 1870. It featured wrought-iron arches two hundred feet wide. It would remain the most elegant in the country until replaced in 1913 by the underground tracks and mammoth terminal of the new Grand Central.

The train entered Manhattan in a paralyzing snowstorm. No traffic moved on the New York streets. It was a matter of two hours before Ward located a black hack driver from Brooklyn who agreed, for an exorbitant fee to make the perilous run from Grand Central Station down to Wall Street.

Ward telephoned Whitney Cushing that he was coming. He requested that the full board of directors of Cushing and Byers be present in the conference room. "And get as many photographers and reporters as you can." Ward said. "We've had ruinous publicity. Now we want equal time."

Gale winds slammed the closed cab, rocking it madly on its thoroughbraces. Within the coach, bone-chilling cold numbed the agriculturists. All attention was centered on the flowers and fruit. The blooms and heavy limbs were carefully wrapped in tissue paper and covered to hold in any faint warmth. Often the driver had to get out and lead his blanket-wrapped horse on the icy streets.

When Ward and the horticulturists walked into the boardroom of Cushing and Byers, Ward wanted to yell out his exultance. The long odyssey had been worth it. The faces of those money-weary, travel-sophisticated, shock-inured men showed disbelief, incredulity, and awe.

Flashes began to explode from news photographers' cameras. The oranges quickly perfumed the boardroom with the smell of ripe citrus. The blooms of the flowers brightened the place, almost shutting out the sleet driven against the windows overlooking deserted Wall Street.

Whitney Cushing looked up at Ward, grinned, and winked. There were formalities ahead, but they were just formalities. Ward had won. He had his financing.

Chapter Twenty-Seven

He SAW HER standing alone in the huge, arched shed of the Grand Central station.

He glanced at her first as he would look at any pretty girl in passing. The only trouble was that pretty was a tawdry, inadequate word for this striking creature, alone and aloof on that platform, carrying several folded New York newspapers under her arm. His gaze touched her, lingered, moved on, and leaped back, held, entranced.

His lips formed the word, "Julia?"

There were—if there remained any essence of the young girl he'd known—only the faintest traces of Dayton Fredrick's daughter. She was far more than breathtakingly lovely; there was idealized unreality in the glazed perfection of her ceramic-gloss skin, her coiffured hair, even of the shoes she wore. She was beauty extraordinary. The full-length coat—Jesus, was it sable?—the triangular, jaunty hat, the very tilt of her head proclaimed her unusual, the ultimate of beauty at this moment in time. He was not the only one staring at her in the crowded shed. The difference between him and this gaping rabble was that he may once have known her.

Was it really Julia? What recollection of the young girl remained to spur any association? Her lips no longer pouted petulantly, but were fuller, the underlip softly curved and touched with lip rouge. Her pug nose had lengthened, her nostrils sharply flared, her face filled out to exploit its delicate, patrician grace of line and proportion. In her green eyes he found the greatest change; that old, wondering, openly challenging directness and overt searching was gone. Those almond-shaped eyes were still green, but this was the only resemblance. This young woman's gaze was undeceived, undeceivable, disenchanted without bitterness, doubting without rancor, sophisticated without dullness. Money and care and conditioners had restored body and sheen to that dark golden hair she'd once sacrificed to sun, sand, and salt water. She still wore it brushed away in soft luster from her face and hanging loose to her shoulders. A small pendant on a filamentlike gold chain around her slender throat was the only ornament she wore.

He sighed, feeling himself respond to her beauty and whatever inner chemistry had intoxicated him, no matter how reluctantly, the first time he had seen her. This response was a thousand times reinforced by her ineffable, remote, unapproachable beauty—and the denial and unhappiness of his own six years of marriage to another woman.

He hesitated beside her. Her gaze touched his. She almost smiled. "Hello," she said.

"Are you really Julia Fredrick?"

She gazed at him for a brief moment. Somehow, it was as if she were memorizing him, making up in her mind for all the long-lost images. "What are you doing in this part of the world?" she inquired. "You're not trying to cheat Commodore Vanderbilt out of *his* railroads, are you?"

"You really are Julia Fredrick." He laughed. "My God, how good to see you."

"I noticed your staring."

"Good Lord, Julia. Everybody stared at you."

"I didn't look at everybody."

"Did you look at me?"

"Certainly. You're still as pretty as ever. You look— more affluent—that's all."

"Are you traveling south?"

"Are you?"

"Yes. Why?"

She shrugged. "So am I. The Sunbird Special. All the way to Savannah."

"How nice. How really very nice."

"Do you think so?"

"You're lovelier than ever. Why wouldn't I think so? You're like some gorgeous older relation of the little girl I once knew."

"And rejected, betrayed, robbed, everything but raped. The only thing I wanted. But of course, you couldn't have raped me. I hate you because you didn't try. You didn't even want to *try*."

"Six years. It's been six years, Julia. Do you still hate me so fiercely?"

"Six years is just a flash in time for me when I hate or love. Didn't I tell you that?"

"Yes, I guess you did."

"You just didn't believe me, did you?"

"I believed you." He grinned. "When Plant outbid me for your father's railroad by a hundred dollars, I believed you."

"Mr. Plant has been very grateful. I'm working for him now, you know."

"Yes, I heard."

"I can't believe you cared enough to ask."

"Can't we call the old scores quits now, Julia, and start new?"

"You still don't know me, do you? You talk about believing I've always hated you for ruining my father and causing his death. And you're right. As far as you go. But how about my secret love for you? Have you ever believed that?"

"No, I haven't."

"Well, you see, that proves it. You don't know me at all. My inner feelings, emotions, conflicts. Nothing about me. You never will. I could meet a nice man and in an hour *tell* him that I loved him. He would believe me too. But it would be a lie. It always has been."

"How many have you told that in six years?"

She shrugged. "What the hell do you care?"

He spread his hands. He tried to visualize her as she had been in the six intervening years since he'd seen her. Growing up, becoming smart and modern in dress, fashion, thinking, and relationships. He wondered where she

354

had lived since her father's death—in how many rich, empty homes, how many hotels, how many steamships to Europe, how many classrooms, and dorms in how many finishing schools? How many men had loved her? How many arms had held her? Well, she was right. He could not care; he did not own that privilege.

"You have a lot of character in your face," she was saying. "You look as if you've suffered—nobly."

"Abe Lincoln said a man already has the face he deserves by the time he is forty."

"I wonder what your face will be by then?"

"God knows, if it's altered by the people who hate you and won't forgive."

"It very likely is."

The conductor called, "All aboard. All aboard, please."

People moved around them, hurrying feverishly, last-minute farewells and sudden tears replacing laughter.

"Are you in the Pullman?" Julia asked.

"I have a compartment."

"How nice."

He touched her arm and entered the Pullman vestibule behind her. He pushed open the heavy glass-and-metal door. They entered the narrow corridor in the compartment area. He paused, waiting for her to leave him. "It's really been good seeing you, Julia. A wonderful surprise."

"Oh? Were you surprised?"

"Seeing you? On a train platform in New York? Suddenly, after all these years? Yes, I was surprised. I never even hoped to see you again—anywhere."

She laughed. "That's funny. I caught this train only because I knew you would be on it."

Caught off-guard, he stared at her, his eyes searching hers. She moved those lovely shoulders in a mild shrug. "Well, it's true." With tapered nails, she tapped the newspapers folded under her arm. "You and your winter flowers are a sensation on all the front pages. Ward Hamilton, the P. T. Barnum of railroading. I'm sure you got what you wanted—as usual. I found out you were returning home tonight, so I cut my own visit short and joined you. I waited, to be sure you didn't have a concubine or two traveling with you."

"Good Lord."

"Many wealthy businessmen do. They don't even consider it being unfaithful; it just makes the trip easier."

"Well, I don't have one." Then he laughed,.puzzled. "I never know when to believe you."

"You may always believe me; you may trust me. I say precisely what I mean, and only what I mean. For good or ill, you may trust what I say."

His gaze loitered across her face. "I hope we'll see a great deal of each other between here and Savannah."

"So do I. Or my trip is wasted, isn't it?"

He laughed again, entranced by her. "May I walk you to your compartment?"

"I don't have one." She met his eyes squarely. "I knew you'd have a compartment, so I didn't think I'd need one."

She gave a porter a half-dollar and asked him to bring her traveling cases to Ward's compartment. Ward. leaned against a window and watched her incredulously. She smiled at him, completely unselfconscious and at ease.

"I'll try to be discreet," she told Ward. "I won't write you love letters to your office on scented pink paper; I won't call you on the telephone; I wouldn't want your wife to find out. I don't believe in hurting people any more than I have to. Even a wife."

"I just can't believe this."

"Why not? Am I inconveniencing you? Am I interrupting something you've planned?"

"I don't mean anything like that. You, here, like this, with me."

"Yes. It is much like a wet dream, isn't it?" She locked the compartment door. "Do you mind? It's drafty in here."

He laughed, delighted but still puzzled, still looking for the joker. "And I thought you hated me all these years."

"Do you want to pull down that curtain? We must stop in sixty stations between here and Washington. I hate little boys and old men staring at me. Besides, I may be naked."

He caught her arms in his hands. "Julia. Why are you doing this?"

She met his gaze without smiling. "Because I've always wanted to, but never got the chance. Because desire and opportunity coincided. Because I've never loved anyone but you."

"Love? The last time I saw you, you vowed undying hatred."

She studied him. "You never wanted me. But if I ever wanted anybody, I wanted you. That's not new and it hasn't changed. Oh, I know I'm a fool to say this, but I've loved you since the first second I saw you."

"But you were a little girl."

"No. I told you, I grew up fast. I had to. I knew at thirteen what I wanted; I wanted you. Nothing has changed that. Not the way you made me hate you, not your marriage, not time, not distance. Only you kept us apart. Only you can do that now."

"Julia, I can't pretend to be clever or smart or even strong, here like this with you."

"I'm glad, because then maybe you'll understand about me and the way I feel about you. I know you're married. I know you are one of the contributing causes of my father's suicide. I loved my father. I've only ever loved you as I loved him, with all my heart. And even that's different. I'll always love my father, and because of my father, I'll always hate you."

"That's what doesn't make sense. That's why I keep waiting to wake up alone, or for you to laugh at me and walk out. Unless you've stopped hating me."

"No. I told you. My hatred for what you've done—the selfish, cruel things—that hatred has not lessened. I don't see how it ever will. But, my dearest dear, neither has my passion and longing for you lessened." She laughed. "That has matured right along with me."

"And with your hatred."

"Yes. Six years stronger, six years more terrible. But I'm a big girl now. I find I can go to bed with the man I hate, if I want him badly enough."

He kissed her, gently at first. Julia's lips were heated, moist, salty with tears. Her slender body pressed against his. As naturally as his mouth covered hers, his hand closed over her breast. He caught his breath at the firm loveliness and felt a shiver run through her body. He felt himself respond, thrust upward, rigid, quivering. She drew away from him and entered the small connecting bath. The crib was too small too move about in comfortably, but she emerged in minutes, her hair loose about her shoulders. Her lace-trimmed gown gleamed, almost transparent. Her nipples stood in bold relief, clearly visible through the fabric, as was the dark mound at her crotch.

357

She tried to smile. "I'm glad you turned down the bed."

"Yes. I didn't see any sense in waiting for the porter."

"That's why you're a rich tycoon." She took his hand, kissed its open palm, and then pressed it hard upon her full breast. "Don't you want to get into something more comfortable? Like naked?"

"I don't own anything as fancy as your gown."

"I hoped you'd like it. I thought about you when I bought it. The salesgirl thought it was shocking because I'm unmarried. But I knew you'd like it."

In bed, he wanted to caress her, to learn her body, to spend a long time fondling her breasts, but her body was fevered, trembling with passion, her hips moving faintly in a way that aroused him as nothing else ever had. "Do it," she whispered. "The first time can't be any good. I've waited too long, wanted it too long, and I don't want to wait anymore." She lay back and opened her body to him, reaching for him, pulling him fiercely to her, closing herself, her thighs and arms and ankles, upon him, her nails raking his back and shoulders, her mouth open, kissing him, frantic and greedy, crying out and whispering and pleading and sighing. She breathed loudly and raggedly and he could feel their hearts pounding against each other, out or rhythm, out of time, battering, and he clung to her mindlessly. She kept crying out that it was the first time for her. The first time. The first time. He understood her. He had never loved before, either, and for him it was really the first time too.

She lay with her head against his shoulder. "I wonder what time it is?"

He smiled, fondling her. "Do you care?"

"I just wonder how soon we'll get into Savannah. Oh God, how I hate Savannah."

"Stay with me."

"I can't."

"Why not?"

"You know I can't go to Jacksonville and become your mistress; I'm not the type. You've got a wife, remember? I've got a job in Atlanta. And I'm going to a wedding in Boston the week after next. I've got to get my nails done Tuesday. Life goes on, my dearest, wonderful lover."

"What's next for us?"

358

"Nothing, that's what I'm trying to tell you. Nothing."

"You'll just say goodbye in Savannah?"

"I may not even say goodbye. I've learned to hate good-byes. It's what you say to people you don't want to lose, and must."

"You can't just walk away. You know I've got to see you again."

"You know better. You're the one who is married."

"And if I weren't married?"

"Don't try to pin me down. I don't know about that. I don't think about things like that. Maybe I will see you again, in some other lifetime."

"My God, just like that? After all we've had? Just go back to Atlanta and never even think about me?"

"I didn't say that."

"Can you really just forget me? Was I really that bad?"

"You know how good you were; you know what you did to me. I don't have to tell you." She tried to smile. "There's a place worn off in the middle of my spine. I'll have that to remember you by."

"Don't make jokes."

"Would you rather I cried or had hysterics? I do have my life, Ward. In Atlanta, apart from you. Always apart from you. I have my job, my problems. In fact, my job is my biggest problem. I'm good at it. I'm one of the best executives they've got. Unfortunately, I'm the first woman in commerce in Atlanta."

"Yes. It can't be easy."

"It's hell. The men all treat me like a whore. Without exception. Even those few who take my work seriously think all they have to do is get me alone and I'll fall on my back for them. I'm scandalous. And I can't be any good morally because I'm a woman and I work."

"Women in business. It's unknown. They can't believe the best."

"The worst, that's what they believe. I've even been attacked a couple of times. Your friend Hobart Bayard wants me to hire a bodyguard just to get me from home to work and back again every day."

"Poor Hobart. He doesn't know what to think about a woman in business."

She moved her hands on his bare body. She said, "Poor Hobart," but she was not thinking about Hobart. She was making love to Ward again, her hands demanding, seeking, her body hungry as if they were less than whole apart.

"The sound of the wheels on the rails," he said. "It makes me want you. Just the sound excites hell out of me, lying here with you, listening to that *click—click—click*."

"Yes, it's our song. They're playing our song."

For the first time in the two days and three nights since they'd departed New York, Julia dressed as the train pulled into Savannah.

"Please don't go," he said. He felt ill with loss.

"I'm going back to the real world," she said. "The world I hate you in."

"Is this really goodbye?"

"Yes, it really is. It's not my fault. You couldn't wait for me, remember? Well, I can't wait forever for you, either." Her eyes brimmed with tears. "You can't ask me to. *I* can't even ask me to." She clutched his hand in both of hers and kissed it, each finger separately, the hairs across its back, the cupped palm. She walked out quickly.

She was gone. He sat slumped, bereft. He could not even look back to the passion and ecstasy. All he could think was of the miles between Savannah and Jacksonville without her. He did not want to make that journey. He knew, now, that God had made Julia for him and for him alone. Without her, he was lost, he had nothing. The world was a black road ahead without her, stretched eternally, hot, empty, and abandoned.

Chapter Twenty-Eight

ROBERT HAMILTON WAS released from prison on the third of April of that year. Thinner than ever, his sinews and muscles hard and cordlike, his face coffee-dark, hatchet-sharp, and set forever in bitter, unsmiling rancor, he wore an ill-fitting, prison-issue tan suit, prison-made brown shoes, and a prison-made wooden leg. He hobbled with swift, determined steps along the street in the overcast day.

The man from the War Department had been waiting for him in an anteroom beside the warden's office. The warden had accompanied Robert into this barely furnished chamber where the prisoner-chaser stood at the window in a warped patch of pale sunlight.

"I'll turn you over to Mr. Schrieber now, Robert. Goodbye, my boy." The warden tried to smile, to demonstrate his humanity in a soulless world. "Like we say, keep your nose clean. Even if it takes both sleeves, eh? And for God's sake, stay out of here. I wish you every good luck,." He turned toward the government man. "Robert has been a quiet, unresisting prisoner. He has been somewhat antisocial and withdrawn, but he served his time quietly, without making trouble."

Schrieber nodded. He waited until the warden had gone out and closed the door behind him. He stared silently at

Robert. If he expected his cold silence and unblinking gaze to disturb and unsettle Robert, he was disappointed. Robert merely stood unmoving and unmoved.

"You want to tell me where that money is now, Hamilton?"

"What money?"

"All right, you bull-headed son of a bitch. Go on, get out of here. We can't stop you. You've served your time. Maybe, in your mind, you think you have earned that stolen money by now."

Robert shrugged.

"Well, Hamilton, I can tell you, we don't think so. The U.S. Army don't like other people stealing from Uncle Sam. By God, we won't stand for it. So I've got a message for you, Hamilton, from the War Department."

Robert waited with that terrible, chilling patience he'd learned over the past nine years in the penitentiary.

"This is our word to you. Some men served their time for their crimes. We say they're free, they've paid society. It ain't like that with you. We're going to watch you, Hamilton. You go near that stolen money and we'll get you. Oh, we'll get you. The minute you touch the first penny of that money, we're coming down on you like a ton of bricks, understand?"

Schrieber waited, but Robert seemed not even to hear him, actually seemed unaware of him. Robert's pale eyes burned now with the soulless inner fire of a fanatic, his gaze fixed on remote distances.

Robert walked the downtown streets until he found a gunsmith's shop. The proprietor recognized the look, the suit, the smell of the ex-convict. But when he doubled the prices of his stock and the one-legged man didn't even blink, he closed his mind to ethics. A dollar was a dollar in these times.

Robert hefted the Colt Model 1872 handgun, a .32-20 with a six-inch barrel, embedded-head cylinder, and recessed chambers. It was a gun, the shopkeeper said, used mostly by gamblers, bankers, and merchants: men who might use it reluctantly, certainly judiciously, but wanted results when they did use it. A steady gun, reliable, that fit the fist well and bucked only slightly.

"Yes." Robert nodded. "I'll take it."

362

With the handgun bulging in one jacket pocket, and the box of ammunition in the other, Robert went out on the street again. He hailed a hack, and told the driver to take him to the nearest livery stable. Here Robert bought a three-year-old carriage horse and a rusted and battered single-seat buggy with a baggage tonneau.

He had only a few dollars left. He figured the days southeast to Jacksonville. He would sleep in the carriage, and husband every penny for grain for his horse. There would be damned little money for food, maybe some soda crackers and rat cheese, washed down with creek water. He could kill rabbits along the way, or field doves. It didn't matter, he wasn't hungry. Well, this wasn't strictly true. He was consumed with a hunger that had nothing to do with food, a hunger that would gnaw at him and drive him, even with his stomach full.

A black butler answered Robert's ring at the front door of Ward's home overlooking the St. Johns River. The sight of the liveried servant somehow enraged Robert even more than the dimensions and elegance of the house and garden.

The servant looked at Robert, his face wrinkling with distaste. Robert had shaved this morning and trimmed his mustache, but his clothing was musky with body odor, and mussed from having been slept in on rainy nights out in the fields. "I want to see Mrs. Lily Hamilton," Robert said.

"Yassuh. You mind saying so's I kin tell her who is calling, suh?"

"Tell her it's Robert Hamilton."

The servant frowned, puzzled, uncertain. The name Hamilton perplexed him. This could be a family member, but little resemblance existed between this brown, shriveled, one-legged tramp and his employer. He solved his dilemma by smiling, but he did not ask the visitor into the parlor. "You waits right heah, suh. I tells Miss Lily."

Thetis was standing beside Lily's chair when Robert was led up the wide stairs along the corridor to Lily's suite.

"Oh, Masta Robert." Thetis ran across the room. "Oh Gawd, Masta Robert." Thetis sank to his knees, crying. He closed his arms about Robert's hips, sobbing and moaning.

Lily stood up. She hesitated, her face pale. She tried to

363

look at Robert's face but her gaze kept leaping down to that wooden leg. She had little memory of the war; she'd been a child. She'd had no experience with returning amputees. If she saw any of them, they were strangers straggling past Errigal, quickly gone, quickly put out of mind. She had been shielded, even during the hell of Reconstruction years, from the brutal aspects of life. A one-legged man was alien to her existence, somehow a freak, no longer quite human; he belonged in a sideshow. She felt pity rush though her, sympathy for the poor wretch who stood staring at her, tears brimming in his eyes, but her grief and compassion were less than personal. She felt somehow detached. Her tears glinted shallowly, shed for her own loss; her dreams were slain. She stared at this man and tried to find Robert as she had known and loved him and courted disgrace and scandal for his love, but this crippled stranger bore faint resemblance to the beautiful, flawless, slender boy she'd loved. "Oh, Robert," she whispered, shaking her head, calling after that boy lost in irrecoverable summer dusks.

"I'm free now, Lily."

"Yes. How good of you to come."

He frowned. "You knew I would."

"Yes. Oh yes. I hoped you would."

"I've dreamed of coming to get you, Lily." His hand touched the kinky thatch of Thetis's hair. "You and Thetis."

"Coming? Coming to get us? Oh, it's been—so long. So much has happened."

"It's almost over now, Lily. You won't have to stay with him now. We'll go away, you and Thetis and me. He won't keep you; I won't let him. He'll never touch you again, never put his hands on you again. He won't be able to keep you from me." For the first time, he almost smiled.

She shivered involuntarily. "But—where would we go?" She looked about, distracted. "Would you take me away from—my house? What would we do?"

"We'll start over, Lily. We'll make up for all we've lost, all those evil years you have been with him. And I—"

Lily's eyes darted from Robert's face to the sobbing Thetis crouched on the floor at Robert's side, to the furnishings of the room, the open corridor door. She spread

364

her hands nervously. "Get up, Thetis, please. If Robin came in now, he would be disturbed to see you like this—crying like this."

"Robin?" Robert straightened. "Is Robin my son, Lily? Where is he?"

She winced, bit her lip, and finally nodded. "He's quite big—almost nine now—but delicate and very sensitive, Robert. Maybe you shouldn't see him until you've had a chance to clean up and change your clothes. I know he will love to see you, but you must understand it's been nine years. He does not know you."

Robert scowled, staring at her. Then he managed to twist his face into the semblance of a smile. "Yes. All right. Robin and I—we'll make that all up . . . as you say. I can wait . . . a little longer. Yes. I'll come back for you, Lily. You and Thetis and Robin. It will be all right then. Everything will be all right."

Ward found the sorrow and tension of his home life bearable only by spending increasing hours away from home and at work. He often prowled for entire afternoons along the piers and scaffolding of his railroad bridge across the St. Johns. The state and city governments were preparing celebrations to mark its opening. Notables, celebrities, and civic and state leaders would ride the first train south across the structure. There would be speeches, a ribbon-cutting, dances, and picnics—a memorable occasion.

Meanwhile, he was plagued by problems of expansion. The money was there now, thank God! Wall Street had agreed to finance him as far south as Lake Worth. He had to keep moving forward with rails because, for every mile of track he laid in strictly stipulated time limits, he was granted five thousand acres of unimproved land. This new land assumed ever greater urgency because grove owners in north central Florida and along the coast as far south as Palatka were accepting his offer to exchange their properties for new land in the Indian River country. All along his extending rail lines, land was being cleared daily, swamps drained and cleared, and small green citrus plants set in carefully banked mounds and unbroken lines for miles in every direction.

He still had to fight his way south. Vandals, thieves, and snipers halted work for days at a time. In a village called

Sugar Mill, just south of Titusville, guerrillas struck from the swamps, laying down devastating shotgun fire across the right-of-way every time work crews appeared. When Uzziah Giddings's men pursued them, the bushwhackers simply disappeared like wraiths in the trackless morass.

Ward rode a work train south. Because Belle threw a tantrum, she accompanied him. He felt guilty because he had neglected Belle. He had walked for two days and three nights into paradise with Julia. He was harassed by attacks on his work crews, drawn fine by time limits imposed on tracklaying by a less-than-friendly Railroad Commission, tense and unhappy at home, deeply involved in work. Belle felt abandoned.

But standing beside the engineer in the work-train locomotive, her face dirty, her pigtails bobbing with the swift motion of the engine, bumping frequently against Ward's knees, she was blissful.

He insisted that she stay in the caboose of the train while he rode with Uzziah and other guards on handcars to clear out the drygulchers so the work crews could proceed south of Sugar Mill.

They approached quietly on the handcars and came unexpectedly upon a camp of embattled homesteaders. The men and their women sat around a campfire, eating smoked venison and sour-milk biscuits, washed down with home-brew beer.

Ward led his men in upon them stealthily. At a sign from Uzziah, the guards shot the horses and mules ground-tied at the edge of the encampment.

The nesters leaped up, yelling, confused. They ran for their stacked guns, and Ward's men laid down relentless gunfire, denying them the weapons.

The nesters, afoot and unarmed, retreated, yelling at each other. Suddenly they wheeled about and ran into the swamps. Four of Uzziah's men pursued the terrorized backwoodsmen in waist-deep, silt-clotted, black swamp water for more than two miles. These guards were as expert in the marshes as the farmers. The nesters could not lose them; they could only run deeper, fighting the vines and tangled growth, their terror mounting.

By the time the guards returned, Ward and the other guards had destroyed the guns and buried all food and other gear. The nesters might regroup, but it would take time and outside financing. He had no doubt they could get it, but this would take time too.

The crews walked diffidently out into the right-of-way. They worked undisturbed, finally able to breathe without tension. Ward sat on the rear platform of the caboose, hugging the meager shade as much as possible.

Belle sat at his feet, unconcerned in the blaze of sunlight, painting a cow in a coloring book. Uzziah slumped against the wall near Ward, his eyes closed, his knees drawn up. Looking at Uzziah, Ward grinned faintly. If Geronimo only had Uzziah for a lieutenant, the Indian wars in the west would go differently for the Apaches.

He looked up, squinting, and saw Robert hobbling toward him. At first he thought it was a mirage, an apparition compounded from weariness, tension, and memories. But the man moving between the tracks was not a phantom of his imagination.

Ward stood up. He grinned and waved his arm.

About two hundred feet away, in the midst of workers who paused, leaning on their axes and shovels, watching the wooden-legged man, Robert stopped, recognizing Ward.

Robert did not smile. Keeping his head up, his gaze fixed on Ward as if afraid his brother might run away, he reached down, unbuckled the wooden leg, and threw it aside.

Then he hopped forward, perfectly balanced, moving easily on one leg. Ward stopped smiling, watching Robert lunge toward him.

Robert moved like a vision of horror through the milling crowd of workers along the tracks. He lunged forward, caught his balance agilely, and lunged forward again. His trouser leg was folded neatly over the stump of his knee and caught with two metal pins along his belt line.

Ward's gaze was riveted on Robert's dark, implacable face, cold with hatred. Then he saw the Colt in Robert's hand.

Uzziah came up on his feet from a sitting position. As Uzziah moved, two other guards stepped out beside the rails in the sunlight at the rear of the train. The three of them drew their service revolvers simultaneously, waiting for a signal from Ward or Uzziah.

367

Ward said, "No."

They seemed not to hear him, or if they heard him, they misunderstood him. Troubled by the sudden tension, Belle jumped up and began to cry. She wanted Ward to take her up in his arms. He shook his head, gripping her hand tightly. "Please, Daddy," she said. "I'm scared. I want you to hold me."

Not less than fifty feet away, Robert stopped, balancing easily on one leg. He was aware of the gunmen beside Ward. He glanced at them, but gave them no other attention. Robert lifted the handgun, his cold face expressionless.

As Robert brought the pistol upward, all three of the bodyguards fired. Their bullets struck Robert in the chest, throat, and groin. He fired the Colt once, ineffectually, into the ground. The impact of the gunfire hurled him backward, seeming to allow him to stand for a moment, immobile, and then go flying backward. Robert struck against workers who lunged away from him. He was dead before he hit the ground.

Belle was screaming in panic and terror. Ward knelt and took her up in his arms. She clung to him, burying her face against his throat.

Ward kept saying only one word: "No . . . no . . . no." He repeated it over and over, and even when his guards finally heard him, they thought he was speaking in panic, not to them at all, but to the man who had come to kill him.

Chapter Twenty-Nine

BELLE WOKE UP SCREAMING. Ward lunged up from his bed and ran, stumbling in the darkness, to her room. He turned on the light as Lavinia entered behind him, her hair in braids, her bathrobe caught in her fist at her waist.

Belle stood up in her bed. It was difficult to tell whether she was awake or asleep. She stood almost as if in a trance, her mouth stretched wide with her screaming. Her eyes were open, but they stared and did not focus. "Daddy!" Belle wailed. "He's coming. He's coming to get me. The man with one leg is hopping at me!"

Ward caught Belle up in his arms. She wrapped her arms tightly about his neck, her legs about his waist, and buried her face against his shoulder. She was chilled and her whole body quivered. "You didn't kill him, Daddy. You didn't kill him, Daddy. You didn't—"

"It's all right, baby. It's all right." His voice soothed her. "It's just a nightmare."

Gradually she subsided, but she clung to him fiercely and he had to hold her until she slept again.

Belle suffered these nightmares frequently for months after Robert's funeral. They did not begin immediately. The day on the railroad car when Uzziah and Ward's guards had killed Robert, Belle had clutched Ward's legs and buried her face against him, but had said nothing.

When Robert's body was returned to Jacksonville for burial and funeral services, Lily became hysterical. For hours she prowled her room in tight circles, stricken, keening, crying aloud, pulling at her hair. Both Robin and Belle were removed across the big old house from her.

Ward suggested that perhaps Lily would not want to attend the funeral services at the gaudy new Magdalena Baptist Church.

At his suggestion, at the tone of his voice, at the very sight of him, Lily calmed and straightened. She stared at him icily. "You'd like that, wouldn't you?" she said. Her mouth twisted bitterly.

"Ward's only trying to make it easier on you," Lavinia said.

Lily's gaze raked Lavinia's freckled face. "Is he? Is that why he killed Robert? To make it easier on me? He deceives you beautifully, doesn't he, La? What does he tell you? That Robert turned three guns on *himself*—killed himself? Is that the lie he tells you? And is that what you believe? My Ouija tells me the truth, and it says Ward killed Robert. It'll say it a thousand times. Ask. Ask Ouija. Ask Ouija."

"We thought you might be more comfortable at home," Lavinia suggested.

Lily tilted her head. "I shall go to Robert's funeral; it is the last thing on this earth I can do for him. None of you can keep me from it."

The funeral services went quietly, with Lavinia's husband officiating. Andrew had never known Robert. It was obvious that he had gleaned his information about Robert's character and good works from Lily.

Lily sat rigidly silent at the church. She was like a pink marble statue, staring straight ahead behind her veil. She moved as her mother or one of her sisters directed. But when the services ended at graveside, Lily ran to the raw hole over which the closed casket, banked with flowers, was suspended, and tried to throw herself into the open pit.

Ward lunged forward and caught Lily's arms, restraining her. She turned, screeching at him, "Let me alone! Let me alone! You killed him! I loved him and you killed him. You killed him because I loved him. You killed him. You killed your own brother. You killed him."

That night, Belle woke from her first hysterical nightmare. The man hobbled, poised perfectly on one leg, toward her and she wailed, "You didn't kill him, Daddy. You didn't kill him, Daddy."

Ward ordered a bed moved into his bedroom, and Belle slept there for the next year with a small night light burning. Her nightmares ebbed and faded only slowly.

Lily protested against Belle's sharing the bedroom with Ward. "It's entirely unseemly," she said. "What will people think, a little girl sleeping in the same room with her father?"

Ward just looked at her. "I don't give a damn what they think," he said. "I don't give a damn what you think."

"That's obvious," she said. "You never have cared what I thought. You want to ruin that child, go ahead, ruin her." She drew Robin hard against her side, rubbing her hands in his thick curls. "You'll never ruin Robin. I'll see to that. As long as I live."

Belle recovered slowly from her nightmares and returned at last to her own bedroom. Life itself held a nightmarish quality for Ward. Lily sank deeper into melancholia, finding happiness only in Robin. She sat with him and Thetis by the hour drawing mediumistic messages from the Ouija board.

Soon after Robert's funeral, Ward returned home one afternoon to find that Lily had locked herself in his bedroom. He tried to talk to her through the door, but she only screeched at him and wailed brokenheartedly, unintelligibly. He sent Belle and Robin out for a carriage drive with Thetis and Luke.

He broke the lock. He, Lavinia, Miz Marcy, and Beatrice entered his room. They stepped inside the door and stared, stunned.

Lily sat on the floor in the middle of the room. She was holding a large pair of shears. She stared up at Ward defiantly. She had cut off every pair of Ward's trousers above the knees. Clothing and lint were strewn about the room.

Ward walked to her and knelt beside her. When he reached out to lift her, she swung wildly at him with the shears, threatening to kill him if he touched her.

He caught her wrist, removed the scissors, and handed

371

them behind him to Lavinia. Beatrice, La, and Miz Marcy were able to quiet Lily enough to remove her to her own rooms where she spent the rest of the afternoon, alternately screaming and singing hymns.

Remarkably, when Phillips Clark arrived after dinner that night to read Robert's will, Lily's recovery was immediate and absolute. Ward told the lawyer that perhaps the reading of the will would have to be postponed, but Beatrice went upstairs and returned in half an hour with Lily, who was now quiet, composed, and even smiling in a fresh new evening dress.

Lily greeted Clark warmly, if sedately and remotely. She sat perfectly still during the reading of Robert's last will and testament, her slender, pale hands folded in her lap.

Robert's will was precise, unmistakable in its intent. Phillips Clark prefaced his reading of the will by saying the paper had been in his possession since before Robert was sentenced to federal prison. It seemed to Ward that a malicious glint sparkled in the lawyer's eyes as he read the document. The whole business seemed to delight the attorney. "That was malice in my smile," Clark admitted to Ward later. "This is one of the few instruments that exudes hatred."

Ward stood at the rear of the room, leaning against the wall. The lawyer read slowly, his mouth twisted in a wry smile: "I, Robert Hamilton, being of sound mind, do hereby direct the following disposal of my worldly goods. To my brother Ward, I leave the sum of thirty silver dollars. To my manservant, Thetis NLN (no last name), I leave the sum of fifty dollars a month, to be paid to him by the executor of this will, on the first day of each month for the term of his natural life, with provisions for suitable burial in the same cemetery plot in which I am interred. The entire remainder, title, and total of my estate, I leave to my beloved (sister-in-law), —addendum initialed and dated—Lily Harkness Hamilton. In the event Lily Harkness Hamilton precedes me in death, I leave my total estate to the Baptist African Missionary Society."

The attorney looked up at Lily and smiled. "You are a very wealthy woman, Mrs. Hamilton. Your brother-in-law's estate is presently valued at one million, two hundred thousand dollars." He waited until the gasps from Lily and her family subsided. He could not resist adding, "It is presently worth more than ten times its original value, thanks to the stewardship of said estate by your husband."

Lily seemed not to hear Phillips Clark. She gazed coldly at Ward. "I always knew Robert hated you," was all she said. "I just didn't know how much."

A week later, Phillips Clark entered Ward's office. "I've just come from visiting your wife," he said.

"How is the lady?" Ward inquired with irony.

Clark smiled. "Filled like a custard cup with malice and hatred for you. She has ordered me to sell, at the present market value, every share of stock she owns in New East Florida & Gulf Central Railroad."

Ware winced but shrugged. "That's a lot of stock to throw on the market at one time."

"I tried to tell your lady that. She seemed to feel that you might somehow steal her money if it were left one hour longer in your control. She has ordered that the proceeds of the sale of NEF&GC stock be placed in savings in the Atlanta Stockmen's and Farmers' Bank. She has named Hobart Bayard as permanent executor of the estate."

"She won't get more than two or three percent interest on her money in a savings account."

"I tried to tell her that too. She feels she can live on the interest of the money. She wants it in 'a safe place.' Translated, this means where you cannot get at it."

Ward shrugged again. "Go ahead. Do as she wishes."

Phillips Clark smiled tautly. "I already have. It was more easily accomplished than telling you about it. I offered the shares, and they were bought, in total, by Henry Morrison Flagler."

Buying one hundred thousand shares of NEF&GC stock proved to be merely one of the less spectacular activities of Henry Flagler in Florida—and particularly along the East Coast route of Ward's railroad—begun that year. "Flagler is breathing down Ward Hamilton's neck," railroad people said. Some of them, Phillips Clark especially, said it to Ward's face.

Ward was preoccupied. He was moving his lines south, mile by mile, day by day. Grove owners were moving into the Indian River country. They looked to Ward for financial assistance, mortgages at low interest, and even, in some cases, for the land-clearing, seedlings and planting costs. Lily became daily more hostile toward him, more withdrawn. Belle was spoiled. No one could control her but him. He realized it, and did all he could to curb her, but failed.

He could not get Julia out of his mind. Riding his own railroad became discomfiting because every click of wheels on the rail joints brought her image erupting vividly into his mind and loins. Her laughter, her kisses, her incredible body, the total happiness they'd known for a little while. It all came racing back with that sound of wheels on rails. *They're playing our song.* Hungry for her, he wrote to her. He begged her to meet him—in Savannah, Lake City, Atlanta, anywhere—but meet him. She did not answer his letters. He didn't even know whether she received them.

He could not put her out of his thoughts; he could not believe she could forget him so easily; he could not believe that he could want her so terribly and that she could be so unaware, unmoved, uncaring.

He tried to consider the affair rationally: Julia was a young, sought-after, career-minded, willful, and headstrong girl. She may once have adored him with a schoolgirl's intensity and abandon, but she was a young woman now. She knew scores of men more eligible. Hell, he wasn't eligible at all, only available. Obviously, his availability didn't move her. Why didn't he put her out of his mind? Why did he even think about her when she'd forgotten him? She had told him she didn't want him, she still hated him because of her father. Except for that brief affair on a train thundering through the night, there was no place for him in her life. She had her executive position with Plant. She wanted money, status, social position, a financially advantageous marriage. There was no place for him in her plans. Why go on tormenting himself, wanting her when it didn't make sense? He knew the answer to that too. He thought about her because he couldn't get her out of his insides. The faint scent of cologne, a remote laugh, the click of wheels on rails, the way some woman walked, or held her head. He could not forget; as long as he lived, he never would forget.

The atmosphere of discontent and insufficiency in which

he lived, at home and at his office, at least spurred him to work harder, longer hours, to keep driving forward until he was too exhausted to think. It seemed a hell of a thing when the best his life offered was the chance to be too tired to think about the state of his life.

He helped more and more north Florida grove owners resettle south in the warm, languorous climate of the Indian River territory. He surveyed, plotted, mapped, and laid out his own town on his rail lines, like a gateway into the new citrus belt, that promised land of eternal spring.

He called his town Winter Grove. He had streets cleared, curbs laid in, and large posts of cement and stucco, ornamented with small statuary, set up as avenue markers. Beside his rails, he ordered constructed the first building of his planned city: the NEF&GC railroad station. Duval, who had designed the Magdalena Baptist Church and other buildings for him, put Ward's ideas on paper. Within weeks, the huge structure took shape beside the ribbon of rails out of nowhere, into nowhere, a monstrosity alone and brilliant in thousands of acres of cleared and planted land.

Built to resemble a Moorish castle, the depot had a rounded, scrolled, and tile-roofed shed overhanging the two hundred-foot-wide platform and the moatlike rails. Glass-and-metal doors opened on waiting rooms floored with tile and decorated with colored clays, fired and laid in Spanish patterns. The two-story walls were gilded, with murals depicting lush orange groves and happy workers, inset windows, and decorative stairways winding upward to sightseeing balconies and a high tower housing a huge clock and below it, the name 'Winter Grove' carved in a marble slab.

Ward surveyed his original acreage and selected twenty thousand acres of the most fertile, watered, shaded, and rolling lands. Some of these he ordered planted in citrus, and rest maintained, parklike, and placed in trust for Belle. The property would be hers at twenty-one. No matter what happened to him, she would be a comparatively wealthy young grove owner and holder of almost forty square miles of prime land. He placed ten thousand acres in trust for Robin, but Lily refused to make the long, hot, and unpleasant trip to view the land, or to allow Robin to

375

go without her, and so the boy barely understood that property was set aside in his name.

When Ward tried to explain to Robin what this would mean to him, Lily cried out, "Don't try to buy my son away from me! Don't think you can make up for your evil with money. Don't think you can buy Robin's love at this late date, any more than you can mine. We have our own money—Robert's money—we don't need you!"

Ward concentrated on Robin, trying to ignore Lily's tirade. He said to the boy. "Wouldn't you like to ride the train with Belle and me to see your property?"

Robin shook his head. He retreated, pressing against Lily. His voice carried the precise tone and tension of his mother's. "No! I don't want to leave my mother! You can't take me away from her! I won't go, you can't make me go!"

Ward felt the nightmarish quality of his life discoloring everything he did, every human contact. He had made his dream come true; he owned his railroad, he was extending it every day, and yet he felt no triumph, no sense of accomplishment. He felt empty.

Daily, his underlings brought him new reports of Henry Flagler's lavish spending in St. Augustine, his announced plans for upgrading steamboat travel in the inland waterway from Jacksonville to St. Augustine, improving roadways, laying spur rails into the resort village, and purchasing more blocks of NEF&GC stock on the open market.

All this remote activity lacked reality for him. The only true realities were his unsatisfactory marriage and the emptiness of his life. He looked darkly at everything. No matter what he tried to think about, his thoughts returned to one refrain: he wanted a divorce.

He was invited to the formal opening of Flagler's two-and-a-half-million-dollar Ponce de Leon Hotel in St. Augustine on January 10, 1888. At first, he decided not to go. There was no reason to believe Lily would accompany him. His trains, however, were booked to capacity, and extra Pullmans, passenger coaches, and even private cars had to be coupled on to handle the influx of millionaires and civic, industrial, professional, and political leaders. All of

376

them exuded laughter and pleasure, while he drowned in his own bile. To hell with it. He was just thirty—young enough to enjoy himself, and too young to pass up a celebration like Flagler's party. Belle was nine that year. He decided to attend and take Belle as his guest.

She was delighted, bright-eyed, awed by the elegance. He decided that it must be, in Belle's young eyes, like the Prince's party for Cinderella. One thing was certain: this elegant existence would be the accepted way of life for Belle; he would see to that. She would live with stars in her eyes. And he had to admit that he was amazed at the opulence piled on richness. What a man could accomplish when money was no object was really still beyond his comprehension, because he had always had to scrounge for every dollar, and justify every dime he borrowed. Here in St. Augustine, the one thing Flagler had not discussed was the price of anything. A festive air of celebration and gaiety overwhelmed guests as they arrived in the sleepy fishing village that Flagler had decided would become a multi-million-dollar tourist mecca.

Guests crowded the corridors of the new hotel, and spilled out into the rotundas and the tropical court. Even the most worldly and sophisticated among them were impressed by the grandeur. The decorations were unusual and breathtaking. A New York City orchestra had been imported for the first season, and its music wafted through the chatter and laughter.

Belle hesitated, then stopped, stunned by the unreal beauty of the sandy-colored, mammoth four-story structure sprawling over most of a five-acre downtown plot as if it had magically emerged from one of her fairy tales. Its medieval towers overlooked Mantanzas Bay, the island reefs beyond, and the Atlantic Ocean. It was a castle from old Spain set down in the midst of the quaint old town. Its courts, its cool and shaded retreats, its towers and fountains and everything glittered like cake icing. The grounds rolled in lush tropical gardens, with orange trees, banyans, and overhanging palms.

Verandas along the street on each side ran off from the main gate. Water-spouting dolphin fountains marked all entrances. Belle stood fascinated by the doorknobs, which were modeled like seashells. The grand archway was twenty feet wide, the rotunda inlaid with richy colored mosaics. Above, the great dome, supported by massive oak pillars, displayed allegorical representations of fire, water, and earth.

Barely breathing, Belle, on Ward's arm, entered the grand dining hall on stairs of polished marble. This hall featured stained glass windows, highly polished floors seventy by a hundred feet, and a seating capacity of seven hundred. Its ceilings were decorated with designs of the sixteenth century, when St. Augustine had been founded by the Spanish.

The guided tour of the facility left Belle speechless. There were 450 elegant sleeping apartments, the furnishings in each room were luxurious and charming, and electric lights glowed everywhere.

The aging Flagler was a proud, expansive, and generous host. He smiled at the wonder he saw sparkling in Belle's young eyes. Belle told him she loved his castle. The old man smiled. "Pretty enough for a princess like you, eh?"

Ward shook Flagler's hand. "You outdid *The Arabian Nights.*"

"I tried to. But we haven't begun, my boy. The only difference between you and me is our ages. We both dream. I saw your monstrosity of a depot sitting alone in the flat wilderness of your projected town. Winter Grove. They're calling it your folly, saying there'll never be a need for it. Maybe not. But they said there'd never be a need for my hotel here, and already we're planning two more. So you're not the only dreamer, eh?"

"I can dream only on the installment plan."

"Perhaps you and I might have a few moments together before you leave town. I'd like to talk to you about your railroad."

Ward felt an odd stricture in his chest. "What could we talk about?"

"About making it the fabulous line it could be. About selling it to me. I could make it the main artery between palaces just like this all up and down this coast." He said this last for Belle's benefit.

Ward managed to laugh. "If you take my railroad, what happens to my dreams?"

Flagler clapped him on the shoulder. "They come true, my boy, in ways you never could conceive."

Ward felt a chill in the music and laughter and brilliance. He could no longer deny what everybody had been saying for the past three years. Henry Flagler *was* breathing down his neck—a hot, billion-dollar, Standard Oil-stoked breath. . . .

After returning to Jacksonville, Ward called Phillips Clark into his office. Phillips tried to inquire about the magnificent new hotel in St. Augustine, but Ward waved this aside. "I don't want Henry Flagler buying up any more NEF&GC stock."

"How are you going to stop him?"

"We'll buy. Whoever is selling, we'll buy. Sweeten the deal a little if you have to, but buy."

"How do you compete with a man who has at least a hundred million dollars in personal holdings? Hell, if Flagler wanted to get Standard Oil, Rockefeller, and allied financing aid, he could bring God knows how many *billions* to bear against you. You start bidding against him and he might do it."

"Just the same, we buy all we can. We hold what we have."

"You'll find that hard to do when Flagler begins to move."

"I'm not going to stand by and see him take over."

"We tried to tell you two years ago: you should never have let Lily sell one hundred thousand shares to Flagler. It's too late to whimper now, but that gave him the first big bite he needed."

Lily . . . Ward felt his belly go empty. If she had deliberately set out to ruin him, she could not have acted more effectively. She *was* deliberately ruining him. He said, "I want you to start divorce proceedings against her."

Phillips Clark was not in the least astonished, but he was pessimistic. "On what grounds?"

"Think of something."

"There are no grounds, not here in Florida. Your wife is ill, mentally unstable. You can't just divorce her in Florida. If you've got an insane wife in Florida, you're stuck with her. The law refuses to permit men to make sick wives wards of the state."

"I'm damned if I'll stay married to her."

"You will, Ward. Face it—you cannot divorce her.

379

You've got one chance—just one: work out something with Lily. God knows it's obvious to everybody in Florida that she hates your guts. But unless she'll agree to divorce you, you haven't got a prayer."

Chapter Thirty

WARD HESITATED OUTSIDE the closed door of Lily's suite—that fragrant and frilled off-limits territory. He drew a deep breath, and rapped on the facing.

"Who is it?" Lily asked from within the room.

Ward opened the door and stepped inside. Lily sat, highlighted in a warped triangle of nebulous sunlight, wearing a pastel cotton dress with a laced choker collar. Her Ouija board was set up on a small, bowlegged, pecan-wood table. Across it, Thetis sat patiently, waiting—God knew for what.

Lily looked up, silhouetted by the sun, her dark hair haloed. For an instant her eyes widened and her mouth pulled into a warm smile. "Robert?" she said.

Thetis caught his breath, wincing in a kind of superstitious terror. "It Masta Ward, Miss Lily."

"It's me, Lily," Ward said. "I want to talk to you."

Lily straightened on her high-backed chair. Her pale cheeks grew even whiter. She brushed aimlessly at her skirt with the backs of her fingers. "Whatever could you have to say to me?"

Ward motioned with his head for Thetis to leave the room. "Check on Robin and Belle, will you, Thetis?"

Thetis nodded, then glanced, troubled, toward Lily.

When she inclined her head in a faint nod, he leaped to his feet and left the room, escaping.

When he and Lily were alone, Ward closed the door, and Lily's head came up, defiant. She started to speak, then changed her mind and bit at her underlip. She assumed a pose of great and long-suffering patience, watching him tautly. He came across the room and sat in the chair Thetis had vacated. He looked at Lily, but she turned her head, gazing through the window. He touched at the planchette with his fingers. It glided like blades over ice on the slick surface of the decoratively printed board. "I want a divorce," Ward said.

Lily turned, caught her breath, and held it, staring at him over the small table. Her eyes raked across his face and she almost laughed, a sound cold with suppressed rage. "Then you'll have to get one."

"You know I can't do that, don't you?"

"Yes. Mr. Clark told me that. And if you think I will *ever* divorce you, you are wrong and stupid. Do you think you can throw me out, disgrace my family with a *divorce*, and break up my home—after all these years?"

"I've got to be free, Lily." He kept his voice low and controlled. Distantly, he heard the children playing on the shadowed verandas. Belle defeated Robin in every contest they engaged in. She left him wailing, pulled his curls until he screamed, or climbed higher than he dared in the oak trees and hung there, spitting down on him until he wept. Every game between them began in laughter— Belle's—and ended in tears—Robin's. "I can't go on like this."

"Why?" Her mouth twisted. "Are you madly in love with one of your new sluts?"

"No. I have no new slut in mind, Lily."

"Then you won't be too disappointed, will you?"

He stared at the sun glinting in the polished surface of the Ouija board. "Why do you want to go on like this, Lily?"

"Because you married me. Because you cheated me of happiness. Because I've *earned* all this. Because my children deserve to live well. Because I will not let you disgrace me or my family in divorce. We *are* married. It is what *you* wanted. We shall stay married. We *vowed*. Till death do us part. I remember, even if you don't."

He laughed at her. The sound of his laughter brought bright blood flushing upward under the fragile flesh of her pale cheeks. "You remember well—what you *want* to remember. What about love? Wasn't love mentioned?"

"What about it?" She tossed her head, her nostrils distended. "Do you call thrashing about—sweating and naked and obscene, like animals—love? Is that all there is to love—dirt and filth?"

"No. There's probably more to love than shared loving. I wouldn't know. I've only been married to you. The point is, you never loved me."

She shrugged, folding her hands in her lap. "You should have known that. If you had been at all sensitive, you would have known it."

"I didn't know it. I didn't know you were incapable—"

"You didn't care. I was the prize your brother wanted. I was something you had to have."

"I thought you might come to love me."

"I told you. I told you I loved Robert. Robert. I would never love anyone but Robert. But you did not care what I felt inside. You didn't know, you didn't care. You wanted to marry me anyway."

He exhaled heavily. "It's too late now for that, Lily. I am thinking about now. Right now. Today. The rest of my life. I am thirty years old. Whatever life has to offer, I have not had it. Or, if I have, to hell with it. It is not what I want. I want my freedom, I want my sanity. I cannot go on like this. I will provide well for you and Robin. You may keep this house—"

"This house?" Her laughter was shrill and contemptuous. "Of course I shall keep this house. And no thanks to *your* largesse. This is *my* house. My home. It belongs to me." Her head tilted. "I've earned it, too, living in hell with you, being humiliated by your open infidelity, your cheap affairs, carried on in public."

"We'll soon be yelling at each other, Lily. There's no sense in this. It is more than your not loving me. My God, you have hated me for all these years—"

"I'll always hate you. Do you think I can ever forgive you for what you've done to Robert, to me, to Robin?"

"Then why in God's name did you marry me?"

Her voice rose. "Look around you. For *this*. For all this. It's mine. It belongs to me. You owe it all to me, for

383

what you did to Robert, for what you did to me. You are my husband. You will *stay* my husband."

"Daddy? What's the matter?"

Ward leaped to his feet. He stared, anguished, at Belle, who had come silently into Lily's bedroom. Or perhaps the smudge-faced, pigtailed child had entered noisily, and he had been so deeply involved in his own unhappiness that he had not heard her. "It's all right, Belle," he said, trying to smile, his face contorted in agony. "It's all right. Go play."

"Your father wants a divorce." Lily's voice lashed at the child. "He wants to leave us, to destroy this home, to run with some sluttish woman. He wants to walk out on us."

"That's enough, Lily. This is between us."

"Is it? Doesn't it concern the children? Won't you abandon them—leave them to strangers to raise?"

Belle stared at him, shaking her head, her eyes bleak. She looked at Lily, unable to believe her, yet afraid to doubt her. She was caught and terrorized in the tension crackling in the room. Her bewildered eyes touched at Ward. She wanted to run to him, as always, to be reassured, but suddenly she was afraid he no longer loved her, no longer wanted her. She sobbed helplessly.

"You don't have to do this to her, Lily."

"Why not? Why shouldn't *she* know the truth about you, too? Why should she go on thinking you're above God Himself? Let her know the truth about you—the rotten, ugly truth about the filthy women you wallow naked with, the way you killed your own brother. Let her know the truth."

Belle staggered forward, weeping, to Lily's chair. She sank beside it, pressing her head against her mother's leg. Lily did not reach out her hand to touch her.

Ward moved toward Belle, then stopped. Instead, he stared at Lily, his face white with rage. His voice rasped, soft and deadly cold, "Some day, Belle will know the truth, and she'll understand me. But if she ever understands the truth about you, Lily, God help you."

He turned and walked out, trembling with anger.

Ward went the next week to Tallahassee, taking Belle with him. His daughter loved him too deeply and wholeheartedly to remain long estranged or alienated from him, or

384

insecure about his love. This was her surest knowledge, the base on which she built her own immeasurable self-assurance. She knew who she was. That moment of terror and loss in her mother's bedroom was like a nightmare, and, as the hours and days passed in Belle's busy young life, its hurt, and finally even the memory of hurt, faded.

They got off the train together at the station in Tallahassee. The legislature was in session and the town was crowded. Belle found the growing, aging town sprawling along oak-shaded hills exciting, as she found excitement in everything new. Ward told her how Florida railroading—almost the first in the entire nation—had begun here with mule-drawn trains to St. Marks in the early 1830s.

Belle found an open hack and engaged it for them. The black driver bowed and smiled, helping her into its tonneau. They drove around sightseeing before they went to their hotel. In the dining room, they had ice cream and ladyfingers. Once, she looked up smiling over her dessert and said, "You know who I love?"

"That's my question," he teased. "I ask that question."

"I learned it from you. But it's mine now."

"Anyway, I'm far too old for you."

"Yes. But look around. See how much prettier you are than all the other men. They all look so *old*."

Ward felt a sense of nostalgic emptiness. Belle's calling him "pretty" brought thirteen-year-old Julia Frederick flashing back into his mind, and recalled her older incarnation as well, hurtingly, almost as if it were a physical presence.

He left Belle with books to read in an alcove off the hotel lobby, while he called on Gates McCall. "Don't take up with strangers," he told her.

"No, Daddy. Not unless they are prettier, or younger, than you."

"All right. With those strangers. But no others."

She waved her arm. "Go ahead. Don't worry about me. I'm used to waiting for you. I've spent half my life doing that."

Gates McCall ushered Ward into his office, asking effusively in what way he might serve his long-time friend and benefactor? But Gates McCall proved to have a laundry list of his own needs. Ward listened, nodding, glad that McCall could obligate himself deeper. He encouraged the

385

legislator to reveal what he had on his mind. At the end of each recitation, Ward nodded confidently and smiled casually. He said, "I think I can help you. I know someone who can handle that; a payment ought to suffice." His contempt for the lawmaker grew. McCall had been too long in politics; he was by now a professional parasite.

Gates was just the kind of legislator he was looking for: the sort who purrs when one strokes him, plays dead, rolls over, fetches, and performs other tricks when one urges him and offers treats.

Finally, McCall laughed and said, "But you didn't come all the way here just to listen to my woes."

"I'm having trouble at home."

"At home? Oh . . . at home. Why, that's too bad."

"I want a divorce. I don't care what it costs me, but I want it."

"My, I'm sorry to hear this. I've never had the pleasure of meeting your lady, but I have heard many times that she is one of the most beautiful young gentlewomen in the South."

"Yes, I'm sure she is. Beautiful."

"Men like you, it's an inner drive with you, ain't it? I mean, you marry the creme de la creme. Puts the final touch on your achievements, eh? Marry the perfect girl every other man cries for and can't touch. I'm truly sorry to hear all is not going well. I don't want to pry, but—is she seeing another man?"

"Not that I know of."

McCall shook his head. "Divorces are plumb difficult to come by these days without sure, cold, probable grounds. Adultery, abuse, or desertion."

"She is mentally ill. A doctor has told me that as long as she stays married to me she is incurable. She is unsettled if I come near her."

"Oh my God." McCall looked pale. He glanced about as if wishing Ward Hamilton and all his favors out of his office, out of his life. "There are cold, hard laws against divorcing a mentally incompetent spouse."

"I know that. That's why I came to you."

"You know I want to help you any way I can. And I don't pretend I ain't indebted to you—"

"Neither do I. . . ."

* * *

Governor Edward Perry was new in office, having recently succeeded Bill Bloxham, whom Ward had come to know well. Though Perry was a Democrat, he was obviously less than fond of Gates McCall. However, McCall's skin was tougher than alligator hide. He listed Ward Hamilton's contributions to the state, and Perry softened noticeably. He was most impressed by the railroad bridge that spanned the St. Johns River and removed the last barricade between New York and direct rail service to the East Coast tourist centers. Further, the relocation of the north Florida citrus growers after the big freeze had attracted the attention of President Cleveland. The President had written to Governor Perry commending Hamilton.

"In the past, Mr. Hamilton has done a great deal of selfless good for this state, Governor Perry. There is a great deal he can do in the future, things he will want to do. Like all of us, he's interested in building this state," McCall said. "He's worked hard and well and successfully for us. He's given up his time and money to help build— and rebuild, especially after the big freeze. We can't afford to throw away a good man like that, Governor."

"No. I agree. We want to do all for him we can."

"Well, he's reached a place where he needs our help. I've agreed to help him, and I hope you'll agree to help me. With all due respect, sir, for you, your office, your obligation to the voters, and the prejudices some voters have against divorce, I feel we have a responsibility to help a man like Mr. Hamilton when he faces a tragic situation."

It took Gates McCall forty-five minutes to state all the facts. After detailing Mr. Hamilton's traumatic marriage, McCall said he believed it behooved the state to alter the law to permit Mr. Hamilton the freedom otherwise denied him. McCall proposed introducing before the legislature an amendment to the present divorce code. "My amendment will state, sir, that if a man has been married X number of years to a woman unable to fulfill the connubial duties of a wife due to an incurable mental state, and where the woman can never conceivably become a ward of the state due to the provisions made for her needs and welfare by her husband, a divorce could be effected."

The governor winced. He believed a doctor or a panel of laymen and experts would have to adjudge the wife incurably ill. "The matter would have to be adjudicated in court. I know it would be easier on all if it could be handled quietly, but marriage is a cornerstone of society. It cannot be set aside any more lightly than it is entered into."

Ward left the governor's office with the promise that if McCall got his bill through the legislature, Perry would not veto or oppose it.

Ward left the capitol building and walked downhill to the hotel. Carriages, street vendors hawking their wares, and pedestrians passed him, but he was unaware of them. He had won at least the first step; he would be free. But he felt no sense of exultance, no pleasure. The world seemed dark and overcast. Inwardly, he felt empty and faintly ill. He did not want to hurt Lily any more than he had to. He tried to tell himself he deserved some happiness in life, something better than he had, but he could not escape the sense that whatever he had achieved, he had not won it, earned it, or especially deserved it. It was handed to him, cynically, because he bought it.

He tried to shake off his dank depression before he rejoined Belle in the hotel lobby. He stood for a moment on the walk outside, composing himself, trying to smile.

When he walked into the small alcove where he'd left Belle, he saw at once that she was not alone. Frowning, he paused, watching her. She sat on the edge of her plush chair, talking animatedly.

Ward crossed the room. He was almost to them before Belle looked up, saw him, and smiled brightly in welcome. The woman in the other chair, with her back to Ward, turned and faced him. "Julia," he said. Then he tried to laugh. "I thought I told you, young lady, no talking to strangers."

Belle laughed. "She said she knew you. She knew all about you. She said she's known you since she was my age. Besides, Daddy, she is younger and prettier than you are."

"Yes." Julia nodded. "You're not nearly as young and pretty as you were when I knew you."

Belle took his hand, and he sat on the broad arm of her chair, still holding Belle's fingers in his, but looking at Julia. "I wrote to you," he said. "Several times."

388

She nodded and smiled, winking at Belle. "There wasn't anything to say; that's why I didn't answer."

His heart sank. It was all over between them. She was lovely, brittle, cool, and lost to him. Belle said, "Daddy, you're holding my hand so tight, you're hurting me."

He kissed her fingers, forcing himself to smile. "I'm sorry baby."

When he looked up, Julia's green eyes were glistening with tears. She shook them away. "Don't mind me. I'm weeping for myself—my own girlhood. I look at Belle and you, and I see myself and my own father."

"Did your father spoil you?" Belle asked.

"Terribly. He didn't know I was a snotnosed little brat who should have been belted regularly on the hour. He thought I was a princess—"

"I know." Belle giggled.

"I took advantage of him dreadfully. That's why I grew up so spoiled. I hope that won't happen to you."

"Where is your father?" Belle asked.

Julia answered Belle, but gazed at Ward. "He died," she said. "Someone hurt him and he died, just when I needed him most."

"I'm sorry." Belle clung to Ward's hand. "I don't know what I'd do if something happened to Daddy."

"You'd live," Julia said. She laughed. "Just don't make all the mistakes with your daddy that I made with mine, making him the center of your life, letting him come to mean too much, and other people mean nothing at all."

Chapter Thirty-One

THE COURTROOM, presided over by Judge Sidney Harlan, was cleared of all but participants in the matter of Hamilton vs. Hamilton. The corridors of the Duval County courthouse were crowded with the curious, the enraged enemies of Ward and his railroad, and reporters anxious to gather new rumor, gossip, and even fact in the matter of the sensational new "Hamilton divorce law" recently enacted in Tallahassee.

Newspapers openly accused Hamilton of "greasing palms" in Tallahassee, buying off the legislature. Governor Perry and State Senator Gates McCall were singled out for especially bitter attack. Almost none of the newspapers took Ward's side in the controversy. To them he was only the latest of the carpetbaggers buying what he wanted and subverting justice. Said one editorial, "This is another case of an affluent and powerful man using his money and influence to pervert justice in Florida. This man has 'bought' his wife and now, tiring of her, wants to 'buy' his freedom. There should not—there cannot—be price tags placed on morality in this state: one set of laws for the wealthy, another for the common man. A rich man doesn't commit a crime; he pays to have the laws changed so that his illegal actions have the sanction of the state and the human rights of others are meaningless. Human rights—the rights of a good and faithful wife—ought to be protected too." One editor did uphold the passage of the amendment. "It is time Florida passed sensible divorce laws," he wrote. But the other newspapers attacked him, accusing him of "selling out" to Ward Hamilton. Some even inquired facetiously as to the editor's "rate" for "paid advertising" on the editorial page.

An editor for the *Pensacola Journal* assigned reporters full time to "bring to light" evidence of Hamilton's "gifts and gratuities" to state officials, to the governors' campaigns, and to legislators, including the financing of pet projects of these lawmakers. The list was formidable.

Entering the courtroom, with Phillips Clark beside him and Uzziah Giddings padding alertly at his heels, was like running a gauntlet for Ward. People spat at him, cursed him, called him a crook, a rich racketeer, an anti-God, and, worst of all, a filthy Yankee.

Clark was not his attorney, but was present only as friend and advisor. Clark had ruled himself out because he represented Lily and had advised her in the past. Even though this was an impersonal matter of law, he did not want to be forced to take sides publicly.

Lily's attorney, Dale Winston, was nervous, confused by the conflicting testimony Lily provided him and by the fact that she had to be helped into the courtroom—wearing mourning black—where she sat alternately deathly still, or sobbing uncontrollably.

Winston was in his late twenties, thin and sharp-featured. He kept running his hand through his brown hair and gripping a pencil between his teeth. He continually made notes with it and absently replaced it in his mouth.

Judge Harlan entered the courtroom, a small, gray, aging man. He slumped behind a polished desk on the raised dais. His accent was exaggeratedly back-country. In his opening remarks he called himself a "good ol' boy who fought against the anti-God Yankees for the preservation of freedom, the sanctity of the home, and the protection of the honor of our Southern womanhood."

He was cold toward Ward, and brusque with Raney MacDonald, a New York attorney brought in to represent Ward. Judge Harlan kept reminding MacDonald, with less and less patience, "You don't need to educate this court on points of the law, suh."

MacDonald, stout, dark, balding, wore expensively tailored suits and rings that glittered on his hands. His manner, dress, voice, and ill-concealed contempt set him and Ward apart in a roomful of shabbily dressed, almost informal people.

From the first, however, testimony damaged Lily. Dr. Dame testified that he had had to ask Mr. Hamilton not to try to sleep in the same room with Mrs. Hamilton, then not to see her at all unless she sent for him, and finally, to stay out of her presence as much as possible.

"And why did you ask a husband not to see or touch or go near his own wife, Doctor?"

"Because his very physical presence in a room upset her. Sometimes his being near made her violent, sent her into tantrums."

"Were you called to the Hamilton residence often at night, for house calls after regular professional office hours?"

"Several times a week."

"For what reason?"

"Mrs. Hamilton would be hysterical, in an uncontrollable tantrum. She suffered delusions."

"You have made recent examinations of Mrs. Hamilton?"

"Yes. I and a court-appointed panel examined her."

"For what reason?"

"To ascertain her mental competency."

"And your conclusion?"

"My diagnosis: dementia praecox. The prognosis is poor—in the present atmosphere."

"Is there hope that Mrs. Hamilton will recover?"

"Recovery in these cases is very rare. Of course, with advances in sciences and medicine, we can always be hopeful. But as long as she continues as she is—in an unhappy marriage, in a state conducive to emotional upset—there is little hope."

"In your opinion, does Mrs. Hamilton require hospitalization?"

Lily wailed aloud, almost an animal-like ululation. "No!" she cried out. "I'm not crazy! I'm not crazy! You can't sit there and order me put away! You can't put me away!"

Dale Winston caught Lily's arms and she sank back into her chair sobbing, her shoulders shaken, her head on her arms. The brokenhearted sound was painful to hear; she sounded bereft, abandoned, and helpless against hostile forces too powerful for her to command. She could not even beg them for mercy; they had none.

Dr. Dame, staring at the small figure huddled at the defense table, winced. "I would not recommend hospitalization for her. No. Not at present. There are more humane remedies for her sad situation. Under controlled conditions, she is quite capable of living a quiet life. She poses no threat to other persons or property. She should be able to live peacefully—if Mr. Hamilton were not permitted either to visit or to disturb her emotionally."

"The law states that a spouse must have been mentally unstable for at least four years prior to filing for divorce."

This provision was met.

"The defendant must be judged insane by a competent court-appointed panel."

"She was so adjudged, three to two."

"An executor and guardian must be appointed to direct her affairs, protect her security."

This provision was met.

"The wife must be provided for financially by the husband. She must never be permitted to become a ward of this state."

"Mr. Hamilton agrees to provide the home where Mrs. Hamilton now resides. Title to this property has been transferred and recorded in her name. She will receive monthly support payments based on a percentage of Mr. Hamilton's personal income. This provision is met."

Lily's attorney called witnesses for Lily. Church acquaintances, Andrew Williams, Hobart Bayard, and others spoke as references for her. All declared her sane, normal, a good, loving, and faithful wife, a churchgoer, the donor of a new church structure, an excellent mother, a competent homemaker, a generous and flawless friend.

Winston tried to keep Lily off the stand, but she was insistent. She persisted until Winston reluctantly allowed her to take the oath and testify.

"Has Testimony against you here been, in your opinion,

in any sense prejudicial, untrue, or unfairly detrimental to your character?"

"It's lies," Lily said. She turned and gazed at the judge. "It's all lies, lies that he has fabricated, lies that he has paid these people to speak against me. He wants to get rid of me. He told me he did want to get rid of me. I begged him not to do this ugly thing, but he said he would be rid of me, he did not care what it cost him. I have given him the best years of my life. I am now almost thirty. I'm old. Who would want me now? He doesn't want me. He has manufactured all these lies against me."

"Can you give the court an example of the lies he has perpetrated against you?"

Lily spread her hands. "They're all lies." She pointed toward Dr. Dame. "Take that doctor—Doctor Dame. He sounds so calm, so righteous, so pious up on this stand. But if you know the truth, it is all different. I can tell you it is all different. Make him tell you how much Ward Hamilton is paying him for his lies against me. I was ill when that doctor came to see me. It was not a delusion. I was ill. But from the first, he has not cared about me. He has worked against me and for my husband. This is not the first time. I can tell you, it is not the first time Ward Hamilton has paid that doctor to try to get rid of me. Dr. Dame, working under Ward Hamilton's orders, several times tried to poison me. I would be dead, but I held the medicine in my mouth and spat it out when he was gone."

"Please, Mrs. Hamilton, can you be more—"

"And Ward Hamilton has turned my friends against me, with his lies and his money. Ladies I'd met and liked and grown to trust, ladies who visited me in my home. He turned them against me. They tried to take my money and give it to Ward Hamilton. But taking my money from me—that was his idea. He put them up to it. I couldn't even have a friend because of him—"

"Mrs. Hamilton, if you could speak specifically—"

"And he was jealous. He was out of his mind with jealousy. He brought me to this courtroom to humiliate me, to make the world think I am insane. And all the time, it's him and his jealousy—"

"Why was he jealous?"

"Because. I never gave him any reason to be jealous. Even when I found out about how unfaithful he was.

Openly. Publicly. With slutty women, he was unfaithful to me. But I never looked at another man. I hoped he would turn from his evil ways. But when the prince expressed his affection for me—"

"Please, Mrs. Hamilton—"

"The prince, Mrs. Hamilton?" the judge prompted her.

"Prince Edward. Why, Prince Edward often expressed his affection. He sent messages expressing his affection. Well, I admitted I loved him—because Ward Hamilton had broken my heart—and I thanked God that I had a decent and loving man to turn to in my ordeal. Not in a fleshly way, but a love of the spirit, of the mind." She wept, her slender body shaken.

"Would you like a brief recess, Mrs. Hamilton?"

"No. I want this to end. I am telling the truth and I want to tell it all."

"Was Ward Hamilton cruel and inhuman toward you?"

"He is a cruel and inhuman man. He is insane on the subject of sex. Filthy sex. Perverted sex. He was openly unfaithful to me from the first. How much crueler can a man be to his wife? I was a young girl and he brought me here and made me the laughingstock of this town. I long ago lost my respect for him as a man, as a husband."

"Mrs. Hamilton, could you—?"

"He even tried to make my sisters undress naked and go to bed with him. My own sisters, in my own house, under my own roof. He dares to accuse me, while it is he who is insane, filthy, cruel, and evil."

Finally, Ward was called to the stand. He stated that he had had sexual intercourse with his wife fewer than a dozen times in as many years. For ten years he had not slept in the same room with his wife. On advice of her doctor, he had not entered his wife's bedroom, except on her invitation. And this invitation simply did not come. Lately, he had not been permitted to see his wife at all because she became emotionally disturbed and overwrought in his presence.

Lily sprang to her feet. Her lawyer tried to restrain her but she shook free of his hands. "Why shouldn't I become disturbed? You tried to force me to do ugly things. You tried to make me divorce you. You tried to take my children from me. Of course I'm disturbed by such cruelty. I would not be sane if such evil did not disturb and distress me." Sobbing, she sagged into her chair. "Don't let him do this to me," she wept. "Oh God, please don't let him do this to me."

Ward sagged behind his desk, emotionally exhausted. Phillips Clark stood at the large window overlooking the terminal yards. "Well, you got what you wanted . . . again," he said at last.

"Almost. I still want Belle."

Clark turned, his voice chilly. "Not going to leave Lily anything, eh?"

"I'm thinking about what's best for Belle."

"Are you?"

"I won't have Belle growing up in that smothering, churchgoing atmosphere. I don't want her growing up in conflict inside herself, believing that the honest emotions she feels, the God-given functions of her body are evil and ungodly. I want her out of there."

"Belle needs basic values."

"She won't get them there."

"Will she get them with you?"

"What the hell's eating you?"

"Nothing. You get what you want, one way or another. You always have. And you'll get Belle. Whether it's best for her or not."

"I intend to."

Clark shook his head. "I don't know why I'm amazed *or* disgusted. But I am. I've always known you were a son of a bitch, but always before you seemed like a likeable son of a bitch. You don't have that likeable quality any more."

"I don't need you to tell me how to run my life."

"I'm not trying to." Clark gazed for a moment at the smoke-blackened train yard. Then he sighed, turned, and walked across the room. He picked up his hat.

Ward said, "Where are you going?"

His hand on the doorknob, Clark turned and gazed at Ward without smiling. "I'm going over to Bay Street. I need to breathe some clean air."

Ward laughed. "There are sons of bitches on Bay Street, too."

"Yeah. But they know what they are."

"So do I."

"Yeah. You know. And they know. But knowing bothers them—most of them. And that's what's different, that's what I like about them."

Chapter Thirty-Two

A LIGHT, cold rain fell, fogging the train windows. Ward sat alone and watched as the coaches slowed, creaking and butting as they rolled into the station at Atlanta. Around him, people chattered and gathered their belongings, preparing to detrain. A porter bent over Ward's chair and told him his bag would be waiting on the platform. Ward thanked and tipped him absently.

He felt a sense of expectancy at war inside him with a premonition of failure, even when there was no reason to fear. He had come running here, afraid, even when his hopes bubbled highest, that the journey was a mistake and would end in nothing. He could not even say why he felt faintly depressed and fearful. Maybe it was just that he could not yet believe that after all these years of denial his dreams might finally come true.

He had wept, suddenly and openly, unabashedly, when Raney MacDonald had reported with a smile that the property settlement with Lily was effected; it was all over. He was free and he had been awarded custody of Belle.

His throat tightened, his eyes burned, and abruptly, without warning, he found himself in tears. There remained many restrictions, constraints, reins, and controls held by the court, but he scarcely listened to the attorney. He was not home free, not yet. But he had his daughter. They could not take her away from him. He did not care about the strings attached to his custody of her. He could listen to all that later.

He telephoned Lily's home, formerly his own. He sat gripping the receiver in a sweaty palm. He was answered by a servant whose voice was chilled and reserved. Finally he was connected with Belle. "Oh, Daddy. Daddy. Daddy."

"Have you heard?"

"Yes. Uncle Phillips called Mother. They told me I'm to live with you. When are you coming for me?"

"Soon. As soon as I can. There are still some legal strings to cut, things I have to do. A house for you to live in, in an approved neighborhood; the right schools; people I have to hire to take care of you."

"I don't need anybody but you." Her voice boiled with laughter.

He laughed with her. "You and I know that. But it's a fuddy-duddy world we're dealing with, baby. The court is very old-fashioned. You've got to have a matronly woman—a nanny and a maid—"

"Sounds wonderful."

"It will be wonderful. Oh, I promise you it will be wonderful. It will take a little time, but at least I've got you. You're all mine, and I am now the richest man in the world."

He had won so much. He had lost much too, immeasurably, but he had balanced the costs and made up his mind; he was willing to pay the price.

He composed half a dozen letters to Julia, and threw them all away. Finally he sent her a telegram, care of Southern Express, Atlanta.

COMING ATLANTA FRIDAY STOP PLEASE MEET ME DINING ROOM HOTEL ATLANTAN STOP

With trepidation, he awaited Julia's reply. He had not seen her since that meeting in Tallahassee. This brief encounter had been unsatisfactory, worse than not seeing her at all. He had wanted so much, needed so much, had so

399

much to say, and they were like remote, polite strangers, with Belle clinging to his hand. Julia was with a business party representing Henry Plant on railroad business, lobbying in the state capital. She could not spare Ward even the time for a dinner. He drew a small gratification from what he read in her eyes. There was no smugness there. There was sadness and understanding—and yes, damn it—longing in her green, almond-shaped eyes. She felt the same pain as he. She was afflicted by loss. She had not for one moment forgotten the time they'd had together. But he could take little pleasure from what she let him see in her face. He could not live on memory. He was alive *now*, in this moment, throbbing and driven with need for loving and sharing. He could not exist on warmed-over images from the past, no matter how sensual or tantalizing. He wanted her now.

When her telegram came, his hand shook. He had difficulty tearing the blue envelope open. Her reply was terse, brief, unpromising:

WILL MEET YOU FOR DINNER STOP

He had three eternal hours to kill. He wandered the downtown streets, unable to walk very far from the Hotel Atlantan. He found the city altered miraculously from the damaged, wounded, struggling site he'd come into in 1875. Every sign of the war was gone, except for the statues and the evocative names of places, avenues, parks, and businesses. The streets were paved with red Georgia brick, wide and clean. New buildings gleamed in the wan twilight. The scars were hidden; for generations they would fester, but they were hidden.

He walked back to the hotel. The Atlantan, once the showplace at Five Points, was getting old. She stood, haughty as an aging matron, already bypassed and half-forgotten by the busy and progressive citizenry. Strange and hard to believe, but the old landmark probably wouldn't even be there in another ten years. Somehow this added to Ward's sense of loss, of regret for things gone and irrecoverable.

He entered the solemn, musty lobby and went into the dining room. It was only five o'clock. He ordered bourbon and water, and sat sipping it slowly. The hands on the clock moved sluggishly. He felt fearful, desperate with hope. He tried to relax but could not help staring toward the arched entrance of the lobby, that path along which Julia would come to him at last.

She paused at the entranceway.

His heart lurched. Weak in the knees, Ward stood up. His napkin fell to the carpeting at his feet. He braced himself against the table, looking at her. She saw him and walked toward him, as gracefully as a ballet dancer.

It was Julia, yet she was not the same. She was a distant relative of the little girl he had known, and her older sister whom he had loved on that train. She was complete now, pampered, indulged, sensual, self-assured. How old was she now? Probably twenty-five, but this didn't matter. Her beauty was ageless, her elegance timeless—every article she wore complemented and accented the loveliest features of her lovely body. He stared, fascinated at the sophistication in her eyes, the firm set of her lovely mouth. Her exquisite perfection dazzled him: the flushed beauty of her cheeks, the simple rings in her pierced earlobes, her hair, darkened now by time, the fur-collared jacket, the mix of richly textured fabrics, unknown to most women. She glowed, attracting all eyes, all attention, all light in the place, relaxed, yet smart and aware of the sensation she created.

The first thing she said to him devastated him. She put out her hand. He took it and found the fingers icy, trembling slightly. She said, "I can't stay. I'm sorry."

Angered, crippled, he lashed out, "Why did you come at all?"

"You asked me. I knew I had to see you, once. I'm sorry I can't stay. I'm truly sorry. I know there are some things I should say to you, things I owe you, things you've wanted to hear me say. I'll say them now. I've missed you since I left you that morning in Savannah. I've wanted you. I've thought of no one, nothing but you." She exhaled heavily. "That's all I have to say. All I can say."

"Sit down, please. There are some things I must say to you."

"Please don't."

He stared at her. The loudest sounds were the remote touch of silver against china, remote fragments of conver-

401

sations, the pounding of his own heart. "My God, I've got to talk to you. I'm free. I've got a divorce from Lily—"

"I've heard that. I'm sorry."

"Why? I was in hell."

"Not sorry for you, sorry for Lily." She sat down on the edge of her chair, uncomfortable, poised for flight.

Ward shook his head, trying to read something in her face. "My God, Julia, is this a nightmare? You said we had no chance because I was married—"

"No. I said we had no chance. You may have told yourself it was because you were married; I never said that. I said we had no chance. We don't. I love you, Ward, with all my heart—as I never loved anyone, as I never will love anyone else. But I hate everything you stand for, everything you do. Your giant railroad, growing bigger, grabbing more and more, pillaging, walking over people. Your divorce is just the latest of the cruel, selfish, and inhuman things you've always done to make me hate you."

"Julia, we can be happy now. Together. I've custody of Belle—"

"Poor little Belle."

"Stop it. Damn it, stop it." The waiter came silently and stood at Ward's shoulder. Ward managed to order another bourbon, and coffee for Julia. He sat, without breathing, until the black man retreated. "I thought—you and I . . . Belle . . . We could give her—"

"You and I can't do anything, Ward. And if you're smart, if there's any human kindness and goodness left inside you, you'll let Belle's mother have her. No matter how ill her mother is, her mother is what Belle needs now, far more than she needs you, far more than you need her as one of your prize trophies to display—"

"Don't—"

"I'm begging for Belle's sake. If I hurt you, I'm sorry. But Belle's life is more important. You mustn't destroy her, just to have your way."

"Destroy? I love her with—"

"With all your heart? Do you? Enough to give her up? For her good? I look at Belle, Ward, and I see myself, eleven, twelve years old. A hotel kid, grown up, smart, and ignorant. I see all the hurt, the mistakes, the heartache. I know, Ward. I've been there. I know how you love her. I do. But let her go."

His voice broke. "Let Belle go. Let *you* go. My God, Julia, what is there for me?"

She shrugged faintly. "I don't know, Ward. You made your life, I didn't."

His eyes filled with tears. "Don't you know how much I love you?"

"If I didn't, I wouldn't be here at all."

"Marry me, Julia. If I've hurt you, I'll make it up to you."

"You could never do that."

"My God, I'd spend my life trying."

She shook her head, smiling sadly. "You'd spend your life building a fortune. Grabbing, extorting, taking, just as you are now. Every time I looked at one of your trains, I'd remember—"

"Julia, I can't stand it without you. I can't spend my life in hell."

She spread her hands. "There's nothing I can do."

"Even if you would."

"Even if I would,"

"Yet you say you love me. Why? To add to my torment?"

She shook her head, "Because it's true. I loved you the first minute I saw you. I loved you because I couldn't help it, not because I wanted to. That has not changed."

"Then come with me. For God's sake, come with me. I need you."

"I can't, Ward. I can't ever see you again after tonight."

"You're walking out on me? Here? Like this?"

"I shouldn't have come here. He would be hurt if he knew—"

"He?"

"Hobart. I married Hobart Bayard, Ward, months ago, quietly. Before your divorce was final."

He sagged, beaten, feeling as if he'd been gutted. "Hobart. You. You married Hobart Bayard. I saw him in Jacksonville. He said nothing—"

"He was there to testify for Lily, against you. He said he saw you for only a minute—in the court."

"But he could have told me. Jesus, why? Why would you marry Hobart?"

"Because he worries about me, about the way men act toward me downtown. Because he has money. Not as

403

much as you, but enough. Because he is gentle and good. Because he's a kind and decent man. Because he asked me."

"Oh Jesus. You haven't mentioned love."

"No, I haven't, have I? I loved you Ward, and look what it got me. Maybe what Hobart and I have is better than love. No, you're right, I didn't marry Hobart for love. I married him for the only reason that truly matters—because he isn't you. . . ."

BOOK THREE:

JULIA, 1890-1900

Chapter Thirty-Three

WARD GAZED DOWN on the swirling tea-dancers as if seeing an unlikely dream coming true. The girls blossomed like blue, green, and amber flowers against the somber grays and blacks of their young men. On a raised dais, the ensemble of black musicians played for dancing, and the dancers spun and laughed like children in a game. The garden and the misty sky provided the unreal setting, without even a threatening cloud daring to mar the texture of the golden horizon.

He smiled wryly, watching from an upstairs window. That radiant scene was more like a dream than reality. This was the ultimate dazzling moment in a dream that had come true, that he had made come true.

He searched among those swirling figures, seeking Belle. She was the unlikeliest part of this dream. Belle—sixteen? It couldn't be true, and yet it was true, and this garden party was the festive marking of that momentous milepost.

He found her on the dance floor. He told himself this was easy because it was like finding an orchid among clusters of marigolds. Dressed in an exquisitie new satin cocktail gown, she pirouetted, smiling up into the face of one of her young men. Around her a soft storm of music, laughter, and whispers wheeled like breeze-tipped leaves.

The warm afternoon winds, blowing across a rolling lawn from the river, drifted her from one smiling set of dancers to the next. Rejected swains, along with jealous rivals—girls who would smilingly hate her until marriage at last took her safely out of their sphere—all gazed after her. From the shadowed window, he watched her glow, loving being the center of her own enchanted cosmos. The sounds wafted up to him, muted piano and violins, subdued laughter, warm, affectionate, low-key chattering, mixed and rising against noises without any apparent source other than the excitement and pleasure of the party.

He turned away from the window, but something shocking and discordant snagged his attention and held him riveted, although the brief scene went unnoticed by the majority of the guests. Another youngster from the eager stag line touched the shoulder of Belle's partner, but this fellow refused to release her. Laughing, Belle tried to writhe free. He caught her wrist and twisted it up her back, forcing her to remain in his embrace.

Ward watched Belle's head go up, her face suddenly pallid. She bit her lip, forced herself to laugh. By this time, the other youngster was abandoned, lost in the wake of the dancers.

Rage flared through Ward. He had never permitted anyone to hurt Belle, even accidentally, certainly not in casual cruelty. He turned on his heel, and strode across the room and down the stairs. By the time he had crossed the living room, the sun parlor, and the flagstone terrace, the music had stopped.

He met Belle and her young man at the rim of the crowd. Most of her male acquaintances were faceless transients who never held Belle's interest long enough to assume any individuality or identity in Ward's mind. This one had a face—a spoiled, petulant, self-indulgent face he would always remember, not because the physiognomy was remarkable, but because this youth had hurt Belle.

Belle seemed to have forgotten the sudden stabbing of pain, the way she'd gone pale, biting her lip to keep from crying out. She laughed now, radiantly, and clung tightly to her escort's hand.

He looked as if he might be three or four years older than Belle. He was tall, almost as tall as Ward, but slender and muscular with that arrogant air of well-being that comes from wealth, ease, exercise, and catered indolence.

"Daddy," Belle said. "I was looking for you."

Ward tried to smile, but could not. He let his gaze rake the youth's face, but the boy was unimpressed by his disapproval. "Are you all right?"

"Of course I'm all right. I've never been happier. It's a super party, Daddy. Everybody loves it."

"I'm glad. Is your arm hurt?"

"What?" She peered up at him, frowning, then glanced down at her fragile wrist, somehow strongly reminiscent of Lily's delicate coloring and supple structure. The livid red fingermarks showed vividly on the clear surface of her forearm. "Oh, that. Just a little show of male dominance, Daddy. It doesn't mean a thing." She glanced up at her young man. "He's just jealous of me, though he'd die before he'd admit it."

"He may die sooner than he anticipates if he hurts you again," Ward kept his voice light, his smile undiminished, his gaze on Belle's lovely face, but his words slapped against her escort—and fell unheeded about his patent-leather dancing shoes.

"Oh, Daddy, don't be old-fashioned," Belle said. "Besides, Laddie has the right to hurt me if he wants to."

"How in God's name did he get that privilege?"

"Because Laddie's different."

With a lurch of recognition, a stab of jealousy and loss, Ward realized that this one *was* different. His name, Belle said in delight, was Laddie. His real name was Beekman Gould McCormick. "But everyone calls him Laddie. If your name were Beekman, wouldn't you be pleased if people called you Laddie?"

Ward shook hands with Laddie McCormick. He studied the youth, trying—and failing—to see what about him set him apart, because he was different from all Belle's other young swains. Ward recognized the difference. The very way Belle spoke Laddie's name set him apart from all the others.

Belle came into Ward's room where he was working over some papers a little after midnight. She wore a pale silk robe over a pastel gown, her hair in braids the way Lavinia had once worn hers. Belle kissed him lightly and sat on the arm of his chair. "What did you think of him?"

"Who?"

"Laddie, of course."

"Not much."

"What a terrible thing to say."

"Well, I guess every father feels threatened when one of the faceless young males underfoot suddenly develops a face."

"Laddie has always had a face. A handsome, distinguished, old-family face."

"A Beekman. And a Gould. *And* a McCormick." Ward smiled. "You can hardly get any more distinguished than that, can you?"

"But Laddie has so much more."

"I see. He's just a cousin? A remote, named-for-the-money cousin?"

"Why do you say that?"

"Because if he were more than a poor relation, he wouldn't need anything more. Who is he, really?"

"He's a wonderful boy—who loves me. And whom I love. His family doesn't have a great deal of money, that's true. They're well-off enough, I guess, but not filthy rich. He's had the best schools and all that. All the advantages. He graduated from Trinity College and spent a year on the Grand Tour."

"What does he do?"

"Do?"

"Yes. He must have a profession, a trade, a job, something?"

"He's an artist and a poet. He paints lovely pictures. He wants to study for a few more years in Paris—"

"Oh, good. He may be leaving soon, then?"

"Daddy! You're tiresome. I've never seen you act like this before."

"And I've never seen *you* act like this before."

"Well, that *is* a switch. I thought you'd be telling me how I've been in love a hundred times."

"No. I've been in love too, a few times."

"You are sweet."

"No, I'm troubled."

"Why? Because I'm at last truly in love? Or because I'm in love with Laddie?"

410

"I would like to know more about him."

"You'll have plenty of opportunity to learn all about him. And when you do, I'm sure you'll feel toward him as I do." She kissed his cheek. "That's what I wanted to tell you. That was Laddie's present for me on my sixteenth birthday. He asked me to marry him."

"I hope you told him you were sixteen."

"He knows how old I am."

"*Only* sixteen. A child. Does he intend to wait for you?"

She laughed. "Sometimes you're even more transparent than mother, and more straitlaced, far more old-fashioned. You really are. Laddie and I don't intend to wait for anything. Your consent would be nice, but we *are* getting married this spring."

He winced, but kept his voice light. He couldn't lock her in her room. He couldn't refuse to sign her wedding application. He couldn't stand to lose her. "That won't give me time to buy you a splendid wedding."

"We don't want a splendid wedding. A justice of the peace will do nicely. A notary, a tugboat captain."

"You *are* in a hurry."

"Yes, I can't wait. I don't want to wait." Her voice had that vein of steel in it he remembered from Lily. "I won't wait."

He felt helpless against her. She was only sixteen, but he could not recall how many years it had been since she had heeded, or endured his counsel. She had a mind of her own, a will of her own. She was capable of violence when crossed. There had been a long parade of servants and governesses over the past five years. They quit or Belle fired them. He went off to work in the morning, with the entire household operating smoothly, and returned to find the place a shambles, all hired help departed, and Belle sitting barefooted, wriggling her toes nonchalantly, consuming a peanut butter sandwich in the wreckage.

Whatever Belle had become, he was to blame. He was too busy, too harried, too driven, to provide an orderly existence for her. He had built a ten-room rambling house on five acres overlooking the St. Johns River south of Jacksonville. He had furnished and staffed it as well as he could. But Belle was less than content, restless, always in motion, refusing to sit still. She cared nothing about learning those genteel arts considered appropriate for every

411

well-bred young woman. She had never learned to boil water, fry an egg, or make toast. She loved horses, and kept a stable of four so there would always be mounts for those screaming, mindless young friends of hers who overran the house. Belle's idea of a slumber party was a Pullman car full of teenaged girls traveling overnight. "I love the sound of the wheels on the rails," she told Ward. "I'd sleep every night on a train if I could. There's the sound of the wheels on the tracks, and the movement, and you're always in some new place in the morning." She went away to a new school each fall, and returned home by Thanksgiving, expelled. He was able to find her a new place by January. She seldom lasted in the second semester past the Easter holidays. There were rules, and rules were stupid, and made for other people.

She was required by law to spend three months each year with her mother in the big old house in Jacksonville. She went reluctantly, and returned miserable. She did not see why the law forced her to listen to her mother talk poisonously of her father, accusing him of all sorts of crimes.

She found some pleasure in trying to make a man of Robin. She broke all his knitting needles, and unraveled miles of his most intricate tatting. With rope sneaked into the house from Luke's carriage house, she tied the sleeping Robin in his bed and stuffed a shirt in his mouth. She hacked off his curls, chopping his hair to within an inch of his skull. Probably she would not have gone to the big old house except for Robin. She loved to torment him.

Ward admitted he had failed Belle. He had protected her—except for three months of each year—from the restrictive and repressive religious atmosphere Lily propagated. But in doing this, he had denied Belle any of those basic values one lived by. Somewhere between Lily's puritanism and his own free thinking lay the moral accountability and ethical integrity he wanted as guides for Belle. She believed in nothing except personal pleasure and self-gratification, and he was helpless against her. He didn't know what to say, even if there had been any means of forcing Belle to listen.

Time had thundered past, like some locomotive out of control, before he could accomplish any of the things he planned. Life itself was out of control for him, at the office and at home. He had reached the apex of his achievement, and ahead yawned only an abyss. He could see nothing else, for himself or for Belle.

He had his triumphs. Belle was one of the most popular, most sought-after young girls in northern Florida. She made the rotogravure sections, on horseback, at parties, boarding trains, alighting from trains, swimming in somebody's exclusive pool in a shockingly brief swim suit. She made friends quickly, aimlessly, and without question, and gave them all her unqualified loyalty. She had attended a dozen esteemed private schools and had collected intimate acquaintances in all of them. Everybody loved her in those schools except the deans. She was forever being invited across the state, across the country, across town for a weekend, a week, or a month. She could not endure one night alone in the house without company. She entertained lavishly and constantly. The house was overrun with bright, scrubbed young faces and strange, discordant accents—New England, Chicago, Texas, Atlanta—like the chattering of migrant birds.

His rails reached slowly south toward Fort Dallas. There was talk that Flagler had become interested in the town and wanted to change its name to Miami. As new freight and passenger markets appeared on the warm south coast, Ward inched his rails out to serve them. He was overextended, deeply in debt. As long as business was good, he met his payrolls, paid his indebtedness, and kept up with interest payments. What he never found was a moment when he could relax, turn his back, or stop running faster and faster just to keep pace. Freight rates were favorable because, with no competition, he set them at what the traffic would bear. But the big systems across the state were growing larger, consolidating the smaller, separate lines under central control. Plant was among the biggest. These huge corporations were able to control and set rates, and sometimes to undercut him, offering his customers lower freight charges over greater distances. Damned few shippers were loyal, even those who owed their second chance to him, when they could save a few cents per carrier ton.

His proudest triumph to date was the village at Winter Grove. The town had begun as the site of "Hamilton's Folly"—the monstrous Moorish depot like a candy castle

413

in the middle of nowhere, the only structure in miles of unimproved land. He had established an electric power plant and a water pumping station. These required operators, laborers, engineers, and executives. They came to Winter Grove to live. He sold the power company and irrigation wells to private companies who opened offices and built warehouses. Homes appeared on the streets he'd laid out. The arrival of people created a need for goods and services. A general store was built a block from the station. It was followed by a vast citrus-packing plant along the tracks. Seasonal workers arrived, black and white. A restaurant, a hotel, and a barbershop opened. More stores and more homes were constructed, more streets paved. Several large groves were now producing fruit, and houses, barns, stables, and outbuildings dotted the countryside. From the farms were shipped tobacco, potatoes, tomatoes, vegetables, flowers, and beef. Winter Grove had become a thriving village.

In the weeks that followed Belle's announcement that she was going to marry young Laddie McCormick, Ward tried to figure out how he could discourage her without alienating her. He had to keep struggling against mounting odds until Belle was married, but not to a rootless, foppish young self-styled artist.

"You're only sixteen, baby," Ward told Belle. "Can it hurt to wait three or four years?"

She shrugged. "It can't hurt me, because I won't do it."

"You're too young yet to know what you want. Give yourself a chance to really know."

"You know better than that. You sound stuffy and tiresome. You know I've always known what I wanted—exactly what I wanted. And I know now."

He hesitated, unable to say aloud that there was a wide gulf between being headstrong and being wise. He didn't want to lose her. Belle was capable of walking out and they both knew it. "A trip to Europe," he suggested.

"A honeymoon gift for Laddie and me? I accept."

He nodded. "If you'll go alone first—for six months. Just six months."

"Well, I won't do that. Oh, I could go, and Laddie could follow me. But I don't want to play ugly games. We're trying to be honest with you. How many times have

I heard you say you waited only to see me safely married?"

"Yes. But the key word in there is not *married*, Belle, but *safely*."

Laddie walked into Ward's office reluctantly, as if fearful of contamination. He wore a dark suit, snugly tailored, tight about the ankles. He was freshly shaven, cheeks flushed and smooth, his nails newly manicured, his shoes polished, and his clothing brushed. He glowed with that idealistic unreality just being introduced into magazine illustration. Ward admitted that Laddie McCormick represented that precise epitome of the beautiful youth who would be adored by sixteen-year-old females.

Laddie set his hat and cane aside and poised himself gingerly on one of the deep leather chairs across Ward's office. Laddie's complexion gleamed; his carefully oiled blond curls waved back from a sculpted profile. His eyes glowed as blue and untroubled as a baby's—and as unaware, Ward thought.

"I asked you down here because I wanted you to see my shop," Ward said.

"Edifying. Quite functional." Laddie obviously was less than impressed.

"I hoped you might like it, find it interesting."

"Why?"

"Belle insists you are to be married. I thought you might want to support her."

"My God." Laddie straightened in his chair and looked around, for the first time actually *seeing* this office, the misted windows, the smoke-clotted terminal yards beyond. He looked as if he might vomit. "Are you offering me a job?"

Ward grinned. "Have I offended you?"

"Well, you haven't amused me. I'd like very much to be on reasonably civil terms with you, Mr. Hamilton. I acknowledge that Belle does idolize you. It would certainly upgrade the climate of our marriage if you and I could be polite, even if we do exist on separate planes. But I must insist that you accept me for what I am."

"Maybe that's why I asked you here. I want to do that. I'd like to understand you. I'd like to accept you—for what you are. What are you?"

"I'm sure your daughter has told you. I am an artist. I write poetry. I have studied poetry at Trinity, and art in the Sorbonne. I am proud of my achievements."

"I'm glad to hear that. Do you earn a good living with your painting and your poetry?"

"I don't think that's any of your business."

"And I think it is."

"I neither write poetry nor paint commercially."

"If you are planning to marry my daughter—"

"Oh, Belle and I shall marry. I assure you of that, Mr. Hamilton."

"I am concerned about her welfare. I believe I have the right to ask how you hope to support her."

"I don't have the same regard for money that you do, Mr. Hamilton."

"I regard it as a necessary evil," Ward said.

"I regard it as an evil necessity," Laddie countered.

"I don't think we'll get anywhere quoting epigrams at each other. You have no job?"

"No. Certainly not."

"And you refuse to accept one here?"

"I certainly do. I refuse to contaminate my soul or blacken my hands in American commerce."

"How will you live? How will you and Belle live?"

"Belle has money, Mr. Hamilton. Belle and I shall not want, any more than we shall compromise ourselves by stooping to soul-robbing, money-grubbing commerce."

"May I ask you one question?"

"I suppose so. I am making every effort to accommodate myself to you, sir; I hope you appreciate that."

"Oh, I do. I realize this is painful for you, and I'm sorry about that. But I also understand you to believe I would not let Belle want for anything, and therefore you have no financial worries as her husband."

"If you want to put it that crassly."

"There is something you should consider. Suppose Belle's money did stop, for some unforeseen reason, and her income disappeared—what then?"

Laddie stood up. "If you are trying to threaten me, Mr. Hamilton, I can only say you're not very subtle about it. But you are tiresome. Next, you'll be offering to *buy* me off—"

"I had thought about that."

"I hope you'll forgive me, but I don't have to stay here and listen to degrading talk like this. You won't pull me down to your level, Mr. Hamilton, no matter what you do."

Chapter Thirty-Four

WARD MET BELLE and Laddie in the terminal at Jacksonville. They had been six months away on a honeymoon in Europe. They had departed in a bustle of excitement, their friends crowding around, the air thick with laughter and newlywed jokes. When Ward had kissed Belle goodbye, she'd clung to him for a moment—perhaps for the last time—as his little girl. And then she was gone, and everyone was talking simultaneously. Amid the shouting and the laughter, Ward felt empty and lost, without real hope for Belle's happiness, though he wanted everything good for her and though he was almost drowned in sounds of pleasure and delight and promise.

He saw them alight now from the Pullman steps to the platform, elegantly and smartly attired in the latest fashions from Paris. Seeing them like that—the pleasant glow of the bride and groom still on them—he felt reassured and happy for them, and faintly hopeful. They were a handsome couple—Laddie aloof, confident, and overtly snobbish, Belle arrestingly beautiful, even if somehow looking far too sophisticated and intense for a teenager.

Ward moved through the jostling, rushing mobs, his gaze fixed on Belle. As another couple stepped from the train and joined them, he hesitated. This couple, somewhere in their thirties, looked fashionable if somewhat eroded away inside, with that essence of breeding and old money that is difficult to fake.

Ward watched Laddie shake hands stiffly with the man, and touch at the woman's smooth cheek with his lips. Belle was far less reticent. She squeezed both of the woman's hands, chattering brightly, and then pressed herself into the arms of the man, kissing him fiercely.

Ward flushed. There was something raw and revealing in her actions, even if they reflected nothing more than her constant need for reassurance and verification of her attractiveness. She was lovely, she was loved; she didn't need to do this. Laddie's farewell had definitely marked the older couple as casual acquaintances, but there was nothing casual in Belle's attitude. It was almost as if she boldly announced that a great deal had passed between her and this older man, even in a brief period of time.

Laddie caught Belle's arm with some violence and broke her free from the man's embrace. There was something in Laddie's attitude that suggested the impatient separating of animals in estrus. The older woman smiled indulgently and her husband dabbed at his rouged mustache with the backs of his fingers. Belle cried out in strident protest and lunged free of Laddie's grip.

His heart pounding, Ward stood in the thinning crowd and watched. He wondered emptily if he were getting a capsule glimpse of the happy couple honeymooning across Europe. Belle was instantly laughing again, shaking hands with the other couple, telling them they must look them up as soon as possible. Laddie did not reinforce the invitation, but remained stiff and taciturn.

Their traveling companions dispersed with the rest of the travelers, and Belle and Laddie were left for a moment alone on the platform, bleak and young.

Belle looked around and spied Ward. Shrieking like a little girl, she ran to him, her arms outflung.

She hurled herself against him as she had when she was five years old, laughing and talking and crying at once. Ward winced, looking at her lovely face. Belle's cheek was swollen and discolored with a purpled, well-defined, and unconcealable black eye, far beyond any cosmetic reparation or disguise known to man. She ignored the shiner, and he tried to.

In the carriage on the way home, she talked animately. They'd seen London, the north of England, and a bit of Scotland. But they'd been alone up there and had soon tired of the quiet backcountry, and had gone to Paris with a couple they'd met on shipboard.

Belle reported, giggling, that she'd waded barefoot in some ancient fountain in Rome and Laddie had painted the Bay of Naples. "Really quite smashing, once you figure out what it is!" They had met dozens of exciting, interesting, and unusual people, too: an English couple they'd both hated on sight and learned cordially to despise, a Frenchman who threw a farewell party for them at Maxim's—which was brand new and *très chic*—and then presented them with the bill! It was fantastic, hectic, ancient, and mildly odorous, and Belle said she was glad to be home, so glad to see him again, she had not known she could miss anyone as much as she had missed him. She did not mention the contusion marring her lovely face, and before they reached the house, Ward had decided to say nothing about it. If they were trying to overlook a bad moment, trying to regroup and live around it, let them. Few marriages are made in heaven, adjustments are always in order, and, whatever their conflict, they would have to work it out.

He stayed, that first night in the home where Belle had grown up, only long enough to drink a welcome-home toast and to turn the keys over to Belle. She wept in delight, gratitude, and pleasure, and begged him not to go. She would miss him. She had lived for the moment when she would get back to him. She did not see how she could get along without him. But as he took his leave, he saw that his departure had been anticipated, at least by Laddie, as nothing less than due, and even Belle looked relieved to see him go.

He felt exiled for the first few months at the St. James. The hotel was aging—as he was!—and he was lonely. But he went out to the house only when Belle invited him. She called him half a dozen times a day just to chat. She came frequently to visit him in the evenings, rushed, breathless, on her way somewhere else, but he looked forward to her coming.

She talked lightly about herself and Laddie. Laddie was

not content; he'd had no success in arranging a New York gallery showing for his paintings. "Don't be surprised if he asks you to underwrite a showing for him. He'll be timid about it. He has a lot of pride. He hates to ask anybody for anything. I know he doesn't want to ask you, but after all, you're the only one who can afford to give him a chance to be seen."

Ward kissed her lightly and promised to do what he could. It was too bad that neither Belle nor Laddie could see that success was seldom handed out casually; it was earned, sometimes cruelly earned. Like all their young peers, born into wealthy and indulgent families, they sincerely anticipated rewards without expending the sweat, effort, or discipline to achieve them.

However, he decided to do anything he could to help them. The strident whispers of their stormy battles and hysterical scenes in public reached him at the St. James. They fought in public places, and created scenes at private parties. Neither of them could hold two cocktails and behave properly, and yet they consumed four and five, until they sagged helplessly and had to be carried home. Sometimes they arrived separately, a whole day apart. Perhaps some constructive accomplishment, a goal on Laddie's part, might reinforce his sagging self-assurance and sense of manhood.

One night, Belle departed his hotel suite, and, within an hour, Laddie was pounding on his door. Laddie came in, wild-eyed and disheveled. He barely spoke to Ward as he looked around the small parlor. "Where is she?" he demanded.

"Belle? She left. Some time ago."

"The bitch. The lying bitch." Laddie looked as if he might vomit.

"Take it easy, son."

"Why? She *does* lie, and she *is* a bitch—a bitch in heat. She says she spends the evenings with you. Sometimes she comes home at eleven, sometimes at one. But do you know where she's been?"

Ward watched Laddie, empty-bellied.

"She *says* she's here with you, but where *is* she? Where is she right now? Do you know where she is?"

Obviously they were miserably unhappy together. He tried to talk to Belle about it, but she only laughed. "It's

421

not the same kind of world you lived in, Daddy. It's a complex existence . . . you wouldn't even understand . . . Laddie and I just have to adjust . . . give us time, Daddy. I am *young,* you know. You said that yourself. I deserve a good time."

Phillips Clark called him one morning at seven. "Maybe you'd better go out to your place this morning," the lawyer suggested. "It's Belle."

He drove out to the old house on the river as swiftly as a carriage could move on the narrow roadway. The day was brilliant, the sun golden, the morning breeze moist and languorous. He was aware of none of it. He drove into the yard, and swung down from the carriage. The immense lawn was unkempt, ragged, and scabrous all the way to the river. The front door was unlocked, ajar, the interior looking as if no servant had cleaned or swept or emptied an ashtray.

"Belle?" he called into the dark house.

There was no answer. His heart pounding, Ward went up the steps. At the head of the stairs, he hesitated and called again. Belle answered this time, from a bedroom.

She lay across a mussed and rumpled bed. Her face was discolored and swollen, her arms bruised. She had been badly and methodically beaten. He sat beside her and tried to smile through the rage that boiled up through him.

"I'm all right, Daddy," she lisped oddly, through a split and puffed lip.

"Yes. You look fine. You look pretty well adjusted."

"Please, Daddy. He didn't mean to hurt me—"

"Thank God," he said in savage irony. "If he'd meant to hurt you, he'd have killed you. I'm sorry, baby. You can't stay here with him. Not until he learns to control his violence."

She shook her head. "This is *my* house. I won't leave. Make him get out."

He nodded. "Why does he beat you?" he asked.

She shrugged, her face turned away. "He's got to fill his bucket somehow."

"You've got to tell me about it, Belle. I can't really help you unless you tell me."

Her eyes filled with tears. She clung to his hands. "Ask him," she whispered. Then she shook her head, pulled herself up, and toppled into his arms. "I'm all right now. Now that you're here. Honest. No, Daddy, don't say anything to him. We've got to work it out. It's between us."

He promised to say nothing. She admitted that all the servants and groundskeepers had quit three days earlier. She had not felt up to dealing with the effort of interviewing replacements.

"Maybe later. I feel better now that you're here. I will. I'll do better. Now that you've come to me, I feel better. I'll be all right. Maybe—maybe I'll get up this afternoon. And I'll hire servants tomorrow, I promise you. It's going to be a whole new life for Laddie and me, I promise."

He held her gently for a long time. She grew sleepy and he laid her down on her bed. He walked downstairs and went out the rear door to the barn. He found an iron crowbar and stood hefting it for a moment. Carrying it like a cane, he returned to the house. He sat on the shaded veranda and waited until Laddie returned with his easel and paints, from the river. Laddie wore Levi's, a blue denim shirt, and an old cardigan.

Ward stood up. Laddie winced at the sight of him, and his face paled, but he remained coldly defiant.

"I don't want you to say anything to me," Laddie said. "I could take you apart, old man, and if you interfere in my marriage, that's what I'll do."

"I'm not afraid of you, son. I know you've had some training in fisticuffs, but beating on defenseless women isn't the same."

Laddie tried to walk past him to enter the house. When Ward stepped into his path, Laddie's face became grayer than ever, his mouth white and taut. "I warn you, get out of my way. I've nothing to say to you."

Ward nodded. "And I haven't much to say to you. But for your own good, I advise you to listen to me." He raised the crowbar in his fist. "There's just this: you can turn around, walk out of here, and never come near Belle or this house again. I'll let you go, and we'll say no more."

"Well, I'm not going to do that. Belle's my wife. This is my house."

"All right. Then you stay. But hear me well: I'll kill you if you ever touch my daughter again in rage and violence. I don't give a damn what she's done; you'll settle it some other way. Your physical cruelty has got to stop. Now. Here. This morning. Do you understand me?"

Laddie stood defiantly for another long beat. His face gave way first. His eyes filled with tears, his mouth contorted, and he sobbed. The sound was heartbreaking. Ward winced. He could not even go on standing there holding the crowbar. He threw it behind him to the ground.

"Is my hurting *her* all you can see?" Laddie sobbed helplessly. "What about me? What about what she does to me? You're right, there's no swelling on my face, no discoloration, nothing you can *see*. But goddamn it, she's killing me. She's killing me, do you hear me? You don't need to threaten me. I don't want to hit her. She drives me— she drives me out of my mind. I don't know what I'm doing. You make her behave. Make her behave. Make her stop humiliating me, cheating and lying and going to bed with every new man she finds . . . make her stop it. Oh, Jesus God, make her stop it. . . ."

Ward returned downtown without even knowing how he got there. He felt helpless—helpless to aid Belle, helpless to bring any relief to Laddie. He just kept going over the same repetitive thought in his mind: rules were for other people, not for Belle. This was the way she'd grown up, and if she remained married, these would be the conditions for her marriage—her own rules, her own laws, her own lack of rules, her own defiance of laws.

He felt exhausted. He even had the terrible sense of reliving his nightmarish existence with Lily. Despite the fact that Lily was fanatically moral and straitlaced and Belle dissolute and insensible to reproof, they were opposite sides of the same coin. Lily was obsessed with prudery; Belle was immersed in laxity of morals, violently opposed to all restraints. It was as if Belle consciously attempted to disprove, discard, and deny every tenet by which her mother lived.

When Ward's secretary announced J. A. MacDonald, Ward could not even remember where he'd heard the name. He could not concentrate; he felt confused and heartsick, unable to give a damn about ordinary commerce. His secretary reminded him that MacDonald was Flagler's executive assistant in his Florida development.

"Mr. Flagler has empowered me, Mr. Hamilton, to meet

424

any reasonable asking price for the controlling interest in your railroad from Jacksonville south along the East Coast. We're prepared for you to hold control of the north central lines to Lake City. Mr. Flagler is interested only in the East Coast south of Jacksonville. He wants to expand and extend the present lines to reach new markets and potential new territories. His building cannot wait for your own expansion program." MacDonald smiled. "He finds it too slow and too conservative. As you know, Mr. Flagler has developed a compelling interest in building lavish hotels along the East Coast. He finds that without owning the railroads which serve the area, he is seriously restricted. I am empowered to tell you that if you will set a price, we'll very likely meet it."

Ward stared at MacDonald, but saw him only through a haze. He could not really even concentrate on what his visitor said. He saw only Belle's battered, discolored face and Laddie's face, contorted and twisted with his heartbroken sobbing. Where could he place the blame? Whom could he hate? How could he resolve a problem without solution?

MacDonald sank back in the deeply upholstered chair and waited with the calm patience of a man with all the time and money in the world. He remained quiet and smiling, waiting for Ward's answer.

Ward gazed across the desk, realizing what MacDonald had said, but unable to care. When you are empty inside, where do you find the resources to go on fighting? "I'm sorry." Ward shook his head and managed to smile. "You'll have to tell Mr. Flagler that no section of NEF& GC is for sale."

"I'm afraid he's not going to accept an answer like that, Mr. Hamilton."

Ward stared at MacDonald, who sat coolly aloof, quietly regarding this purchase as an accomplished fact, with only the details to be worked out. For the first time he saw the deadliness in a powerful man's amiable smile; it was nothing to be shared. It was not meant to be shared. It was like an escutcheon worn in battle.

"I'm trying to be friendly, Mr. Hamilton," MacDonald continued. "Mr. Flagler intends to have this property. Owning it is crucial to his development plans. Trying to work around this railroad while you control it has proved to be a major stumbling block. We tried to convince Mr. Flagler of this as long as three years ago, but now he has finally understood. You are in our way."

"Well, I'm sorry as hell about that."

"I don't mean to sound facetious, Mr. Hamilton. I assure you, I am quite serious. We need these railroad lines. We are going to have them. If you cooperate with us, I can almost guarantee that you can name your own price—as of now. That way, you will emerge from all this a very wealthy man. If you oppose us . . ." He shook his head, continued to smile, and said nothing more.

Ward gazed down at his hands. They shook. He could not concentrate on J. A. MacDonald, Henry Flagler, or thinly veiled threats. He could think only about Belle. "I began in this business dealing with men like you before breakfast, Mr. MacDonald."

"What does that mean?"

"Please don't threaten me. It won't help a thing."

MacDonald dropped that inscrutable, unshared smile. He shook his head. "Please don't misunderstand me, sir. We are not bluffing; we are not trying to strongarm you. In all friendliness, I'm trying to lay the facts before you. We want this railroad. More than that, we *must* have it. One way or another, we'll get it. You can come out of this smelling like money, or you can crawl out on your belly. That's up to you."

Ward shook his head, feeling the faint fluttering of panic deep inside. "I'll just wait," he said in a low voice, "and see what you fellows can do."

"This may be the most costly decision of your life, Mr. Hamilton."

"What the hell? It's only money."

Chapter Thirty-Five

THE DIRECTORS WELCOMED Ward warmly in the board room at Cushing and Burden. Perhaps warmth was overstatement. They smiled, these men around the conference table, and made a place for him. But he was at last truly aware of smiles not meant to be shared.

The man on Ward's left inquired if he'd seen Roosevelt in Florida? Ward answered that he didn't know Teddy Roosevelt, that the great man and his Rough Riders were across the state at Tampa, a distance of a hundred and fifty miles.

"I hear there is yellow fever among the troops at Tampa," someone else said.

Others chimed in:

"Florida is a pesthole for yellowjack. That state will never have a real potential until the malarial plagues are eradicated."

"And Cuba is worse. Teddy needn't fear Spanish bullets as much as the diseases that will kill his men."

Another long silence ensued. Whit Cushing asked Ward if he had seen any of the new plays on Broadway; Maurice Barrymore's *Ben Hur* was still running, and over forty theaters in Manhattan that year offered everything from farce to Shakespeare.

Ward shook his head. He hadn't seen any new shows; he had been working with his accountants and bond attorneys, trying to decide how to answer the bondholder's petition for default on his corporate indebtedness.

Everybody shifted slightly in their chairs; the change was barely perceptible in the atmosphere, but a new tension hung charged in the expensive blue wreaths of cigar smoke. They had him where they wanted him; *he* had initiated discussion of finances. This was an important condition. It was like a move in chess; ground rules required that he introduce topic A. Though Cushing and Byers was a financial institution, one somehow felt that actual discussions of money and debt were almost obscene unless the guest brought up the matter. He had been maneuvered into broaching the subject; he had betrayed his weakness.

"I'm sorry to do this," Whit Cushing said from the head of the table. He didn't sound unhappy; he sounded totally unconcerned, almost disinterested. "Officially, Ward—and this is a corporate decision—we can't carry you financially any more."

"*Carry* me? I've never missed an interest payment in twenty years."

"But you have often let the principle ride. Not once, but several times."

"Always with the full consent of this board. With the blessing of this firm."

"Under different conditions, old man. When you—or your company—looks bad or weak, even less than firm, we take a new look. That's what's happened here."

"You're trying to force me out."

"Not at all. Your bonds are bad. It's not as sinister as you suggest, or very complex. Your bond issue is in default—"

"Technically."

"Technically. Nevertheless in default. Bondholders have petitioned against you. Some of these investors are cherished clients of ours. The word is around that your railroad is in trouble. You don't have a reserve account equal to two years indebtedness as your indenture requires. You're in default. Everybody is hedging. Cushing and Byers is going a step further. As I say, it's a corporate decision to call our loans with you."

"You've never lost a penny on my railroad—"

428

"Yes. Well, as I say, there has been a restructuring here, Ward, a reassessment. New thinking. We are trimming away the questionable accounts. As I said, a corporate decision. An accomplished action. I regret there is nothing I can do."

"Even if I am able to refinance the bonds?"

"I am sorry."

Ward stared around the table. "Can't you even tell me why? I've been a customer of this firm since 1878—twenty years. Don't I rate the courtesy of some explanation?"

"I have explained it. It's a corporate decision. You have been lopped off in a general restructuring. We do make reassessments, at our discretion. There is a national depression. Your corporation is one of the weakest of our accounts. Depression, a shaky account, if you will see that as an explanation."

"I don't. Freight business is up eleven percent in this quarter."

"Florida has always been a high-risk area, Ward. This can't come as any surprise to you. You knew that from the first. The board okayed you only reluctantly. But we entered into our association with your firm under a more favorable climate—in different times, under a different set of circumstances."

"Those are only words, Whit."

"I'm sorry." Cushing shrugged, his face darkening. "You asked for an explanation; I tried to give you one. I'm not required to, you know."

"I wanted the truth."

"I rather resent your implication." Whit smiled tautly.

"I know. But this is my very existence we're discussing so casually and so politely. I don't want politeness. I want the truth."

"Now I do resent it."

"I still want you to tell me why I'm being frozen out like this."

Cushing no longer smiled. "As I told you, termination was a corporate decision. The decision has been made and implemented. That's all I have to say."

Ward could not keep from looking at the others along both sides of the table, separately and for a long time, holding their gazes challengingly, and feeling their chilled stares on him. Only Whit Cushing did not look at him;

the others, by their cold glances, exposed the ultra-civilized savagery of their benign contempt, the deadly kind of violence practiced in these rarefied arenas. He could not help thinking they were not as far removed as they believed from the wolf pack turning on a wounded member; those deadly eyes voted his extinction. If they'd been members of the notorious Black Hand Society terrorizing the slums in many big cities, he could expect the kiss of death from one of them. But these men were Brooks Brothers and Yale and Princeton and Harvard and the Exchange. They didn't kill with slashing incisors or with knives or guns. They killed with credit, by withholding it.

He met their remote, disinterested gazes. These men killed by staring through you without recognition, acknowledgement, or compassion, or any memory of twenty years of association. No Black Hand victim was ever executed more effectively; only here it was done without blood. There was no other difference; they were all killers if you opposed them, wolves snarling over a wounded member, the Society disposing of a defector, the securities people removing a competitor. They smiled when they slew you, smiled and passed the word at lunch, over the bridge table, in steam baths, or on commuter trains, and you no longer existed in their world, in any of their worlds.

Whit Cushing did not bother to say goodbye or that he was sorry or that he remembered raucous all-night poker battles as far back as twenty years. Whit remembered nothing. Ward winced. It didn't matter, but Whit had at least attended Dayton Fredrick's funeral. Well, Cushing had been younger then, still carrying a gram of rebellion under his establishment exterior. He was a distinguished, gray, imposing figure now, as remote as statuary.

Because he could not simply roll over and play dead on command, Ward canvassed the other financial houses: Seligman, White, Harriman, and Morgan. They spoke to him, but they did not really see him; certainly they didn't listen. Some even gave him that patented smile as they ushered him out. No one was going to help him. The answer was simple. Someone wanted him out of the way and he was being removed as if he'd never existed. Cold eyes, dead handshakes, empty smiles. It was like something orchestrated. Only it was no game, but a deadly, vicious business, because it was his life and everything he'd worked for that they so casually denied and denigrated.

He sat unseeing, unaware, on the train south to Savannah, his bonds in default, his debt service terminated. He had one chance to stay in business: he had to come up with enough cash to clear the fund of its immediate indebtedness. This meant a shifting of debt from one set of creditors to another, but only this would buy him the time he needed to save himself.

He walked into the quiet and somber atmosphere of the Atlanta Stockmen's and Farmers' Bank two days later. He was exhausted from travel, tense and depressed, afraid that the smell of defeat was on him. He had showered and shaved, and been massaged and manicured. He tried to laugh when he shook hands with Hobart Bayard, saying, "I got all dressed up and smelling like a whore just to visit you, Hobart."

Bayard's face creased into a trouble smile. He had grown portly. His lank hair still toppled over his bulbous forehead and the dark rings under his protuberant eyes were blacker than ever. His suits were more expensive now, but still off the rack, though he was president of the bank.

Hobart discussed the weather. He reported that the Harkness farm at Errigal was productive and successful, far richer than it had ever been before the war, when it had been worked by slaves. "It was a magnificent thing you did, Ward, sending agricultural experts up there to develop your father-in-law's farm."

This delay, this polite conversation, this warm smiling, were bad omens. Or maybe defeat bred defeat. He wanted to get down to business, but this seemed the last thing Hobart Bayard wanted. "That was a long time ago, Hobart. I was still married to Lily."

"But you didn't stop the experiments after the divorce. That was magnanimous of you."

"No, practical. Lily was still Robin's mother. Belle's mother. Her family was dependent on her unless that big farm was made productive and profitable again. It was just good business."

"I'm sure there's a golden crown waiting for you—up there—anyway." Bayard smiled.

"If it's a Baptist heaven," Ward teased, "I'll never be allowed in long enough to see it."

"We Baptists aren't that bad, Ward. I know you think we're intolerant. Maybe our sure knowledge does make us a little smug—"

"A *little* smug?" Ward laughed. "Let's don't discuss religion, for God's sake. Religion is one reason Lily and I got divorced. I need you."

"Yes . . . well." Bayard smiled, his fat lips puffing. "How long will you be in town?"

"That depends on you, and how long it takes you to say yes."

Bayard seemed not to hear him. Ward's hands clenched. He'd seen enough—more than enough—blind, deaf, unheeding men in the past week. He wanted to yell across that sleek desk at Hobart, *Look at me, damn you. Listen to me. I'm here. Look at me.* He sat unmoving, realizing that Hobart was inviting him to his home for dinner. "Julia would love to have you. She keeps up with you—as well as we can. She says she's known you since she was a young girl."

"Yes. Twenty years."

"You'll come then?"

Ward shook his head. He didn't want to see Julia, not now, not reeling from unseen blows about the head and heart and kidneys. He didn't want to see her at all. Recovering from Julia Fredrick had been the toughest battle of his life. "I'm afraid I won't have time, Hobart. Apologize to Julia for me—right after you remind her of who I am."

"She'll be disappointed."

"So am I. Does she really like being a *hausfrau,* after having been the first liberated female in commerce at Atlanta for so many years?"

Hobart exhaled heavily. "She's never stopped working. She never will. She's quite exalted in the Plant System. Much higher in rank than she ever had any hope to advance. But Plant's whole system is shaky. Plant himself may be dying. That's what I've heard. He's quite ill. He's almost entirely relinquished control of his empire to underlings, and this can't be hopeful for Julia. But despite all I can say to her, Julia persists in her quote career unquote."

"Why do you waste your energy opposing her?"

"That's a good question. She is willful and headstrong and determined."

"She hasn't changed."

"No, she hasn't changed, but she places herself in jeopardy everyday by persisting in an atmosphere where she is resented, mistrusted, misunderstood—"

"Misunderstood? Julia? She's quite easy to understand. Simply stand well back and don't oppose her."

"Yes. Superficially, that's a true assessment of her. But she is just a woman, weak and not *physically* equipped to protect herself."

"Equipped to protect herself? From what?"

"From men without morals or moral fiber, men who look at her and see—a whore. A lovely, fashionably dressed whore, but a whore. In the past two years alone, she's been assaulted—assaulted, mind you—twice on downtown streets when she's worked after dark at her office. Once it was quite nasty. A policeman just happened . . ." Hobart broke off. "But she has been attacked in her office, five or six times, by men who simply refuse to believe she is there for any reason except male sexual gratification."

"Can't you make her give it up?"

"Did you ever try to get Julia to do anything?"

"Once. I see your point."

"Thank God for the telephone. She calls me now when she works late and I meet her at her office."

Ward sighed. "Nothing's ever easy. Please give Julia my best. But I must get back to Jacksonville. I'm in serious financial difficulties, Hobart. Bonds in default, outstanding debts being called."

"I heard."

"Did you? I know news travels fast, but—"

"I may as well tell you, Ward. We are affiliated with a New York bank chain now. The old regime at Stockmen's is out. I am almost the only one of the old group left. We are now owned and controlled by the Morgan Trust."

Ward felt as if he had been struck viciously in the groin. He understood now why Bayard had discussed crops, weather, Julia—anything in God's world except money and credit. He spoke, his voice brittle, sounding strange in his own ears. "I need cash. More than a million dollars, Hobart. I need it at once."

433

"I'm sorry."

"Hobart, this bank has assets of hundreds of millions. Part of that growth you people owe to me."

"Nobody denies that. But the old management is out, Ward. All of them. I could have stood on principle and gone too, but I can't afford that luxury. I'm hanging on because that's all I can do. Hang on. Take orders. Whether I like them or not."

"And your orders are to cut me loose. No credit, no loans, nothing."

"I am sorry, Ward. The Morgan people bought Stockmen's. We were big before, but now we're the biggest bank in the South. Still, I take orders."

"The Morgan banks have nothing against me."

"But they have connections, Ward. People who don't like you, people who want you out, people who honestly believe you a bad risk. I'm being indiscreet. In the name of our long friendship, I'm telling you more than I should. I owe you that. I sit here today because of you. But I am helpless. There's nothing I can do. I'm sorry."

"Sorry? What does that mean? I established a line of credit here twenty years ago—"

"It's been rescinded, Ward. I am sorry. I am sorry and I am helpless."

Chapter Thirty-Six

THAT ANGUISHED MOMENT in Hobart Bayard's office ended Ward's passive acceptance of the shattering blows that threatened ruin for him.

He caught the train to Jacksonville that night, cold rage propelling him. He stood alone, apart from the crowds, caught up in his thoughts about what was happening to him, and what he could do to end it. His defeat was executed like a well-planned chess game with all the moves worked out in advance. Somebody with power and influence wanted his railroad system, and all steps toward acquiring it were minutely orchestrated. The investors had decided he was technically in default of his term bonds though only principle was due at year's end, more than six months away. He was technically in default, but no more than he had been at any time over the past ten years. No one held as binding that indenture clause promising a reserve account equal to two years debt service requirement. That capital couldn't sit idle; it had to be out working. Investors knew and until now had accepted this. Suddenly they wanted to deny and disapprove his use of this capital. This was the decision against him. Next, as if on cue, Cushing and Byers recalled their loans. Two days later, a bank in the Morgan chain rescinded an old and established line of credit and called for immediate payment of total indebtedness, interest and principle.

Hell, it was obvious, there was planned action to destroy him. He couldn't prove it, and even if he could, who would listen? Tell the chaplain. Tell God.

The fact of the matter was that he'd always been an outsider—tolerated at best, even at Cushing and Byers—in financial circles. He was not affiliated with Gould's railway system, or with Vanderbilt or any of the big railroads. He was an independent, one of a vanishing breed, and both bankers and bond investors could declare blandly that they closed on him for one reason: his operation was shaky and suspect.

Hell, where was the news in that? He had started out on a shoestring and brass guts. He would go out fighting just as hard as he had fought his way into the transport industry. Powerful conglomerates suddenly opposed him. They may well take his railroad from him, but, big as they were, they'd know they'd been in a fight. He needed cash to fight them because they denied him access to credit. He would get cash. . . .

He did not sleep on the long and uncomfortable journey southeast across Georgia to Jacksonville. Because ten miles was the limit for ordinary travel by horse, small towns appeared every ten or fifteen miles, and each of them built a depot and required a stop. The train seemed forever slowing, straining into forward motion, bumping, rattling. His eyes were dry, hard, and haggard, and his mouth was set in a grim, gray line, but he had stopped being afraid, stopped retreating, and overcome the panic churning in the pit of his stomach. He'd made up his mind now what he was going to do.

He was surprised to find all lights burning in his St. James Hotel suite. He was fine-drawn with fatigue, his mind completely involved with his options and his pressures. He stopped inside the door, set down his suitcases, and stared numbly about the small, brilliantly lit parlor.

"Well, what's the matter? Aren't you glad to see me?"

Belle swung up lithely from the small loveseat where she'd been curled under a comforter with a novel by John Fox, Jr. She wore a gown and a silk robe.

Ward laughed and held out his arms. "Hello, baby."

"I guess you can see I came to stay for a while." Belle kissed him and clung to him for a moment, trembling.

"Are you all right?"

She laughed. "No broken bones, no black eyes, no bloody nose, no split lip. For Mrs. Beekman Gould McCormick III, I'm in surprisingly good shape."

"What are you doing here?" He glanced at the half-empty bottle of bourbon on the coffee table. "Besides drinking all my liquor?"

"You've got plenty of liquor. I checked that before I decided to stay. Laddie and I are all right. Really. We just need time—away from each other. Time to think."

"How wise is it coming here, if you hope to repair things with Laddie? You know he never believes you're really here when you say you are. He believes I would lie to protect you."

"What he believes. What he doubts. That's part of the reason I am here. He's got to get his head on right."

"And you think he'll do it with you here?"

"If we don't make it this time, it just cleans his plow. With me, anyway. If there's any hope for us, he will accept me for what I am, and where I am. I'm sorry, Daddy, I've just about reached that terrible place where I just don't give a damn anymore."

She ordered fresh sandwiches sent up by room service, along with fresh coffee. He was trembling with exhaustion; he could not even remember when he had slept last. Belle did not see his fatigue. Her vision was turned inward. She wanted to talk. They talked until daylight. She fell asleep finally, with her head in his lap, as she had when she was a little girl.

Ward stared down at her lovely face, her complexion clear and young and stunningly beautiful. His eyes burned with tears. Where could he place the blame in a hurtful situation like this? Where could he find helpful answers? She was willful, headstrong, and spoiled, and obviously had the morals of a mink. A hell of a judgement to make on one's own daughter, but he could not help her if he lied to himself, though he would go on lying to her. She was still his impeccable little girl. It was almost laughable, in an agonizing way. Lily would say coldly that Belle was *his* daughter, if Lily would say anything to him.

Or could he place the guilt on Laddie—jealous, spoiled,

violent-tempered, immature? He had been jealous of Belle long before they were married. He should have suspected, even then, something of what she was like. Still, the light flirtations of her girlhood were hardly comparable to the destructive and adulterous affairs she flaunted in Laddie's face now that they were married. When they'd been children, they'd played children's games, they'd fought as children, but now their battles were cruel, demeaning, and dangerous. Laddie had hurt Belle physically when roused to jealousy long before they were married. Had she believed marriage would somehow change his personality?

He sat holding her, smoothing her lovely, rich hair back from her forehead. His mind wheeled and spun, skidding from agony and concern for Belle and the unyielding pressures of the prospect of facing, tomorrow and next week, men who were out to ruin him.

He came into his office at noon, groggy with fatigue, but coldly determined to hold control of his railway system. For the moment, Belle was content. Three of her oldest acquaintances would have lunch with her in his suite and they would spend the afternoon shopping. She had regressed to that secure time when she was under his protection. "I feel good again, being home with you," she said. "I feel like I'm your little girl again, and that you'll take care of me, and I don't have to be afraid of anything."

Phillips Clark, Bracussi, and the rail system lawyers and accountants awaited him in the conference room. Exhausted as he was, he saw in their faces that they had the news from New York and Atlanta—from wherever bad news emanated. In their minds, behind their smiles, they were looking for jobs, preparing resumes, clearing out desks. Even Phillips Clark looked as if he were prepared for the postmortem. Where do we send the body?

Ward spoke first to Bracussi: "I want a total accounting of our assets. I don't mean railroad equipment or rolling stock; I'm talking about the diversified businesses and holdings we've accumulated over the years."

"All of that will go," Clark said, "when they foreclose on you."

Ward's head jerked up. Exhaustion made him hoarse. "Yes. When they foreclose on me. In the meantime, they are viable assets: a lumber company, a mill in Lake City, a naval stores company, logging operations."

"There are also all the farms and grovelands along the Lake City line, groves between here and Palatka, land you took in trade for Indian River properties. The groves haven't been any good since the freeze, but the land itself has an appreciable market value, as do the houses and other improvements on most of the groves and farms."

"Get me the best possible market price on everything."

Phillips Clark sat up straighter. "You're going to liquidate—"

"That's right. Everything that isn't part of the operations of NEF&GC goes on the block, for sale immediately. We may not get the top prices we could command by waiting, but we'll get enough to refund the bonds, pay off outstanding principle and interest due—"

"You can do that." Clark nodded without enthusiasm. He agreed it was a feasible plan and would buy them out of their present bind. "But what then?"

"The present bind is what I'm caught in," Ward said. "If I am operating my trains, I'll take in operating capital."

"And you'll be living on your cash flow—"

"But the word that has meaning for me is *living*. I'm still alive and I still hold my railroads and I'll stop those sons of bitches. I've still got my company. I'll show those bastards one more time that I'm better than they are. They've got nothing but money. And I've got nothing but brains." He laughed. "What we've got is a Mexican stand-off."

"You want some very carefully considered legal advice?"

"All right."

"I had thought about liquidation as a way out. Bracussi can provide you with all the information you need today because I've already ordered him to break it all down."

"Then I want every one of you to get to work on this project. No matter what you were working on before this morning, forget it. I want these properties liquidated at the best possible price, at the earliest possible moment. And I want it started now."

Clark sat forward, his voice hard. "You still haven't heard me out."

"I'm listening, Phil. But barely."

"Well, that's where you're wrong. You ought to listen good. As I said, I considered liquidation, but I looked beyond liquidation. To what? To next year. The next time they bring a petition of bond default against you. They're nipping at your balls, Ward, and they're going to get you. It's no longer *if* they get you, only a matter of *when*. No independent has been able to stand against them. Even Plant, as big as he is—"

"Plant is a sick man. Dying. I'm not."

"But Plant is a hell of a big independent, and you're not. You need capital credit to keep extending your lines. If you stop extending your lines, you're through. Where are you going to get financing? As towns grow and markets appear farther south—as far down there as Fort Dallas—where will you get the financing?"

"I'll keep building and I'll keep my trains running. I'll keep getting land grants with every mile of track I lay. That land will appreciate in value. I'll improve it and I'll sell it, and my railroad will attract new investors—"

"The investors your railroad is going to attract are the people who mean to force you out. Flagler's people are buying up every share of common stock on the market—at any asking price. All right, you can stop them for the moment. They tried the direct body blow—denial of credit, petitions of bond default, called loans. But even if you stop them now, it's only temporary, Ward."

"And your advice? Cut and run? Liquidate, but don't sink that money into this railroad? Bank it in numbered accounts somewhere? Is that your high-priced advice?"

"You could save your ass that way. You could come out of it a wealthy man."

"You think I haven't thought of all that? I was so damned tired and beat that all I *could* think was take the money and run. There's just one thing wrong with your plan. It would be admitting the big boys are smarter, after all, than I am—"

"No, just richer. Just one hell of a lot richer."

"The other thing is, I won't do it. I'll stop 'em now, and when they come at me again, I'll stop 'em again."

Phillips Clark shook his head. "Well, like I always say, I'm glad I've got a front row seat. I don't want to miss this."

Although he hadn't slept, Ward returned to his suite at the St. James only a little before midnight, refreshed and exultant. His people had located immediate buyers for his naval stores company, logging operation, and lumber yard, at better prices than he'd dared to hope. At least his precarious position wasn't yet common knowledge in the state. This was a trump card his opponents had neglected to play.

He called a press conference, with champagne, a free buffet, a wet bar, and beautiful hostesses. When the reporters were in an affable mood, he announced a new fifty-mile extension of rail-laying to be initiated immediately south of Melbourne. He grinned coldly. He'd give the boys on Wall Street something to think about with their coffee and mineral oil in the morning. Sometimes the best revenge is to live well.

Belle and Laddie awaited him in the parlor of his suite. Their reunion was tearful, with both of them vowing to change.

He saw that Belle's bags were stacked near the door for the bellhops. She and Laddie had waited only to share the good news with him.

"I'm going back home with Laddie," Belle said. "I didn't mind his having the house, but I'm damned if he'll get custody of my horses."

He saw that they'd killed off a quart of bourbon. He said nothing about it, but smiled and closed his arms about both of them.

"We'll make it," Laddie said. "We've been fools. We know better."

"Sure you will. Give yourselves a chance," he said. "You've got to let her grow up, Laddie."

"I know."

"I tried to tell you, but you wouldn't listen. Sixteen—that's not a ripe old age, no matter what a sixteen-year-old tells you."

"I know I've been wrong," Belle said. "Really, I do."

"Okay, sweetheart. Just remember, you're not the only one who feels pain."

"Nobody's going to be hurt anymore," Belle said.

"Well, physical pain is just one kind of hurt. Maybe the easiest kind. And that's my wisdom for the night."

Belle kissed him, clinging to him, wanting him to believe, to share their triumph. "Laddie and I have decided to have a baby," she said. "Maybe a baby will make a difference for both of us. And think how proud the kid will be to have a grandpa like you."

Chapter Thirty-Seven

WARD STARED AT himself in his shaving mirror and grinned through the lather. A week had roared past in which he'd savored his triumph over the moneylenders. At first no one could credit that he had accomplished the impossible. His efforts had been harrowing, but he had prevented what everybody had seen as inevitable.

His enemies still crouched like jackals, waiting to pick his bones. It would be running from the truth to believe otherwise. They'd assumed he was dead and, unlike Lazarus, unable to rise again. As he paid off creditors and funded his bonds, the truth slowly dawned on them. He wasn't dead, not yet. In the distance, he felt he could discern the drone of savagely polite and cultured voices, dispassionate, disbelieving, plotting calmly as they waited, setting contingency moves against him. The hell with them. They'd fought fiercely, if silently, but before the first week was out, they were already backing away.

Gradually, the robber-baron conglomerates realized he would not simply disappear because they wanted him to. His business improved because, for the first time in more than ten years, he went out personally and beat the bushes, pressed the flesh, met the competition's best rates, called on potential customers, and brought in new accounts himself. He prepared four-color brochures advertising farmlands, improved and unimproved, with improvements available to suit the buyer.

He felt good, physically and mentally. He was able to laugh again, to find humor even in threatened disaster. Hell, it was great to laugh, to feel strong and unbeatable. All he'd needed was to get out on the front lines and face the fire and the challenge. He felt twenty years old again, and not forty-four.

He believed now, for the first time, that he would win. New lines of credit had yet to be established, but there were banks and smaller loan institutions who would deal enthusiastically with a twenty-four-year-old firm. He would need more lenders; the old, easy time with Stockmen's and Farmers' was past. But maybe that was best. He'd grown soft, he'd gone to flab, he'd forgotten to stay alert, he'd stopped running for his life.

The telephone rang. With lather splotched white and fluffy on his cheeks, he crossed the bedroom and answered it.

"Daddy?"

"Belle. Are you all right?" Jesus. Always the first question, that gut-gripping stricture.

"Oh, yes. You've got to stop worrying, Daddy. We're all right now. Laddie and I are fine. If we go anywhere, we go together. That makes Laddie happy. It bores me a little, but what do you always say—everything has its price?"

"No. I always say, 'I love you.' " He sighed heavily. "And I'm glad you're all right."

"I'm better than all right. I'm getting so damned healthy. I ride my horses a lot. When I'm home, I'm out riding along the river—"

"You be careful."

"Oh, Daddy, you know I will."

"I don't like it, you riding alone."

"Oh my God. As soon as I get Laddie off my back, *you* start preaching."

"No. I won't say a word. If Laddie is happy, I'm satisfied."

"Laddie is happy. While I ride my horses, he paints. Maybe we've found the prescription for the perfect marriage. He goes his way, I go mine."

444

Listening to Belle chatter happily, Ward glanced up and glimpsed a portly, balding man across the room. Startled, he looked again. Good God! The man had shaving cream on his face. Jesus. It was he. He was truly forty-four years old. His hair was graying around the ears, receding at the temples. He felt a stricture with that shock of recognition. Forty-four years old. And worse than that, he looked it.

After his conversation with Belle, he returned to the bathroom, feeling mildly depressed. The lather had dried. He would have to spread new cream before he could finish shaving.

He stared for a moment into his own reflected eyes. Shocked, he bit back an exclamation of terrified disbelief. For that instant, he didn't recognize his own eyes. In the shadowed mirror, those reflected eyes were not his. They belonged to someone he knew, but not to Ward Hamilton. His heart beating raggedly, he bent forward, staring. Then he recognized those eyes, faintly bloodshot, haggard, with a wariness glittering deep in them, a disenchantment, but, most of all, a conscious, flat emptiness, like an opaque curtain drawn so no one could see beyond them.

He felt as if he had been struck. He shook his head, faintly ill. "Those aren't my eyes," he whispered aloud in horror. "They're *his* eyes—Dayton Fredrick's eyes."

Deeply disturbed, he retreated a step. It was as if he had looked into the clouded mirror and seen, instead of his own reflection, Dayton Fredrick's—the surface sheen of self-confidence, the go-to-hell grin, the steely strength, and those damaged, carefully shielded eyes, reflective panes beyond which no one was ever permitted to probe.

From the vaults of time, he heard Julia's scathing voice: *You don't truly know how it is with my father because you've never really looked into his eyes, or seen him when he's dead tired and scared.*

He shook his head, trying desperately to escape this overwhelming cloud of depression. Slowly the clouded depths of the mirror lightened, and he recognized himself again, but he remained shaken by his vision. He shaved hastily and got out of there.

He couldn't get Dayton Fredrick out of his mind all the rest of the day. Superstitiously, he felt it was an omen of evil, a foreshadowing of doom, that he had come to

445

resemble that man of surface charm and inner panic. He tried to tell himself he was simply exhausted, under fearful pressures, but he avoided every mirror.

And he was less than astonished when reports came of stoppage on the rail work south of Melbourne.

"It's yellow jack," Bracussi said. "Thirteen men down in one day. Panic has hit the work camp. It's hard keeping men down there."

"Jesus," Ward whispered. "I can fight Morgan and Rockefeller and Cushing and Flagler, but not you too, God."

"What?"

"Nothing. I'll take the next train down there."

"You don't have to do that."

"I don't? Will you go? Or Phillips Clark? I've got to keep that track moving. If I miss a deadline, I lose land bonuses and even the franchise."

"I know that. But I also know it's an epidemic, Ward. It started in Tampa, and killed off God knows how many soldiers stationed over there waiting for boats to Cuba. Now it's spread to the East Coast like a goddamn plague."

Ward and Uzziah Giddings were on the eleven o'clock train south. Ward had discussed the yellow jack and malaria epidemic, via telephone, with half a dozen Duval County doctors. None was hopeful. There were no answers to these killing diseases. There were many theories about the cause of yellow fever: the night vapors from swamps; germs in the fouled atmosphere itself. A Cuban doctor had named mosquitoes as the disease vectors more than fifteen years ago, but few reputable medical men put credence in such a farfetched notion. The medics could tell him only one thing: one should stay clear of infected areas; the killing plague came suddenly with the onslaught of summer heat and rains.

He arrived at the campsite at dusk. Work had stopped completely. Foremen finally admitted to Ward that no serious tracklaying had been undertaken for the past three days. The ill were isolated and left to die. The well stayed drunk, or abandoned camp during the night.

"Rain, too, has stopped us. The wind gusts up to fifty or sixty miles an hour. We're slogging around in bogs up to our asses. The goddamn mosquitoes blow in in clouds, sometimes so thick you can't breathe."

The rising wind had whipped the canvas top off the large, screened-in wooden barracks, which had been converted to an emergency isolation ward.

Doctors from nearby towns had visited the work camp, and had left quantities of laudanum to relieve the fearful, bone-wracking chill and fever. They had departed, refusing to return. They believed yellow jack was transmitted on night breezes, and they refused to remain in the pestilent area after dark. Also, they had no proof that both malaria and yellow fever were not highly contagious. They'd left the campsite in greater turmoil and worse panic than there had been when they had arrived.

Nobody wanted to go near the isolation hut. The sounds from there were agonized screams from some pit beyond hell. The strongest men turned gray, refusing to step inside the barracks where the plague victims lay dying in their own vomitus.

Ward crossed the compound in driving rain. He opened the door and stepped inside the hut. Sick and dying men were sprawled everywhere, covering almost every foot of space. Most had turned a dull bronze color. They threw up black gorge and died where they lay.

Dead men lay on fouled cots or frozen in rigor mortis on the stinking wooden flooring.

Fighting back sickness that burned up into his throat, Ward retreated. He ordered the healthy men who had not yet decamped to dig six-foot burial trenches alongside the right-of-way. The men agreed to do this, but refused to touch the dead bodies.

Digging the slit grave proved almost impossible. Men stood with lanterns as the rain increased in intensity, slanting in across them. As the excavation was opened, it filled immediately with muddy water, or the earth caved in on the sides.

Raging, the men tried to throw down their shovels and get inside the tents, away from "this pestilent swamp gas."

"Keep them digging," Ward told Uzziah.

The half-breed nodded. Ward plodded through the rain to the isolation tent. Inside, he grasped one of the corpses by the heels, and dragged it out of the tent and across the encampment to the burial site.

447

Finally, two of the foremen, with bandannas tied across their noses and mouths against the stench and contagion, entered the hut with him and began to drag out the dead.

The rains increased in fury, seeming to whip in from every direction, wheeling, whirling, and bending elders, willows, and bay trees along the right-of-way. Lightning cracked across the swamps, turning the encampment starkly white for moments. By the time the last of the dead had been buried, six inches of black water swirled in deep sloughs across the compound and the cleared right-of-way.

Despite the savagery of the gale winds, Ward continued to work in the isolation hut the rest of the night. The two foremen, gray with fear, worked with him and Uzziah. With tubs of scalding water from the mess tent, they scrubbed away the filth. The surviving men were given heavy doses of laudanum. Canvas sidings had been lowered over the screens, but, by midnight, the wind had ripped those curtains to shreds. Lamps rocked and swung in the tents, or were hurled from their nails and shattered.

"Hurricane!" one of the foremen yelled at Ward. "Got word yesterday from Fort Dallas that a big blow was forming out in the Atlantic. Had no idea it was going to hit land here. Looks like we're going to get it head-on!"

Rain slanted in almost horizontally on the howling gusts.

"Batten down!" was the only order. But it was useless. Canvas tops, of the mess tent, the barracks, the work offices, were ripped free. The wind raged so fiercely that wooden-based shacks were torn from their moorings and upended. Men ran to the freight cars, clambered in, and closed the sliding doors against the raging gales. The big cars shuddered and wavered on the rails in the wind. The men huddled inside the rocking cars, waiting for the gale winds to topple them from the tracks.

Ward, the foremen and Uzziah carried the few surviving patients to a freight car and made them as comfortable as possible.

By one o'clock that morning, any activity on the grounds was impossible. A man could not stand or move against the force of the wind. The wind-driven rain cut like slashing razors, blinding and painful. Uprooted trees toppled and then were lifted and hurled across the compound like limbs.

Water rose from the swamps on both sides of the right-of-way. The filled and raised railbeds were undermined and then washed away in the torrential flood. The freight cars rolled helplessly; some struck face-forward into mud, while others were overturned and lay in the rising water.

The right-of-way became a raging torrent of white-capped water. Every piece of equipment, from huge graders to handcars and wheelbarrows, was washed away on the current or buried in mud. The big machinery sank in the deep water, and inched and twisted along in the mud and irresistible currents.

Walls of water rolled in across the encampment, and the rising black tide inundated the right-of-way, turning the whole swamp into a raging lake of mud. By four A.M., the men who were still alive climbed out on top of the overturned freight cars. They lashed themselves down with ropes and crouched there, battered, whipped, and slashed by wind and rain.

Thunder boiled up from the bowels of the earth. Bolts of lightning cracked, blindingly white and breathtakingly savage, revealing the destruction for long moments and then plunging the whole world into cavernous blackness.

The rains diminished by ten o'clock that morning as the eye of the hurricane moved inland. Gradually, the water subsided. The rail line remained, a twisted black stream through the swamp, while raindrops splashed lightly on the whitecaps.

Ward decided that the survivors could link themselves together with rope and try to follow the cleared right-of-way north to Melbourne.

He opened the door of the car where they'd bunked the epidemic victims. There was nothing more he could do for them; there was no place even to bury them in this raging sea of black water. They had drowned when the freight car fell off the broken, undermined rails and slid into the deepest water in the ditches. "We'll have to leave them here until we come back," Ward said.

"Shit," one of the workers said, slashing downward with his arm. "Who's coming back here? What's to come back

449

for? Hell, you couldn't force me back to this place with a gun."

Linked together by ropes, the survivors plodded, waist-deep and sometimes shoulder-deep, along the washed-out railbeds. One of the foremen said, "Rails and ties we've laid for the past month are gone. Whatever rails are down there are so twisted they'd be useless."

Every railroad bridge was out, completely demolished. The men swam the creeks, unable to find pilings or concrete abutments. All signs of bridges and rails were gone.

Ward plodded silently. If he had hoped to find an end of the destruction at Melbourne, he was disappointed. Tracks set on solid ground remained like islands on the broken, rutted, gouged-out right-of-way. All the way to Cocoa, only small sections of the line, and no linking bridges, remained.

One of the first people to call on him at his office in Jacksonville was a representative of the Flagler interests. The man offered his condolences in a flat, unemotional tone, and then got down to the reason for his visit.

"Mr. Flagler sends his deepest regrets. He realizes that millions of dollars will be needed to restore the rail lines, at sixty thousand dollars a repaired mile. He offers to take over the line immediately, replace all demolished rails and bridges, and extend the lines so that land bonuses or franchise rights need not be forfeited."

Ward managed to shake his head. "Tell Mr. Flagler thanks, but I'll come to him when I need help. And don't worry about my land bonuses or my franchises. I haven't forfeited them yet."

Into his mind, at that moment, flashed an image of Dayton Fredrick, bluffing, laughing, lying smoothly in the face of ruin, with only those hurt and wounded eyes betraying him. He stared down at his own hands.

Ward had never conceived of a day when he would return to Lily's home, seeking help. For days he had moved in a kind of catatonic trance, a state of shock that had settled over him as he waded and plodded and swam north along his ruined rail lines until finally he could board a train north at Cocoa. All he could think was that he was beaten, finished, unless he could repair, restore, and replace his lines and finance immediate new extensions.

A servant whom Ward did not know answered the door. After what seemed an interminable delay, Ward was ushered into the sun parlor. A deep, forbidding silence settled over this old house where he had lived twelve years of his life, if it could be called living. A breathless tension hung in the room.

Finally, Lily came into the sun room with Robin at her side. Robin was tall, he looked like a thinner, more fragile, less virile, delicate carbon copy of Robert. Robin bowed slightly toward Ward, but did not smile, and did not offer to shake hands.

"We heard about your—disaster," Robin said.

"Yes. I am deeply in trouble, or I'd never have come here." Ward studied Lily. She seemed thinner, more breakable, her black hair faded and streaked with gray. There was an almost enfeebled tranquility about her. She sat in terrible calm, her hands in her lap. Ward went on, "I have been to every banker, every moneylender in Jacksonville."

Lily nodded as if something she had contemptuously envisioned for a long time had come to pass. She was not surprised, she was not moved. "I knew you'd come about the money," she said at last.

"I do need help, Lily."

"No." She remained icily serene, marble-cold.

"I can promise you—"

"I don't want to hear your promises. Your empty .promises. Your lies. It is *my* money, Ward. Mine. Robert left it to me. He meant for me to have it in my—"

"There's more than a million dollars, Lily. Robert left a hundred thousand—"

"It's mine." Her voice rose slightly. Her white, almost translucent hands trembled in her lap.

"Please don't upset my mother," Robin said.

Ward stared at Lily, wishing to God there had been something in their years of marriage, or even in the years they had now been apart, which had united them, even for a little while. There was nothing. They had nothing to look back on. She had not forgiven him anything, nor would she, ever. "I know the money is yours, Lily. I would not jeopardize it for anything. But I do need to borrow from you. Secured loans, at interest. I assure you, anything

451

you'll let me have, I'll double for you. It's just that I am strapped at the moment. My back is against the wall, Lily, or I wouldn't be here. I can get funds, but only matching dollars. I would use your money only to get matching funds. It would be returned to you with interest, but without it I can't get matching dollars—"

"I don't know what you're talking about."

"I swear to double any money you might lend me."

"I won't let you have anything."

"Cash will save me, Lily. Only cash. If I can get established again, get my line open, I'll be all right. I know you don't give a damn about that, Lily, but I need your help. I have nowhere to turn."

Lily shook her head. "It's no use, Ward. Robert left that money to me. To me. I feel it's like a holy trust."

Exasperated, frustrated, defeated, and recalling all the fruitless times he'd tried to communicate with Lily, he laughed at her.

Lily's face went gray and her lips whitened. Her hands clasped and unclasped frantically. "Get out."

Robin said, "Don't come here again. You upset my mother. I won't have that. Don't come to this house again."

He walked the five miles back downtown to his office. He moved numbly, his gaze turned inward on his own defeat. By the time he'd reached his office, he'd made the only decision left to him.

He walked tiredly down the corridor to Phillips Clark's office. He rapped on the door. Clark said, "Yes? Come in."

Phillips had stacked packing boxes on his desk, conference table, and chairs. He sorted through papers, saving some, throwing others into an oversized trash barrel placed near his opened desk.

"Where are you going?" Ward asked.

"I'm catching a train later tonight, Ward. To New York City. I won't lie to you. I was coming in to see you before I left. I've had an offer I can't refuse. I've been offered a full partnership in the Wall Street law firm of Selig, Dillham, and Roth."

"I know them—"

"Yes. I won't lie about that, either. They represent Flagler, in bonds and other matters. My railroad experience was most impressive and interesting to them."

"I need you."

"No, Ward, you don't. Not anymore. I wouldn't walk out on you, but there's nothing here to walk out on. It's over, Ward. Finished. I've had my front seat for a long time at your wondrous magic show. I've watched you pull all the rabbits out of all your hats. There are no more rabbits, no more hats. We can't lie to ourselves about that."

"They haven't beaten me yet. That's what I'm in here to talk to you about."

"Ward, for hell's sake, take what you can. Get out. Now. Try to salvage something. They've got you now. I admit it took a yellow jack epidemic and a hurricane to knock you over, but they'll tear you apart if you go on fighting them."

"Is that the real reason you're getting out?"

"It's the real reason. Look, I know these men. They have no mercy, no compassion, and no principles when they grab something. Newspapers and yellow-sheet sob-sisters call them robber barons—because that sounds romantic and not as vicious and evil as thieves, murderers, and crooks."

"And so you're joining them?"

"Hell, what I just gave you was a recruitment speech. I've one chance, Ward: smell like flowers or push up the daisies. Go with the prestigious Wall Street firm of Selig, Dillham, and Roth—at one hundred thousand base a year, plus full partnership—or I can eventually find myself disbarred—if I'm lucky. Anyhow, as your attorney, I'm finished. They told me that, in so many words."

"And what did you have to do to get this partnership?"

"We don't have to end in malice, Ward. I didn't *do* anything. I didn't double-cross you; I didn't sell you out—though you won't see it that way."

"You sold your NEF&GC stock."

"Yes. It was down to par, Ward. Going off the board. I got ten dollars a share."

"From Henry Flagler?"

"Yes. But that's not important. I would have sold it to Jesus Christ at ten dollars a share. The stock would have been worthless by tomorrow morning."

Ward sighed heavily and walked to the window. He

453

stood staring down at the train yards. "You just about gave him controlling interest."

"That's what I'm trying to tell you. I didn't sell you out. He would have had control anyway. I'm sorry, Ward God knows, I tried to tell you."

Ward returned to his own office. He spent the next ten hours talking on the telephone. He called every railroad system operating in the South. He offered his Jacksonville-Lake City line for a million dollars. He got five flat refusals from men who told him, in effect, that they would wait and pick up the system from receivership—at ten cents on the dollar. South Georgia Railroads and the Tallahassee, Pensacola & Mobile lines were interested. They knew his position; they knew he was on the brink of receivership. However, the route into Jacksonville from the west was vital to both of them. Ward's hold on the north central line and the rails south across the St. Johns had been his strength. Both South Georgia and T.P. & M agreed to deal with him. But a million dollars was a matter requiring overnight board conferences; both promised to submit firm bids before ten the next morning.

He had to be content with this. He faced the prospect of losing the rich freight-hauling business from the lumber, tobacco, and naval stores and the vegetable-producing regions of the state. But the future, the big money, his only hope of staying alive, lay in the North-South connecting rail links between New York and the growing resort and tourist towns along the East Coast. The sale of the Lake City lines would secure his position in Jacksonville and south. He could restore his broken lines, replace bridges, and extend new lines deeper south toward the village of Fort Dallas.

He prowled his office, too exhausted to think, too keyed-up to rest. The building settled into silence, and grew shadowed and tensely quiet. At last, a little before midnight, he went down to the street and found a hack in which he rode to the St. James.

He went in the elevator up to his room. Inside, he turned on only one small lamp. He undressed, yawning helplessly. But when he fell across his bed, he lay sleepless, staring into the purple darkness. Distantly, he heard the clangor of fire bells, and even his room seemed oddly pink, but he was too tired to care. He fell asleep finally, with the fire sirens wailing, wailing, and spinning inside his mind.

He never afterwards knew how long he'd slept—a few minutes, a few hours. He awoke to someone's savage beating upon his door facing, yelling his name almost hysterically. Over the voice rose the screams of fire sirens, the shrilling of night disaster whistles on every factory building, the rattle of heavy equipment racing through the streets. "Mr. Hamilton! Fire! The whole town's on fire! You must get out of the hotel! At once!"

He dressed hurriedly and went out of the hotel in trousers and shoes and a shirt open at the collar. The town writhed and coiled and raced in mindless panic, flames shooting upward hundreds of feet into the air, gutting buildings, devouring everything in its path.

He was unable to learn where the fire started, only that it was out of control. The town was being evacuated. Police ordered him to keep moving with the crowds of refugees away from the spreading fires. During the rest of that night, the flames swept an area of 148 blocks, destroying 2,368 buildings. Before it was over, nine thousand would be homeless.

He tried to break through fire lines to get to his office building. Police refused to let him pass. "Nothing down there, sir. It's all wiped out." The railyards and everything on the wharves, Bay Street, and the waterfront were burning, with fearful loss of life.

He kept walking in a roundabout path, going always toward the river, drawn there irresistibly. He finally reached the waterfront, from which he could see the flames consuming Bay Street, crumbling buildings. The wide body of water reflected the fires in orange and green and cerise. Docks, piers, and wharves, eaten by flames, buckled and sank, smoking, into the water.

He kept stalking along any open street, across Market, Liberty, Adams, Washington, going around police barricades, drawn toward the place where his railroad bridge spanned the St. Johns.

He could not get within five blocks of the bridge and railroad piers. He did not need to. Fires illumined the night brilliantly. From where he stood, he could see the wooden pilings, the trusses, and the trestle, consumed by flames. It was all reflected, as if in savage mockery, on the black face of the firelit river.

He stood unmoving until the supports burned away to the waterline and the rails crumpled, sizzling and flaring, into the river. With the loss of the bridge, his last hope died. There was no way he could rebuild that bridge, and without that link, he was lost. He was finally and totally beaten. He went on standing there, staring at the seared posts of the bridge across which his beautiful trains had once raced south and north, as if in a dream.

Chapter Thirty-Eight

THE TRANSFER OF control of NEF&GC to Flagler's company was accomplished smoothly. As if poised for weeks, an army of accountants, lawyers, and railroad experts assumed command. Ralph Bracussi was retained; on the first day, all signs of NEF&GC disappeared. Almost at once the new name, Florida East Coast Railway, appeared, as if it had always existed.

Flagler's people moved swiftly and competently. Within a week, the charred bones of the old drawbridge across the St. Johns were cleared away, and, within a month, pilings were set for the new multi-million-dollar steel span.

The rebuilding of the razed city was undertaken at once. Armies of laborers came in and rubble was leveled and removed. A twenty-five-million-dollar reconstruction program was initiated on the cleared ground.

Labor disputes ended Ward's control of the Lake City lines. All land bonuses had to be forfeited because of delays and stoppage caused by the hurricane, floods, and fire. Ward was unable to find credit or underwriting. Rolling stock was chained to the tracks under judgments obtained by creditors. The line was taken over in foreclosure and sold off to a corporation that became the Jacksonville, Tallahassee, Pensacola & Mobile Railroad.

Ward, numbed by loss, was unable to feel the new agony. When he returned to the small house he'd been able to rent outside Jacksonville, he found half a dozen scrawled messages delivered by the Duval County sheriff's deputies and pushed under his door. He knelt, took them up, and read them: *Get in touch with Sheriff Bullock at once. Urgent.*

He stood for some moments without emotion. What could possibly have urgency for him now?

He walked out to the small stable behind the cottage, and hitched the horse to his single-seat buggy. He drove along the potted roadways slowly, as darkness settled in around him. He gripped the reins, hardly aware that he held them, unconscious of movement or of where he was. People passed him on the wrecked and burned-out streets, but he did not see them.

His gaze fixed on some black hole an infinite distance away in the darkling sky, he kept his head up, his jaw thrust forward. People, seeing him pass slowly, distracted, paused and watched him talking to himself.

They saw him suddenly raise his arms upward, his hands clenched into fists. People stood unmoving and stared, awed, driven to laughter and yet for some reason not laughing, but chilled at the sight of him, lost in his own rage. There were many wild, mindless people loose in these streets after the holocaust.

His voice was low, but raging. He sobbed, not in weakness or self-pity, but in fearful and soul-wracking passion. His bitterness poured out, snarling and defiant. They saw no adversary, but the man in the carriage did.

"You hear me, goddamn you?" he wept. "All right. You beat me, you son of a bitch. You beat me down. You. No man *you* made could do it. No corporation these puny bastards *you* made could do it, but *you*—you did it. *You* tore me down. You beat me. But that changes nothing, you hear me? Nothing. You're still a son of a bitch, a mindless son of a bitch."

They heard him in horror and retreated, shocked at his impiety, his blasphemy. In dread, their flesh creeping, their hackles standing, they saw he was talking to God—not as a supplicant, a petitioner, or a humble worshipper, but as an outraged equal adversary, a general who has weathered a ruinous seige, the worst the enemy could heap upon him,

458

and yet stands unbowed, threatening, begging to be struck dead rather than go on living cravenly in servitude.

The onlookers backed away, apprehensive, retreating in terror, just as the first men ran from thunder, lightning, storm, and fire. They watched him silently intimidated, waiting to see him struck dumb, blackened with warts, blinded with cataracts, crippled, maimed, covered with festering sores. . . .

He sat for a long time outside the county building. When he was at last in control of his emotions, he tied the horse at the hitching post and entered the building.

A deputy asked his name. When Ward told him, and handed him the messages he'd received, the deputy nodded and winced slightly. "I'm afraid there's been some trouble, Mr. Hamilton."

Unamazed, Ward nodded numbly and waited. "It's your daughter, sir. A Mrs. Belle Hamilton McCormick? Is that your daughter?"

Ward's heart stuttered; his eyes burned. "Belle," he whispered, anguished. Always that immediate stricture of terror. He nodded. "Yes. What's happened to my daughter?"

The deputy exhaled heavily. "It looks like she's killed her husband, Mr. Hamilton."

Ward sagged. He looked around helplessly. He wanted to sink to the floor but he merely stood, waiting, his face pallid. "Is she here?"

"Yes, sir. She's been arrested."

"Could I see her, please?"

The deputy led Ward to the women's detention area. It was a malodorous, clamorous place, a way-station on the road to hell. Belle couldn't stay in this place; he had to get her out of here.

The deputy, accompanied by a stout, heavy-shouldered matron, unlocked a cell door. Ward saw Belle crouched on a prison cot. She was disheveled, barely aware of her surroundings. Ward said, "Belle."

She looked up, her face twisting. Suddenly she sobbed. She looked like a little girl in terror and agony. He put out his arms. She ran to him and pressed against him. She clung to him, trembling violently. "Oh, Daddy," she whispered. "Get me out of here. Get me out of this place."

He did not speak. He had no promises, no resources, no reassurances left. All the rabbits had been pulled out of all the hats. He could only hold her, smoothing her hair with his hand.

When he tried to hire expensive legal counsel to help Belle, Ward learned how helpless he was, how low he had fallen. Doors that had always swung wide open for him were closed. State officials who had extended glad hands, palms up, suddenly refused even to see him. He was unable to arrange bail for Belle; he could not get her released into his custody until her trial. Worst of all, the top-flight defense attorneys he tried to bring South refused even to accept the case without an advance retainer fee of one hundred thousand dollars.

For the first time, he realized he was powerless to aid Belle. When she needed him most, he was unable to help her. He sold her house on the river. Because of the demand for housing after the fire, he was able to command a good price for the property. A criminal law firm in Jacksonville accepted the entire amount as a binder fee on their services.

After the first week, Belle stopped begging Ward to get her out of the prison. She accepted the place—the smell, the filth, the casual inhumanity, the dehumanizing treatment, the vileness of the inmates. She no longer cared where she was. She did not comb or brush her hair. She sat staring into the past, barely aware of people around her.

Her trial created the wildest sensation since the fire. People crowded into the courtroom: strangers, the curious, the vindictive, the morbid.

Belle sat silently at the defense table. She had lost weight. Shocked, Ward saw for the first time how much Belle resembled Lily in the early stages of her illness. He shuddered. In his mind he saw Lily as she'd stood, a lovely young girl, slender and reedlike, shielding her face from the sun, the first time he met her at Errigal. He saw Belle now, slumped, thin, and withdrawn.

The state presented its case against Lily methodically, impersonally, and in detail: the police, who had answered the call and found Laddie, his face shot away, on the

460

drive outside the elegant home; the medical examiner, who had fixed the time and cause of death; the coroner, who had performed the autopsy. McCormick had died from gunshot wounds in the face and head. The arresting officers testified that Mrs. McCormick, in her riding habit, had awaited them in her living room. She appeared to be in a state of shock. She offered no resistance. She admitted having shot her husband. "I rode into the yard. He leaped out of a hedge and grabbed my horse's reins, and tried to pull me from the saddle," she had said, "and I shot him."

Finally, the defense put Belle on the stand.

"Why did you shoot your husband, Mrs. McCormick? Was it in self-defense? Did you feel your life was threatened?"

"He threatened me. I thought he was going to kill me."

"Why would your husband want to kill you?"

"He was enraged. Suspicious. Jealous. Insanely jealous. He had started trailing me, sneaking around, following me everywhere. When I rode my horse and thought he was contentedly painting, he was stealing around behind me, spying, hiding, following."

"When he grabbed your horse, did he threaten you?"

"Yes. He had beaten me before. With his fists. Many times."

"Did you know he had been following you on the day of the shooting?"

"Yes. I'd found out about his following me several days before. Every time I went out on my horse, he followed."

"Did you ask him why he followed you, hiding and spying?"

"He accused me of meeting—some man. What he said was—*men*. He accused me of meeting men in secluded places along the river."

"Were you alone that day of the shooting when you returned home?"

"Yes."

"Yet he grabbed at your horse, threatened you, and tried to pull you from the saddle?"

"Yes."

"Had you been alone all that morning?"

Belle hesitated. "I—met some—people—on the bridle path. I rode with them for a while."

"But you returned home alone?"

461

"Yes."

"What did your husband do?"

"He hid in the hedge beside the drive. He leaped out at me, cursing and threatening me. He frightened my horse. It reared. He went on yelling at me. Cursing. He grabbed the reins, started hitting at me, clutching at me, trying to pull me to the ground. I shot him."

"You had a gun with you?"

"Yes."

"Did you always carry a gun?"

"I had lately. Since the fire—there had been tramps along the river. And sometimes snakes crawled into the bridle path and frightened my horse."

"And for those reasons you carried a gun?"

"Yes."

"And for no other reason?"

"I carried it only for—self-protection."

"Did your husband know you had a gun with you that morning?"

"He must have. He knew I carried it."

"Yet he wasn't afraid? Of the gun? He had no reason to believe you would use the gun, even though you carried it for self-protection?"

"I didn't know I would use it—until he grabbed me and tried to yank me to the ground."

"You had not thought about using that gun—against your husband?"

"No. Never."

The prosecutor hammered at Belle about the gun and her reasons for carrying it. Had she not started carrying the gun only three days before the murder of her husband? Had she not bought the gun the same day she learned that her husband was following her every time she left the house on horseback?

At first Belle denied that her carrying the gun had any connection with her anger at her husband for shadowing her, but the receipt for its purchase was dated three days before the murder. The prosecutor waved this piece of damaging evidence in her face, shouting at her. He alluded to the receipt, her denial, her using the gun coldly, premeditatedly, repeatedly in his summation. The jury found Belle guilty of second-degree murder. Three weeks later, the circuit judge sentenced her to ten years in the

462

women's correctional institution at Lowell. Here, he said, she would learn discipline, that she was not above the laws of God and man, that there was no special disposition for those who flaunted the rules the rest of us have to abide by.

Ward went out to Lowell on the train each Saturday morning. He visited Belle on Sunday, taking her gifts and a picnic lunch, which neither of them touched. He returned to Jacksonville by train on Sunday night and began the long week of waiting again for Saturday.

He was dead inside, emotionally numb. He hated himself for his failure and his inability to aid Belle. Worst of all, he blamed himself for her having slain her husband. He had failed her most tragically by trying, from the time she was a little girl, to free and insulate her from the rigid, prudish, puritanical conventions her mother lived by. He'd done that, all right, but he'd rendered her morally bankrupt. She'd had no rules or virtues or ethical concepts to build on, lean on, fall back on. She'd believed only in her own rules, her right to live as she wished, exempt from all narrow restrictions, and her father's infallibility, strength, and influence.

His life focused on his visits to Belle at Lowell. He wanted only to spare her as much as he could, aid her as much as he could, shield her as much as possible, and assure her she was not alone, that he shared her imprisonment.

Nothing else could touch him. From former railroad acquaintances, he learned that Hobart Bayard had been slain outside the Southern Express building in downtown Atlanta. According to the report, Hobart had been delayed by a business conference at his bank. His wife had been waiting at the building entrance. She was attacked by two men, who tried to drag her into an alley. Hobart, arriving in his carriage, ran across the walk, flailing with his cane. The two men shoved Julia against a wall and turned on Hobart. Even in rage, Hobart fought ineptly, though with great courage. He swung futilely with the cane. One man kicked Hobart in the groin. As he fell, the other hit him across the head with a paving brick and then kicked him when he was down. They stomped him to death, while his wife, pressed against the building wall, watching in horror.

Ward heard this, but felt nothing. The whole story concerned strangers from a part of his life that was past and dead. It was like reading of a monsoon in Calcutta, famine in China, or the fall of Troy. Distant, remote, unrelated to his existence.

He grew steadily more deeply troubled about Belle. She continued to lose weight. She refused to eat, or to obey the most innocuous rules of the prison. He gazed at her, despairing, frightened. She had not lived by rules in childhood, in the dozens of finishing schools he'd found for her, or in her marriage. She would not live by rules, even in prison.

One Sunday, he left her and walked slowly, head down, along the dusty, late-afternoon road toward the train depot at Lowell.

He felt lost, empty. It grew dark. He would miss his train, the only one going east that night. He could not care. He found no reason for life, no hope, no feeling. He stared upward toward the blackening sky and saw, with a faint sense of irony, that his own private star was no longer there in the deep heavens. He could not care. It did not matter anymore.

Chapter Thirty-Nine

His life was concentrated in the prison and the train depot at Lowell, in the burned-out shell of Jacksonville. The two places were connected by the thin steel rails. He came alive only when he was with Belle. He tried to smile, to lift her for a little while from her despair. When he was away from her, he existed in a void. He retreated from human contact, shrank from the sound of laughter, the swell of music, the demands of relationships. He avoided anyone he had ever known. He spent his time away from Belle alone, waiting, cold, and empty. He was dead inside.

When he saw the Jacksonville Union Depot, the rail lines south and west that he'd once controlled, he felt neither rage nor regret, but only sadness. A deep melancholy came over him and he wondered how could he go, uncaring, from the place where he had towered like a giant and ruled for so many years. The hurt and loss went deep, the wounds in his spirit would not heal, the agony remained raw. He had spent twenty long years in that place, and now the days in exile were long and the nights interminable. He tried to put his failure from his mind, but who could walk away, without tears, from the pain of defeat? He had left too much of himself, his energies and his dreams and ambitions, all scattered, littering this place where he was now a stranger. He could not let them go without grief in the blood and heart and mind. This was not something he'd acquired easily, a bargain cheaply won, something to barter and cast aside without mourning. Although it was relinquished, gone beyond hope of restitution, it was like flesh torn from his body, an eye gouged out, a heart squeezed dry. Unlike hunger, it could not be appeased, and it was no thirst to be slaked at some fountain.

It was raw pain to be endured in the slow hours of everlasting nights. He existed between agony over Belle and the empty torment of regret, of what might have been.

He wandered empty roads, depressed, his mind turned inward on itself as if on a treadmill, obsessed with *what if?* What if he'd acted differently, done thus-and-so instead of such-and-such?

He tried to clear these thoughts from his mind. There was no sense in thinking about what he should have done. All those chances, options, and opportunities were gone; they belonged to the dead past. And yet the man didn't breathe who could refrain from chewing over old mistakes. He had done what he had to do, but for every road he'd walked, he could now see a hundred paths he should have taken.

The bitter truth was, he'd lost the dice. They'd taken the game from him. In his mind he heard Dayton Fredrick's warning: *Don't let them take the play away from you.* And Dolly Marsh: *There was no second chance for Dayton. There's no second chance for anybody.*

They had taken the play from him. Tough, impersonal, disinterested men. When they took the play away from you, you were finished. You had the dice and you controlled the game. You had your chance, and when you lost it, you were lost with it. Nobody permitted you a second chance in this world, not in the real, competitive world where a man rolled over his adversaries or knuckled under and was flattened and finished. There was no place for hesitation, weakness, or compassion. Hell, hesitation and compassion *were* weakness.

He felt as if he stood on the platform of a lonely way station in the black and empty Florida night. The train had roared past him and wasn't coming back. Not for him. The night was a void and the black rails stretched, eternally, to nowhere. Inside, he was whatever he had been—all the strengths, any goodness, any decency, any cunning and evil, the black and the white, the gray—only nobody gave a damn. He had wasted all his substance fighting and winning the showy little battles, so he had no strength left for the important confrontations. He'd fought until he was unable to fight anymore, and the battle had moved on beyond him. He was through, finished. There remained only one thing he could do now: face this truth.

But it was not that easy. He was still young and vigorous and driven. He was not like other men, made old and weak and ill by defeat. He laughed savagely. Jesus! How many other old bastards had *died* saying those very words?

Yet the past remained, fragmented, but inescapable—scenes to be replayed, the past an illumined stage behind his eyes, parts recast, actions rescinded and avoided, names spoken that had never been spoken before, evils amended.

Or had he been doomed from the first? Was it that he belonged to that army of doomed pioneers who simply came too early into Florida? Hamilton Disston, owning huge chunks of the state, but almost lynched, finally, by his own workers, when he failed. Dayton Fredrick, who saw his dream washed away in a tidal wave. Henry Plant, who died leaving his estate entangled in litigation that would persist for years in the courts. Demens. Tuttle. Brickel. They had all come striding South with their dreams, as he had, and had been denied at the last, as he had. . . .

From somewhere he heard that the Reverend Andrew Williams, pastor of the Magdalena Baptist Church, had preached a sermon of which he was the unnamed, but minutely detailed, inspiration. Reverend Williams had talked to a fascinated congregation for almost two hours on evil men who go against God in their obsession with worldly power and success and immorality. Such a man who apparently succeeds against incredible odds and obstacles, only to find his dream a nightmare because he has flaunted God's will, finds his success tainted by the corruption that won it and threatened by the greed of other godless men. But it was not the opposing human forces, Reverend Williams shouted, that had exacted the terrible price for godlessness, visiting Biblical wrath as old as

Genesis upon the godless. The forces of god Himself destroy the evil men among us: storm, fire, hurricane, and flood—the invincible weaponry of God against which a puny man cannot fight, cannot stand.

Ward shrugged. Reverend Williams's sermon was a sensation, reprinted in newspapers, quoted on the streets. Andrew Williams could speak from his heart in rage against Ward Hamilton, because this good and righteous Christian man had never forgiven Ward Hamilton, and he never would.

Ward gazed in his mind's eye at the other faces of those unforgiving people standing with Reverend Williams against him. His own mother had died, unforgiving; he had destroyed Robert's opportunities in Lumberwood, and she could never forgive that. And Robert. Hatred almost as old as he was, reinforced all along the line. Baxter Marsh, hating him for taking Marsh's wife, for being young, virile. And Dayton Fredrick, losing one more chance to recoup his failing fortunes because of Ward's bid against him. And Julia, unable to forgive him, even when she loved him, for contributing to her father's death. Simon Shaffer, despising cunning in other people. General Maitland O. White. Lily. Sorry, you'll have to stand in a long line, Reverend Williams.

And no other human being could ever hate him as he hated himself for failing Belle. He had robbed her of those values and virtues everyone needed to grow with, and when she was in desperate trouble and needed him most, he'd been powerless. It seemed to him he had been all his life on a locomotive out of control, racing toward this moment of loss and retribution.

He went over and over it in his mind. If only he'd had the money and influence and power he'd wasted all these years, Belle would have been released in his custody before her trial, and she would have been freed in that courtroom because she *had* killed in self-defense. God knew she had. But that jury had to be made to *see* the way Laddie McCormick had beaten her, threatened her, followed and harassed her until she lived in terror of him. But he had been unable to buy Belle an adequate defense. He had spent everything he had left, but it was not enough, and he could not forgive himself.

On the anniversary of the first railroads into Jacksonville, a reporter from the *Times-Union* called on him. He could not listen to her questions, or answer her intelligibly, or even care. He could not tell her he was dead and empty inside. He could only get up and stalk away, leaving her there, astounded.

He had no friends, and wanted none. He remembered Robert's telling him that day would come when he could not even pay people to remain in his company. "You've got leprosy of the soul," Robert had told him. Maybe Robert was right. He wandered, between visits to Belle at Lowell, alone, unwanted, unforgiven. But not even this mattered. He was too numbed with loss and grief over Belle to care.

He sat alone on the veranda of his cottage when the sheriff's carriage stopped out front. He remained where he was. The sheriff swung down from the coach, and crossed the walk. Ward watched him, unmoving.

"Mr. Hamilton." Sheriff Bullock cleared his throat. Ward felt that old electric stricture of terror flash through him. "I've been sent here on a sad mission, sir. It's my duty to tell you that your daughter Belle—well, sir, Miss Belle is dead."

Agony roiled deep in Ward's belly. He stood up and said, numbly, "Dead? Belle?"

"Yes, sir. Miss Belle was killed."

"Killed?" Torment wheeled faster, burning and churning in his guts.

Sheriff Bullock nodded. "Well, sir, Miss Belle was leading a riot. A riot of inmates up there at Lowell. In the fighting, a gun was fired. Several times. It may have been a matron, a guard, or another inmate. That hasn't been determined fully yet—"

The loss and agony and sickness rushed upward from the pit of Ward's belly. He sobbed, and sank, crying, to his knees. He slouched there, sobbing it all out—the terror, the heartbreak, the loneliness, all the cold and empty numbness of his soul.

Chapter Forty

FOR A LONG TIME, Ward remained in a terrible calm that is like the eye of a hurricane.

His recovery was slow, his return to human contact gradual, but it all began, a painful journey, that dark afternoon when he learned of Belle's death. There is in a man's life a sorrow too fearful to contain, too terrible to stand against. Belle's death was that moment for Ward.

He sank to the lowest depths of despair. When he learned of Belle's death, he wept out the grief and, along with it, the agony and regret and ache of exile. He reached, in that moment, the place where he could either end his life or go on living, but he could not remain dead inside. The pain was too intense, like the crisis in a fever—the patient lives or dies, but the fever breaks and he is no longer the same.

The funeral for Belle forced him into action. His grief was too devastating to be borne alone. Friends, family acquaintances, many of the men he'd known in the transport industry, they all came. Their compassion touched him and lifted him, at least a little. Later, there were Belle's papers, visits to her lawyers, talks with Laddie's people. None of it was easy, but all of it was necessary and time-consuming. All of it forced him out of his shell of hurt and more and more into human contact.

He had lunch with former business associates downtown. He talked with men who were rebuilding the city. He ate lunch at a club where railroad men gathered, though he had sworn he never would again. There were committees, and someone was forever urging him to chair one, and even though he refused, he was once more among the quick, the public-spirited, the builders, the doers, the vital men of action who accepted him unquestioningly as one of them.

When Belle's attorney read her will, Ward sat with tears in his eyes. She hadn't accumulated or stored up much in worldly goods, but what she had, she'd left, or returned, to him. The largest package, one he'd forgotten in his grief over her imprisonment, was her twenty thousand acres—over thirty square miles—of citrus land in Winter Grove. He'd long ago set it aside in trust for her. Had he found the parcel among his assets, it would have gone for Belle's defense. Sitting there now, he wondered if she had known all along, and refused to touch that rich property, wanting to leave something for him? He would never know, but it was good to believe it.

The following week he hosted a party for his old railroad friends at the club. He didn't call it a farewell party, or speak any epitaphs, but secretly he told them all goodbye, the men he'd known, fought against, and fought beside, for more than twenty years.

The next day he caught the Florida East Coast train at Jacksonville Union Depot, crossed the river on Henry Flagler's magnificent new steel bridge, and rode south to Winter Grove.

Like Napoleon going into final exile, he stepped from the train and stood on the platform of the Moorish-castle station until the train disappeared, a single red lamp winking its way south. Since Ward had last been in Winter Grove, Flagler had built a resort hotel, the Palisades, on Main Street. The hostelry was small, as Flagler's inns went, and its best view was along a palm-fringed park to the Moorish-style depot.

He lived in the Palisades Hotel until builders completed a fieldstone cottage on the wooded area of his grovelands.

471

The day after he moved into his new home, he received a delegation of visitors.

Wearing a blue denim shirt, Levi's, boots, and a two-day beard, Ward stood on his veranda and stared at the squad of elegantly attired business executives dismounting from the carriage.

J. A. MacDonald introduced the company. Henry Flagler remembered Ward warmly, and regretted the untimely death of Ward's daughter, whom he remembered as a "little princess" at the opening of his Ponce de Leon Hotel in St. Augustine. The other men were top-level executives with Flagler's burgeoning development and railroad corporation. Ward had difficulty rounding up chairs for all of them. He tried to smile. "If I'd known you were coming, I'd at least have baked some cookies."

Flagler glanced around, neither displeased nor impressed by the view. "Are you really planning to—retire here? A man as young, as vigorous, virile, and talented as you are?"

Ward shrugged. "When you're hated soundly enough by competitors, it takes something out of you."

Flagler shook his head. "Sometimes it's not hatred so much as jealousy that turns men against you. I've lived too long and been a target too often to be disturbed by jealousy or petty hatreds. I don't know anyone who has been successful who was not compelled to pay some price for his success. Some get it at the loss of their health; others give up the pleasures of home and spend their years in offices, forests, or mines; some acquire success at the loss of their reputation, others at the loss of character, and so it goes. There are many prices paid, but there is one universal price that I have never known any successful man to escape, and that is the jealousy of many of the men among whom he moves."

"I've retreated anyway," Ward said.

MacDonald said, "We've come to rescue you from all this, Ward—from what each of us sees as a fate worse than death—buried out here in the middle of an orange grove."

Flagler laughed. "You can't even see your monstrous depot from here."

"Thank God."

When the dutiful, good-humored laughter ebbed,

MacDonald said, "Mr. Flagler wants you to head the East Coast Railway, Ward. Executive vice-president. That's the top office."

Ward's heart lurched. He caught his breath, obviously astonished. The men around him smiled warmly and glanced at each other. MacDonald continued, "Mr. Flagler empowers me to offer you $100,000 per year."

"Good Lord." Ward smiled. "What would I do that would be worth a hundred thousand a year?"

"Start by dropping all false modesty. We believe you're worth it. We want you to run and build and expand this railroad. Mr. Flagler will tell you, as he told me: his paying you a salary of $100,000 per year will remind him that he respects you and your judgments, and it'll remind other people that he respects you." MacDonald laughed. "But most of all, it will remind *you* how much he respects you."

Another executive said, "You know this East Coast—the market, the needs, the potential, the business. Employing you is a unanimous decision among Mr. Flagler's brass—one of the few unanimous decisions we have made. That should make it easier for you, at the start."

"We want the best," MacDonald said. "We're smart enough to know you are the best."

"You will answer directly to me," Flagler said. "As a matter of fact, you answer to J. A. MacDonald here, but since he is my executive right hand, you will in reality be working only for me. I want you to oversee my road construction south, Hamilton. You'll be there in Miami after all, when we rename Fort Dallas, just as you planned, on the first train into town. Our train. Our town. It's only a fishing village of a couple of families now, but I honestly believe it will grow."

Ward thanked them. He promised an immediate decision. They smiled and shook his hand. Each of them welcomed him into the force and said they looked forward to working with him. His acceptance was just a formality. Flagler and his brass picked a couple of bags of oranges and departed.

Alone, Ward stood at his gate staring after them until the carriage disappeared in a diminishing cloud of sun-flecked dust.

He wanted to laugh, to cry, to yell aloud, to tell

Belle—to tell somebody—about this wonderful happening. It wasn't what he wanted, it never would be what he wanted from life, working for another man, taking orders when he'd never learned to take orders. He hated even the thought of it, but this at least was a vindication. They respected him. They wanted him. It gave direction and purpose to his life. It ended his long exile. It provided him with a second chance when nobody believed there was such a thing.

These men did want and need his abilities, his strengths, his experience, his know-how. They confirmed it: he was the best; they needed him.

He exhaled heavily. Maybe that was what it was all about, after all. Not whether you worked for yourself or another man. But being needed. Having inside you the power and vigor and knowledge and guts that set you apart. They *could* get along without you, but they didn't want to, they knew better. They needed you. You'd paid your dues in blood and tears. But you had not lost everything after all. You got another chance, another roll of the dice. . . .

Hell, who knew to what heights he might rise now?

Sighing heavily, he returned to the house, but he could not sit still; he could not concentrate on mundane matters like food, rest, a book to read. He looked about, feeling cramped and crowded. He walked out of the house, and prowled the groves. He felt constricted, as if he could not get a full breath. When he returned to the cottage, he saw a second carriage at the gate, a woman standing alone on the veranda. He hesitated, disbelieving. It was Julia.

"I hoped you would come to me," Julia said. "It would have been easier. For me."

He shook his head. "I came to you. God knows how many years ago now. You threw me out."

"Yes. But that was in a different world. You were a railroad tycoon, robber baron, transport potentate. You owned the world—half of which you had stolen. Besides, I didn't know then how good you are. Oh, I knew how *good* you were. Oh God, did I know! But I didn't know how good you are, inside. That's what I wouldn't believe, what I refused to believe. It had to be proved to me."

"Do you mind telling me what you're talking about?"

474

"I'm talking about forty-three thousand dollars; does that ring a bell? Money you lent my father. A check I gave you in rage to repay it. A check you never cashed. A check now long outlawed. I only found it out because I was in trouble financially after Hobart's death. You see, Hobart was important in the bank, but he was comparatively a poor man, living on a banker's salary. I didn't even suspect how poor we were until he was killed.

"I scrounged around looking for money to live on. I still had my position, my career. But after Hobart was killed, it was never the same. The price was too high. I lost my taste for a career in a place where I wasn't wanted, except for one thing. I wanted out. Only I couldn't afford to quit now. I was almost broke after settling Hobart's affairs.

"I went to the Stockmen's Bank to borrow some money. The executive asked why I wanted to borrow a few thousand when I had an old, unused checking account with slightly over forty-three thousand dollars in it.

"I stood there in that bank and felt my heart sink to my shoes. My tears ran down my face. They thought I was happy and relieved to get that money. But I was crying because, suddenly, like a bolt, after all these wasted years, I'd found you. The real you."

Ward made coffee. He cooked steaks and made a salad. "I learned, living alone," he told her. "You learn to cook or you starve. It's really not all that difficult."

"I'll take your word for it." She stood watching him. "Are you going on being polite? Treating me like a stranger?"

He spread his hands. "You said yourself, it's been a long time."

"A long, wasted time. We've already wasted too much time—we can't even stop to decide who's to blame. I've come to you—if you want me."

"I've always wanted you."

"Then act like it."

He laughed. "I'm in my forties. I'm out of practice."

"It's like swimming, you never forget how."

"Maybe you get afraid of deep water."

"You just let yourself go. I'll teach you. The real reason I'm here is to ask you to go somewhere with me."

He frowned. "Go? Where?"

475

"I want to catch the morning train to New York."

"Why?"

"So we can catch the next train back here from New York. Six days and six nights aboard a train, getting acquainted again. And we'll never leave our compartment. Then we'll come back home here. We'll come back here and watch the oranges grow, and make love, and make up for what we've lost. We'll make love while the oranges blossom. Maybe, once in a while, we'll go out and pick an orange. We'll have the finest orange grove on the Indian River . . . and we'll have each other."

"Sounds like heaven, the way you tell it."

"It *will* be heaven. It had better be. We've worked hard enough getting here."

He went to her, the coffee and the steaks and the salad forgotten. He didn't tell her about Flagler's offer. He didn't need Flagler's job now, or Flagler's railroad. Not anymore. He had all he needed: proof that Flagler wanted him, and respected him and his abilities. He had what he truly wanted at last. Here, in his arms. What had Julia's father said? *The Fredricks hate well, but they love even more intensely.* And somebody else had said the world is well lost for love, and he believed that. He would send word to Flagler tomorrow—from the train. *Find a new boy.* And tomorrow morning he would start again, to regroup, rebuild, return. Tomorrow. He would start anew in the morning, but for now, for tonight, he was content.

THE VAN RHYNE HERITAGE

BY LOUISA BRONTE

The family that became a railroad dynasty, driven to greatness by daring dreams and bold desires...
THE VAN RHYNES—

They began on a humble dirt farm and became the millionaire titans of the industrial age. A family like no other, a law unto themselves, they would stop at nothing to win the golden prizes of ambition and desire.

With ruthless courage and pride, they built an unshakable dynasty and forged an American empire of passion and steel.

B12043105 $2.25

Available wherever paperbacks are sold

Second volume in
THE AMERICAN DYNASTY SERIES
launched by THE VALLETTE HERITAGE.

jove

NT-35